Ethna's Journal

Corinna Newton Downes

Edited by Jonathan Downes
Cover and internal design by Jon Downes for CFZ Communications
Using Microsoft Word 2000, Microsoft Publisher 2000, Adobe Photoshop CS.

First published in Great Britain by CFZ Press

CFZ Press
Myrtle Cottage
Woolfardisworthy
Bideford
North Devon
EX39 5QR

CFZ PRESS

ISBN: 978-1-905723-21-8

For my beloved daughters, Shoshannah and Olivia –
they are, and always will be, my constant sunshine
and
for Jonathan
he is, and will ever remain, my guiding star

Corinna Newton Downes was born in 1956. She was originally from Middlesex, but moved to Stamford in Lincolnshire in 1985 and lived and worked there until May 2007, when she married Jonathan Downes, director of the Centre for Fortean Zoology [CFZ], and became their Administrative Director.

She has two daughters, Shoshannah and Olivia, who lived with her after her divorce from her first husband in 1999, and are both currently (2007) at university working hard at their respective studies of Veterinary Medicine and Psychology with Criminology.

She lives with her husband and an ever-changing collection of animals and men at the CFZ headquarters in North Devon, where she follows her interests in writing, medieval history, archery, and baking.

To my dearest Mother,
for her strength and bravery

Hereafter, find my Journal.

What has bidden me to pen these words, I know not, but henceforth, I feel bound to scribe this for whoever may feel compelled to read it.

First Entry

*U*pon this misty afternoon in late autumn, I did see you for the first time. It was just before dusk when you did arrive at Cragnuth, our small town, looking for shelter for your small company of five men and yourself for the night. From out of the vaporous clouds of mist that hung low across the river, and stretched over the flat lowland that bordered our walls, you came forth into my world. You sat astride your grey mare, and - with a wave of the hand - gestured your men to halt at our gate.

I had been tending to my own mare, Beda, after returning to the village only an hour or so before. Upon leaving the stables, as usual after a brisk ride, I was hungry, so I had decided to visit old Seren, who makes the most delicious biscuits in our village. Not that our own cook, dearest Martha, cannot make wonderful biscuits too. It is just that Seren's are... oh dear how can I write this? Well, they are unlike any others I have ever tasted, and this is no bad reflection at *all* on Martha's own.

Seren's house is to be found near the Main Gate, and is one of the last in a small alleyway of buildings, where live the tradesmen and women of the town. As always after visiting old Seren, all evidence *has* to be eaten before returning to the keep, so *that* is how I happened to be passing the gate at the time of your arrival. I did see you emerge from the mist, and had watched with interest as you approached. Your armour was mud-splattered, and the dark hair that hung from under your helm clung, dampened, by the wet air, to the pauldrons that protected your shoulders, and clumps of dirt scattered the scant parts of your face that were unprotected from your helm.

I am used to travellers using our small town as a brief respite to their journeys, but in *you*, there was a difference. I feared that the daughter of Lord Edric should not be caught rapidly cramming a freshly baked biscuit into her mouth if you were as important a guest as you *appeared* you might be.

So, as you halted, I had walked briskly along the narrow lane that runs between the scant wooden houses that make up our tiny town, nibbling away at my purchase. A guard ran passed me, moving as fast as he could in the direction of the keep. I reached the well where children were heaving their buckets of water ready for the night ahead; struggling back to their homes, desperately trying not to spill a drop. My pace quickened, as I entered into the bailey through its outer walls, and on past the smithy, where Tarek was still hard at work, with sweat gleaming on his face and torso, despite the cold and damp air outside. He noticed me as I hurried by, and I responded to his quick wave, as I carried on up the cobbled slope to the keep, where I pushed open the heavy oaken door into the Great Hall.

By this time, there was immense activity inside. The guard who had passed me had delivered his message, and preparations were hurriedly being made for your arrival at my father's home. I had enquired of my father as to your identity, but had been met with the quiet, stony face I have become used to, and was brushed aside as he waddled towards the open door; his gait reminiscent of a Yule-fattened goose a few days before its neck is wrung.

"You are most welcome", I heard him say, and - from where I stood in the far corner of the hall - I saw you approach him. You had removed your helm, and I was quietly amused as to how you towered over my father as he bowed low before you in greeting. Many years of over-eating, and an unhealthy love for wine and ale, have left their mark on my father's girth. He is not blessed with a great height either, and looked rather diminutive against your tall, slim, frame.

Apart from your armour and your stature, it was clear that you are of noble birth, for my father has never fawned quite as much before as he did this eve. It was embarrassing - yet amusing - to see him ingratiate himself before you. It saddens me to speak of my father as such, reader, but he is - indeed - a cruel man, and I feel no love for him at all. He is outspoken, arrogant, and vindictive to those whom he deems have erred against him.

Whilst he was showering you with compliments and good grace, I slowly, and quietly left the shadows, and approached my father and our guest. As I walked, I became conscious that - after my ride - I must appear windswept, and in all probability, in a state unbefitting my station. I should have returned to my chambers immediately

upon arriving at the keep to make myself more presentable, but it was too late now. As I walked, I began smoothing down my skirts, and ran my hand across my hair, to carefully tuck any loose hairs back into place. My cheeks still felt flushed from the afternoon's exercise, but I could but hope that no-one would notice.

I feel that I cannot fully explain why, but I felt immediately drawn towards your presence. But, after writing this, and upon thinking more deeply, perchance I *can* explain. I am the daughter of a nobleman, and however badly he thinks of me, and treats me, there is no reason at all why I should not be presented to a visitor *as* such a lady. I, in the absence of my mother, *am* the 'Lady of the Keep' and should, therefore, greet any traveller who happens upon our hospitality.

I stood silently a few feet away, and my eyes took in every contour of your face: the small scar that ran from the bottom of your right cheek and disappeared into your dark beard, the white teeth that gleamed as you smiled - a smile that made your face soften and your whiskers turn up slightly to the left. Your long dark hair, now freed from the restrictions of your helm, still clung to your shoulders, apart from a thin strand that had escaped such confinement, and curled down over your left eye. Oh, and *such* eyes do you have. A darker brown I have *never* beheld.

And so, Arthyen you are apparently a nephew of the King. I have never been in the presence of royalty before, and I was nervous to curtsey before you. Many people have I met in my twenty years, but our town is on the very edge of your uncle's kingdom, and from my memory, none so noble has ever past through.

It was but a fleeting glance you gave me as my father introduced me as his daughter, before ushering you into the hall for warmth and food. But *in* that glance, I felt myself drawn towards you, as I have never been drawn to another person before. I feel as if I have known you for all of time, and that we have just been waiting for this moment to meet again. You did bow your head to me as I rose before you, and your dark eyes smiled. I wonder. Did you feel the same notion of recognition?

You recounted that you are sent to scout the lands for the enemy, that has - of late - been attacking villages and towns on the outskirts of your uncle's kingdom, razing them to the ground, and - without quarter - slaughtering every man, woman, and child in their path. Not many have survived to tell their story; but those that have done so, have spoken of such terror as makes the blood chill. It would seem that you might hope to use our home as a garrison for a few weeks to come.

Before taking supper, which would be some time yet, my father ordered one of the several waif-like boys, who scuttled back and forth all day doing his bidding, to take

you to your allotted chamber in order for you to refresh yourself. You strode after the boy, as he led you up the steps at the back of the hall. I watched the flickering light of the candle, which the boy held aloft as he led you down the corridor, throwing eerie shadows on the walls, and - in an instant - you had gone from sight; the dimness descending once again.

The kitchen had been in turmoil upon your arrival. The table of my father is always plentiful, due to his gluttonous appetite, but the advent of *such* a guest had brought a great panic, and there was much to be prepared. As we live by a river, we are lucky to have a fresh supply of fish every day, and so - upon entering the kitchen - I had been greeted by the sight of two large salmon, and a sturgeon, being gutted and prepared, along with three large loaves of bread being thrust into the ovens. The three chickens that had *originally* been intended for the evening meal were already cooking on the spit. The fat spat on the coals, as Hannel, who intermittently wiped his brow from the heat, occasionally turned the scrawny-looking fowl.

At five years of age, poor Hannel is the youngest son of Hamel, and his wife Martha; head cook of our household. And he constantly ends up with the most menial of tasks. My heart always goes out to him when I see his small frame sitting by the hearth. He was born with one leg shorter than the other, and - although he tries very hard to do as much as any boy of his age - he is restricted by his deformity, and hence; is always to be found in the kitchens at the time of day when his two elder brothers are helping their father in the kennels. As always, I went up to him, and - kneeling beside him - tousled his blonde locks, and kissed his tiny forehead, and - as ever - he gave me a big grin in return. Despite the cruelty that nature has bestowed upon his tiny body, he is such a happy little soul, and I have a very great affection for him.

I had looked across at his mother as she was busily stuffing one of the salmon with a mixture of herbs and freshly churned butter, as she sang happily to all who cared to listen. Her belly was heavily rounded with her fourth child. When she had realised she was once *again* with child, she had confided in me that she hoped *this* would be the daughter that she longed for.

I admired her bravery at the prospect of another birth, for I had assisted at the arrival of Hannel. He had been a difficult child to bring forth into the world, and I knew - as Martha must do - that to endure another labour could be very dangerous to both her, and her unborn offspring. Her time was near, and, if providence allowed, by Yuletide there would be another mouth to feed for her and her husband.

Martha had stopped singing in mid-chorus, and had looked up at me and asked, "So

My Lady. Our royal guest. Is he handsome?" I had felt the heat rise to my cheeks, and had opened my mouth to stutter a reply, when she had laughed loudly. "I see by your blushes that he is", and she went back to her fish, and resumed her singing. Embarrassed, I had stood up and hurriedly left the kitchen to return to the hall. Just as I did so, you were descending the steps. The sound of Martha's question returned to my thoughts as I saw you, Arthyen.

You had discarded your armour, and did wear a long, dark-red tunic over your dark, brown, woollen hose. Without its armour, your body moved lithely, and with a regal grace. In a moment, I took in your broad shoulders, and your toned torso beneath the shirt, and your long, lean, legs, still encased in their long, leather boots. Your hair was now dry, and it naturally fell in slight waves to just below your shoulders.

When you came upon me at the foot of the steps, you had raised your right hand to your chest, and had bowed. I noticed how your knuckles and finger joints were gnarled with battle scars. Then I had seen the ring. It was made of gold, and had an outline that I could not quite make out engraved upon its face. I must have been squinting at it quizzically, because you told me quietly that it was of a dragon's head. At the sound of your voice, I took a step back and was about to apologise to you for being so rude as to stare, when my father strode up to us, and, engaging you in conversation, managed to usher you away from my company.

I knew then, that Martha's judgement of my blushes was correct!

Despite my status as the daughter of the noble Lord Edric, I had long been expected to wait at table along with the kitchen servants. Even when company was present, my father deemed it right and proper for me to do so. And so, upon this evening, I did find myself pouring wine into your mazer, when - to my embarrassment - you did ask my father why I was doing such a thing. To which he replied "Why not? She does not have much else to do".

For a brief moment I noticed the look of astonishment upon your face, as you stared at my father at this utterance. In fear of any possible retribution from my father at your defence of my status, I quietly said, "It is of no matter Sire. It is my honour to serve such a guest," and - the wine poured - slipped away to my place at the far end of the table.

I was not hungry, but forced myself to take a few mouthfuls of the food before me. My dearest hound, Orvin, settled himself across my feet under the table. Orvin and I have been together now for ten years; he has been my constant companion, and has helped make my life bearable in this barren place.

My cheeks do redden, even as I write this, when I think of how often I did look at you at table this eve, but you must forgive me, for I could not help myself. I do not think you caught me looking through lowered lashes but the once. 'Twas only when you took the mazer to your lips, that our gaze did meet for the briefest moment before I turned away. Upon looking once more, I did realise that your gaze was still upon me, and I did blush and tentatively smile. The smile you did return was such to make my heart pound so loud in my breast, I did fear that all present would hear it.

Second Entry

*I*t was the strangest thing this damp morn, that - when I did awaken - my first thought was of you. As I did stretch the sleep from my body, my ears were filled with the sound of activity in the courtyard below my window. I knew that you were leaving, and with this thought such sadness and panic came upon me. I left the warmth of my coverlet, and on tiptoes ran to the window. Oh, how cold the floor was on my skin, but for one last glimpse of you I should bear it. Orvin sat beside me, and as my hand caressed his soft head, my eyes searched the throng below. The horses were restless, and wished to be on their way; they skitted around their riders, awaiting the weight upon their backs. My eyes found your grey mare, but they could not find you. But, upon straining my ears, I did hear your voice, and that of my father in reply. I shifted position, and in my haste did knock the candle-holder. To my horror, I could do nothing but watch it fall from the window, and clatter upon the steps below. I did jump back into the shadows, but knew that my father would have no doubt as from whence this object had come, and a dread filled me at the thought of his sharp tongue and heavy hand.

I heard you shout, "We ride!" to your men, and once again I peered from my tiny window; at last to see you mount your horse in readiness to leave. Then, quite suddenly, you did turn your mare around in my direction, and looked up at my window. You threw me such a warm smile as did make my heart melt, and my hand cover my lips to hush the sigh as it tried to leave them. Then, with a slight bow of your head, you turned your mare around and led your men down through the town, on to the

main gate and beyond. It was as if I heard you whisper, "I shall return" on the cool breeze that then swept across me, and made me shiver. I did not move from my vigil until you had disappeared across the river. A silence filled my bower, and I waited for the heavy footsteps of my father to come upon me. Long did I sit on the side of my cot, shivering in the morning chill, but - strangely - those footsteps did not come.

I entered the great hall with trepidation, some time later, and hurriedly dispatched myself to the kitchens, where I took of my breakfast away from the unloving eyes of my father. I have never been in any doubt that he did lay blame at my door, because my twin brother, his only heir, had died at birth whilst I had lived. He has made this known to me from the very beginning of my memories, and it is something that I shall undoubtedly have to shoulder until the last breath does leave my body. Our poor mother was also taken into darkness upon that day, and I have been made to live with the responsibility of their passing for the last twenty years. The cruelty of my father has never allowed me to wipe it from my memory. How I wish my dear mother were here today, and that I could have grown up with my dearest brother, but alas it was not to be. Time cannot mend all things. Already, once in my life, my father has tried to give me away in marriage, but on that occasion my future husband was killed whilst hunting. That was four years ago, and I did not shed a tear, for my intended was thrice my age. Each day since, upon waking, I have been filled with the deepest dread that it will be the day that my father announces that he has found someone *else* to whom he can give my hand in marriage.

That was this morning, dear journal; now the golden sun has reached its zenith, and has begun his descent into the west for another day. Now I have realised why I received no harsh reprimand, or beating, from my father this morning. It would seem that he had already satisfied his thirst for retribution, and I am writing this entry, as he discusses arrangements with my cousin Margh, of my impending union with him.

Yes, my cousin arrived late this morning. Sent for by my father, no doubt. It would seem that he has Margh firmly fixed in his mind now, as the man who will take his wicked daughter away from his presence for good. Upon reflection of my earlier writing, I think that I would probably have preferred the hapless hunter to that slimy toad, Margh. His touch makes my flesh crawl. His breath makes me want to vomit. And when he looks at me with those cold, blue eyes; it makes me want to plunge my fingers into them, whilst wiping the smirk away from his lips with the palm of my other hand. I detest the vile creature, and pledge now that I shall never give myself up to him. I would rather throw myself into the quagmires on Blackditch Moor, than become his wife.

My head is full of plans of escape as I pen this, but - alas - I fear that I shall not be

able to flee quite as easily as I would have hoped. Any journey from this place would be hazardous on one's own, and my father would be sure to send his henchmen after me, who would - I fear - be unforgiving in their treatment.

Somehow, though, there seems to be some light in my world; ever since yesterday evening when the strangers from the south came into our village. Although, today, my heart is full of dread when it thinks of Margh, the previous day's events have also given rise to some kind of hope. But I know not what or how. I can almost sense it trying to smother the dread which is trying to encroach upon me. I am certain that my heart is trying to tell me that I shall find a way out of this trap that I now find myself caught in. I know not how this will happen, but I believe that if I listen *long* enough, it will tell and show me the way.

I am so tired, and my head is thumping from the fretting to which I have subjected myself. How I wish I had my dear mother with me now. I am sure that she would know what to say to calm me, to soothe away my fears. I choke back the tears, as I write this, at the thought of the mother I have never known. A mother must be the dearest person in anyone's life, and I miss that closeness immensely.

It will be time for supper soon, but I shall not take any food this eve. I do not wish to be in the company of those who plot against me. No, I shall stay in my chamber, and stitch my cloth by candlelight, and wait for the tiredness to take me away from here, to the land of dreams.

Third Entry

erhaps, here, I should explain how Orvin came upon his name. I am not certain it will be of much interest to some who may come upon this journal, but I shall record it nevertheless. I have told already how he has been with me for ten years - it was a few days after my tenth birthday that he was born in the kennels, along with his five brothers and sisters. He was - as Hamel, Martha's husband and keeper of the hunting pack, had told me - the runt of the litter, and would probably not survive. A tiny little bundle of fur; he was always the last to get to his mother's teats, and had to battle his way through the throng of his siblings to get a drink of his mother's milk. Even though there was plenty of space for him, he always seemed to be pushed out of the way by his other stronger kith and kin. He may have been the smallest of the litter, but - even through my childish eyes - I could see from the beginning that he was determined to survive.

When it had been time to wean them off their mother's milk and take meat, it was heartbreaking to see his tiny body being pushed away by the others, as he fought for his fair share. So I took it upon myself to sneak in to the kennels at the end of the day, with leftovers from the kitchen. I can still remember Martha - who was carrying her first child, Willard, at the time - giving me a wink every evening as she passed me a bundle of whatever suitable food was left. I do not know to this day whether she ever told Hamel what I was up to, but as a ten year old I did not even think about such things. All I knew was that this little pup deserved the right to live, and I was determined to ensure that he was given that chance.

Orvin - but why that name? Ah, well that is easy to explain. It was one of those days when the wind howled, and groaned, around the crags upon which our township is

built. I had been on the archery range practising with my bow, more of which I may explain in a later entry, for I am not inclined to go into more detail at this present time. I shall note however, that it was not a very good day to be practising, as the wind was creating much difficulty with the flight of the arrows. They were simply not flying as true as they should. I had tried and tried to aim further to the right to compensate, but had grown tired of my failed efforts.

The banners that flew from the keep, however, seemed to be at their best, being stretched to their fullest extent to display my father's coat of arms. This being a brown hunting dog on a green background on the lower half, the top half being yellow with a black sea serpent - to dramatic effect. Suddenly, out of the corner of my eye, I noticed that one of them became unattached from its pole, and was caught on an updraft. I watched as it was taken by the wind. It finally came to rest just outside the kennel doors, where it seemed to snag on something on the ground. Giving up on my bow for the day, I had decided to retrieve the banner, and take it to my room to repair in order to present my father with my handiwork. I thought that he would then be pleased, and bestow upon me some kind words and affection - in those days I was still trying to please him, for I had not yet learnt that it was a hopeless task.

I had unstrung my bow, and slid it into its bag. Quickly I had wrapped up my arrows in their bag, being careful not to damage their goose-feathered flights, and had made my way down to the stables eagerly. The banner still lay where it had fallen, the wind still trying to take it on another skyward journey. The wind was unsuccessful though, due to the banner being held down by something unknown to me at that time.

To a ten year old, this presented many wonderful thoughts to fill my imagination. Perhaps the little faerie folk that Martha had often told me stories about were holding the material. Visions of tiny hands holding on to the silky material took seed in my mind. How many little hands would it take, I had wondered, to hold such a thing in such windy weather? Were they, perchance, trying to take it away to make clothes with? Or perhaps they were going to make bedding for their children? Oh, and such tiny children they would be. I can remember that I had giggled to myself as I pictured Martha as one of the faerie folk. I had thought that she would make such a wonderful plump fairy, with her rosy red cheeks, and sparkling eyes.

My childish fantasies were broken, however, when, upon reaching the banner, I had discovered it to be snagged on a piece of wood that had broken loose from the fencing around the yard. Bending down, I had begun to loosen it when, from out of the kennels came a growling, snapping, small bundle of fur. To a puppy, I expect that this flapping piece of material must have seemed like some wyrd creature come to at-

tack his territory, as it flapped, and billowed, stretched against its wooden captor. Such a brave little dog deserved a brave name, and so Orvin he became - a name I had heard tell of in stories shared at great feasts in our Hall, since my earliest memories of such occasions. Orvin had been a brave man who had battled sea serpents, on a great journey across the sea many, many, years before on his way to our lands - hence the origin of the serpent in my family's banner. I shall not attempt to relate the whole saga here, as I fear it would take me far too long to write out. Perchance, I shall leave that for the old warriors; they could tell it much better than I could ever do.

The sound of barking had brought Hamel from inside the kennels. Standing with his hands on his hips, a broad grin creasing his face, he had announced that - as I had named him - then Orvin should be mine! I realised in later years that in reality he had been given to me as he would not have been good enough for hunting; being too small and puny in the eyes of a hunting master, and would probably have had his throat slit in the next day or so.

However, a ten-year old girl was very happy that day, as she bundled up both the banner and her newfound companion in her arms, and skipped back towards the keep, bow and arrows slung across her back. She may not have met any faeries that day, but somehow that did not matter, for instead she had certainly gained a loyal friend.

Oh, I must add that I *did* repair the banner, but no kind words did utter forth from my father's lips.

Fourth Entry

This is the first entry I have been able to make for a few days. The reason is, as I shall write below.

Orvin and I arose early on the Friday morning of last week and, together with my horse, Beda, didst slip away, whilst the household was still asleep. My father and Margh undoubtedly had much wine and ale to keep them in sleep for many hours before they arose, and by the time they did I would be well out of their reach. I kept to the lowlands, where I would be in open country, and - hence - able to keep a watchful eye open.

By mid-morning, I found myself on Blackditch Moor. There was a chilly autumnal breeze that whipped across the moorland, but it was good to be out of the confines of home. I had looked to the east, and knew that somewhere, out there, was a man who had been constantly in my thoughts for the past two days. I cannot, nor would want to, clear my head of your presence, Arthyen. Your name goes around and around within my head. I can see your face before me when I shut my eyes, and can hear your voice when all about me is quiet.

Dismounting, I had led Beda for a short time, before sitting down to rest awhile, and eat some of the food I had taken from the kitchens on my departure. I had slept fitfully the night before, and after the food entered my belly, I began to feel tired, so decided to lie down amongst the heather. I knew that Orvin would keep an ear open for anything untoward, so I had closed my eyes for what I had intended would be just a few minutes.

The sound of distant growling had brought me back to consciousness. I thought that perhaps I had been dreaming, but upon opening my eyes I realised that it was, indeed, Orvin who was growling. I dared not move at first, but lay prone and listened carefully to what sounds might be around me. I knew Orvin was standing at my head, as I could see his tail in the air over my face. Beneath me, I could feel the ground shaking to the movement of hooves. This meant they were not upon me yet. So I rolled over on to my belly, and peered through Orvin's legs. The late afternoon autumn sun was reflecting off the armour, of what I thought were three or four riders coming over the moorland. My hand instinctively drew my sword from its scabbard, as I searched for the exact location of Beda. I could see her only a couple of feet away to my left. I estimated that I could probably reach and mount her before the riders were fully upon me, so - with a deep intake of breath - I leapt to my feet, scrambled across the scrub, and putting my foot into her right stirrup, hauled myself into the saddle. I yelled to Orvin to follow, and urged Beda into a fast gallop.

She did as I bid, and soon we were flying across the moorland. But I was a long way from home, and turning in my saddle, I could see that the riders had given chase. I could also see that I had miscalculated, and that there were in fact ten of them. They were yelling as their large mounts gained slowly on my little mare. I knew I was doomed, and that it would not be long before they over-ran me. Dearest Arthyen, I have never been as scared as I was at that moment. I half-expected an arrow to pierce my back at any moment; its cold metal head embed itself into my flesh, perhaps even break my backbone.

Oh Beda, I did not want to run you so fast over such unforgiving ground, so full of rabbit holes. When you tripped, and I heard the snap of your leg, my heart stopped beating for what seemed like minutes. You fell screaming to the ground, my dearest Beda, and you could not help but fall on me, trapping my leg underneath you. You were galloping so fast that you hit the ground with such force that you broke your neck instantly. At least the end came quickly my faithful friend. You did not suffer the agonising pain of slow death. But I am so sorry that it was me who killed you.

When you fell, the grip on my sword had loosened, and I felt it fly from my grasp. Frantically, I had searched for it, and at last saw the glint of its steel just out of my reach. Turning, I saw the riders nearly upon me. I desperately tried to free my trapped leg, and reach my sword - such a tiny weapon against ten men with swords double the size. Eventually, I managed to ease my leg from underneath your broken body, and grabbed the hilt of my sword. Pulling myself to a standing position, I faced the men - weapon ready - and Orvin snarling at my side. We were not ready for death, and would not die without a fight, as weak and one-sided as that would be. I could almost hear the men laughing at me as they came closer and closer.

It was only then, that I realised, that behind these ten riders - slightly to the left - came another group. My heart sank. I knew very well that, as a lone woman, I was an easy target, and that my antagonists would surely have their pleasure before dealing the final blow. I was about to plunge my own sword into my breast to deny my enemy such gratification, when I realised that at the head of this second group was a grey horse that I recognised. They were close enough now for me to hear their yells. I was not the only one to hear them. The ten riders suddenly turned their horses in a wide arc around me, and with a blood-curdling cry, urged their mounts back towards the others.

It was as the last of these men rode close past me, that I felt a dull thud on my upper arm. It knocked me forwards, and I stumbled to regain my balance. At first, I thought his horse had knocked me. But then I felt a stinging sensation, and felt a warm trickle down my left arm. The limb felt heavy, and a searing pain overwhelmed me. I looked down at it, and saw the crimson fluid oozing down to my hand, and dripping off my fingertips. I looked up in a daze, just as the two groups crashed into each other, and I could hear the sound of metal upon metal as their swords met. I heard the grunting of the horses as they pounded into each other. Then everything went hazy, and I saw no more.

I can remember only the smallest details of the remainder of that day. I can recall feeling a great pain in my left arm, and someone calling my name. The memory of a familiar voice, and the dark brown eyes in a face I had, of late, seen in my dreams. The pain of being lifted astride a horse and the tenderness of an arm around my waist, the weight of legs wrapped around mine to keep me straight in the saddle. Through the pain and half-lidded eyes, I recall seeing the familiar battlements of home in the near distance and then being carried in someone's arms through the hall - I remember the smell of the wood smoke in the great hearth. I made out Martha's worried voice and above all, the whisper of my name from a voice that made my life suddenly worth living again.

It has been Martha who has told me of the events of those days since I was brought back home. She has told me that I had been delirious with a fever for four days, brought on by the poison that had entered my bloodstream from the blade of my assailant. Old Jenifer had administered a herb poultice; a skill - which has been handed down from daughter to daughter for many generations - her mother had taught her. A skill no man may ever know, and no woman ever tell.

I was not surprised to hear that my father and Margh had come to visit my bower but only once or twice since my return. They had preferred to spend their time hunting, eating, and drinking. It had been a surprise to learn that you, Arthyen, had been the

one who had spent many hours by my cot, as my body fought against the pestilence that had invaded it.

It would seem that you and your men had spent every day since the skirmish, riding out; scouting for signs of more of the enemy that had come upon me. Martha had learned from you, that you had been tracking the group for some time, and that it had been purely by chance that you had caught up with them when you did.

She told me how every evening she would wait at table, and see you sitting with my father and cousin, politely indulging in conversation whilst the meal was eaten, and then would make your excuses at the earliest possible opportunity, and return to my chamber, where you would sit in the corner and read.

Martha had smiled with a twinkle in her eye, when she recalled how - in the darkest hours of my sickness, when it was not certain whether my body would give in to the icy grip of death or manage to fight it off - she came upon you seated on the side of my cot; my hand in yours, as you wiped the sweat from my forehead. How once she had crept in, before she herself had retired to her own cottage and bed, and without you knowing she was there, you had placed a kiss on my forehead.

Fifth Entry

his evening, I did rise from my bed for the first time in a week, and did slowly dress myself. I was unsteady on my feet after lying down for so long, and felt very light-headed. Martha and the other women were busy preparing supper, and there was no one else to assist me, so the procedure took what seemed like an age to complete. My left arm was heavily bound, which made the prospect of placing it into a sleeve one that I did not relish. I decided upon the loosest shirt I could find, over which I could put my kirtle. This would not be the most elegant of clothing, but it would suffice, and had the added advantage of requiring no buttons or laces to be secured.

My arm ached, but the sickening pain had long left me. Nonetheless, I found raising it above my head proved more painful than I had thought it would be. I had gritted my teeth, both against the soreness, and also in my determination to join you at supper. If it had been just my father and my cousin, I would have stayed in my chamber for longer, but I wished to share your company, as - since it had been clear that I would survive my ordeal - you had not come to my room to visit me. I know that you could not, Arthyen. It would not have been proper for you so to do. But I have missed you these past few days. My only news of you has been through Martha, and I only see her but briefly when she has a few minutes to spare out of the kitchen.

When she has had the time, my dear Martha has combed through my hair every day since I have returned from my delirium. She had tended to it a few hours earlier, so I managed to tidy it up quite simply with my right hand. At last, I felt respectable enough to try to take supper in the Hall.

Gingerly I had stood up, but felt giddy, and had to sit back down again. Orvin whined as he stood by my bed. After a few deep breaths I tried again, and although I still felt as if my head did not belong to me, I remained standing. I took two or three tentative steps away from the bed, towards the chair where you had spent many an hour reading, and upon reaching it, placed a hand on its arm to steady myself. I felt as if my body was getting used to being upright again, although my legs were still slightly shaky, so after a few minutes I had taken another deep breath, and had managed to reach my door. It was difficult to do everything with my right hand, but I eventually positioned myself, and - half-balanced against the wall - opened my door, and stepped into the corridor, Orvin loping on in front of me.

I shuffled along the corridor, leaning against the wall for support. The closer I got to the steps to the Hall, I could hear the hubbub below, and the smell of the food as it wafted up towards my nostrils. Each step I took became easier, and by the time I had reached the steps I was able to walk more normally, although still drunk with the effort of walking. The problem of descent, however, had been something I had neglected to think about in detail. I found myself faced with a dilemma.

But Orvin seemed to have an idea all of his own. I watched him as he trotted off down the steps, and made his way across the Hall, oblivious of the other hounds that lay sprawled across the floor, and that raised their heads from their dozing to observe him. He completely ignored my father and my cousin, and slowly walked towards the person standing by the brazier. Orvin then sat down by the figure, and uttered forth one short bark. Upon recognising Orvin, you turned around instantly, and saw me wavering at the top of the steps. Patting him on the head, you walked back through the Hall, and approached the stairs with a slow, easy, gait.

As you passed my father, you said loudly: "My Lady Ethna, it is good to see you well enough to join us again. I am sure your father is delighted to see you recovered". At this, my father had coughed and spluttered into his mazer, and Margh had shot you a glance of poisonous dislike.

Bounding up the steps, two at a time, you greeted me with a warm smile, and offered me your arm. I thankfully wrapped my good arm round yours, and leant into your body, as you slowly escorted me down the steps. Out of the corner of my eye, I caught sight of Martha and a couple of the younger girls watching us from the entrance to the kitchen. Martha was clapping her hands quietly, bobbing slightly up and down in her excitement. At that moment, I felt sure that, knowing my dear Martha; she would have something to say about it later.

Orvin was sitting waiting for us at the foot of the stairs, and jumped to his feet, wag-

ging his tail when we reached the bottom, and I told him how clever he was. You then led me down the length of the Hall to the warmth of the brazier, and sat me down in one of the seats nearby, before disappearing into the kitchen. As I sat in the half-shadows, Orvin resting his head on my knee, I noticed Margh confide something in my father's ear as you passed them.

I noticed you re-enter the Hall, but as you walked by the other two, my father stopped you and engaged you in conversation. Soon afterwards, Linette, one of the girls from the kitchen, came to me to offer me some wine and had said how good it was to see me up from my bed. She assured me that the wine would help fortify me as she gave me the wooden cup. From behind her skirt, I could see a wisp of blond curly hair poking out. "Is that my Hannel?" I did ask quietly. Grinning - as only he could - he jumped into sight, and limped over to me. I asked how he was, and - as he tried to clamber into my lap - told him how I had missed him these past few days. But Linette had taken hold of his tiny hand, and led him slowly back to the kitchen, before he could make himself comfortable, patiently slowing her own gait to accommodate his lopsided walk.

I have no idea what conversation had passed between my father and my cousin, but whilst you were trapped by my father, Margh came and settled himself opposite me. To my great displeasure he did take my right hand in his, and place his other hand on my knee. I jerked my body away; his hand fell, and he withdrew it. I had shuddered at his touch, but I could not free my hand from his sweaty grip.

I glanced to where you and my father were standing across the Hall. Cleverly, my father had been sure to place you so that your back was towards me; hence, you had no notion of what was occurring behind you.

Angrily I had demanded of Margh, "Unhand me cousin, or I shall set Orvin upon you".

Coldly, my cousin did reply: "And then I shall have to slit his scrawny throat".

I had recoiled at this statement at first, but, upon composing myself, replied as calmly as I could, "And then, with my dagger, I should pierce your heart as you slept, *dear* cousin. Then I would cut it out to feed to the hounds that lie hereabout. Perhaps, though, even the dogs should find it too bitter to digest".

He did not flinch at my words, but just smiled and tightened his grip on my hand, until it turned white as the bloodflow became restricted. I became nauseous as he squashed the bones together. Tensing my body, my injured arm began to ache again,

and at my protestations of discomfort, Orvin stood and snarled at Margh. This sound had aroused the curiosity of the other dogs in the Hall, and one or two of them barked, prompting my father to yell at them to be silent. They obeyed instantly, presumably with an inherent fear of my father's wrath should they not. But Orvin continued his threat to Margh, who eventually released my hand, on realising that unwanted attention had been aroused.

Supper was a quiet affair. My father had placed you on his right, and Margh had made sure to escort me to the farthest left, with himself seated next to my father, hence you and I were as far apart as was possible. I managed a few short mouthfuls, but my arm had begun to ache terribly, and I found myself wishing that I had remained in my bedchamber after all. As usual, the wine flowed freely into the mazers of Margh and my father, but I noticed that yours hardly rose to your lips.

As my relatives belched their satisfaction of the meal, I arose from the table, and - with Orvin following behind me - I made my way slowly to the heavy doors to get some much-needed air. The doors were made of oak, and the thought of opening them one-handed was, in itself, a daunting task.

"You find the air in here stifling also?" you had asked, as you appeared beside me. I nodded, as you pulled open the huge doors. "May I bestow myself upon your company?" you continued. Turning to look back at the table, I saw that the other two were still seated, oblivious in their wine-sotten state to take any regard of what we were doing. It is a strange thing that a liquid can change the state of mind of men so quickly and so easily. A few short hours ago, the thought of you and I being together so intimately would have prompted much plotting and planning to separate us, but now it was as if we did not exist.

"I should be honoured", I replied.

Our only company being Orvin, we slowly walked together around the Keep. We did not speak of many things, but just seemed happy to be in each other's company. You had asked me of my life at Cragnuth, and gave me a brief account of your life at King Ulmar's court. I was not familiar with being with a man in such close company, and did not know what to say to you. But strangely I felt completely at ease, and did not feel that there was any need to try and make conversation with you just for the sake of it. After completing our second tour of the Keep, we sat on the steps outside the doors, and you explained how - with the dawn - you would again be riding out with your men on one last scout, before returning to the King to report on your findings. This information made my heart sink, but I did not show my dismay. To my embarrassment, however, I could not stop myself from stuttering that we would miss

your presence, to which statement you had taken my right hand in yours and kissed it softly.

"If I may be honest," you had said. "Cragnuth is a cold and barren place."

I knew not what to say in reply to this honesty, but before I could respond, you had continued, "But there is warmth that follows when you enter a room, and it is this that I shall miss greatly".

We had been seated together for I know not how long, when Martha interrupted our solitude, as she made her way slowly down the steps on her way home. I knew she must be exhausted, especially in her advancing pregnancy, but was not surprised when I heard a low chuckle emit from her as she passed us. I had smiled inwardly, as I again imagined the teasing she will surely inflict upon me on the morrow. It would be too much to expect her to resist such a temptation.

Unwittingly she had broken our tryst, and it was if a spell had been broken, and we had been brought back to reality at that moment. You told me of your concern for my well-being, and that I looked tired, and should return to my bed. Dearest Arthyen, I was *very* tired - indeed I still am as I pen this - but I shall not rest until I have written all that I have to say. My arm still ached, and I *did* want to return to the warmth of my coverlet, but more so, I did *not* want to leave your company. I sti-fled a yawn. After you had told me that you and your men were to leave us in a few short hours, I was not sure when - if ever - I would see you again, and my heart still felt heavy. I wanted to stay with you for as long as I could.

However, as Martha disappeared into the darkness, you rose to your feet and helped me to mine. I had hoped that my father and Margh were asleep by now, at least slumped at the table if not in their cots, but it was still wise to try to open the door slowly and quietly. Creeping gingerly through, like two naughty children, we were immediately greeted by the sound of snoring, and - smiling at each other - we crept through the shadows at the side of the Hall, and made our way to the stairs, Orvin trotting silently behind us. One of the large dogs was sprawled - fast asleep - in our way, and whimpered in its dreams as we stepped over it. Eventually we reached my chamber, where you kissed my lightly on the back of my left hand, before making your way further up the hall to your own room.

I can hardly keep my eyes open, so I must lay me down my head to sleep. Surely, fate would not bring us together, only to wrench us apart forever after such a short time? As I close my eyes, I shall will myself to awaken early, in the hope of seeing you on the morrow before you leave.

Sixth Entry

As soon as I had awoken this morning, I wrapped myself in my cloak, and rushed down to the kitchens in the hope of arriving there before you did. I had assumed that you would call in for some provisions for the day's ride. However, upon reaching the kitchen, I was most disappointed. Martha told me that you had passed her not ten minutes earlier. You had gone to the stables to collect your horse, and your companions, who had been given shelter there since your first arrival at Cragnuth many days before.

Martha told me that you had been quite polite to her, and had wished her a very good day as you had met. She thought you very gallant, and with a wicked twinkle in her eye, she proceeded to quiz me on the night's activities that she had happened upon on her way home. She sat me on a stool by the fire, which was already busily sending flames roaring upwards, and emitting a comforting heat. Then she patted my hands in my lap, and sat expectantly.

"Well?" she had asked after I had sat silently for a minute or two, too cosseted in my own thinking of how much I would miss you, to be able to answer her.

As usual, not able to sit with idle hands for a moment longer, Martha suddenly rose from the stool opposite me, and gathered up a dead duck from the table. She deposited herself on the seat once more, and began to pluck the lifeless body, while she waited for me to compose myself.

"You were like two peas in a pod when I saw you", she ventured. "Well-matched I should say, if I were to be so bold as to offer my opinion".

Downy feathers wafted around Martha's stool, and some floated onto my lap. I could faintly hear the sound of quills as they were being plucked from the fowl's flesh, but still the sound seemed to be far off in another world. I was still with you, Arthyen, in my own world. I was back outside last night with you as you had kissed my hand. I could still see the expression upon your face, as you had spoken of my warmth. Did you mean what I thought you had meant? I wished so much that I could turn time backwards, and be in that moment with you once more. I let out a long sigh.

"It is of no matter, Martha, for I fear that I shall never see him again", I eventually answered quietly.

She must have taken pity on me, for her voice altered, and she soothingly said, "Now, now, My Lady. Don't be talking like that".

The plucking stopped as she laid her hands on mine. "I have a feeling in these ageing bones that you will. Yes, *that* is what they are telling me. You and him will meet again. Mark my words".

I did look up at her, and at that moment, for the briefest passing of time, I believed her... and smiled.

"I hope your bones are right, Martha".

"They usually are in these things, My Lady," she grinned, and resumed her plucking whilst repeating, "They usually are".

I left her to her chores, and went to search out Airic, the chandler. For, apart from the fact that many of the candles needed replacing in the Hall - which I had been sure he would attend to - I also needed some new ones for my chamber. I was anxious to get them renewed, as the sky outside was overcast, making my room too dull in which to stitch for any length of time.

Airic was in his middle years; a tall thin man with dark hair and whiskers, and dark brown eyes. Although Airic has been with us for some nine years or so, I do not know much of his background. He is a quiet man who relishes his solitude. I have often wondered whether he used to be a monk, for he moves around in such a quiet, lonely, way. Do not get me wrong, reader. He goes about his business perfectly well, and I have no complaints about that. I have no complaints that he likes his own company occasionally either, but it would be nice to be able to get to know him a bit more. I have come to realise, though, that he *does* have a wonderful wit, and he has made me laugh on those odd occasions that he has been willing to openly engage in

conversation. Sometimes though, when he does not think anyone is near, he has a habit of muttering to himself. It is as if he has been having an unspoken conversation in his head, when occasionally an answer to a question in his mind is uttered from his lips by mistake. It is most odd.

Airic lives in a small cottage at the foot of the motte, just inside the bailey wall. Here he makes all the candles, using the tallow he has rendered from the fat of our slaughtered animals.

I am happy to have him around, and he usually does his job - however menial - perfectly well. I assumed that his late arrival this morning was due to the fact that he visited the tavern over-long last night, and was perchance suffering from a heavy head, but I was certain that by mid-morning the candles would have been replaced.

I did not have to search for him for long, however, as Airic soon quietly entered into the Hall, carrying a basket laden with candles. As ever, he had seemed completely engaged in his own thoughts, as he had placed the basket on top of one of the benches. I could hear him humming quietly to himself, and he seemed surprised when I approached him. I apologised for having startled him, and asked if I could have four of the candles.

"My Lady", he answered, offering me four of the waxy objects, which I took with a thank you, before taking them to my room where I have remained since.

It is now time to take supper, and my eyes are tired from the stitching and writing that I have been labouring at these past hours. Tonight, this is all that I shall write.

Seventh Entry

oday I visited Tarek in the smithy, for I have a mind to go for a ride tomorrow if the weather is bright enough. With this thought in mind, I needed to get my blade sharpened.

Everyone calls Tarek 'tiny'. This is, however, a term of affection for he is one of the biggest men I have ever known. He is a jolly fellow, slightly hard of hearing in one ear, but always with a kind word for everyone, and never without a tale to tell. He has a mass of dark hair that falls to his shoulders, and a beard and whiskers, which - strangely - are a different colour to the hair on his head. He has kindly blue-grey eyes, and always has red cheeks, which is hardly surprising, from the heat given off from the furnace. He is of a great girth and height, and towers over all our villagers. When I was a young girl, I used to ride on Tarek's shoulders, and felt I was a giant among the 'little people'.

Upon feast days and celebrations, Tarek can always be seen above everyone else, with a child upon his broad shoulders, their tiny feet wrapped around his neck. At Yuletide, the elected 'Prince or Princess of the Bean' sits aloft, a crown upon their head, as Tarek parades them around their 'subjects'.

I shall add here - for those of you who do not know - that at Yuletide we play a game called 'King of the Bean'. This entails a small bean being baked inside bread or cake and whosoever finds the bean, is crowned 'King' of the Yule feast. One year, the children's version was introduced, and the girls and boys now get their own chance of becoming 'Prince or Princess of the Bean'.

One of Tarek's greatest gifts, is his ability to weave stories to the children, of how his

37

giant ancestors built a great raised road, which he calls a 'causey way', in his country of birth, and that he is the only one of his kind left. The children sit wide-eyed and open-mouthed, as they listen to him narrate tales of heroic giants who battled against yellow-haired marauders from the northern seas, who came upon his shores in long ships, with a lust for blood and land in their eyes. It is strange, but sometimes I do wonder whether he really *is* the last of his kind, for oddly, none of his offspring seem to have inherited his stature.

As ever, he greeted me cheerfully as he hammered away at his anvil. I presented him with my sword, and asked him to sharpen the blade, which he tended to immediately. His craft had been handed down from his own father, and over the years he has perfected that skill, and it is a pleasure to watch him at work. He makes it all look so easy, and it never fails to impress me when he produces a blade out of a piece of shapeless metal, or a horseshoe that fits so well to the hoof for which it has been cast. Tarek came across the sea with his father when he was a boy of around five, and he had been quick to learn our language - something his father never quite managed to do very well - but older people always seem to find it harder to adapt to change, do they not? Even today, Tarek still speaks with a strange lilt to his tongue, but we have all become used to it.

This is of no matter, as he is a man of few words anyway, as he goes about his daily toil. But he is sometimes given to singing a raucous song of battles won, and of strange beasts slain. After a few ales in the tavern, he has also been known to sing a few songs of women won and lost. He has obviously led an interesting life, and has had three wives who have produced ten children between them. His current wife, Myrna - who also comes from the land of his ancestors - shares his cottage with him, and these children; two of whom she has borne. I have no idea how Tarek stands up inside it, let alone how they all fit into such a tiny cottage. But they all seem happy and content. Sometimes, when you walk by, you can hear Tarek and Myrna shouting over the children in their native language. I must admit that it does have a strangely calming note to it.

Eighth Entry

I have *such* interesting news to record tonight, that I fear it will take me many hours to pen, and it also means that from this moment on that I must make sure that I hide this journal for fear it should fall into the hands of those who may do you harm, my dearest Arthyen.

The day was bright this morning when I awoke, and the ground was covered in a light coating of frost. I decided that it would - indeed - be a good day to take my new mare, Elwine, out for a ride, for I had not as yet been able to do so. Her mother was the same mare who had birthed Beda four years before, and I had been pleased to be able to acquire Elwine, for this reason above all else. She is chestnut, just like Beda, but with four white socks and a pink nose, which our marshal, Wilf, has warned me, not to let the sun burn in the summer months. Apparently, pink noses are very susceptible to the harshness of the sun's heat. Information like this is one of the reasons he is keeper of the stables I expect, for his knowledge of horseflesh is never-ending.

I like Wilf. No-one really knows how old he is; in truth I do not think he knows himself, but he is grey-haired, with a long grey beard that reaches down to his chest. In his last battle, a sword that had left a gash down the right side of his face, had blinded him on that side, and had left him with only the one good eye. Rumour has it, that when he was a young warrior, he would plait his beard - which apparently was jet black back then - and tie bones into it that rattled together when he ran into battle. I have never been able to find out whether these were human finger bones, as is the tale, or chicken bones. I like to think that they were the former, as it gives him a more fearsome character. If I am to be blessed one day with children of my own, that

is what I shall tell them; for I know that children love to hear such tales.

To look at him now, you would not believe that he could have been terrifying in battle. To me, he has always been dear old Wilf in the stables, who loves all the horses in his care, and treats every one of them as if they were his own children. He was as upset as I was when he heard of Beda's death, but I do not think he blames me for what happened. He lives on his own now; his wife Udela, left this world around this time last year, and they never had any children, which I have always thought is a shame, as he would have made a very good father indeed.

I decided that I would take Elwine and Orvin, and ride to the forest which lay to the west. I would take my sword, and bow, and some food for the day. My experience on the moor has not dampened my desire to be alone with Mother Nature, and her glorious world, and I am determined not to let it make me a prisoner of my own home. Besides, there was no-one to stop me; no-one who cared enough to forbid me from going, in case some evil befell me. Apart from dear Martha, of course, who gave me a worried look as I packed my provisions. I kissed her on the cheek, and told her not worry - I would be back before nightfall.

I reached the forest about half-an-hour after leaving Cragnuth. It felt good to take shelter beneath the boughs, from the cold wind that had swept across the lowland. A thick layer of brown needles coated the forest floor, and the steady sound from Elwine's hoofs became muffled, as we made our way down a deer-path. I knew exactly where I was, and also where I was in mind to end my journey, deep in the middle of the forest. There was a deep pool I had been visiting for many years, which had its own magnificent waterfall carved out of the mountainside. The cooling waters fed the river that - in turn - meandered to join that which ran alongside Cragnuth. There, I had intended to sit and eat some of my food, and had hoped to see some of the deer that live deep amongst the trees.

I was not prepared, however, for what I did find in a glade about an hour's ride into the forest. At first, I thought I had been hearing things. But it was definitely men's voices that I could hear, along with the occasional whinny of a horse. I became wary, and was about to turn Elwine around and return to the safety of Cragnuth, when I decided that I should try to learn whom these people were. If Cragnuth was in danger, I felt that it was up to me to find out and warn the town if I could. I had dismounted Elwine, and had left her secured to a low branch, before taking Orvin with me, and had quietly approached the glade; my sword drawn in readiness for an attack. Peering through some bushes, I could make out a huge encampment of at least one hundred men and horses. The banners flying on some of the poles depicted a blue dragon on a yellow background. There were several lit campfires, but I knew that

these would not be seen from Cragnuth, as this part of the forest was around the side of the mountain that bordered the town on the western side. Whoever these people were, they were definitely hiding themselves well.

All too late, I heard Orvin emit a low warning growl, and I sensed that someone was behind me. Turning sharply I found myself confronted by three burly men, all with swords drawn, gazing at me in disbelief. One of them held Elwine's reins. They exchanged glances between each other, as if they did not know quite what to do, but then one shrugged and gestured with his sword for me to enter the clearing. There was not much else I could do, and I assumed that, as these men had not killed me straight away, that perhaps they were not the enemy after all. A lone woman and her dog, albeit an armed woman, could not do much against their heavy steel blades, and warrior strength. If they had been going to kill me, they would have done so by now. I was certain of that. I had to be - it was the only idea that would keep me feeling brave.

Once in the clearing, I returned my own blade to its scabbard, and gestured for Orvin to sit. I awaited my fate, as a mass of armed men circled around us. Yes, I was scared! Of course I was! But I am the daughter of Lord Edric; a woman whose forefathers were great warriors, and I was not going to dishonour them by behaving like a coward. I stood defiant.

I heard a familiar voice shout, "Stand down! Move away and give them space! The woman is known to me."

The men slowly began to move away. I heard someone mutter, "What a fine woman she is too", followed by a low snigger from another. "Yes, a fine warrior woman. I would not mind teaching her how to use that sword", muttered another. "By the look on her face, I would not like to think where she would stick it", came the low response. "I fear she may slice off your cullions", the voice continued with a snigger.

Again bellowed the voice, "Show some respect, men. For she is a woman of noble birth".

"Move... Now!"

The circle of men seemed to shudder as one, and began to widen quickly, as you - Arthyen - walked forward, and bowed your head. "My Lady Ethna. I must apologise for the coarseness of my men".

I was aghast at seeing you. I had so wanted to believe you, and believe in you. I had

so needed to trust you, and trust in you. My heart wanted me to do all these things, but my head was screaming at me not to. You had deceived me. Anger welled up deep inside me, and I could do nothing but ignore your courtesy.

"I do not understand, Lord Arthyen. I thought you and your *five* men had left to seek your uncle's counsel many days ago," I said, sarcastically emphasising the word 'five'.

"And I am not foolish enough to think that there is any way that you could have done so, and returned this quickly with so many men".

"I would never have assumed that you would be", you had replied.

"I am not in the business of allowing myself to be duped, My Lord". I had said angrily.

"And I am not in the business of deliberately wishing to dupe you", you said. "I have only wished to spare you the consequences of my..." you hesitated. "Shall we say, indiscretions?"

I did not reply. I *could* not reply, for fear that my anger at being taken for a fool, would erupt in the form of tears. No, I would stand quiet; as I wrung my hands behind my back, and willed those tears to stay away.

You continued. "Forgive me, My Lady, but from the very first time I met your father and cousin, I had an instant mistrust of them. I told you once of the coldness of Cragnuth did I not?" you asked.

"You did", I had to admit.

"I did not add that I also sensed deceit, for I feared it would upset you to speak of your father in such a way".

"My father means nothing to me", I replied quietly. "It is the deceit you have shown towards me that wounds".

You clicked your tongue. "My Lady, if you can still bear to be in my company, then I invite you to join me in taking food in my tent. There, I shall attempt to explain my actions, in the hope that I may restore what trust you may have had in me, and take away the pain that I have obviously caused you to suffer."

I knew that, if I had wished so to do, I could have taken my horse, and left the encampment. And I knew that I could have done so without any hindrance from you, or your men, but I wanted so much to have my trust in you restored. It was important to me that I could rid myself of the feelings of mistrust and anger that I felt towards you at that moment. So I responded with a curt "As you wish", and had followed you to your tent.

You had beckoned me to be seated, and had waited for me to do so before you had seated yourself. You did offer me food, but I did decline. I found that I had no stomach for sustenance at that moment, but had - however - taken the offer of water with gratitude, for my mouth was very dry.

"My Lady", you began, as I drained the cup of its refreshing and cooling liquid. "I am sorry that you have come upon us this day, in such a way".

"I am sure that you are", I replied sharply.

"Madam", you continued. "I realise that you are angered, but if you would let me explain, I would hope to quell your resentment".

"Please carry on", I said. "I shall try and curb my hostility while you do so".

"My thanks", you continued. "I did inform you that my men and I would be returning to my uncle. It is true to say that my five men did, indeed, do so. However, I did not accompany them."

I had been tempted to interrupt here, but refrained from doing so. It would seem that you had expected me to, for you paused in your explanation for a moment, before carrying on, "These men that you have come across today have been hiding in this forest for the past two weeks, as their numbers did increase each day. We have been scouting as I had told you; that much *is* true. But as we did so, at every town and village we came upon, we have recruited more men. Some of them have joined us from my uncle's castle, some of them are farmers, and some of them are free lancers whom we have met on the road. All have pledged allegiance to me, in the name of King Ulmar, and will fight with me to secure these borders, and dispel the evil that threatens these lands."

"Why such secrecy?" I asked.

"My uncle is aged, and his mind is addled", you continued. "He does not realise what is happening to his lands. His advisors are crooked, and are not to be trusted. I be-

lieve the enemy has bought them. They seek to prosper with land taken from my uncle. I was sent out to scout, presumably on the promise that I would be slain."

Here, he paused briefly, while he took a drink from his own cup.

"You see, My Lady", he went on. "The King has a daughter, the Lady Igerna. The laws of the land will not allow her to rule upon his death. I am his only surviving male relation".

"You are to be King?" I asked, knowing full-well the answer.

"I am his heir, yes", you replied. "And it would suit them to have me killed, conveniently, on this reconnaissance of the borders".

"The King is unaware of this?" I asked. "Surely there is someone who can warn him of this treachery?"

"He would not take heed, My Lady", you said. "He is but a puppet now, and hardly is aware of what day it is".

My mood had begun to soften at his explanation.

"I have always been known as hot-headed, so now I am acting in such a way", you said with a half-smile.

"So, if I guess correctly," I began. "You are gathering your own forces, to try and destroy the enemy without your King's favour?"

"Exactly", you responded. "And that is why I could not say anything to you in case we were overheard at Cragnuth, for although I know I could put my trust in you, I am not sure of where the allegiance of your father or cousin would lie."

"I understand, My Lord", I said, and added: "Nor any of the other townspeople either, no doubt, although I would like to think that they would support you".

"I think if they knew who my father was, they might", you said.

This statement had intrigued me. "Who was he?"

"I am Arthyen, son of Beroun", you began. "I know not whether this name has ever been spoken to you. He was once King of this Lower Kingdom, while his brother-

in-law, my uncle, was King of the Upper Kingdom. My father was slain by the same enemy that are threatening the borders now. That is why we ride under the banner of my father, rather than the King".

I remembered your ring with the dragon's head, and the connection with your banners became obvious.

"I am here to avenge my father's death, and also to protect the lands which are to become mine, by birthright as well as by default. If I am to die doing so, it will be under the banner of my father. For, in the first instance, it is for him I am fighting".

I had heard of the tales of Beroun. He had been a great King, but legend had it that he had been slain by a great dragon that had swooped out of the north. Great tales of heroic deeds always become twisted in translation as they are handed down, but Beroun's death had not been one of those ancient tales. This was more recent, and I was not sure how to approach the subject with you, but it would appear that you had read my mind for you had continued:

"When my father was killed, my mother fled, with me still in her womb, back to the safety of the castle of the King - her brother. I was brought up in the halls of the King, and was taught how to read and write, how to ride, and how to fight. It was not until my mother lay dying, that she told me about my father, and my birthright. I was in my sixteenth year before I learned the truth".

You had risen from your seat, and had begun to pace up and down the tent.

"You do not have to continue, My Lord, if you do not wish to", I offered, at the sight of your obvious agitation.

"It is important that I continue My Lady," you replied. "It is important to me, to our friendship, that you understand *exactly* why I am here, and why I have had to deceive you. I shall not rest if I do not continue".

"I have no wish to become parted from your friendship, My Lord. Pray continue if you feel you need to, but I have no wish to cause you discomfort".

"My forefathers ruled over the Upper and Lower Kingdoms for many centuries. They lived in the age of dragons, but lived in peace and harmony with them. Hence the dragon has been our family emblem, handed down from generation to generation."

"But I have heard tales that your father was killed..." I began.

"...by a great dragon?" you interrupted. "My Lady, the enemy that comes before us is led by a great wizard. He thought it would be a cruel trick on my father, to be killed by the very beast that had shared our forefather's lives so happily for so long. So he decided to conjure up one last dragon to slay him".

I gasped audibly.

With horror, I realised that, not only are you, Arthyen, in mortal danger from this wizard, but also that if he had done it once, he could well call upon such a beast again.

"His mistake was that he had failed to anticipate the chance that my mother could be with child, so - when she escaped - he thought no more of it".

"But why has he waited so long before trying to take over both Kingdoms?" I asked.

"To conjure such a beast took a lot of energy. I assume that he has had to take time to regain his strength, and amass an army. I have heard that he has recruited from lands across the seas, and has had to pay out large amounts of gold, and promise much in return."

"And now he knows about you?"

"There were other people at my mother's deathbed apart from me. Her dying confession to me was overheard by many who would plot against me".

"I am sorry to have not trusted you, My Lord", I said, standing up. "I offer my allegiance to you, and will assist you in any way that I can".

"You must keep yourself safe", you replied, taking my hands in yours. "Until I came upon Cragnuth, I had only vengeance and possible death in mind, but now I have met you, Ethna, and I have realised that there is a chance for more. After the incident on Blackditch Moor, and you were caught in the icy grip of death I realised that you had touched my life in a way I had not thought possible."

I had blushed at your words and bowed my head. You had placed your hand on my shoulder. "I have no wish to cause you embarrassment, My Lady. I shall say no more".

 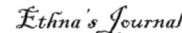 

At that point, one of your men-at-arms entered into the tent, clearing his throat to gain your attention. "I think our position has been discovered, Lord Arthyen. Two men have been sighted leaving the forest, heading for Cragnuth at great speed My Lord."

"I am sure I was not followed", I pleaded.

"You were not, My Lady," the man said. "We were following you from the moment you entered the forest, and there was nobody behind you. These men must have come across us by chance. Perhaps hunting?"

He looked at you, Arthyen, but you did not speak.

"I do not know how they got past our look-outs, My Lord", the man-at-arms continued, in a tone that seemed as if he felt personally responsible for such an occurrence to have happened.

"What is done, is done", you had said. "It is getting late, and you, My Lady, should be getting back to Cragnuth before you are missed. It can only be hoped that you were not spotted here, but be on your guard. I shall have men escort you to the forest edge. I trust that you can make it home by yourself from there?"

I had nodded to you, and prepared to take my leave. I had expected a proper farewell from you, but realised that you were now deep in thought as to your next move to escape further detection.

"Farewell, My Lord Arthyen," I said as I left the tent.

"Farewell, My Lady Ethna," you replied as you disappeared to the small table at the end of your tent.

So here I am, back in my chamber, reflecting upon what has occurred. My head is spinning, and I am not sure what to do. But I know that, at least, I must attend supper as if nothing has happened.

So, for now, I shall leave my writing and descend to the Hall.

Ninth Entry

s usual, the wine did flow freely across the lips of my father and cousin last night, and - as usual - I left them long before they were ready for sleep. Neither had questioned me on my whereabouts yesterday. I know not whether they knew, or whether they did not care, but was only relieved that I had not had to make up any excuses.

I know not how they managed it; the wine had taken its toll, I could see, and it made me smile at their obvious discomfort, but - not long after dawn - my father and cousin took of their leave, taking with them six of our best soldiers as protection on their journey. As usual, I was not privy to their destination, but I have heard from others that they have decided to seek counsel with the King themselves. I have a feeling that it is not with good intentions towards you that they ride.

My heart is heavy with longing, and my head is tormented with thoughts of your safety. My day has been filled with such menial tasks as to keep my mind busy, but now, as the rest of the township settles down to its slumbers, I know that it is time for me to rest my head upon my pillow, and hope that sleep can find me once more.

Tenth Entry

I knew it would take my father and Margh three good days' ride to reach your uncle's castle, and I felt compelled to ride out to the forest to try and warn you of the likely reasons for their sudden departure. But I knew, deep in my heart, that you would no longer be there. It was two days ago that your camp had been discovered, or perhaps so, for it is still not certain whether the men seen riding out of the forest had, in fact, seen or heard anything at all. However, you would not have remained in the clearing - you would have taken your men to another place and, unfortunately, I have no way of knowing where that place could be. All I can do is wait here at Cragnuth, and hope that you are safe.

One of the daily routines of Cragnuth is the sword practice. Ever since I could wield such a weapon, I have stood in the arena with the soldiers, along with any other able-bodied men of the town, as often as my other duties allowed me. My father may have no living sons, but I have endeavoured to be as much of a son as I possibly could by learning how to defend my people. I am not a very good sword-maiden, but I have learned the basic skills that, perhaps, will keep me alive for a few minutes longer than if I had not. I admit that I have not enough strength in my upper body to wield a sword for long periods, but I have picked up many tricks from my fellow comrades-at-arms. They have accepted my presence amongst them, and have learnt not to hold back if pitted against me. They always win in the end, but I have managed to wind a few in my time.

So today, I decided that I should attend practice, as I have a very strong feeling that some day soon, what skills I *do* possess, may well be called upon.

As I have been blessed with a not too tall body, my speciality is the upward thrust -

very good when up against an enemy brandishing a shield, as a sneaky, well-aimed thrust upwards underneath the shield, can do a lot of damage. I am also lighter than the average soldier, and am - therefore - slightly more nimble on my feet, which again can be quite an advantage.

And so it was that, whilst I was attempting a particularly vicious - and I must add most un-ladylike - thrust underneath poor Unga's shield, I had the oddest feeling that I was being watched. I must add here that we did not, of course, use our full strength in these practises; goodness no, or otherwise there would be none of us left standing! Occasionally some of us received injuries, but these wounds were purely accidental and no-one harboured any ill-feeling against those who had caused them. I have had blood drawn on two or three occasions, but have survived perfectly well, and am, in a strange way - although this does sound very conceited - quite proud of my scars.

Indicating my retreat from the practise, I removed my helm, and had scanned the perimeter of the enclosure, but could see no-one other than a few children who were playing with wooden swords, whilst their fathers or elder brothers used the real thing within the enclosure. Further round, I could make out two women chatting to each other as their offspring clung to their skirts, one of whom I could hear crying very loudly, even over the noise of the men, as she had obviously grown tired of waiting for her mother to finish her conversation. Certainly, I had discerned no-one there who was in the slightest bit interested in what I was doing.

However, that feeling had still been present, and it had begun to irritate me that I could not discover from whence it came. My eyes searched further away from the enclosure - there were many folk going about their daily business and it was nigh on impossible to make out anyone acting strangely in the crowds - until I made out a figure leaning against the door of *The Serpent's Nest* - Cragnuth's tavern. From where I could see, this figure looked to be cloaked from head to foot, and certainly seemed to have their gaze set in my direction. I had decided that the only way to find out was to approach whoever this person was, and see what occurred when they realised I was coming upon them.

Still the figure did not move, and it was not until I was within an arm's reach of this person that they raised their head slightly to reveal, from under the hood, a pair of brown eyes that could not be mistaken.

My hand had flown to my mouth as I had gasped.

"My Lord", I had whispered. "Is that really you?"

A hand shot out from under the cloak and wrapped itself around my arm. "Come", you said under your breath. "We must speak," and you had led me around the corner to the alley beside the tavern.

You had checked that we had not been seen, or followed, before removing your hood.

"It is dangerous, My Lord, for you to be here," I began to gabble. "My father left yesterday to meet with the King. I am not certain, but I think it may be in connection with you".

"I know", you said. "I saw them leave. I have been awaiting a good hour to come here to speak to you".

"But you should not be here. You should be far away from Cragnuth by now", I said earnestly, for I was indeed afraid for you.

"My men have left ahead of me," you explained. "They are many miles from here by this time, and I shall leave to join them after we have spoken. You may rest assured, My Lady, that by nightfall I shall be well on my way".

"Then you are still set upon your mission? You will take your men to fight without the King's knowledge or blessing?" I asked.

"It may well be without his blessing, yes, but I fear that once your father reaches him, it will certainly be to his knowledge, although I do not think he will understand. His advisors certainly shall though, and it is *they* that who are not to be trusted."

How tired and troubled you did look, my dear Arthyen. Would that I could have eased your anguish.

"You are quite a skilled maiden with the sword, My Lady", you continued, changing the subject. You smiled.

"Not really, My Lord, but thank-you." I smiled back.

"I could not leave, My Lady Ethna, before saying farewell to you properly. I fear that I was rather preoccupied when you left us the other day".

"I realised then that you had more important things to think about My Lord." I had answered. "The safety of all of your men should be paramount in your mind at such a time".

"Yes, it is true. I have one hundred and fifty men who follow me, and it befalls upon me, as their captain, to lead them, and ensure that they do not fall into any traps."

"I am sure they trust you, My Lord", I said softly.

"And do *you* trust me, My Lady?" you asked as you took a step towards me.

"I think, my Lord Arthyen, that I would trust you with my life", I had answered.

"I should tell you, then, that there is another reason why I am here", you continued. "As we speak, I have men talking to your townsfolk and soldiers to see if there are any amongst them who are willing and able to join us."

"Oh", was all I could manage in response.

You must have sensed my surprise at this confession, for you had continued, "This is wrong of me I know, My Lady, and as, in your father's absence, these people are under your guidance alone, I feel it right to ask your permission first".

I thought for a moment.

"We shall, of course, not take many with us, and shall not leave the town unprotected", you carried on, as I contemplated what he had said.

"I know that there will be many here who will be honoured to follow you, My Lord," I said at last. "If they wish to leave, then I shall not stop them."

You bowed your head to me in thanks.

"But I shall only allow it on one condition", I added, trying to look at stern as I could.

You looked quizzically upon me before asking, "My Lady?"

"I insist that you and your men rest here and take food before you leave. You cannot ride on empty stomachs. What say you?" I smiled.

After a brief pause to gather your thoughts, you smiled back at me, your brown eyes sparkling, before answering. "I think, My Lady that a good deal has been struck. If we leave before light tomorrow morning, it will not put us much behind. It also means that I shall have a few more hours in your good company, which, I cannot

deny, is excuse enough to delay my departure."

I knew I had blushed, but I had no control over such involuntary actions.

"It is settled then. Martha can be trusted not to speak of your presence here," I said, confident that I was right. "How will you tell your men?"

"Leave that to me, My Lady. I shall return in a short while. I presume they may stay with Wilf? From what I have been told of him, he is one of the old warriors, and can be trusted?"

"Indeed he can", I answered on behalf of the marshal. "As can most of the town, My Lord. There not many here who would not follow under the banner of the King - or your father - by all that I have heard."

"Whilst I believe that is true," you answered, "I still have to be cautious. This cloak is to disguise myself for *your* safety, My Lady, for I know that if I am recognised, and word gets back to your father that we have spoken, then I shall have been responsible for placing you in possible danger. That is something which I have no intention of doing".

What happened next I had not expected. We were so close at that moment, and I was not sure what to say or do. I had thought that you would leave to find your men, and tell them of the change in plans but you did not. In truth, you took one step closer to me, and before I knew what was happening, I felt you slide one arm around my waist.

I find myself in need of laying my quill down momentarily for I am not entirely clear how to write the continuation of this entry. It concerns me to write such intimate thoughts, but I realise that not to do so would give whoever may read this journal an incomplete account, and I feel it only right and proper to record as much as I dare.

To this end then, I shall continue.

For a hand that has carried a sword so often into battle, your touch was feather-light and gentle against my cheek. As you had caressed my skin, it had sent a tingle down my backbone, and I found myself erupting in goose-bumps, and overcome by such a wonderful sensation that I have never before known. Your fingers traced down my jaw-line, until - upon reaching my chin - you had tilted my head slightly upwards. A cooling breeze had swept around us as you bent your head down, and had brushed your lips against mine.

I shall never forget those words you whispered, dearest Arthyen. So softly you had spoken. Perhaps too personal to record here, but write them I feel compelled to do. "Ethna, in these last few days, you have captured my heart and I give it to you willingly", you said. "I am a warrior, fearless of battle and death, but I have now found myself in the strangest position. I feel complete when I am in your company, and I find myself pining for you when I am not. When I awake from my sleep, I sense you are there to greet me, and when sleep takes me, I swear I can feel your breath on my cheek as you whisper good night".

I had opened my mouth to reply, but your lips sealed them before any words could utter forth. It was so soft that caress of your lips on mine, and in an instant it washed away the fears that have clouded my thoughts of late. I know not from whence it came, but a tear meandered down my cheek. As you drew away from me, you had looked deep into my eyes, and pensively wiped away the droplet with your finger. "What say you, my dearest Ethna? Is this a tear of despair or joy?"

I had placed the palm of my hand on your cheek as I answered you. "It is of joy Arthyen, because after all these years I have at last found you. I have searched through the gloominess of life to find you for so long, that I had long given up hope of ever finding you. And yet ... it is also of despair."

At this, you had taken my hand in yours, and a look of deep concern furrowed your brow. I continued: "Despair that we have met in such perilous times that I know not what is to become of us. My father has put me up for sale, and a man I detest with all my heart has bought me. You and I have been brought together, and it would now seem that my father is intent on pulling us apart".

No man has ever shown me such affection, my sweet Arthyen. This day you pulled me towards you and held me in your embrace, and for the first time in my life, I felt empowered to take a hold of my destiny.

I answered your original question, "Arthyen, it is true that we have only known each other but for a few brief days, but I am bereft when you are not with me. What say I? My heart is yours, and I know that you will not treat it unkindly."

In a low voice you carried on, "There is a malice riding on the approaching winter winds, and I am certain that war will be riding with it. When the battles do rage they shall take me far from these walls. But know this, My Lady, that although I may be many miles from you, my spirit will always walk with you." You kissed the back of my hand, and then placed your lips upon mine once more.

"As for your heart," you continued, "I shall lay down my life to protect such a delicate and precious thing."

We stood wrapped in each other's embrace for only the briefest moments, before you had broken away from me.

"I must warn my men," you said. "They shall be wondering what has occurred with me".

Replacing the hood over your head, you were gone from the alley in an instant.

It did not take you long to return, and we made our way as unobtrusively as possible up to the relative safety of the Hall, where Martha was only too happy to be involved in such a secretive alliance.

Supper tonight was so different to what it had been the last time you were here, Arthyen. We could sit openly together and dine, and did take much pleasure in each other's company. We both knew that this would be the last time for many days, or even weeks, before we would be able to see each other again.

Martha spent the evening happily clucking around us, and seeing to our every need. She is a very dear woman indeed.

And so, reader, here I am now in my chamber as Arthyen sleeps further down the hall, before riding in a few hours to join his men. I wonder how many of our townsmen will be following him? Who will they be? He has said he will not take many, but how will he choose who can go, and who must remain? I shall hope for their safe journeys.

I know I must close my eyes soon, but how can I sleep when I have such great concern for his safety? How I can I close my eyes without seeing his face before me, and wishing it to be real? Would that I could feel his hand against my cheek, feel his breath against my skin as he whispers those sweet words in my ear.

Eleventh Entry

As I awoke on this grey morn I did think that I had encountered such a wondrous dream. My skin did tingle and my heart beat furiously within my breast. As my eyes grew accustomed to the grey light, I did behold a figure leaving my chamber, the candlelight flickering on the hilt of a mighty sword. Such joy I did have - 'twas not a dream - those sweet kisses had, in truth been placed upon my skin by the gentlest lips of my noble lord. I did whisper your name but you did not hear me. I did leap from my bed and did run after you but you had gone. Through the village did I run barefoot, scattering chickens as I went, to see you join your men at the banks of the river, where they had been awaiting your arrival. I watched as you turned to look back. Did you see me My Lord?

Oh, if you could have tarried but just a moment longer, I should have laid my hand across your troubled brow, and kissed your lips in farewell, but there I did stand at the edge of my village, and weep as the other women do for the safe return of their men. My cloak was wrapped tightly around me against the drizzle, so that it did not wash away the warmth of your caresses on my face and shoulders. May your sword keep you safe My Lord, my dearest Arthyen, and may your horse carry you safely in battle and back to me.

Long did I stand out in the cold fine rain and watch, as you did lead your men across the river, and into the dark wood beyond. The last man had long disappeared into its murky depths, before I did return to face my daily toil. Oh my sweet Arthyen, how slowly has passed this day, not an hour has gone by that I did not think of you. Now darkness has fallen, and the skies have cleared. A thousand and

more stars do shine above and the moon does bathe my face in its pale light. I am comforted by the thought that this same light shines down upon you, as in some small way it does bring us together this eve.

Would that I could take up my own sword and follow your road, but I know that I cannot. We know of the terror of raiders who ride from out of the sunlight to wreak death and destruction upon poorly defended towns and villages. Alas, although we may boast some protection from our outer wall, we find ourselves such a town. Our roofs are of thatch, and the buildings are built from wood, the keep included. Several boldly aimed, blazing arrows, and all would be soon laid to ruin. I know that I must stay with my people, and prepare to fight here if necessary. I shall meet my fate, boldly, and without fear, beside them if that is what is written.

Twelfth Entry

t is several days since you left us, Arthyen, and my father and cousin are expected to return any day. I know neither what news they will bring, nor how my father shall react when he discovers that men are missing from the town. Perhaps I should record that fifteen of our men have followed you; five soldiers hand-picked by your men-at-arms and the rest members of the town - ordinary men and boys who decided they wished to try their luck in battle.

Tarek had wanted to join you, but Myrna would have none of it. She told him, directly by what I have heard, that she would not be left to look after ten children all on her own. I must admit that I do not blame her for such an outburst. Besides, Tarek's skills are needed here, and I feel sure that you would not have allowed him to follow you, even if his wife had done!

Despite having the use of only one eye, Wilf, however, did join the march under your father's banner. I had thought he would choose to do so - Wilf is a warrior first and foremost, and although running the stable at Cragnuth has its responsibilities and a fair amount of high-standing in the town, I had known that the chance of one last battle would prove too much of a temptation for Wilf.

He has left the stables in the capable hands of young master Gryffyd.

Gryffyd is now fifteen years of age, tall and lean as a pole, and is the second son of Seren and husband Gryffold. He has been working under the watchful eye of Wilf these past four years. It is an unspoken expectation that Gryffyd will take over the role of Cragnuth's marshal when the situation arises. He is an eager young man with a mass of red curls upon his head, and his face and arms are covered in freckles.

When he was a little boy he used to be teased, for most of his body is covered in these tiny patches of darker skin. His complexion is such that he cannot remain in the sun for very long in the summer months, as his skin does turn red so quickly, and causes him much discomfort.

Carrow, the tanner, has seen his two elder sons - Milyan and Gorlas - leave to follow you, and Seren has made Wilf promise to look after her elder son, Peder, along the way. Joining them are Aedd, Bowen, Cullen, Lennox, Meryn, Oran and Tormod.

The five men-at-arms who have left are, of course, very well-known to me as we have shared many a bruised morning together. They are Unga, Kendrick, Quinn, Bledri and Gethin. I hope their swords keep them all safe and well in battle.

I am sad to see these people leave us, and I pray for their safekeeping and safe return to their families and loved ones. I do smile also, though, when I think of Wilf. I have it on good authority that he did plait his beard once more, and did, in true fashion, thread it with bones. I have been assured, however, that these were chicken bones, not those of some unfortunate human.

Thirteenth Entry

The first snowfall, heralding the coming of winter, has come upon us this day, and in its wake has come the dark cloak of death. It was not yet dawn, when I was awoken by a frantic shaking by Bertha, one of the girls from the kitchen, who is also the elder daughter of Hildred, the village midwife. As I suddenly left my dream world, I could sense that the world outside was eerily muffled, and I knew immediately that this was because our lands were covered in snow. Bertha had gabbled her message that I was needed at Martha's home, for the infant was on its way into this world. I had jumped out of my bed, my head thumping at the rapid change from sleep to wakefulness. I had dressed in my warmest clothing as quickly as I could, and had followed her out of the keep into the early morning air. It was still snowing thickly, and all around, the new-laid snow was glistening like a thousand jewels in the pale light that had emitted from the door, as we had left the Hall.

From the frightened look on the young girl's face, I knew that all was not as it should have been at my destination. She had told me all the while that Martha had started the pains late yesterday evening, and that to begin with, all had been well. It was only in the early hours of this morning, that it had become obvious that Martha was in difficulty. I had been prepared for the worst, as I have recorded before, but had always hoped that Martha would be spared a difficult birthing.

Once inside her home, though, the smell of blood and imminent death was overwhelming. The air inside was stifling, made the more so by the heat from the fire, and the presence of so many people in the small area that made up their tiny cottage.

Poor Martha was prostrate upon her cot, glistening with sweat, and looking as weak

as a newborn lamb. Hamel, her husband, was sitting in the opposite corner, his head cradled in his hands, as he sobbed quietly. The two older boys - Willard and Rafe - were standing on either side of him with their heads buried in his shoulders. My eyes had frantically searched for little Hannel, and had just made out his small frame huddled in the darkest corner. As my eyes became adjusted to the dimness in that part of the cottage, I could just make out his eyes staring, not looking at anything in particular - just staring.

The sheeting on which my poor dear Martha was laying, was soaked with blood; its crimson stickiness was seeping down her bare legs. The village midwife, Hildred, was standing at Martha's head, shaking her head, as she wiped a damp cloth across Martha's forehead. I had looked across at Hildred for a sign of hope, but was met with a look of none. She whispered to me that the child was not turned properly, and following her gaze I noticed one tiny, bloodstained foot emerging from between Martha's legs. It was clear, in that instant, that there was no hope left for either the child or for Martha. She was quite obviously exhausted, and could push no more. All she could do, now, was wait for her life-blood to drain away.

Looking down at her, I could see that she was already quite pale, and was shivering - an obvious sign that it would not be long. I took her hand in mine, and told her that I was with her. She half opened her eyes, and softly smiled, tightening her fingers slightly around mine, with as much strength as she could muster. Her breathing was shallow, and she groaned with pain.

The sobbing in the corner grew louder, and it took a great deal of strength from me not to let the tears come to my own eyes.

You tried so hard, dear Martha. Just before death took you, you had tried once more to push your child into this world. The scream you uttered forth will stay with me until my own final parting on the wings of death.

It had been little Hannel who had caused the tears to come. An icy cold draught had swept across the bed as Martha had breathed her last. It had chilled me to the bone, and I had been startled when Hannel limped suddenly past me, and had thrown him-self on to his mother's breast, calling out to her plaintively. I had touched his head gently, at which he had left his mother's body, and had wrapped his arms around my legs, and clung to me. I stood there for what seemed like a very long time, the tears running freely down my cheeks, before I gently had released his grip, and had bent down to cuddle him, before picking him up in my arms, and taking him to his grieving father and brothers. There, I left him.

It took Hildred and me quite a while to clean up the deathbed, and make Martha more comfortable. I realise that it may seem a rather odd thing to write, reader, but there is no reason why - just because she breathed no more - that Martha should not lie in a clean bed. She looked serene in death, and her face showed no sign of the pain she had endured in her last moments. Many would come to visit and pay their respects, as she was a well-known - and much-loved - member of our village. She will be sorely missed, and my heart is heavy with her loss.

It had stopped snowing, and daylight was upon the land by the time I left the cottage. News of Martha's departure had already reached many of the other townsfolk. There was a silence as I had walked back to the Hall. There were no children playing in the snow, and it lay as it had fallen, untouched by the usual eager footsteps of the young.

You will forgive me, but I can write no more today.

Fourteenth Entry

I have not written here since Martha's death. She was committed to the cold, hard soil yesterday, with her unborn child still in her womb. Hamel and his two elder sons are coping with their loss as well as they can - there is plenty of work for them with the hunting pack to help keep their minds occupied. Little Hannel, however, is finding it all very difficult, especially as he used to sit with his mother in the kitchen every day while she worked. He has still been coming and sitting by the hearth, turning the spit, or helping with the chores, and the other girls have been very kind and patient with him.

Tilda has temporarily taken Martha's role of cook. As Lady of the Keep, the hiring of the staff would normally fall upon my shoulders, but I have had to explain to Tilda that, although I am perfectly happy for her to take on the responsibility, the final decision will have to rest with my father upon his return. Tilda was quite content with my explanation, and has happily continued where her mentor left off. I can see no reason why my father should not let her continue, but I have learned over the years not to take anything for granted where he is concerned. It would be just like him to deliberately go against my wishes, and decide upon someone else instead.

The return of my father is long overdue. I had fully expected him to arrive back here a day or so ago. The waiting is interminable. I would rather have him arrive, and do his worst regarding the missing men. The anticipation of his reaction is far worse than his expected actions. I have been told by many that, "I was not to concern myself," and that "things have been taken care of".

Apparently, it is to be related, that you had stolen into the town just as the gates had

been closing, and had done your recruiting under the cloak of darkness. It was to be told that you and your men had intercepted a few regulars of *The Serpent's Nest* as they arrived for their evening ale, and that the recruitment had then spread by word of mouth. This would mean that I would not be implicated in any untoward activities, and also that there would be no single person to blame either, especially as the two gate sentries themselves were two of those who had joined your army.

The past experiences of my father's wrath have always preceded him, and it is a sad fact that the townsfolk had long ago learned to spin a yarn in cases where this ire could be fuelled.

Fifteenth Entry

I am beside myself as I write this entry tonight. I know not where, nor whom, to turn to for comfort. I do not understand the politics of war, but to hear of the ultimatum of banishment threatened towards you, does seem too much to bear. My father and cousin did return from the King's Counsel this eve, and did bring such news to my ears. It was Margh who took great pleasure to impart this news to me at supper. He smirked, and seemed to relish the discomfort it caused me, although I tried very hard not to let my true feelings show. I cannot understand how the King could bestow such a denunciation on his own kith and kin, when it is only for the future of his kingdom that you do search out your enemies now, and I told my father and Margh my thoughts.

This had been a mistake, for I fear my defence of your actions did not please my father. As hard as I did try to remain unbiased, I believe that my eyes did betray my affection for you. Alas, to this end I fear that my father will encourage my cousin's irksome attentions even more.

What shall you decide to do, I wonder? The messenger should reach you by nightfall. Shall you choose this exile? Shall I never see you again? I am sure that my heart could not bear such a separation.

Now I do pace my chamber with much anxiety. Oh, but for a word of your safety should reach my ears, that I could rest tonight in the knowledge that your heart still beats within your chest, and that you are not lying in some blood-soaked field.

Sixteenth Entry

s I did stand in that barren place, I did see you walk over the brow of the hill leading your weary horse with one hand, the other trailing your bloodied sword. I could not move, but seemed rooted to the spot, the howling wind whipping around my bare feet and ankles. I did wrap myself tightly in my cloak, and did squint against the biting wind. I could but watch you approach slowly, and with great effort, until you stood but a foot away from me, and still my legs would not move. Stepping forward, you brushed your lips against mine, and it was as if a hundred butterflies were released within my stomach. I blinked and you were gone. I did open my mouth to cry out, but no sound did utter forth.

Such was my dream.

I awoke before dawn, a cold sweat upon me, and did lie in my bed staring at the candle in the window, as its flame did melt it slowly into oblivion. Orvin was stretched across the foot of my bed as usual, and as I stirred, he raised his head briefly before returning to his own dream world. Soon his legs were twitching, as he began chasing something in his sleep - his nose twitched, and he began to make faint barking noises in his throat. How I envied him his slumber. Gazing at the candle, I longed to be shrouded in darkness once more. I wished to be joined with you again, even if only in my dreams, but was scared that I would encounter you in such a way as I had done minutes before. I know you are somewhere out there, and that you have given your heart to me, as I have given mine in return, but sometimes, in my desperately lonely hours, it sometimes seems not to be enough. I need to see you, be with you and touch you. Arthyen, my heart yearns to bond more tightly with yours.

My body still aches with the chill I did catch on the morn of your departure those long days ago, but I shall endure my discomfort silently, as I know that you do endure more. My own physical discomfort shall soon pass, but I know not how you shall endure the pain of your betrayal. My own needs are small compared to what you have to bear now.

I shall remain in my chamber today, with just Orvin for company. I have tried, during these past hours, to rid myself of the horrors of my nightmare last evening, but have failed. I do not wish to be in the company of anyone else; I wish to be alone with my thoughts of you. I am of the mind that if I can think of you without interruption, the negative visions of last night will dispel.

I shall, later, endeavour to inscribe some more, when I hope to record my father's reaction to the departure of our fifteen good men and boys.

I have sent word to the kitchen with Anfeald, one of the lads who run errands here, that I wish to dine by myself. Anfeald's father is Bledri, and you may recall that he is one of those men who have recently left us. Bledri is a tall, stocky, man with black hair and beard, and the most astonishing green eyes. His voice is as deep as that of a stag in the rutting season when it bellows its threat to likely usurpers. Anfeald is only seven years old, and has been with us in the Great Hall only for a few months, but he does seem to be doing well against my father's outbursts of vindictive behaviour - he takes it all in his stride.

And so, whilst I am awaiting my food, I shall continue with my writing as promised earlier.

When my father had learned of their leave-taking, his immediate response was to declare every one of them as traitors. As expected, he had readily tried to lay blame at my feet, but I am indebted to a surprising intervention by Airic, for - at that exact moment - he had entered into the Hall to go about his work of tending the candles. It was he who had told my father the agreed story. I do not know whether my father truly believed him, but his accusations towards me ceased. Poor Airic. My father had blustered on to him about how these men did tarnish the name of Cragnuth, and that of his ancestors, by following this outlaw, to which Airic had responded in his usual, slightly uninterested and unassuming way, "Oh didst they, My Lord?"

I had stood there waiting for my father to finish his tirade against the men, for I had wished to inform him of other matters. Eventually he ran out of words to use, and Airic managed to slip away to proceed with his work. As he passed me, he rolled his eyes to the heavens, and half-smiled at me.

It was then that I had told my father of the death of Martha, and of my decision - as Lady of the Keep - to bestow upon Tilda the position of cook. To my surprise, he did not disagree. I think his mind was too full of the perceived treachery that he felt towards the so-called traitors, for him to be bothered with such relatively small details.

Seventeenth Entry

Keowyn, son of Aeldred, did come upon our settlement this day, and did dine with us while breaking his journey overnight. He is the messenger who had been endowed with the task of delivering the threat of exile to you. My father did ask him quite blatantly at table, whether he had succeeded in his King's duty. My Lord Keowyn had informed my father that he had, indeed, carried out his duty many miles from here, and that you were still resolute upon your course. Whereupon my father did throw me a stern glance, and I could but lower my head for fear that my eyes would betray me again. Alas, my cousin did hear the sharp intake of my breath as you were spoken of, for he did lay his bony hand over mine as it rested in my lap. As his hand clenched my fingers tightly, he did then, with great smugness, tell of his total agreement with the King's rule of banishment over you, but no words of support did return at this news; in truth an eerie silence did descend upon our table.

Upon glancing at our visitor, from his expression it does seem, and hearten me, that you, my dear Arthyen appear to have the support from the noble Lord Keowyn. I sense that the task he had been set had not sat well with him. Many times this eve I did try to speak to him alone, but it was as if my cousin knew of my intent, as he did not divert his attentions from me, until at last, weary of my thwarted efforts, I did retire to my chamber away from his evil stare and unwanted advances.

I hope that tomorrow I shall be able to seek counsel with my Lord Keowyn without such attention.

Eighteenth Entry

An icy dawn was upon us again this morning, and I did stand apart from the others, as Keowyn prepared to take his leave. Gryffyd emerged from the stables with his horse, but before Keowyn mounted, he purposefully approached me, and kissed the back of my hand in farewell.

"My Lady Ethna," he said quietly. "I know that my task of messenger is not one that has brought joy to your heart, and my friendship for the recipient has made it an onerous one for myself also."

I glanced behind Keowyn to where my father stood. It would not be long before his suspicions at our conversation would be aroused.

"My Lord Keowyn, it does please me to hear of your words, and I thank you for telling me. I felt last night that you did not agree with the sentence over Lord Arthyen".

"He has been like a brother to me for many years My Lady, but my relationship with the Lady Igerna, the King's daughter, has put me in a rather delicate position," he continued softly.

"I am understanding of your position My Lord and I am sorry that your friendship as been placed under such foreboding," I told him.

I could see that both my father and Margh were beginning to grow suspicious of our conversation. Gryffyd must have noticed my concern, for he manoeuvred Keowyn's horse so that it stood between them and us, his face beaming with mischievous de-

light.

"My father will approach soon, I fear, My Lord. Please give me some news on Lord Arthyen," I uttered quickly. "Is he well? I do so fear for his safety. How did he take the news?"

My dearest Arthyen, it was then that he did speak softly the words I had longed to hear. That you had been well when last he did see you, and that the news had come as no shock to him. My sweet Arthyen, you had entrusted with him this message for my ears alone, and I thank fate for keeping you safe thus far. I did ask him to tell you, if your paths do perchance cross again, that I do think of you greatly.

"It is unlikely that they will", he replied. "But yes if that should occur, then I shall give him your message. If you will forgive the familiarity in saying this, he was right in his description of you, My Lady".

He could say no more, for at that moment my father did then approach, and My Lord did take his leave, but not before he did kiss my hand once more. As he did so, I felt him press something into my palm. Instinctively I closed my hand around the object. I looked at him enquiringly, but he simply bowed his head and smiled.

From its shape, I thought I knew what it may be, and my eager curiosity willed me to open my clenched fist and look at it, but I knew it would be wise to wait until I was in the safety of my own company, before I could investigate further. Before that time arrived, I carefully placed the object into the purse that hung at my hip.

As our visitor left through the gates, I made my way back to the keep with Orvin, only to be joined by Margh, at which point Orvin emitted a low growl. I hushed him, for - although I appreciated his ever-present loyalty - I did not want to cause a disturbance. I wished only to reach my chamber as quickly as I could.

Margh was irritatingly attentive as usual, and at first I considered whether he had witnessed the hidden exchange, but I rejected the thought as swiftly as it had descended upon me.

Perhaps here I should tell you a bit more of my cousin, although it displeases me to have to waste my precious ink and parchment so to do. Moreover, as this is a brief record of my life during these days, it is only fitting that everyone involved should be described in a manner that befits his or her character and involvement.

Margh is the son of my father's second half-brother. I shall attempt to explain.

When my father's mother, Edwyth, died, my father's father, Aewel, married for a second time. This second marriage to Wilfrida brought with it her two sons from her first marriage, Harian and Baldric. Margh is the son of Baldric, and is, therefore, a cousin only by marriage, rather than by direct bloodline.

I have already written of how I find Margh detestable and slimy, and I stand by those words. But I should perhaps try to describe him more fully, and in a less intolerant manner. Margh is five and twenty years of age, and has blue eyes that are as cold as the waters of the river in winter. He has a nose that protrudes like the beak of a hawk, and it sits between two sunken cheeks in a long and bony face. He has lank hair the colour of a fieldmouse, and it hangs limply to his shoulders. He is not of a great height, and is only about one inch taller than I am, although he tries to make himself taller by walking with his shoulders back and chest puffed-out, like a cockerel on parade to his hens. Alas, it would seem that I am not making him out to be very pleasant, but what I have written is a fair description of the features of the man.

I can only assume that the combination of a promised, handsome dowry upon his union with me, and the fact that it is not likely that he will find a woman who would voluntarily give up her single status to wed him, have helped to urge him forever onwards in his odious advances towards me.

I do wonder, Arthyen, that if I had not met you, would I have accepted my fate with less dissent? Would I be more inclined to try to see the good in him? Perhaps I would have been worn down in time; my fighting spirit and resolve broken, to finish my days as his chattel. There is still a fear in my belly, that he may yet succeed in his, and my father's, aim.

So, Margh accompanied me back through the streets. Several times, I tried to deflect him by explaining that I had errands to run, but he would merely stand and wait for me outside the various establishments that I visited. Eventually I gave in, and we walked back in silence to the Hall, where I at last left him, and brought myself here to my room.

So, reader, I am at last at my small desk writing this report for you. I am sure, like myself, you may have already speculated what gift I had placed in my purse earlier, and as I sit here now, my sweet Arthyen's signet ring is before me with its dragon head gazing up at my face as I pen this.

I shall carry it with me at all times, Arthyen, but not on my finger. Even if it did fit, it would be far too dangerous a thing to wear in public here at Cragnuth. I shall wear it around my neck every night whilst I sleep, and, indeed, on most days, but on those

days when my clothing would make it noticeable, I shall keep it safely in my purse, which never leaves my hip. It will give me comfort to know that something of yours is with me wherever I am, and I can but wish that I could give you something in return.

Nineteenth Entry

 great army does follow your command, but I know that you shall not hide behind their armour for protection. I know, my brave Arthyen, that you shall ride out in front and face the battle boldly, with no thought for your own safety.

I do miss you so much my dearest Arthyen, and I cannot help but wonder whether I shall see you again. The times we are living in are indeed dangerous, and life is such a delicate thing at the best of times, but when war rages it becomes even more fragile. It can be snuffed out as easily as a candle flame, and in such violent ways. I cannot imagine what life would be like without you in my world. These dark thoughts do cloud my head, and make me despondent. It is at times likes these that I begin to think it would have been better if we had not have met, for then I would not have such dreadful thoughts to concern me. Such a singular thought I admit, but life would be much simpler.

Oh, but no, for if you were not there, life would have continued to be so unpleasant. It would be just an existence, not a life at all.

Half of me urges me to pull up the drawbridge to my heart, so as not to be hurt, but I am afraid that it may be too late, for the bridge has been down too long, and its length and breadth has already been walked upon.

My ranting tonight, must make me out to be a woman possessed. However, dear reader, I am not. It is just that when I am on my own, I sit and think - perhaps I think too many thoughts too often, for I cannot think of one thing and let it be. I have to continue with the consequences of where one path of thought would lead,

and then compare it to where another path would lead, and so on and so forth. Such torment I do cause myself by thinking too much. I fear that too much of this solitary life here in Cragnuth has caused me to look inwards.

My father has succeeded in taking away what self-worth I had, and although to others, I put on a brave face and go through life's calamities with strength and fortitude, inside I am awash with self-doubt. This self-doubt leads me to question whether you and I shall ever be together. Whilst I know there is no reason why we should not be, I cannot believe that love has come into my life after all these years.

Yes, I have known many good people in my life - I have made many friends at Cragnuth whom I love dearly as brothers and sisters - but the special love between a man and a woman is something that I did not imagine I would ever experience. I had begun to think that a union with my cousin would be all I could hope for regarding a marriage and a future.

Forgive my despondency this evening, but I am sorely worried for your safety, Arthyen, and I am sorely tired also.

Twentieth Entry

I know not for how many days I have known you, Arthyen, nor, then, for how many days I have been writing this journal. There have been many days, or even weeks, that I have not put nib to parchment at all. Since my last entry had been so negative, I had thought it best not to write for a few days, and hence this is the first time I have sharpened my quill for three days and nights.

I wish I could give some encouraging information as I resume my record, but we have received news of an attack two days ago on our nearest neighbours, a little settlement in the west called Sith Hill Fort. We only heard today of its total destruction, and the ill-tidings have brought fear and unrest to our town. Our physician is presently tending to the bearer of such news, a young peasant by the name of Walt. It would seem that he should live, as the sword that sliced at him only managed to peel off the top layer of skin where it struck, and did not succeed in harming anything of importance within his body. A poultice has been applied, and it is now just a matter of waiting.

It is all the more difficult, as my father is not at present here at Cragnuth, for he did leave but two days ago - I believe he has gone to visit his half-brother, Baldric, to whom I introduced you briefly in an earlier entry. I can only presume that this visit is in connection with my supposed marriage to Baldric's son, my cousin Margh. This has placed me in a very uncertain position, for I know not what to do for the good of the town. In my father's absence, I feel that I need to guide the people, but I do not know whether I should wait to see if he returns, before making any decisions. In this, though, I have no way of knowing how long to wait. Are we in imminent danger, or is this threat still days - or even weeks - away? It is plain to see that

Cragnuth is in grave danger from this foe, but - to put it quite simply - there is no place for the people to go; they would become banished people with no livelihoods, wandering the hedgerows and fields, with the prospect of no homes to which they could return.

For my part, it would be a sad day indeed should I have to say farewell to my home, without knowing if I shall ever look upon it again. My time here may have not been entirely happy, but it is *still* my home. I know, however, that if the enemy continue their swathe of destruction unchallenged, then it is only a matter of time before Cragnuth will fall. Even if we *do* stay to defend it, we simply do not have enough men to protect against such a force, and it would be foolish heroics to even attempt to do so. But I do not see that we have any other choice. We need more men, more defences, and a lot of good fortune. Although we do have hope and courage, I fear that this will not suffice if the enemy launch an attack upon us.

Ever since Walt arrived with his tales of the massacre, there has been unrest in the town. I have noticed a few peasants have already left with their families, their carts loaded with as many possessions as they could take, or - as in most cases - as much as they could themselves carry. I cannot say that I lay any blame upon them, for I would probably do as they did, if in their situation.

I, however, am the daughter of Lord Edric, sword-maiden of Cragnuth, and shall stay, fight, and die if necessary, under the banner of my ancestors. If I should die here, then I shall join them in the 'Great Halls' knowing that I have not dishonoured their name - I shall be able to walk among them without shame.

I write as if I have made my decision, but in truth, I have not. I think I shall ponder upon my actions, and call counsel with the elders of the town tomorrow morning.

For now I shall rest.

Twenty-first Entry

After a sleepless night, I arose this morning with a great tiredness, but also with good expectations. During the cold night hours, a tentative idea came upon me, and I know not why I did not think of it before.

Many years ago, when we were but children, I used to explore the lands outside the town walls with a very dear friend of mine, Leif. I have not mentioned him before, but Leif and I went everywhere together for several years, during that period of time when we decided that exploration outside Cragnuth was far more exciting than learning how to read or write with Father Lorcan, more of whom I shall try to tell you about later.

On this particular foray into the unknown, in the first days of summer, Leif and I decided that it would be fun to explore the forest - the same forest where I came upon you, Arthyen, all those days ago. We had slipped passed the sentries, and out of the gate early, and had arrived at the edge of the forest long before Father Lorcan would have realised we were missing from his lessons. This was great sport for two nine-year-olds, who thought themselves very clever for accomplishing such a daring feat.

We had spent all morning weaving in and out of the giant trunks of the pine trees, having mock sword fights with fallen branches, or racing each other from one trunk to another, until we had come across a beautiful glade deep in the centre. It was as I have described it earlier, but on that occasion, we discovered - quite by chance - that there was a path, albeit a very slippery and narrow one, that disap-

peared behind the waterfall. We decided to follow this trail, and to our amazement, it opened up into a huge cavern behind the cascading waters. This was simply too much for us not to investigate further, and so off we went deeper into the chambers. For some odd reason children never seem scared of getting lost on such adventures, and we were no different, for we kept on walking deeper and deeper inside the labyrinth that opened up before us, the sound of the waterfall fading behind us, albeit still faintly audible.

I seem to recall that we walked for ages and ages, but it was probably only for about half an hour or so in reality, before we could feel cool air on our cheeks. Had we discovered another land on the other side of the waterfall? Or had we merely gone round in a huge circle, and come back out into the forest in another place? We had not been prepared for the sight that befell our eyes on that day.

Opening before us was a huge valley - a giant chasm cut into the mountains around us. We could see at least two great waterfalls that were feeding their waters down deep into the valley below us, and we could see the sunlight shining on a great river that meandered through the bottom of the valley. This seemed to disappear into the sides of the very mountains themselves.

We stood in awe at the size of it all - we had never seen such a sight in our lives before. We had, indeed, found a magical world beyond the waterfall, and wondered whether it was full of strange creatures and people. We could see a myriad of caves dotted along the mountainside nearest us, and our imaginations created great winged creatures living deep inside these caverns.

Leif suggested that we made a blood pact with each other not to tell another living soul about what we had found. I had agreed eagerly, upon which Leif had drawn his small dagger, and had cut the palm of his hand; a line of crimson liquid erupting along the wound. He had then passed the weapon to me, whereupon I had done likewise, before we placed our hands together, blending our lifeblood, and swearing total secrecy on our honour, and the honour of our ancestors. We had become blood brother and sister.

Until this day, journal, I have kept that secret. As for Leif - well my poor dear friend died not many months later, when he fell out of a tree and did break his leg upon hitting the ground. Although it was thought he would recover, his blood did turn bad, and he died. Even now, I still think of his sweet face framed by a mass of light brown curls. He was shorter in height than I was, but it was nearly always Leif who won the races we had, for he seemed to have longer legs than I did. Ah well, I must let Leif lay to rest in my mind for now.

As I had intended doing, I called for a council meeting with the elders this morning, and told them of my plan to temporarily relocate the townfolk. As I described the secret land beyond the waterfall to them, they seemed unwilling to believe me at first. But after a while decided that they would go and see for themselves whether the land I had told them about, in truth, did exist as I had described it.

And so, it was that they left that very forenoon, and returned later in the day, all fervent believers, and thinking that I had come across a very good idea, indeed.

Here I must add reader, that when Leif and I came across this land we were but nine years of age, and to us, this land seemed like a magical kingdom. It is, of course, merely a valley that is found in the midst of a range of mountains, and, although as far as I know, it can only be accessed through the cave system that Leif and I discovered, it is quite possible that there could well be another entrance to the valley.

The counsel members agreed that my idea of moving the people of Cragnuth into the forest and through the cave system was a worthwhile one. The people would be safe from attack, and also not too far away from their homes. The message was sent around the town, for those people who wished to leave, to pack up as many of their belongings as they could carry, for we were to relocate to a magical kingdom. I would not force any person to leave their home if they were disinclined to do so, but I hoped that most would follow me.

It is expected that we shall leave tomorrow. This will be my last entry again for a few days. It will not take us long to reach the valley, but I am not sure how far into it we shall roam before settling. I shall endeavour to write again as soon as I am able.

Twenty-second entry

Everybody carried as many possessions and provisions as they possibly could, with others being carried on the backs of every spare horse. No carts or wagons could be taken where we were going, so many people had to leave many possessions behind, just as I have had to do. I am sorry to report that I have had to leave my writing desk and chair, and I am finding it sorely difficult to write now without them. However, I am well aware that others have had to leave more.

That morning, our procession of baggage began its short journey down across the flatlands towards the forest to the west. From my position at the rear, I could see the snake-like column of people come to life ahead of me, and I had waited patiently for all those in front take their turn in joining the departure of Cragnuth. It seemed to be taking an eternity, and the back of the line had still not taken a step, when a rider did burst forth from the wood to the east and rode with great speed towards us. He did slow down only briefly to splash across the river. I did raise my hand to shield my eyes from the winter sun, and for one brief moment did think the rider was you, as his stature was so much like yours. He did thunder past our pitiful procession, sending frozen divots flying in the air in his wake. Midway he did alight his horse, and begin to speak to each villager in turn; but was met with a shrug of the shoulders, or a shake of the head. They were all too miserable or frightened to take notice of a stranger's questions on a day such as this.

He was obviously searching for someone, and I was intrigued to learn to whom this bedraggled soldier wished to speak.

It was Tarek, our blacksmith, who did - eventually - turn, and point in my direction.

The realisation that this man was looking for me hit me like a bolt from a thunderstorm. I could not move from my saddle, for my head was full of thoughts of some bad news of you.

I was too scared to move forward.

I fingered the thong around my neck, and pressed your ring against my skin where it hung 'neath my shift. With dread in my heart, I slid from my horse's back, and did wait for the messenger to reach me. 'I am she,' I replied in confirmation of his enquiry.

Everyone around me disappeared in a haze as I prepared myself for the worst. But then he did give me your message, and oh, I fear, dear Arthyen, that I did make him blush, for I did fling my arms around his neck on hearing of your safety, and plant such a kiss upon his cheek.

He told me that you had intercepted the small group that had attacked Sith Hill Fort and had destroyed them. This meant that, for now, Cragnuth was safe!

The message also brought a warning, though; that the enemy's forces were moving slowly westwards, and that we should remain vigilant. After delivering his message to me, the soldier then enquired as to my father's whereabouts, and I informed him of his absence. I thought how much this would irk my father when he hears of it - on two counts; the first that you had instructed your messenger to speak to *me* first, and secondly that it was *you*, sweet Arthyen, who had saved Cragnuth from imminent destruction.

I watched as the messenger returned across the river, and it did cross my mind to follow him and plead - or even demand - to be taken to you. But I decided that it would not be good to do so. It would not be honourable to leave these people now. There was also Hannel to watch over, for he had become a very pale and withdrawn little boy since losing his mother.

I could spare but one man to send as a messenger to Baldric's Manor to warn my father of the evacuation of Cragnuth. I had been of a mind not to inform him of our whereabouts, but the Elders had insisted that he should know. I had, therefore, reluctantly despatched the message forthwith.

It seemed to take us a long time to cross the lowlands to get to the forest; due simply to the large amount of people. I was concerned about us travelling on such open ground, and wished to get everyone to safety beneath the shelter of the trees as soon

as possible. I rode up and down the line, urging everyone to walk as quickly as they could. I had positioned the men-at-arms on the flanks, equally spaced as to give the people as much protection as possible. We had but fifty armed men to protect around one hundred townspeople, and I knew that if the enemy came upon us now, that we would not stand a chance for survival.

The weather had also turned against us. As we had departed Cragnuth, the skies had been filling with heavy clouds that foretold of a blizzard on its way. It was freezing cold, and as the people breathed, the air was full of the vaporous clouds of the warmth leaving their bodies. By the time the first of the exiles reached the forest, the snow had begun to fall, and the wind had begun to whip around us. Great white flakes danced on the gusts, and settled so quickly that soon the world about us was white.

This also was dangerous; for our passage through the snow would be easily seen by anyone who came across it, leading the enemy straight to us. I urged the people to hurry, and could but hope that the snow continued to fall and obscure the tracks.

I had galloped Elwine to the front of the procession to lead the way through the trees. I felt humbled that these people trusted me enough to take them away from their homes, and follow me to an unknown place. It has been such a heavy burden upon my shoulders, and I hope that I have done the right thing.

Slowly, we made our way down the deer-path towards our destination. We passed through the glade where you and I had met, Arthyen. I looked to where your tent had been - the ground still had the faint outline where it had been pitched, and all around the glade there were scorched patches where your campfires had blazed. I had heard some people say that it had been the enemy who had been here before us, but I was quick to explain that it had been *your* men who had camped here, and that the enemy did not know of this place.

We were nearly at our destination; I knew because I could hear the sound of rushing water. Once there, I had instructed a soldier to remain at the mouth of the entrance, to encourage those who were afraid to walk behind the water to conquer their fear. This he had to do several times, and when - at last - all the townsfolk had disappeared into the caverns, the poor man was soaked to his skin.

I ordered fires to be lit in the cave as soon as possible, in order that everyone could dry themselves as well as they could; for I did not want anyone to catch their death of cold. There was a flurry of activity within the caverns, and soon the fires were lit, and each one quickly had a circle of cold, damp, people huddled around. I decided that

we should remain in here for the rest of the day, in order that everyone could thoroughly dry out. There is no real urgency, for we are, at least, now relatively safe from our enemy.

For a while, I sat in one of the darkest corners, and watched my people huddled around their tiny fires. Steam ascended from their clothing as they began to dry out. I looked at the faces of my people - some of them looked frightened, some of them seemed quiet and withdrawn, whilst others chatted amongst themselves as if resigned to what may befall them. A few of the children started to grizzle from the cold, and their mothers wrapped them in their arms and held them close. Most of the sobbing died down, but there were still one or two children who seemed intent on making their presence very much known indeed. From the opposite side of the great cavern, I could faintly hear a mother singing a lullaby.

The horses had been settled at the back of the cave. The other livestock was still at Cragnuth, but much had already been slaughtered for our winter provisions anyway. It had been decided that we would return and collect the few that remained in a day or so when the people had settled more, and after proper enclosures had been made to keep the animals from wandering.

I felt vulnerable. What have I done to these people? I have torn them away from their homes and livelihoods. I have been telling myself that I have made the right decision - it had to be the true course, for at least if Cragnuth *does* get attacked, these souls around me will not meet their deaths at the hands of our enemy; an enemy that marches across our lands with a black heart. This foe has shown itself to be merciless, and there is no reason to assume that it will alter its stance.

The flickering light from the fires danced across the cavern walls and ceiling. I had forgotten quite how big these caves were, and my thoughts then turned to Leif once more. He had been the same age as me; he came into this world two weeks after my ill-fated entrance. His mother had been employed to wet-nurse me, so he and I had been together right from the beginning. As I sat there, I smiled to myself as I remembered some of the scrapes we used to get into.

I can recall the time we went fishing in the river, and Leif's hook got caught in some weeds at the bottom. He tugged so hard that his line broke, and he was flung backwards into a gorse bush. He had shouted so much and had jumped up and down, with his hands grasping his buttocks. Oh, how I had laughed at you then, my dear Leif.

You had chased me around the bush, still with one hand on your bottom, but before

you could catch me, we had both collapsed to the ground with tears of childish laughter running down our flushed cheeks.

Orvin and I had sat there quietly in the cave. I sat with my legs tucked up under my chin, my arms wrapped around my knees. Gazing into nowhere, memories came flooding back. I shall tell you of one more occasion when Leif and I, together with some two of three other children, were playing the game of hoodman's blind. We were in our seventh year, and for some reason we were near the stables at the time - it was on Midsummer's Eve and there were great celebrations and feasts at Cragnuth. We spun you around so much you could not walk straight, and you fell straight into the biggest pile of freshly laid horseshit that ever there was. It had been a hot day, and you had been running around with just your breeches on, and when you had fallen sideways into the clumps of dung, it had covered your chest and face. You stood up, took away the cloth covering your eyes and beamed. How you did smell! Your mother had cuffed you around the ear, and declared that you were the most tiresome of children. She had led you by the ear to the trough, stripped you off in front of everyone and had ordered you to 'wash that stink away from here'. You had just laughed at your nakedness, and had run around the trough a couple of times before she could catch you again.

Oh Leif, you always saw the funny side of everything. I think the only time I ever saw you sad was the day you said goodbye to me. Your mother had known you were soon to depart this world, and had sent for me, for she knew our bond was strong. You had lain half-awake on your cot, as the fever took hold of your body, and had told me how frightened you were of leaving. I had lain beside you during that night to keep you company, and had put my arm around you.

I spoke to you of our many adventures, and as you listened, you lay your head on my shoulder. Your body was hot with the fever, and I soothed you as your mother continually bathed your body with a damp cloth as you lay helplessly waiting for release. When I had awoken in the morning, you had left this world for the next, your frail body still in my embrace and your mother gently weeping at your side.

I do miss you.

I do not doubt that you would have grown-up and left Cragnuth to make your own way in the world by now if you had lived, Leif. Who knows? Would you have joined with those who left with Arthyen?

I hope you are happy where you are Leif, and that you are free from pain and sorrow. Perhaps you are fishing with your ancestors? Or perhaps you are sitting on a rail, idly

dangling your feet, smiling down at me at this moment. I hope you are smiling, Leif. And that you do not mind that I have broken our pact after all these years. I hope you understand that it is for the good of the people of Cragnuth that I have done so.

The recalling of my memories was broken, and I was brought back to reality by a slight shaking on my knees. A small hand was placed across my own, and I could hear a tiny voice speaking to me. It was little Hannel come to find me.

I tousled his hair as I always did, and wrapped my arms around him, pulling him in towards me.

"What is it, my Hannel?" I asked him.

"I am cold," he said.

"Poor Hannel," I soothed, pulling him closer, and wrapping my cloak around his frail body. "There, is that better?"

He nodded quickly, and snuggled himself into my warmth. I found myself swaying slightly side-to-side, as if rocking a baby to sleep, and I rested my cheek on the top of his head.

"Story?" he asked of me. "Tell story to Hannel?"

"Oh dear," I had replied. "I am not very good at telling stories, Hannel. You need to ask Tarek. He is very good".

"Tarek stories scary", Hannel said.

I could not understand what Hannel meant at first, as he had always enjoyed Tarek's epics before. However, since his mother's death, Hannel has become a very nervous little boy. I presumed that Tarek's tales of giants and battles were a bit too much for his sensitive nature at this time.

"I shall try and tell you a story, Hannel, but I warn you that it may not be a very good tale", I said to him.

I had looked around for a subject, but my eyes had beheld none. I thought for a moment before deciding that I would try to tell him the story of the eagle and the crow. I had recited one or two paragraphs of this story, when I had realised that Hannel had actually fallen asleep. I sat holding him for a short while, before gently rising to

my feet, and taking him back to where I could see his father and brothers were sitting.

After leaving little Hannel with his family, I despatched several soldiers back into the forest to see if they could kill any food for my people to eat, to add to any supplies that had been brought with them. It did not take long before two of them returned, each with a doe draped across the back of their shoulders. These were soon being drawn and paunched, and prepared for cooking, but would not go far amongst the great number of mouths to feed. However, it was better than nothing, and it went towards feeding those people who had not managed to bring many provisions with them.

Twenty-third Entry

Many had gasped in astonishment at the valley; some just shrugged their shoulders and continued to trudge ever onwards down the path, their heads bowed against the icy winter winds. It did cross my mind to wonder how this path came to be, but I can but assume that some creature most likely created it in a similar way to the deer paths in the forest. The snow from the day before had not been disturbed, but it was plain to see that the way was definitely etched into the side of the mountain.

With great care and attention, we did file down towards the valley bottom, for the way was slippery and treacherous. The old warriors who had come to investigate this place two days ago, had discovered the caves Leif and I had seen when we had come here. These were all along the mountainside path that ran from where the cavern opened into this valley. They had decided that the people could live temporarily in these caves, for they would clearly provide natural shelter from the elements, and so this is where we were heading that first morning after leaving Cragnuth.

We have settled quite well, and yesterday the animals were brought across the lowlands. We now have some dairy cows, some sheep, goats, and many chickens for our eggs. The swine that were brought across are proving to be very difficult for our swineherd to tend, for they keep trying to escape their pen, and run with their wild cousins in the forest.

Accompanied by Orvin and five men-at-arms, I have been making daily forays further into the valley. It was on one such journey today that we did first see the fires in the distance.

Fine wisps of smoke were being blown across the valley. These immediately pan-icked all who saw them, including - I am ashamed to admit - me. Instantly, the word passed around the men that we were doomed, and that the enemy were already in the valley before us. My first thought was that I had led my people into a trap, and that we would all be cut down most bloodily. My biggest fears had been realised. I had let the townspeople down; they would all die, and it was solely my fault.

Mustering my resolve, and wheeling Elwine around to face my men, I glared at them and ordered them to hold their wisht, and hush their words of malcontent. I told them that it may *not* be all as it would seem, and that we would wait, and - under cover of darkness - work our way nearer to where the smoke was originating from.

I had instructed them not to speak of what we had seen when we returned to the others. I told them that if I heard one villager mention it, that I would know from whence the information had come, and that I would deal heavily with the culprit. They all bowed their heads in acknowledgement of my orders. I then signalled for them to return back to the caves.

I had not relished having to be so harsh with them. They are good men; honourable and true, and I know all of them so very well. However, I could not let them see the fear in my eyes - I had to be strong. If I am to lead them in the absence of my father, then I *must* prove myself to be a worthy heir. If word were leaked that I am weak, then I would have naught but dissent and rebellion.

This entry I write before we leave for our journey deep into the valley. If I do not return ever to write again, then I shall take my leave of you now, by inscribing a note of farewell to all that I love who may read this, and also to all those I do not know who may come upon my journal in the years to come. I do not know the reason that I began to record this small part of my life, but have felt compelled to do so, upon seeing the figure that sat upon his grey mare all those long days ago. I have lost many good friends along the way in my short life, but if I am - indeed - not to return after this eve, then I shall hope to be able to meet them again when I cross over the swords into their world.

So, I bid you farewell.

Twenty-fourth Entry

I t had not been my time to jump across the bloodied swords quite yet, as I am here now to write this. I do so fervently, for I have much to tell.

A dilemma had confronted me on the evening we had left. I did not know whether to just take the five men who had been with me earlier, or to take more. If I took more, and we were correct in our assumption that the enemy was here in the valley, then that would leave the townspeople with too few arms to defend themselves if the need arose. However, if we discovered that it was but a small group of the enemy, if I had more men we might well be able to destroy them. I decided - in the end - that the five men would be all that would come with me. If necessary, and, if we went undetected, and if it proved possible, we could then return to collect more men, and attack under the cloak of darkness the next evening.

So, we had departed quietly. We had the minimum of weapons - just swords, bows and spears, but alas, we could not risk torches to light fire-arrows. What we had would have to suffice, so we rode silently; each one of us alone with our own personal thoughts. Your ring was with me, Arthyen, and it hung, nestled between my breasts, close to my heart. It was comforting to know that in some small way you were with me on this perilous journey into the unknown.

We had picked our way slowly down the path; it had been a clear night, and a heavy frost had made the path treacherous for our horses. But we eventually entered into the valley, and made our way in the direction of the origin of the smoke.

We soon came upon the river, and followed its banks towards the flickering orange glow of the fires ahead. One thing became plain to us then, and a dread filled my

heart. By the number of fires that I could make out, this was definitely a major encampment that we were approaching. I had hoped that by coming upon them at this
time of night, most of whoever they were would be asleep, but as we advanced towards the camp we could make out the voices of many men.

'Perhaps this enemy never sleeps', I had thought to myself.

It also occurred to me how open these people were about their existence here. They
obviously did not expect to be located, and were - in a way - like us, in sharing the
belief that we were the only people to know of the existence of this valley.

The river bore sharply round to the right, and we found ourselves having to travel in
single-file, as the side of the mountain left only the narrowest passage for us to nego-
tiate. I could sense that we were close, so, using only hand signals, I indicated to the
men to follow me as quietly as they could. We needed to be vigilant, for I knew not
what would confront us once we had travelled around this bend in the river. There
would be sentries posted at some point on the edge of this encampment, and I
wanted to make sure that we saw *them* before they heard or saw us.

I had sent Orvin ahead of me. He may not be one of the hunting pack at Cragnuth,
but the instinct is still within him. I knew *he* would sniff out danger before we could
become aware of it.

I was correct. For as we followed the river, the narrow track gradually began to open
up again, and there - standing in the middle of it - was Orvin; his head up as he
sniffed the air, his body rigid. I halted my men with a raise of my hand, and listened.
I could hear a faint mumbling, but it was the smell of wood-smoke that wafted on a
sudden breeze in our direction, that reached my nostrils first. We had reached our
intended destination.

I had not thought this far ahead, and I did not know what my next plan would be. I
knew that I could not just turn my men around and return to our own makeshift settlement, without trying to find out *who* these people were. True, there were many
more of them than I had at first anticipated, but we needed - somehow - to get close
enough to see their colours.

The sudden arrival of a hungry creature of the valley, determined the course of events
that did follow. An owl silently flew past me on its nightly search for food. I had
been so engrossed in my pondering of how to proceed, that its arrival had startled me.
In my quivery state, I had instinctively drawn my sword, thinking an attack was upon
us. I winced at the sound of the metal scraping against metal, as my blade left its

scabbard.

I had hoped that the sound was not *really* as loud as it had seemed to me, but within minutes I heard rustling ahead, and a loud voice booming, "Who goes there? Identify yourself or be damned".

"We could try and flee, My Lady," Alger offered behind me.

"I do not think we would get very far, for it is dark, and we do not know the road well enough," I replied.

"But that could work in our favour, My Lady," came the response. "If it is dark, then they cannot see us."

"They have the advantage, Alger, of torches and more men," I replied, pointing in the direction of the small line of flickering lights coming our way.

"You should listen to the woman," interrupted an unknown voice from our left. "It would appear that she does speak some sense. There are indeed more of us than there are of you."

I had heard Alger growl and draw his sword.

"I believe", the voice continued, "that you are outflanked". As he had said this, a party of about twenty mounted men came into view, each of them holding aloft a flaming torch. I had looked behind, and found - to my dismay - that they were all around us.

I looked at Alger, and shook my head. To my relief, he sheathed his blade.

The sentries had reached us by now, and we were once again asked to identify ourselves.

There was not much else for me to do, so I sat as upright as possible in my saddle, and, pulling back my hood, replied in as confident a voice as I could muster: "My name is Lady Ethna, daughter of Lord Edric. We are from Cragnuth, and have come in search of peace in this land".

"I have heard of such a place, but if you come in peace, My Lady, then why do you skulk around under cover of darkness?" the horseman who had spoken before asked me.

His words were true, of course, and I was at a loss as to how to answer, but answer him I knew I must.

"We came here this eve," I continued, "to try and establish if you were friend or foe."

"Mmm", he began. "I see. Would not a visit in daylight have established that in a more congenial fashion?"

"Most certainly not, Sire", I answered. This man had begun to irritate me. "We are a peaceable people, and if you do know of Cragnuth, then you will also know that it is not a heavily defended township. Would it not have been foolish of us to walk straight into your camp, not knowing whether you were friend or enemy, when you could quite obviously snuff us out like a candlewick, with as many men and weapons that you appear to have?"

I had baulked at the idea of admitting that we did not have many weapons, but it did not seem important now. If, after all, he did know Cragnuth, he would already be aware of that fact. If not, then telling him now would not change anything, for we would be killed, and our people searched for and destroyed.

"Sir," I continued in the absence of a response from my interrogator. "I have answered your questions politely, and with honesty, as befits my station. Perhaps you will give me the courtesy of introducing yourself?"

He kicked his horse forward, and circled around me from behind. He pulled his horse to a halt in front of me, before urging it on, and settling on my right side with his mount's head against Elwine's rump.

Now I could see him quite clearly. Apart from the arrogance that seemed to ooze from his every pore, he was - actually - rather a handsome young man. He had thin, dark, whiskers and beard on a rather long face. I could not see what colour eyes he had in the light of the torch, but I could see that they were closely set together over an equally long nose. His eyebrows, I did notice, joined in the middle. This, I had always been told by the women back home, meant that the owner of such eyebrows had a temper, and should not be trusted.

My scrutiny of his features had been reciprocated with his of mine. Eventually he answered my question.

"My name is of no consequence, My Lady," he began. "We ride in the name of King Ulmar, and under the banner of Beroun, once king of the Lower Kingdom."

At this news I heard my men sigh with relief. For *my* part, I tried to keep my voice steady, when I responded: "I know of this banner, Sir. You have some of my men from Cragnuth marching beneath it".

He looked at me questioningly.

I named them all, before adding triumphantly, "and this ring that hangs around my neck bears the head of the dragon, and was given to me by your Captain". I pulled out the ring, and showed it to him.

At the mention and sight of this, the horseman flinched slightly before composing himself again. "We shall check to see if what you say is true, My Lady. Wait here".

He walked his horse back to where his men were waiting, and muttered under his breath to two of them, who then rode back towards the encampment.

"We shall wait here until my men return. If indeed any of those you mentioned are with us, then *they* will confirm your story".

We could do nothing else but sit on our horses and wait. It was freezing cold, but in some way I was content in knowing that our *hosts* must also be as cold as us. I smiled inwardly that this arrogant man was probably wishing that he had gone himself to check our story, so that he could have warmed himself, and sent someone else back in his place.

After some while, the two horsemen returned, and spoke quietly to him. He nodded to them, and signalled for his men to leave. He then approached us.

"It seems that such men are known in the camp, My Lady. As to the origins of the ring, those I cannot vouch for as I am not privy to Lord Arthyen's private affairs," he stated. "You are free to do as thou wilt, My Lady".

It had occurred to me that this man might well be deceiving us. There was no *real* way of knowing whether his men had checked for those carrying the names I had mentioned. It could just all be a trap. They could have made up the story of riding under the banner of Beroun, and be pretending that these men were with them, in order that we relax our defences, such as they were. I had made up my mind on insisting in seeing a banner, or in finding Wilf, or one of the others.

When the horseman had mentioned *your* name however, I began to wonder if he was telling the truth. After all, I had not given him your name, when I had shown him

your ring.

"Thank you, Sire," I said to him, bowing my head slightly. "I shall indeed pass on tidings of the courtesy bestowed upon us by you, to Lord Arthyen when I meet him next".

This obviously unnerved the man even more, for he bowed his head, and said most pleasantly, "You and your men are most welcome to stay at the camp for the night, My Lady, if you so wish."

"I thank you for your kindness, but we shall return to our own camp tonight," I had replied, equally pleasantly, but with an icy tone.

"As you wish, My Lady", and he clicked his horse into a walk, back to the warmth of his tent.

"I shall perhaps return on the morrow," I called after him, "for I would like to speak to those I know".

"As you wish", he shouted back, as he disappeared into the darkness, his torch-flame flickering in the breeze.

Calling to Orvin, we had left for our journey back here to the caves, somewhat confused as to how we had come across the army of Lord Arthyen, in a place that we had thought uninhabited, and unknown by anyone other than ourselves.

Twenty-fifth Entry

oday I did - indeed - return to your camp. I followed Orvin, and trusted in his hound's nose to take us on the correct path, but the way did not look familiar to me in the daylight, until we came to the bend in the river.

I had decided that neither the men nor I would mention what we had discovered last night. I had thought it best not to let the people know yet that your army was here. It was a beautiful, crisp, morning, and for the first time in many days I felt happy. I was looking forward to seeing you again, and hoped that I would find you in good spirits when I reached your camp.

I had been pleased, if not more than a little relieved, to see that the sentries had been warned of my possible arrival, and that they happily gave me instructions as to the correct path to take. In the daylight, I could see the magnitude of what lay before me. There were so many tents and men milling around, that I could not possibly attempt to say how many I thought were there. Some men were sitting outside their tents, while they tended to the necessary mending of clothes or armour. Some were just sitting talking to each other, and laughing loudly at some funny story told.

I did not know exactly where I was aiming for. Somehow, I had thought it would be much easier to find you, or someone else that I knew. Orvin trotted slowly beside Elwine, ignoring the odd barks from countless camp dogs. I decided that I would stop and ask if anyone knew the whereabouts of any of the people whose names I would give them. Most of them were pleasant in giving their negative responses, although they were surprised to see a woman amongst them. I could feel a hundred pairs of eyes following me, as I made my way down, what seemed to be, the main

path through the camp.

To my great relief, at last, I heard a voice I recognised call my name from the masses.

"My Lady Ethna, what a sight for sore eyes indeed you are," came the familiar voice of Wilf.

I had pulled up Elwine, and turned my head in all directions to try and locate him, and eventually saw his familiar figure walking briskly towards me from the very bowels of the mass of tents.

I slid from my saddle, and waited for him to approach; a huge smile on my lips at seeing his friendly face. As he came closer, I could hear the faint knocking of the bones in his beard, and this made me smile even more.

"I had heard that you were in the valley, My Lady", he announced as he took Elwine's reins, and tied them loosely around the hitching-rope that was strung across the gap between the nearest tents.

He took my hand, and placed a kiss upon it, whereby I wrapped my arms around him and gave him a big hug in welcome.

"I hear you met Caswyn last evening?" he said, with a wry grin upon his face.

"He would not give me his name, Wilf, but if you mean the young arrogant who came upon us, then yes, we did meet him", I answered.

"Ah yes. That would be him," Wilf grinned.

"I presume that he is someone of high rank?" I asked, as we began to walk together.

"He likes to think he is, My Lady", Wilf replied. "But he is just a young lad of noble birth, who thinks 'ee a bit more special than others. In time he will learn. I do not think he has actually *seen* battle yet, and when he does, I reckon it'll come as a bit of a shock, My Lady."

"I see. Then he was not amongst those who killed the enemy that attacked Sith Hill Fort?" I had asked.

"Oh no, My Lady," he was not there. "Not rightly sure *where* he was on that day. Battles are for men, My Lady, and I think that when it comes to his turn, he will

probably run and hide afeared. I can remember wanting to do that the first time I came face to face with a bloodied sword."

"Well perhaps, if he survives, it will make him a little wiser, and a little more amenable, Wilf", I said.

"Ha", Wilf snorted, and then said in a jolly way, "I have not introduced you to my new friend, My Lady".

"Oh, no you have not, Wilf," I responded looking around for someone.

Wilf put his fingers to his lips and whistled. A moment later, a small dog appeared, rushing through the legs of the men and horses, its tail wagging furiously, to a hail of verbal abuse, and shying horses.

"Meet 'Vala', My Lady", he introduced the little tan and white dog.

"She is very sweet, Wilf", I had replied. "Where did you find her?"

"More like she found me," he began. "T'was after the fight at Yeo Bridge. On that day we had put to rout the small enemy troop, and were finishing off the stragglers, when we came across these folk that had been caught by the retreating foe. I will not tell you what we found, My Lady, for it was not pleasant, but this little dog was the only creature left alive. She was sitting by the body of her mistress, My Lady, just a little girl of about six I reckons."

Wilf had paused for a moment, before continuing, "As I say My Lady, I will not tell'ee what the beasts had done to that little maid and her family, but after we had given them burial, and were on our way again, this little dog began to follow us. She seemed to take a liking to me, and has been with me ever since".

"She is very bright, My Lady," he said with a note of cheer in his voice. "It is good to have such a companion after so many months of being alone".

He had seemed lost in thought at the memory of the little girl and her family.

In an attempt to distract him, as we walked along I said, "Oh, dear Wilf, it is good to see you again. I see you are still rattling your beard at the enemy".

"Aye, My Lady", he smiled through his beard. "I like to frighten the living daylights from them with my rattling".

"I am glad to hear they are only chicken bones, Wilf," I continued. "Although, of course, the enemy do not need to know that! Your secret is safe with me," I smiled.

"But they be not all chicken bones, My Lady," Wilf had replied with a glint in his eye. "One of them is the real thing. The bone from one of the damned digits that helped do this to my face".

This was news indeed, and I was eager to see such a bone. "But which one is it then?" I asked him. "They all look much the same, and are very difficult to tell apart".

He stopped walking, and I halted beside him, and looked closer at his beard while he thought. "Hmm," he said, scratching his head. "Do you know," he continued slightly bemused, "I do not think I can rightly recall which one it is, My Lady". He had looked at me out of his good eye, and I could see mischief dancing in it.

I laughed at that. I laughed so loudly, that even Wilf's little Vala stopped in her tracks to see what was amiss. I do not think I have laughed so much for a long time.

"Oh Wilf", I said - slightly out of breath from my amusement - placing a soft kiss on his hairy cheek. "You are such a dear old friend, and you *do* make me laugh. I hope you are taking good care of yourself".

"I am, My Lady, I am", he had replied. "It is indeed an honour to ride under the banner of Beroun. I cut my teeth on battles under that banner."

"Is that where you lost them also?" I giggled.

Wilf had roared with laughter at that, and had slapped me rather over-enthusiastically on my back, for I nearly fell over, and he did have to steady me, before we both started laughing again.

Whilst Vala went eagerly on ahead of us, Orvin stayed close by my side. The young dog's antics seemed of no interest to him at all. In fact, I rather think that he thought the whole episode rather tiresome; a bit like an older brother looks down upon his younger sibling's play-acting, with a certain air of misplaced superiority. Poor Orvin - my dear companion.

By now, we had reached the furthermost perimeter of the encampment, and so turned around to make our way back to where I had left Elwine.

After composing myself, I asked Wilf in a more serious tone: "And what of your new Captain? How do you and the other men consider him?"

"Lord Arthyen is a skilled captain, My Lady, and a worthy son of King Beroun. He has shown himself to be a good tactician, and a brave leader. He treats his men well; as equals, My Lady," Wilf replied.

I had searched into the middle distance as Wilf spoke of you. I had been hoping to be able to meet with you again once at the encampment, but so far I had not seen you. I was not even sure that you were here. I had not seen your mare amongst those tethered to the rope that had been stretched from one tree to another near your tent. I knew it was *your* tent, for I had recognised it from the afternoon in the glade. It was the largest here, and unlike the others was not striped but made of a plain, cream-coloured cloth, emblazoned on alternate panels with the sign of the dragon.

I ventured to enquire of Wilf as to your whereabouts. "Is Lord Arthyen here?"

"No My Lady, he is not with us as yet," came the answer. "He took his best men-at-arms, and rode west, when we all took the east road here into the valley. I am not certain where he went, My Lady."

Vala ran ahead, joyously sniffing her surroundings, stopping every so often to relieve herself in her excitement. Occasionally, she would give chase to a leaf as it fluttered across her path. Then - completely without warning - she would suddenly stop dead in her tracks to investigate another interesting scent, completely forgetting about the previous object of her desire. Wilf laughed at her as she found a stick - he told me that this selected missile would be the only one she would chase today - no other would do. Wagging her tail, Vala presented the stick at my feet, and - jumping up and down on her two front legs - she seemed to be grinning as she barked her request that I throw it for her. This I did. Off she raced at high speed to retrieve it. Soon she returned, and went through the process again, her dark eyes gleaming with de-light. Thus it had continued for about ten minutes, until - to the sound of a sympathetic groan from Wilf - I miss-threw the stick, and it landed in the centre of some impenetrable undergrowth, and hence, was lost forever. I even found myself feeling guilty at spoiling the little dog's fun, but she soon seemed to recover, and by the time we had returned to the camp, it would appear that the whole episode had completely gone from her memory.

I had tried very hard to hide my disappointment at not being to see you today, Arthyen. I do not think that Wilf noticed the change in my demeanour on hearing of your absence. We had spent a good hour talking about events that had occurred at

Cragnuth since his departure, and he had assured me that all those who had gone with him that day were well.

We had taken of our leave in good spirits, but as I returned to my people, I could not help but feel guilty at not letting those concerned know the whereabouts of their loved ones. I was still not sure that it would be a good idea to tell them that they were only less than half a day's ride from those they held dear, for they would only have to say goodbye all over again, when the men left, and it would put more of a strain on their hearts.

I shall visit again tomorrow, in the hope that you have returned.

Twenty-sixth Entry

I did awake this morning more sluggishly than of late. The wind had howled outside the cave all night, which had caused me to endure a disturbed sleep. On top of this, it had seemed colder than usual, and I did not want to leave the comfort and warmth of my blankets earlier than was necessary. However, I had also wanted to revisit your camp to see if you had returned, for, apart from wishing to see you, I had also had an idea last night, and was eager to share it with you. Four day's time will see the Yule fire-festival upon us, and I had thought that the celebrations might be shared between the townspeople, and your men in some way.

So, off we had gone; Orvin, Elwine, and me. As before, we had been waved through by the sentries, and were soon well into the heart of the camp. It was oddly quiet that morning - I never did find out why.

To my delight, I spotted your mare tethered outside your tent. She was dozing, and did not move a muscle when I tethered Elwine beside her. I signalled for Orvin to sit, and walked up to your tent. Upon reaching the flap, I was suddenly at a loss as to quite what to do. I had expected you to have a sentry outside, but there was no-one. I did not want to simply enter into your tent, for I knew not what I would find inside. You may be working, sleeping or in conference with someone. It would be rude of me to walk in unannounced.

Trying to knock on the material would have made no sound at all, so I decided to clear my throat, and cough a few times to see if that attracted any attention from inside.

Nothing.

"E're what be'ee doin' by Cap'n's tent?" came a gruff voice.

"Why is the Captain's tent unguarded?" I retorted sharply, and I thought, rather quick-wittedly.

"Er, I had to go and take a piss... Er, relieve myself, My Lady", came the reply.

"I am sure that your Captain would not be pleased to know that his life had been put in possible danger because you had gone for a 'piss', Soldier", came another voice; one that I recognised as that of the arrogant young man from the other night.

With all the activity outside your tent, it was not surprising that you had been disturbed, and it had not been long after the exchange outside began that you appeared, looking unkempt, and dishevelled, with sleep's dew still upon your eyelids. Once outside, you had squinted against the sunlight, whilst rubbing the sleep from your eyes.

"What the fuck is going on out here?" you demanded, wrapping your cloak around yourself tightly against the frosty air.

It was then your turn to look aghast, when you had seen me standing there.

"My Lady Ethna", you said startled. "Forgive my appearance - and my language - Ma'am, but if I had known you were visiting, I would have been more suitably prepared".

At this last statement, you had half-laughed, "That was a rather dull-witted thing to say, My Lady. Forgive me, but you have caught me off guard. I have no idea why I would have been expecting a visit from you, as I was not even aware that you *knew* of this place".

You had seemed rather embarrassed that I had come upon you in such a way, and I suddenly felt rather awkward myself, and began to think that it had been a mistake to come after all. Perhaps I should have stayed away, and ignored the fact that you were even here? Eventually you would have learned of my visit the other evening, and perhaps then, you would have paid a visit to me.

"I am sorry, My Lord", I said, "It would seem that I have rudely awoken you. I should not have come unannounced, but I had hoped that you had been warned of

my existence here in this place", I said looking across at Caswyn with a scowl.

"You have no need to be sorry, My Lady Ethna," you replied. "But my men and I did not return until the early hours of this morning, and I have not spoken to anyone about anything that may have occurred here in my absence".

"Nevertheless, My Lord, I feel that I should leave you to your business", I continued.

You ushered the errant soldier away, and took Caswyn aside. He then nodded his head and left, but not before casting a glance of disdain upon me.

Now that we had become alone, your voice had softened, and you became more personal in your address, "You must be freezing standing there. Please, come and share the warmth of my tent, and tell me how you come to know of this place, for I am much intrigued. I had thought that no-one knew of this valley apart from me."

We had entered your tent, which was almost as cold inside as out. As you had gestured for me to sit, you apologised for the coldness and explained that whilst the brazier in the very centre of your tent would normally have been lit, as you had arrived back in camp sooner than warned, it had not been tended to. I watched you as you crossed to the opposite side of the tent to where a bucket stood, its icy water awaiting your morning ablutions.

"You look so tired, My Lord Arthyen", I said softly, as I had watched you smash the ice on the water bucket with the hilt of your dagger.

"I am indeed tired, My Lady," you said as you tossed the chunks of ice on the ground, at the back of the tent behind the bucket. Discarding your cloak you continued, "But there will be plenty of time to sleep when the battles are over, or when I am dead. Whichever is first." You began to splash the icy water on your face, before placing a hand on each side of the bucket, and standing hunched over it for a second or two as if deep in thought.

I blush as I remember gazing at the contours of your naked back, with its perfectly curved spine. I had seen the scar that ran from your left shoulder down towards your bottom rib, and, Arthyen, how I had longed to trace my fingertip down that scar.

"I have missed you, Ethna", you said quietly, with a large sigh. "I have missed you greatly, more than I could have thought possible."

I was surprised, yet pleased, at the familiarity in your address. "And I have missed

you greatly Arthyen", I responded likewise, taking a step towards you. Before I could reach you, however, you moved away from the bucket towards your bed, where you had discarded your shirt the night before.

With your back to me, you had eased it over your head, and - pulling it down over your torso - un-tucked your hair from its collar, before turning to face me.

Before having the chance to speak more, a voice from outside announced the arrival of the errant guard. You had given him permission to enter, and we both watched in silence as he lit the brazier with the burning faggot he had brought. The wood refused to co-operate at first, and it took many attempts from the poor guard to finally get it to burn. He eventually made a low bow, and took of his leave as quickly as he could.

You had seemed embarrassed at his presence, and whilst he had made his efforts you had withdrawn to the other side of the tent, and had busied yourself with shuffling some papers across your writing table, flashing the occasional look of impatience in his direction. When he had left, you seemed to relax again.

"Bring the seat closer to the warmth, Ethna," you beckoned, as the heat began to pour forth from the blazing logs.

You smiled softly as I did so.

"You are warming up?" you asked coming towards me.

"Yes, I am. Thank-you".

"Now tell me. How do *you* come to be here?" he asked. "I am, truly, greatly interested in how you know of this place."

I told you briefly how Leif and I had discovered this valley when we were younger. You had seemed intrigued to hear of Leif, and seemed genuinely sorry when I had told you of his untimely death.

"I am impressed at your valour, My Lady", you told me, when I explained how I had made the decision to leave Cragnuth.

It was then that it had dawned upon me, and I was shocked.

"My Lord, I have deceived you!" I cried in alarm.

You had leant forward from your stool, and had asked me what had caused this outburst.

"I had to send a message to my father and cousin of our whereabouts, My Lord," I had continued. "It means that I have led them straight to you. They could arrive here any day, and you will be discovered".

I jumped up from my stool. "Oh no, what have I done?" I had cried. "You must leave immediately."

I had begun to pace up and down your tent, wringing my hands in front of me at my stupidity, whereupon you had intercepted my movements, and had taken each of my hands in yours. "You have done nothing for which you should reproach yourself, Ethna. You did not know of our presence here when you sent the message, and cannot be blamed for anything that may happen because of it".

I had shaken my head in denial.

"My sweet Lady Ethna", you carried on. "I am sure that your father shall not venture out of his step-brother's manor in this weather, with the threat of such danger around him."

I had looked up at you.

"Well - do you?" you asked grinning. "Do you *really* think your father or cousin would make such a treacherous journey, just to get to sleep in a cold and draughty cave?"

The fear left me, as I gazed into your eyes, and saw your grin. I chuckled. You took me back to my stool, and sat me down again.

"Now, tell me more about your journey here the other night".

I retold how we had come upon the camp under cover of darkness, and had been confronted by Caswyn.

You had laughed when I mentioned that name, and had told you how arrogant the young man was. "That fellow seems to be forever raising the hackles of those whom he comes upon. I really must have a quiet word with him sometime about civility". "I have not been sure whether to tell the people that you are here", I said. "I did not want to create a problem with families visiting the camp".

"You may as well tell them, My Lady," you had replied. "I am not certain how long we shall be here, and there is a chance that eventually someone from either camp will bump into someone from the other. Besides, I may wish to visit you myself," you continued, smiling. "And how would you explain *that*?"

This had been the news I had been hoping for. Firstly, I could now go home and let everyone know that we were not alone in the valley, and that the men from Cragnuth were all safe and well. It would be something else to celebrate at Yuletide. Secondly, dear reader, the news that my Lord Arthyen may wish to call upon me, brought a great joy to my heart.

I told you of my idea for Yuletide, and you were pleased. It would help lift your men's spirits, you had said. To be in the company of women and children at such a time of goodwill, would remind them that there is another aspect to their world, other than the pictures of death that had been all to frequent of late, and you had said that you would ensure that word was passed around your men.

We sat opposite each other, and I watched you gazing into the embers of the fire. You looked so distant, Arthyen, as if you were a thousand miles away. You sat hunched with your hands clasped together across your knees.

"You are troubled, My Lord," I had said gently. "Is there any burden I can help share?"

You did not appear to have heard my words. I arose from my seat, and knelt before you, "My Lord?"

You started and blinked. "I am sorry, My Lady. I do not mean to ignore you".

"I know", I had reassured you. "You have many trials to face, My Lord, but please know that I shall help you in any way I can. You *do* know that, do you not?"

"My dearest Ethna," you began, looking at me, and placing a hand on my cheek. "I know that you would, but I fear that there is not much that you can do. I am in exile by my own doing. I must face the future with an uncertain heart, but I *know* that the path I am following is the true way".

"Then you should, indeed, follow it," I told you. "Those who manipulate your uncle shall be uncloaked when you have triumphed, Arthyen, and then your uncle will lift the exile, and you shall be able to return with honour".

It sounded so easy, but I knew that it would not be. You knew also, but you were kind enough not to give voice of your doubt about my words of comfort. Then you had bent over, and placed a kiss on my forehead, and bade me rise from my knees. Smiling gently at me, you had said, "Forgive me Ethna for not being of good company. I am tired, and my mood is suffering for that".

"You have no need to apologise to me, Arthyen, for I understand how tired you must be," I responded quietly. I felt that I should leave you to your thoughts - it was not fair of me to divert your attentions away from more pressing matters.

I had gathered up my cloak, and arose to leave. At which point you had risen to your feet also. "However, I feel that I have taken up too much of your time. I think that I should return to my people, and give them the news of your presence here. I trust that this will be in order, and that you will not mind if more visitors do arrive upon your encampment?"

You had seemed slightly surprised that I should be departing so soon, but you did not offer any invitation to stay longer.

"I shall instruct young Caswyn to pass the word around to the men that people of Cragnuth share the valley with us, and that they can expect the townspeople to visit," you had told me as I left the tent.

"I shall think upon the matter of the Yule feast some more", you had added, as I had mounted Elwine".

"As you wish, My Lord", I had replied. "No doubt our paths shall cross again before then, and perhaps we can discuss plans in more detail at that time. For now then, My Lord, I shall bid you farewell".

"I hope those paths cross very soon, My Lady", I heard you say, as I turned Elwine in the direction of home.

I do not recall much of my journey back to the caves - I had been lost in an inner despair at the pain you must be suffering. I do wish I could help out in some way - however small - to take some of that burden away from you.

I know not what to do.

Twenty-seventh Entry

On returning yesterday, I did make it known to everyone of the existence of you and your men. Great excitement did ensue at this news, especially from those who had loved ones marching under your banner. I explained that they would be welcome to visit their kin, and that they would meet with no hindrance if they wished to do so. This news had seemed to breathe a new life into the whole of our small, displaced township, and I left everyone to his or her plans.

I did not speak of the possible celebration at Yule, as I had not felt it fair to mention it last night. It was, after all, something you had said you would still think upon, and I did not want to raise any false hope among my people - they have had plenty of false hope of late.

Although I had wished to visit you today, sweet Arthyen, I did think that it would be prudent if I left you with the business of war, as I did not wish to be a diversion to your plans, as I had been yesterday. It had been very wrong of me to arrive unannounced, but you did treat me as courteously as you could. However, I had lain on my bed last night, and these thoughts that did trouble me had made it very difficult to enter into the realm of dreams. I had found it difficult to get into a comfortable position, and had lain staring into the darkness around me, listening to the distant sound of snoring, and the sound of babies crying for their night-time feeds.

It is also at these times, in the darkness and loneliness of night, that I wonder whether I am doing the correct thing for my people. Are they *really* better off here away from their homes in Cragnuth? What of their livelihoods?

As I lay there in my dark solitude, I had made the decision that I would ride to Cragnuth - I wished to visit my mother, brother, Leif, and Martha where they lay in our

119

burial ground. I needed to sit amongst them, and ask them for guidance - I yearned to feel the comfort of their presence around me.

It was one of those crisp wintry days today; when the sky is blue, but there is no heat from the sun, as it hangs low in the sky. As I had stood at the entrance to my cave, my arms wrapped around me in an attempt to keep out the cold, I watched a lone eagle hanging lazily in the sky above the valley. Occasionally it would flap its huge wings slowly to gain more height. I did wonder what things it could see from such a height, and I had wished that I could become as one with it, and soar high above my troubled world.

Leading Elwine out into the cold air, I had smiled as I had noticed some of the villagers slowly making their way down into the valley towards your camp. They were going to see their friends and loved ones, and I found myself wishing I could do the same. I had listened to their excited chatter as they passed by - they could not know how envious I was of their journey. The only person who would have perhaps known, now lies in the cold earth at Cragnuth.

I had mounted Elwine, and with Orvin - as ever - by our side, we made our way up the path towards the cave entrance, and out into the forest. We were soon on the lowlands. It was good to see Cragnuth's rocky shape in the distance - I had not realised quite how much I had missed it in such a short period of time. I had urged Elwine into a gallop across the lowlands, Orvin loping beside us. It had felt so good to feel the wind against my face, as cold as it was - I felt free of all my burdensome thoughts.

Cragnuth's burial ground lies just outside the walls, on its east side. This quiet place is to be found in a sheltered spot, away from the harsh winds that blow across the lowlands. In the spring, the ground is covered in tiny blue flowers, and yellow wolfsbane that make a carpet on the paths between the mounds. In the summer, each of the mounds is covered in tiny white flowers. Children like to pick them, and make chains out of them, which they then place on their heads like little crowns.

When we had reached the entrance, I had dismounted Elwine and left her loosely tethered. My dear Martha's burial mound is still fresh, and has not yet properly settled - its lumps of frozen earth are not yet covered in the grass that shall eventually smother it. I was sad not to have been able to bring anything to lie across the earth for her. I had knelt beside her place of rest, and laid my hand on the mud. "Dear Martha," I had whispered. "Why did you did have to leave so suddenly? I *do* miss you". I had then found Leif's place and again did lay my hand upon it. "I hope you are happy, dearest Leif," I softly said.

Taking a deep breath, I did find where my mother and brother do lay. I sat down on the cold earth, and lay across their special place to send them an embrace. I had then sat next to them, my hands in my lap, for I know not how long. Orvin lay down beside me, and rested his head on my knee, and I had sat there stroking his head whilst quietly talking to my mother. I did ask her to help give me the strength to lead my people in the absence of my father. I did find myself telling her all about you, Arthyen. I described you to her in every smallest detail. I did tell her that you are very handsome, and that I find you to be such a brave warrior, and that I was sure she would have liked you very much, had she been able to meet you. I did also tell my dear brother that he would have found you to be such an amenable friend. All the words seemed to tumble from my lips with such ease, and my tears did fall freely down my cheeks.

I had seen Orvin raise his head to look in the direction of the entrance, but had dismissed it as a movement from Elwine catching his eye. I had continued with my conversation, totally oblivious to all that was around me.

It was only when Orvin had whined, stood and wandered off in the direction of Elwine that I realised that I might not be alone. I could not see the entrance from where I sat, so I had crawled alongside the mound next to my mother's, and had peered around it, to see what or who had caused Orvin to wander off.

I had not expected to see the grey mare standing patiently in the frosty air, her rider sitting astride her, with his arms crossed over his saddle, as he sat equally as patiently. I could see that he was searching the burial ground, and I knew also that he could not see me. I did not want him to see that I had been crying - I knew that my eyes would be reddened and swollen. I did wipe my eyes with my cloak, but the fabric was so rough, that I did fear that it would make things worse.

I knew that there was nothing that I could do to hide my sorrow.

I stood from behind my hiding place, and straightened my cloak and skirt. You saw me immediately, and dismounted Acha, but you did not enter the burial ground. You stood next to her, and waited for me to approach you.

"Forgive my intrusion, My Lady", you said bowing your head in greeting. "I had no wish to disturb you. Had I realised that you were paying your respects to those departed, I would not have come".
"You are not disturbing me, My Lord", I answered.

"I became concerned when I was told that you had ridden this way", you did con-

tinue. "I had visited the caves to see you, and was told of the direction of your journey. I must tell you that it is not safe for you to be here".

Your concern for my safety did bring joy to my heart, for I knew then that the flame was alight within your breast, as it was in mine.

"I am grateful for your concern, My Lord," I replied. "It was, in truth, not a wise journey to make, but I did so feel the need to visit those I have loved and lost".

You had nodded in concord at my reason.

"My Lady Ethna. I would enquire of you as to whether you have a mind to journey with me for a few hours? If you are warm enough, and would tolerate the coldness for a while longer, I would be honoured to have your company".

"And I should be honoured to accept your invitation, My Lord Arthyen," I responded with a smile. "I am quite warm enough, thank you, and would be pleased to accompany you."

You had taken my hand then, my dearest Arthyen, and had led me to Elwine. As I had placed a foot in a stirrup, you had placed your hands on my hips to assist me upon her. I had missed this closeness with you.

We had ridden briskly back to the shelter of the forest. This provided refuge, not only from any enemy eyes that may be watching, but also from the icy wind that had begun to gain in strength. We walked through the trees slowly, enjoying the respite given by the forest of the wind. Many times, you had looked across at me as if about to speak of something important, but each time you seemed to change your mind.

"You do seem to have many more men in your camp, than were there last time I came across you here in the forest?" I had asked, to which you had replied: "We have been lucky enough to recruit nearly fifty more men, My Lady. We are now nearly two hundred men strong, but I know that this is not enough to defeat the army that marches upon us."

I knew that what you said was true. What could two hundred men and boys *possibly* hope to achieve against a fighting army of more than twice that many war-hardened warriors? It was a hopeless task, surely. I did feel my heart sink when I thought of the reality of what was expected of your men, and - indeed - of yourself.

We had reached the entrance of the caves, and had dismounted to lead our mounts

behind the rushing water. Elwine's eyes rolled in terror at the sound of the water - she had done the same on our way out earlier this morning. I did talk to her quietly, and led her into the caves as quickly as I could. Acha did not seem as concerned, but merely did walk quietly as you had led her through - a true warrior's horse, I had thought. But then Elwine is but young, and still has a lot to learn about the world around her.

I had been about to remount Elwine, when you took a hold of my arm. "My Lady", you said. "I have been trying to tell you something ever since we met this morning".

"I have known that there was something you wished to say, My Lord Arthyen", I replied, gently smiling at him. "It is clearly a matter that troubles you".

"It doth indeed trouble me, Lady Ethna", you did reply, frowning. "It would seem that a small group of the enemy are heading for Cragnuth. My scouts have informed me that they shall be there by Yuletide morn."

I did gasp at this news. So it would seem that my home would fall after all. And on such a day?

"That is why I was so concerned for your safety, My Lady", you had continued. "They may well have sent out a scouting party, and they could have crossed your path this morning."

I still could not speak.

I knew not what to say.

"We shall, of course, be sending out a reception party to meet them, My Lady", I did hear you continue. "We shall not let Cragnuth fall that easily."

"You are to fight them on such a day?" I asked.

"The day is not important My Lady. We shall fight them on any day in order to defend the freedom of the people of Cragnuth, and of any village or town they try to destroy. Surely you would not have it any other way?"

"No, no indeed I would not," I agreed. "What is your plan?"
"We shall await their arrival at Cragnuth - they will not be expecting us," you had replied. "I am sorry to tell you such news when you had hoped for better things than battles for that day".

I did place my hand upon your cheek. "I shall hope that Cragnuth can be spared, My Lord, and that you shall safely return, but know this, that I shall ride with your men."

"Indeed you shall not", your retort was immediate, as you took a step backwards. "Battles have no place for women".

"Indeed I shall, My Lord, for I have the right to defend what is mine", I replied defiantly. "If I am called to fight as such, then I shall stand with the men and do so."

I did put my hand in yours. "You *cannot* deny me my right, My Lord."

"I know that I cannot deny you that right, My Lady Ethna", you replied, "but it is simply my wish that you stay safe".

My dearest Arthyen, I do believe that you did really mean what you said. However, I know also, that I cannot stand by and neglect to take my place in the defence of the land of my forefathers, but I did realise from your expression, that to speak more on the matter would not do.

"The light will be leaving us in a few short hours, My Lord," I said swiftly. "Come, should we not make haste, if we are to make good our hours together?"

You had nodded, and seemed relieved not to dwell more on the coming battle. You helped me upon Elwine, before seating yourself in Acha's saddle.

Our horses picked their way slowly down the mountain track that ran by the caves. Some of the townspeople stopped and waved as we passed, but most seemed busy with their own tasks to take much notice. We were soon returned to your camp. I had thought that we would stop here, but you urged Acha onward and I found myself following the same path that Wilf and I had walked upon a few days ago. I could not help but notice the increased activity around us.

The middle of the day was upon us as we rode further north, following the river as it twisted its way idly through the valley. I had asked you where we were going, for it seemed that you had purpose in your direction. You did tell me that you wished to show me something that you had come upon by chance yesterday, after I had left you. You had ridden out to try, and clear your thoughts and had seen a small island shrouded in a low mist in the middle of the river at its widest part. Or, you *thought* you had seen such a thing, for when you had approached it, it had disappeared. You told me that you had been sure that you had heard your name spoken on the breeze.

You pulled Acha to a halt. "It was in this place", you said.

I had looked across the river - I could see nothing but the other bank. I had looked across at you, and seen the look of disappointment upon your tired face.

"Perhaps I did dream upon such a place after all", you had said despondently. "Or perhaps I am battle-weary, and my mind is playing tricks on me".

As you had spoken those words, I had looked again across the river. A low haze had descended before me.

"I think not, my Lord Arthyen." I said in disbelief. I turned to look at you. "Look, yonder". I had pointed towards the incoming haze. Goosebumps prickled on my skin at the eerie sight.

We had both sat astride our mounts and watched as the mist thinned to reveal an island. You had not been mistaken, Arthyen. I too, heard your voice spoken in a low whisper, that hung on the mist, as it crept across the river towards us. It seemed as if to beckon us closer.

As it cleared, the fog revealed a line of stepping-stones that stretched from our side of the river across to the island - I know that this does not make any sense, and many would say we had been bewitched by the faerie folk, but I promise that I do write the truth.

We had dismounted, and stood at the edge of the river. I had wanted to cross the stones, but was too scared of what may befall me. Would they disappear, and leave me stranded on this strange place? I held your hand, and looked at you. "What think you? Shall we cross?" I had asked.

We did not have to make a decision, for at that moment our choice was made for us.

From out of the swirling mist, six shrouded figures approached silently across the clearing on the island. They halted at its shores, their faces hidden by their hoods. All stood quietly, until at last one spoke; her voice a whisper on the still, damp air.

"You have returned, Arthyen, son of Beroun. They call me Rhialdaron, and we give you welcome - we have been expecting you," she said, as she crossed the stones to our side of the river, introducing her companions with a wave of her hand.

You looked strangely calm, and bowed your head in greeting and reverence of the

shrouded figure before you.

"Many years have passed, and your time has come to reclaim that which was lost to the darkness," she had carried on, lifting one hand to rest on your head. "Come, walk with me Arthyen".

Her five companions had waited on the island in silence. I remained where I was, and watched as you followed her across the stepping-stones to the bank across the river. As she turned to wait for you, I felt her gaze rest upon me, but I could not see her face, for it was still shrouded in her hood. She had beckoned me to follow. I felt her power over me, and - although still unnerved by the sudden appearance of this mystical place - I found myself following the two of you across the stones.

We walked in silence along an overgrown path, which passed under a great stone arch that hung with ancient vines. The stems entwined with each other, causing huge knots to cling to the stonework. From their appearance, they had been here for many years, and yet the island did not really exist. Or did it?

The other five figures walked silently ahead of us. We followed Rhialdaron, and found ourselves ascending a small flight of worn stone steps. We entered into a small round temple, circled by stone pillars covered in trailing ivy that seemed to be holding the columns together. Atop the entrance to this temple, was a great stone dragon's head - its jaws open, displaying great carved teeth, snarling down at all who passed beneath it. Ivy trailed out of its jaws, and hung across the entrance like trails of green spittle.

In the centre of the temple was a great, carved tomb. Seated in front of each pillar was a small, stone dragon, each one facing the tomb. They all seemed to be alive, although I knew that they were made of stone. However, I could swear that I could see the beat of a heart within each one's breast.

It had been then that Rhialdaron had raised her hands, and removed the hood from her face, and gestured towards the tomb. As her hood fell, masses of red hair cascaded in ringlets down her back. As she raised her arms, she glanced across at where I stood and smiled softly. She was the most beautiful woman I had ever seen - her face was pale, almost deathly in appearance, but yet she seemed so alive in spirit. When she spokem her voice surprised me, for it was deeper than I had imagined it could be for such a delicate creature.

"Here lies Beroun. He has rested in this temple these past five years and twenty awaiting your return. It is time for you to avenge your forefathers, Arthyen, and for

you to take up the sword that has lain here in this tomb of marble for so long."

With her long, thin fingers, she beckoned you to approach the tomb. The cold, white effigy of your father lay atop the large tomb, his arms across his chest. His stone hands held a great carved sword, the finest detail on its hilt having been delicately and finely worked. You placed a kiss on the cold marble forehead, and knelt beside your father's last resting place.

I am hesitant to write of what did happen next, dear reader, for I do not know if you will believe what I say. It was a most strange occurrence, but I do promise you that I do write the truth.

The five shrouded figures began to chant in low voices; their words I could not understand, for they were in an ancient, arcane, tongue. Rhialdaron had outstretched her arms across the tomb, and joined in the low chant, her emerald eyes gleaming. I had remained near the doorway into the temple, but I could still see the marble begin to crack, and fall away around your father's effigy as the chanting continued. You too, had watched in amazement, and you had arisen from kneeling as the marble began to crumble from around the outline of the sword. I watched as rose to your feet, and backed away. I do lay no blame upon you for being wary of what was taking place before you. The chanting had grown louder, and its pace had quickened as a cloud of dust encased the tomb, hiding it from sight.

We had both watched as Rhialdaron slowly raised her arms higher, and bid the voices to fall silent. The dust continued to swirl around the room, sweeping around the bodies of those present, including me, which caused me to gasp with fright. The dust came to rest in front of you, Arthyen and shaped itself into the form of a man. I saw the mouth open, and heard a deep voice speak to you. "It is I, Beroun. My son, how long have I waited to see you". You stared into the face of your father, and dropped to one knee.

"My son, you need not bow before me; it is I who should bow before you, for it is you who can succeed where I did fail. The evil that sets its eye on Graelin, is growing in strength. The evil needs to be halted, but it is spreading like a pestilence across these lands. Graelin must not fall, but the King is under the spell of this evil wizardry."

"Father", you spoke hesitatingly. "I have come upon these lands to rid it of this evil. I ride under your banner, and am proud that the same blood rushes through my veins as that which ran through the veins of my forefathers. I shall fight to keep these lands safe, and free Graelin from the grip of destruction."

"It is as it should be," the vision spoke. "You have the strength to succeed my son, but it is not you who shall have the power to destroy."

I had noticed your questioning look at this remark.

"That power falls upon the shoulders of someone else. Do not search in your past or your future for this person, my son", the vision of Beroun had continued, "They themselves do not know the responsibility that doth lie before them, but their path has already merged with yours."

It was at this moment that the body before you began to fade, and your father's voice grew faint. As the dust began to regroup over the tomb, I heard the last words that Beroun spoke to you. "May the souls of your ancestors watch over you my dear son. May you defeat those who sinned against them, and rise above the dark fog of evil, as the rightful King of Graelin".

I walked over to stand by your side, as the dust settled, and dissipated into the cold white stone of the tomb.

The temple had fallen silent. All that remained was a faint breeze that blew the dead leaves across the temple floor, and rustled the ivy against the columns. I had shivered, but not from the cold - from the eerie silence that descended upon us. With my eyes still transfixed upon the tomb, I felt for your hand, and wrapped my fingers in yours.

It was then that Rhialdaron took a step closer to the tomb, and to our amazement, lifted the double-edged sword - stone no longer - from where it lay upon Beroun's chest. "Do not be afraid of what lies ahead," she said in a low voice. "Approach, Arthyen, and take your legacy."

I released your hand as you walked towards her, and watched as she passed the weapon to you. You did wrap your fingers around its hilt, which I could see was engraved with the finest detail. Passing your other hand down the flat of its blade, your fingers traced around the stone of amber set in its pommel. I could see an inscription running down the length of the blade, but it was written in an ancient runic script, and I could not understand it. I could see, however, that it was from the mouth of an engraved dragon, that these written words did come forth.

"In your hand is the sword of Graelin, Arthyen," Rhialdaron continued. "It has lain here in this temple for many years, ever since the kingdom fell to the evil powers of darkness that killed your father. Your birthright awaits you, son of Beroun. The

road ahead will be full of hardship, danger, and temptation, but the blood that runs through your body is strong, and you can triumph if you will but trust in yourself."

Rhialdaron laid her hand on your shoulder. "You have many questions in your head, but listen to your heart, and one shall be answered this very moment," she smiled.

You had looked at her, before turning your head in my direction. I am not sure what her meaning had been, but I did feel at that moment, that somehow I was to play an important part in what lay ahead.

Rhialdaron retreated to where her companions awaited her, and then all six of them left the temple as silently as they had arrived.

You and I also left the temple, and retraced our steps down the path towards the river. We saw Rhialdaron and the others cross, but when they were half-way they simply disappeared into the icy mist that arose from the river. Continuing, we crossed the river to where Orvin was sitting patiently with our horses. We had walked in a stunned silence. I am not certain as to whether either of us had really known what had just taken place, but you carried in your hand a great sword, and that – assuredly - had not materialised from nowhere.

Once on the other side of the waters, we turned to look at the island. Neither of us seemed at all surprised to see that it was no longer there, and that the river carried on its journey to the edges of the valley, without stepping-stones to hinder it on its way.

You looked pale, my sweet Arthyen. For my own part, my heart did beat fiercely within my breast. You stood staring at the weapon, and then looked at me. I saw the tears in your eyes, and I embraced you.

Twenty-eighth Entry

Today you will leave the safety and secrecy of the valley, and await the enemy behind the gates of Cragnuth. I have spent the day thinking about my own plans for the battle ahead. Arthyen, you have told me that you do not wish me to be involved in such a thing, but I am determined that I shall not be left out of the defence of my home. I believe that what I have a mind to do may even be successful. I shall put my trust in the skills of those of the remaining members of Cragnuth's garrison that stay with us, and also in the bravery of those townspeople who will agree to follow me on the morrow.

Today, also, my thoughts have been with you, Arthyen, and your mysterious meeting with your father yesterday. I still cannot quite believe that it really occurred, but when I left your tent last evening, the sword laid on your bed as proof of the afternoon's events. It is, indeed, a beautiful piece of workmanship, and I do but hope that it does keep you well in battle.

There had been a name mentioned by Rhialdaron that I had not recognised - Graelin. You will know, reader, that it is not a name that I have mentioned in my journal thus far. Upon our return to your camp, sweet Arthyen, and the privacy of your tent, I had questioned you about it. You did explain to me that Graelin was a name given to the Upper and Lower Kingdoms as a united land. Your forefathers had once ruled over both these kingdoms as one; it had not become divided until the time of your father's father. This division had occurred due to your father's father being a twin son. His brother had demanded that he be able to rule as the rightful heir also. Even though your father's father was the first born of the twins, to save bitterness he decided to divide Graelin into the Upper and Lower Kingdoms.

By the time the sun had set this eve, I had made my plans known to the men, and to all those who wish to take up arms against them who threaten to destroy our home. As I write this tonight before I retire, I know that I have fifty men of the Cragnuth garrison behind me, together with at least *thirty* men of the town, armed with bill-hooks, spears, forks - anything they could find that could do damage to the flesh of our enemy.

You had left under the cover of darkness. We had stood at the mouths of the caves, as you had led your men up the path, and into the cavern, before dousing the flames of your torches, and emerging into the world outside. I had stood at the mouth of the cave where I had been playing a game of stones with Hannel. We had heard the sound of horses climbing up the track, and had made our way - with everyone else - to wish you and your army well. It did take a very long time for your men to pass us on their way into the cavern at the top of the trail. The mounted men had to ride single file, but the foot soldiers were two abreast. You had ridden, of course, at their head - I felt sad that I had missed you. I also felt miserable that you had not stopped to say goodbye.

As Wilf passed us, he had jumped out of line, and presented me with Vala's make-shift lead. "Don't want her to be caught up in battle, My Lady", he had said with a sad look in his eyes. "You will look after her? She is a dear little dog, My Lady".

I had nodded at him and smiled. "I shall look after her until your return", I said. He had then bent down and kissed little Vala on the top of her head, before jumping back into the line of men working their way up the path, causing a ripple down the line as each man had to re-adjust to his new marching partner.

Eventually, the last of your men passed us by, and as all disappeared into the darkness of the cavern above, there was quiet again. The light from their torches was gradually going out, one-by-one, and I knew you had all gone into the forest; and perhaps to your doom.

I had been about to return inside, with Hannel, to resume our game, when he did point up the path. Following the line of his finger, I saw a light growing larger in the darkness of the cavern above us - a figure then emerged on our side. My heart raced, and I knew immediately that it had been you, Arthyen. I had watched as you urged Acha slowly down the rocky path, your arm holding the blazing torch aloft to light your way. Acha picked her way slowly down the loose trail, her sure hooves kicking up small stones as she did so.

As you came alongside me, you did not dismount, but sat firmly in your saddle. You

looked ahead into the darkness. In the torchlight, I could not help but notice the deep thought etched across your brow.

I had reached out, and gently caressed Acha's neck. Her skin rippled under my touch, and she exhaled noisily in the cold, night air. She chewed at the bit in her mouth, and stood patiently for your further command.

The gladness upon seeing you, though, did begin to fade into fear. From the look upon your face, and the distance you seemed to place between us, I could not be certain as to why you had returned, for you did not seem to wish to speak.

"My Lord?" I had asked of you, wishing to either confirm or disprove my worrisome beliefs.

These few words were enough to disturb your thoughts, and with a swing of your right leg, you dismounted from Acha's back.

"I have seen your preparations, My Lady Ethna," you said - somewhat coldly - with your back still towards me.

You had taken me aback with such words, not only for their lack of affection; I had not expected your first utterance to be so direct, but also because I had thought my plan was still unknownst to you. I had gone to great pains to keep all my arrangements hidden from sight. I felt the heat rising to my cheeks, as you continued to tell me that you knew, that despite your advice, I was determined upon my madness in joining in the fight on the morrow.

I felt anger well up inside of my breast: "Is it madness, My Lord Arthyen?" I retorted vehemently. "Is it madness, to wish to fight for my land, and my people's freedom? If this is so, then surely you are equally guilty. Is it not madness for *you* to fight for something which is not even yours?"

"You forget, My Lady, that Cragnuth is built in the lands of my forefathers", you had replied - somewhat churlishly I had thought. As you spoke these words, you had turned to face me.

I knew that this was true, but your protestations concerning my part in any fight were beginning to become irksome. I was tired, and wished to be done with this, the day before the battle. Reader, it is the waiting that is so wearisome - it preys on one's mind, and makes one of a sour disposition. But, I did not want to be irritable with you, sweet Arthyen. I searched in your eyes for the affection that has so often been

there of late. I could see from those dark eyes, that my tone of voice had surprised you. It did make me feel instantly wretched, and I did wish to reconcile with you.

Placing my hand on your arm, I had agreed with you, "Forgive me, My Lord. I know this to be true".

Your expression had softened at my touch, and yet I could still detect the hurt in your eyes. I know not if this was due to the sharpness of my tongue, or due to the fact that I was determined in my intentions on the morrow.

"Your stubbornness in the matter is worrisome to me, my sweet lady, but it seems that we have reached a stalemate", you said, sighing quietly, as you did take my hand in yours, and kiss the back of it softly. "All I can hope then is that, in one world or another, we shall meet again tomorrow".

My dearest Arthyen. I knew you were irritated with me, but I could not discern whether the look in your eyes was of anger, or of hurt. Were you merely angry with me for disobeying you, or were you concerned for my safety? I wish you had been able to tell me, Arthyen.

Before I did have a chance to respond, you re-mounted Acha. You had reined her around, and with a click of your tongue, you did urge her onwards back up the path. I am greatly troubled as I write this. Our parting should not have been thus. My heart did ache, and I did try so hard not to cry, as I stood and watched you disappear into the cavern. I had waited, in case you would stop and look back, before leaving, but you did not. The tears fell, but I had wiped them away in anger, for I did not want to admit to such weakness.

I cannot make any sense of your sudden coldness towards me today, Arthyen. I understand that you were tired, and that you were much pre-occupied with matters of war, but the sudden loss of words of affection had confused me. You have told me in the past of how you feel, but I find myself wondering whether it *was* from the heart that you did speak these words, or was it just that you have roamed so long on your own that to find someone of like mind, brings comfort; perhaps the comfort of friends, rather than of a future together as something more.

Perhaps it is my fault, and I have read too much into your attentions of late. Perhaps what you felt for me was not *really* love at all, but merely a passing wish for such? Do you feel that you are unable to give fully of your heart? Or perchance you are still in love with someone who has crossed your path before I? Did she leave you with a broken heart, which is now yearning to be healed? Do you think that I can help heal

that wound? Alas, I do not know whether I can or, indeed, whether I should want to repair that which has been so recently given to, and rejected, by another.

Perhaps you still whisper sweet words to another in your dreams? If so, then when you speak such words of affection to me, they are empty, for they no longer have meaning. Once spoken to another, whether in a dream or not, erstwhile you tell them to me, they no longer have a special place in my heart, for they are shared, and thus are deemed worthless.

I am in despair, and suffer from such great sorrow and anger at the judgements I have made. Once again, I am at the mercy of my innermost feelings, and do need to rid myself of them. Why do I torment myself so? If it is correct what I think, then surely I should never wish to lay sight upon you again, dearest Arthyen? If your feelings for me are not true, and are not for me alone, then I will be but a fool.

Enough, for now... at least!

We are ready to ride tomorrow. To death, or to victory; I know not which. I have willed myself not to think of you, and of our bitter parting this eve. Would that I could take a dagger, and plunge it into my breast, and cut out this heart that beats within it; wrench it from my body, so that it does prevent the pain that it doth cause me when I think of our parting. My eyes are heavy, my head doth ache, but my resolve is strong.

I shall lay down my pen, and try to rest. I cannot sleep, for we need to be in our position tonight, in readiness for whatever may occur tomorrow.

Whoever doth read this, I know not if, or when, you shall hear from me again.

Twenty-ninth Entry

Many long hours have passed since my last entry. The oily, black smoke from the death-pit is still thick around the walls of Cragnuth. We do not bury our battle-dead, but send them to their ancestors by burning their bodies, and thereby scattering their ashes on the four winds. I have not yet learned how many of your men were lost, my Arthyen. I do know that we lost eleven of our garrison, and five brave villagers who gave their all for the defence of their homelands.

Much of this day is but dimness in my memory, but I shall try to record as much detail as I can.

I, indeed, did not sleep last eve, but did sit in the darkness of the cave, away from everybody and alone in my solitude. Try as I might, I could not rid my thoughts of our parting, Arthyen. Sleep would have been a welcome relief, for, when left thinking for too long, my thoughts seem to become all too real, and I find it difficult to shake them. If I had been allowed some respite from the world, even if for only the briefest of time, it may have dispelled my dark thoughts of your feelings towards me.

Forcing myself to forget them, I mustered the men as the middle of the night came upon us. We rode in silent contemplation up the path to the cavern, and into the dank forest beyond. The villagers, who followed us with whatever form of weapon they could find, did join us on foot. We had secured our horses in the trees - Gryffyd was in charge of their safekeeping until we needed them. They were not far out of reach, but far enough to be shielded from sight.

I lined-up the men at the forest edge, their bows strung and their arrows standing in

137

the ground before them. My dilemma was how to the keep the light from the torches hidden from beyond the trees. Their glow would be seen from afar, and all might well have been given away. I had come upon the idea of hanging blankets from one tree to another, in the thickest part of the forest nearest to us, and keeping the torches hidden behind these, with the four bearers - Burl, Deman, Medwin and Odo. I did hope this would work well enough.

I did notice that several members of the garrison had huddled together in a group. At first, I did think they were keeping close together to share of their warmth, but it became apparent to me that they were whispering and plotting for, every now and then, one or the other did turn and look in my direction, before continuing with their secret talks. It did soon become plain that their discussion was about me. I did feel sick in my stomach that these men would turn against me, and that all would be lost. 'Tis true that my self-doubt had been gnawing away at my thoughts since I had made the decision to join the fight, but I had also managed to keep a grasp on a tiny thread of confidence, that what I was embarking upon was the correct path for me to take. In a moment, the asides of those who seemed to be making plans against me, began to hew away at this confidence.

I knew, however, that there was nothing I could do, but prepare myself for the worst from these plotters. I would have to keep my eyes open, and my back covered. I became despondent, and felt sad that these people should turn against me now. I was aware that to show my vulnerability would be just what these men were wishing, so I stood as self-assuredly as I could. I needed to fool *myself*, in order to fool those around me that I was sure in my intended actions.

It was cold. We could have no fire. I told the men to take turns in warming themselves by the torches - it was of little comfort, but it helped. The rest of us stood stamping our feet in the snow, and rubbing our hands up and down our arms in an attempt to keep warm. It was not an easy task.

As hard as I did resist, after my musings of last night, I did find myself thinking often of how you and your soldiers were keeping warm, wherever you were. I liked to believe that you had gone inside the town. The enemy would be expecting a small garrison perhaps, and a township of not many people - most of whom would be unarmed and vulnerable, but they would not be expecting nearly two hundred and fifty well-armed men behind those walls. This would seem to be the best surprise. If this were the case, of course, then you would have fires for your men, and with this thought firmly in my mind, I was satisfied.

I had charged Willard with the task of being my messenger, and he did stand by my

side all this time. He was to run back to the torchbearers as quickly and quietly as he could, when I gave him the word, to summon them to our line of archers. Our first volley would be our arrows of fire. This hail of fire would be our weapon of surprise - all arrows after that would be expected by the enemy, but I did think that if we could manage to let at least ten arrows fly from each bow within the first minute, then we might cause some damage amongst them. The timing would be crucial - they must not detect our presence, but we must not let them out of our range. Did I have the patience and the nerve to hold fire until the last possible moment?

I did not have long to test out my fortitude.

We did not hear them, but just before first light, we saw them. Mostly on foot, they silently made their way across the river to the east of us. I could not count how many there were - they massed together like a swarm that cut a swathe across the lowlands. I knew then that Cragnuth must surely fall - of this I had no doubt.

The skies were against those that came upon us, however, for as they were crossing the river, the clouds did clear, and the moon did shine her pale light down upon them. We then, for the briefest of moments, saw them before they disappeared again into the shadows, as the clouds once more covered the moon.

The dark shape of bodies was nearly at our walls, when I did see the sky above light up with streaks of flame, as your archers, Arthyen, let their fire-arrows fly. Whether it had caught our assailants off guard, I did not know. Nor did I care. I nodded to Willard, and he ran back into the darkness of the forest, to find the others with their torches.

Our foe was occupied with the unforeseen attack from Cragnuth, and I knew that *this* was the moment for us to arm ourselves. The boys ran up and down the line, lighting our arrows as they went, until we all stood, arrows flaming, ready to let our own shafts fly. We would only have the chance to use the flames once - it would take too long to light the arrows again, and once the element of surprise has been delivered, it is no longer unexpected, and would be wasted against the shields of those we try to destroy.

I took a deep breath, and called down the line for all to draw. We all stood with our bowstrings pulled back to our ears. I did then shout for all bows to be raised to the sky.

I had shouted the release, and fifty arrows soared upwards into the night sky, leaving trails of flame and smoke in their wake. Before they had reached their highest point,

our bows had been loaded, drawn and fired again. Before the first lighted arrows had begun their descent, we had released another flight. And so, we had continued, until our five hundred arrows had all been sent forth.

I could see our arrows fall into the unsuspecting enemy, and I could see that the walls of Cragnuth were still spewing forth a deadly rain of arrows from your bows.

The grey light of dawn was now upon us, and it unveiled the dark hours' work. Bodies of our attackers were strewn across the riverbank, where our arrows had found their targets, and I could make out more twisted carcasses under the walls of Cragnuth where your arrows had done their labour. I could make out some bodies - still alive - writhing in torment, as the flames devoured their entrails. I could still see, however, that there were still many more men left standing, and it was some of these that suddenly turned in our direction.

This is what I had both feared, and half-expected. Half of my men had already retrieved their horses, and were mounted, awaiting my word, with their swords drawn in readiness. I could not retreat now. I had to finish what I had started! I gave the order for them to ride into the approaching enemy.

I watched as my riders slammed into the attackers. I could see their blades hacking into all around them. Behind the mass of bodies, I could see the gates of Cragnuth open, and did see your men pour out of the town into the fight outside. The sound of their shouts was so loud, it did reach my ears, and I watched them hurtle into the enemy.

A shout next to me dragged my attention back to my own immediate situation. The group of assailants, that had broken away, were nearly upon us - there were enough who had escaped the assault of our horsemen to give unto us great harm. Those villagers who had followed us, emerged from the darkness of the trees, and took their places at the edge of the forest, beside my remaining men-at-arms... and me.

To watch this enemy descend upon us did fill me with a great dread, and I knew that my companions must have been feeling the same. I turned to them, and drawing my sword, did let forth a cry of battle. I did do of my utmost to make this sound as strong as I could, but I do fear that my voice did waiver. It did seem, though, that the others did not notice - they did join in my cry, and - as one - we ran forward into the oncoming enemy.

I do not understand from whence it did come, but as I began to run, another feeling did overcome my fear. I cannot write what it was, for I know not how to name it.

 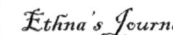
But it did make me feel as one with my blade. Mine eyes were set upon a figure that did bear down upon me, and I did feel such a battle-lust, that I did shout ever more loudly as I did near him. I do wonder now, as I write this in the aftermath, did he think me an easy kill?

I had stopped dead in my tracks, as he had swung down his sword to smite me, but I did dodge the blade and jumped to my right. He grunted, and then tried again, but once again did miss. I ran around behind him, and managed a quick stab at his side as I passed. He snarled, and lumbered his big frame around. I curled my lips, and snarled back at him; crouching, ready to spring to the side at his next lunge. This came, with his full force behind him, but again I managed to dodge to the side. I knew that I did have the upper-hand over him, as I was smaller, and lighter, than he was. I could run faster, and I was wearing no heavy armour. I did know, however, that I could never deliver a fatal blow through his armour. I thought that I would try to bring him to his knees, so I again danced around him, and as I did so, I lunged at the back of his knees to deliver the cut across the hamstrings that would render his legs useless.

As I did so, I shouted at him "Come, feel the coolness of my blade against the warmth of your blood; the sharpness of its edge against the dullness of your skin. Feel it pierce your flesh". I knew that he did not understand me, and he spat out his response in his own tongue, but I would not deterred by these barked words.

I heard him grunt, as my blade cut his flesh, and I watched him fall to his knees. He did try to stand, but he could not. I stood apart from him, regaining my breath. I knew that I had to deal the mortal blow, but hesitated. Could I really end another's life? This was what I had trained for, for nearly every day since I could hold a sword, but now the time had come for me to use it to kill, I was not sure that I could do it.

I heard the sounds of cries around me and saw one of the villagers fall to the ground, his hand clawing at the gash in his throat as his life-blood pumped out into the face of his killer.

It was then that I *knew* that I could. And not just that I could, but that I *must*.

I looked at my erstwhile assailant, as he tried to crawl on all fours towards me. Raising my sword, with both hands clasping the hilt, I shouted, "I am my father's daughter! Be gone with you from my lands!" I brought down my sword with all the force I could muster from my tired limbs. At that moment, thoughts of all that I hated rushed through my head. I felt my blade's progress hindered, as it cut the flesh on the back of his neck. Then I felt it meet bone before sensing its freedom, as it left

his body, and hit the ground below him. I fell to my knees. I saw his body twitch, and for the briefest moment did think that *somehow* he was still alive. I knew that he could not be, for his head sat where it had fallen about six inches away from the rest of his body. Through his visor I could see, the look of surprise in his dead eyes.

I did not have time to think, as I knelt there beside the body of my first kill. For I sensed someone behind me. Half turning my head, I saw a figure looming over me. I did roll on to my back, and did thrust my blade upwards into the groin of my attacker. I did feel his warm blood trickle down on to my hand. He began to fall towards me, his own sword approaching my belly as he did so. I did withdraw my sword quickly and rolled out of his way as he fell to the ground. I stood, and swung my sword - and winced - as I heard the thud of metal against bone. He turned, and looked at me in disbelief, and then down to where his arm had once been. He frantically clutched at his blood-soaked stump, his life-blood pumping through his fingers. I did raise my sword high over my head, and with all of my waning strength, I did sweep it down with a thrust into the back of his neck, to make sure of his departure from this world.

I felt like a wild animal. I then did know how it must feel to be a beast cornered by the hunters. I was shaking. I could feel the sticky crimson liquid on my hand, and wiped it on my skirt. The sounds and figures around me did merge into a haze. I knew not what was taking place around me. I saw another man approach, and did raise my sword above my head, before screaming, and running towards the figure.

It was the call of my name that halted my rush. As the mist in my eyes did clear, I did see a familiar face before me. It was the young upstart, Caswyn. He did stand before me, his hands raised to stop my assault, with a frightened look upon his face. I do think that he really thought I would kill him at that moment.

Poor Caswyn.

I heard him tell me that I could lay down my arms, for the battle was over.

I stood with my sword at my side. I did feel cold and vulnerable - I was shivering as if stricken with a fever, my body did ache from its terrible exertions, and my sword hand was bruised and numb. Looking around me, I could see broken bodies strewn across the land between the forest and Cragnuth. I could see some of your men walking through the bodies, checking for any signs of life. Occasionally, I saw a sword being raised, before dealing a fatal blow. Whether these life-taking thrusts were relieving the black-hearted enemy of their souls alone, or whether any of our own men were being aided on their last journeys, I know not. I am sure that there

were many wounds that could not be healed, and a swift end by the sword is surely a far better means of leaving this world, rather than waiting for a slow death to take you whilst you suffer in unrelenting agony.

Taking in a deep breath, I lifted my head, and could see smoke rising from the roof-tops of some of the cottages in the town. I was relieved - and surprised - to see that, for the most part, Cragnuth appeared unscathed from the attack. We had defended her well.

But it was clear that this would not be the end of our fight. I am not certain whether any of our attackers did escape back to the main army, to report on the failure of the attack. However, if they did not, it will be obvious to their leader, whoever he is, that the assault had not gone well, when his army does not return. Our only hope, for now at least, would be that the smoke rising from the smouldering rooftops, along with that which will rise from the funereal fires from the burning of the dead, will give the enemy a false hope of victory. It will be seen for many miles, and may fool them, allowing us to regroup, and form our next plan.

The wounded that could walk, were being helped back towards our town. Those who could not, were carried. The battle had not lasted for long, but I did know that it would take the rest of the day to retrieve the wounded and dead. Our fallen friends would be sent to the other world, in the pit that was being prepared not far from our walls. The carcasses of the enemy that had fallen would be taken to the south shore of the river, where they would be piled together, and left to the crows and the weasels, before being burnt like the vermin they were. A mound was already being formed, as I stood, unmoving in the bitter air, and watched. I blinked, shivered, and left Caswyn to his business, as I returned to those of my brave men-at-arms who had fallen, to see if there was any hope for any of them who were still alive.

I could not speak, for my voice did seem to have left me. I think it was from the screams that had been uttering forth from my lips since the battle had begun. It was, perchance, just as well - I did not wish to speak, for there seemed to be no words that I could utter forth, that could make the sights I saw any softer on the senses.

Amongst the groans of the injured, and the caw of the crows that had arrived for easy pickings amongst the dead, I heard an unfamiliar voice speak my name. He introduced himself as Leofric, and had told me that you, Arthyen, had sent him to seek me out. He was to report back on my safety, as soon as I had been found. Your concern had given me renewed hope that my ideas of last night may be false, and I did ask of him as to your own well-being. And he did recount that you were well, and had not sustained any injury. I did say that I was glad to hear of such news, and that

I did hope to see you later in the day, when the business of giving succour to the wounded was over.

News of the battle's end had reached the women who had been left behind in the caves. Those brave enough to face the waterfall were already beginning to emerge from the forest, to help tend to the wounded. I could hear the wails of those who had discovered that a loved one had been killed. Poor Hilda found her husband, Botolf, flat on his back in the mud, with a spear in his chest. When they tried to lift him, they found the spear was embedded in the mud below him - such was the force of the hand that dealt the blow.

I had seen Odo walking in a daze, holding his hand to a gash on his forehead, which was oozing blood between his fingers. I had taken his hand away, and looked at the wound, but it was not as bad as it had at first seemed. I lifted my skirt, and ripped off a piece of the material and proceeded to dab at the gash. I told him to press down on the material so that the bleeding would cease.

Poor Odo. I knew that he must have been suffering from a bad ache in the head. Odo is fifteen years of age, but is not blessed with a lot of sense. He is a bit slow in everything he does, but that does not mean that he does not do things well - only that he does them slowly. I did not think that this was the place for him to be; I had not realised that he had left the safety of the forest, and had thought that he would have slipped quietly away, back to the cavern once his errand of lighting the fire-arrows had been accomplished.

I did feel sorry for him, so I dispatched him back to the valley, to collect my dear Or-vin and little Vala. He seemed pleased to be able to leave this place of death for a short while, and he ran off into the forest. As he did so, I did smile, for it seemed to me that his aching head had been miraculously cured.

On your orders, all of our wounded had been taken to Cragnuth, where they could be given much better care than in the cold, damp, caves in the valley. I had had to agree with you - I did welcome the chance to see my home again. I had gone to the Hall with the other women, so that we could tend the wounded and dying, where they had been laid-out; some of them spread across the floor, and some on the tables at the side of the Hall.

It was well into the afternoon before all the enemy dead had been piled on top of each other in two large mounds. The torches had been lit, and the bodies were soon ablaze, sending plumes of black smoke billowing upwards - the fires were left to send their burning victims to whatever afterlife vermin inhabit. No-one stayed to mourn

their passing.

We did send our own departed to their ancestors shortly after dusk. They had been laid, side by side, in the pit that had been freshly dug for them that afternoon, along with those of your own men, Arthyen - warriors all, who had laid down their lives for the good of those left behind.

I did listen as you said words over their bodies. You declared them all good men, brave and selfless, and did thank them for their sacrifice. Women wept over their loss, and children clung to their mothers' skirts, and wept with them. I did stand slightly apart from the others, my arms crossed under my cloak, with its hood pulled over my head, to hide my own tears. I felt personally responsible for the deaths of some of those whose bodies burned. I was not - and as I write this, I am still not - sure that I had done the right thing in making our stand that day.

I have not had any man or woman come to me with any signs of hostility. In truth, many have given me their support. Even the three men from this morning have begged my forgiveness for their doubt of my qualities as a leader, and skills as a fighter, and I was embarrassed at their discomfort for having doubted me. I lay no blame upon them now for questioning my abilities, for I am but a woman, and they are used to being under the command of men.

I returned to the Hall to aid in the tending of the wounded and dying. It was then that you did find me for the first time since we parted company yester eve. I bowed my head to you in greeting, but no words left my lips, for I was uncertain how to address you - our leave-taking had been on such cold terms. My thoughts of the night before were also fresh in my mind still - however foolish they may be.

Raising my head, all the unhelpful thoughts that had filled me with despair last eve, were overcome with your appearance before me - how exhausted you looked, Arthyen. Your face was smeared with dirt and blood, and I could see a bruise across your forehead. I wished to embrace you, and tell you of my love for you, but I dare not utter the words I wished to, for I knew not what your own feelings were. To avoid your eyes, I simply knelt down on the floor to tend one of the wounded. I felt oddly unsettled. I wondered whether you would chastise me for my actions in the fight.

I think you were just as uncomfortable as me, Arthyen, for you too seemed unable to speak. You appeared taken off -guard when I ignored your presence, as I continued with the care of the sick. I kept my gaze to the ground, but with my eyes, followed your feet as they paced up and down a few times, and then I heard you clear your

throat. I cannot help but smile now, dear Arthyen, as I write how suddenly the words flew from your lips.

"My Lady", you began. "I beg your forgiveness for the discourteous manner in which I addressed you when last we spoke. I was concerned for your safety, but I believe it may have not been understood as such."

"'Tis true, My Lord," I replied, looking up at you. "I did think your manner some-what sharp."

You were chewing the inside of your cheek, as you pondered over how to respond. Lowering your head slightly, your hand gathered up the hair that had fallen over your eyes, and smoothed it back over your head.

"Undoubtedly, My Lady," you said quietly, and sighed. "I can only repeat my offer of an apology, and thank you for your assistance in the battle. I was wrong to doubt your skills as a warrior."

I began to feel dreadful, as it was plain that I was making you uncomfortable. I could see that you were exhausted, and in need of rest and this was no time to play games with words. I was tired also, and had no wish to bring discord to our friendship.

"My Lord Arthyen," I replied. "You have no need to apologise, for I know your intentions were well-meant. Today, I have done what I had to do for those that I love, and for the land that is my life. I am only too glad to have been of aid in whatever small way."

You seemed to relax visibly at these words. "Then my words did not offend you, Lady Ethna?" you asked.

"No, Lord Arthyen, they did not offend me", I smiled at him.

"I am glad to see the warmth of your smile upon your lips again, Lady Ethna", you softly spoke. "I greatly missed it, and had yearned for it last night before I left".

"As I had yours, Lord Arthyen," I responded quietly in case we were overheard. "The uncertainties of what may have occurred today, did cause us disagreement, did they not? It is forgotten, and I smile now, My Lord, for I am so *very* glad to see you here before me again".

"As, Lady Ethna, am I so *very* glad to see you again, for I was afraid that I would

not," you responded quickly. I saw the familiar smile in your eyes, and knew then that our bond had not been broken. However, our moment of intimacy was sadly interrupted.

At that moment, the young boy - of about seventeen - whose name I did not know, and whose head I had been cradling in my lap, suddenly coughed his last breath. I smoothed his blond fringe out of his eyes, and closed the lids with my forefingers. I sighed, and kissed his forehead, and noticed a tear escape from his right eyelid from where it had been nestling, as I rocked him gently as he lay dying.

He was one of your archers, and you did bend down, and remove his body from my lap, placing it gently on the floor beside me. Taking my hand, you urged me to stand.

"This is no place for you. Come", you said.

"My place is with my people," I replied tiredly. "I cannot leave them now - some of them are here because of me".

"Many more are here because of me," you had answered. "You cannot dwell upon such thoughts, if you are to lead your people and have their respect. They fight under your command because they trust you. They follow you because they believe in you. They know that they may die, but they are willing to do so, as they believe that what they are fighting for is worthy of such sacrifice. To show doubt now, is to show weakness."

"Perhaps, then, I am weak", I had responded.

"No, My Lady", you told me earnestly. "In truth, you are, indeed, a most remarkable and courageous young woman, and it has been a great honour to have fought in battle, with such a stout heart as yours alongside me."

Weakly, I did smile at you, sweet Arthyen. Your words did bring me cheer, but my heart was heavy with the loss of so many. My body yearned to rest upon my bed, and my head longed to shut away the events of the day, and escape to the kingdom of sleep. I had thanked you for your gallant words, and - as hard as it had been - had then excused myself from your company, to continue with the toil at hand.

Yet, you did follow me saying, "My Lady Ethna, you should take some rest, and some food. It will not do the others harm for you to see to your own needs for a short while."

You had taken my arm to halt my progress. "I insist," you said gently.

That is why I am here now, once more in my chamber, writing this before I lay my head down upon my pillow. You did bring forth from me a solemn oath that I do rest for an hour or two before taking food, and had escorted me to my room. I am sure you did not think that I would be sitting here writing this, but I smile as I do so, for I am aware that one day you may read this, and then it shall become known of my wilful disobedience. My oath will stay true, however, albeit somewhat delayed, Arthyen, for once I have completed this sentence, I shall indeed rest for a while.

I do wish that I could draw a line through what I wrote last night, reader, but to do so would be a falsehood. This journal is intended to be a *true* account of all my thoughts, feelings, and ideas, no matter how mistaken, or unfounded they may appear to be.

Thirtieth Entry

I do find myself writing this, my second entry today, as I wish to record your decision to remain at Cragnuth with your garrison for a few more days. The wounded that can be moved shall leave tomorrow for the valley, but those who cannot, will stay here - some of them have injuries that are far too severe, and it is plain that some may yet leave this world.

At supper this eve, you did tell me of your desire to keep your army camped in my home. It is obvious that there is a chance that another attack may come any day, and for the moment, you have an advantage over the enemy by staying behind Cragnuth's walls. I did offer you the arms of the town's own garrison to join with yours, as I do think that, as long as the townspeople are hidden in the valley, no harm should come upon them. I would instruct the less injured of those warriors who would return, that they are to be responsible for the welfare of the men, women, and children, in my absence.

They are to return to the valley at first light on the morrow, under the guard of an escort, who will then return to Cragnuth with what meagre supplies of food can be spared, for those remaining here. You did graciously accept my offer of some of our meat to feed your men. I am only too glad to be of help to you, Arthyen, and would offer more if I was able.

Four of the older women had asked to stay with the wounded, and I had pleaded their case to you. They were not bound to anyone in the town - two of them had become widows after the battle today, and the other two had lost their husbands during the last winter. I know that you had not wanted them to stay, but you did understand the reasoning behind their request, and did reluctantly agree to let them re-

main.

I have a feeling, my dear Lord Arthyen, that you did wish me to leave with the others, but you did have the respect not to ask this of me. I do feel that you knew that I would protest most strongly, and that you would lose this particular fight. Hence, no words on this matter had passed your lips.

After we had eaten our meagre, yet most welcome, supper of bread and potage, I had taken Orvin for a walk around the keep before returning to the sick. You did join us on our walk, and it had brought back memories of a happy time that seemed so long ago, when we had done the very same thing, only this time there would be no Martha to interrupt us as she ran down the steps on her way home. My thoughts turned to Hannel, and I hoped that he was safe and well with his father and brothers.

We had stood on the steps and looked towards the river - the glow from the death mounds was beginning to fade, and soon the cloak of darkness would descend upon the lowlands. I slipped my hand into yours, and rested my head upon your shoulder.

And so, dear reader, this has been Cragnuth's day of Yule. What should have passed as a day of celebration and rejoicing, has passed as a day of death but, at least, also a day of victory.

Thirty-first Entry

My father and cousin did return amongst us today. One of your scouts did bring us the news of their approach, and the news did cause much turmoil and apprehension within the walls of Cragnuth. I was not sure how my father would react when he realised that you were here. It had been something that I had thought about ever since I had mentioned it to you a few days before. It would have been difficult enough for my father to accept that you were in the same valley as us, but the situation as it was today was much more serious. I know that you would have every right as the ancestral King of this realm, to billet yourself in Cragnuth, but as - in my father's misguided eyes - you are a traitor to the Crown, I knew not how he would take this news.

Upon the arrival of this warning, your first thoughts had been to leave Cragnuth and return to the valley, but you were not sure whether there would be enough time to muster all your men, and retreat, before my father returned. I knew that you did not plan to retreat to the valley for your own safety - Cragnuth was still in mortal danger from our enemy, and you are still prepared to defend it as, and when, the need should present itself. It was for my own safety, and that of your followers, that you did think of such an action. You had explained this to me earnestly, as you issued your orders to your men - via Caswyn - that you knew that my father would try to enforce some kind of imprisonment upon you, should you remain.

However, you also knew that this course of action on his part, although quite probable, would take much time to organise, as the ride to the King would take several days at least, although he could quite easily order your captivity in a room in Cragnuth, until such time as reinforcements arrived. You had told me that my father may well decide to imprison me also as a traitor for having made you welcome here. So

151

you would take your army and make camp again in the forest, where you would also be able to keep watch for any further attacks on the town.

I had been greatly relieved to learn of your intentions. I knew that, although there were only two of them, my father and cousin could well send for reinforcements from the King, to arrest you and, no doubt, claim a substantial ransom for doing so - I know there must be a large sum of coins on your sweet head, Arthyen.

The scout had told us that my father and Margh would arrive in the lowlands within the hour. This had not left us much time to prepare ourselves. I would have to ride out to meet them, and inform them of our return to Cragnuth, and the battle that took place yesterday. This, hopefully, would prevent them from having to enter the valley - I did not wish either of them to know of its exact location.

I am sure, as you read over this journal dear reader, that you can imagine how much my mind was in turmoil upon this day. I was well aware that my father and cousin were returning from the house of Margh's father, after bartering over my intended union with this odious cousin of mine. For all I knew, an announcement of such would be forthcoming this very day, and this possibility did weigh heavily upon my mind.

Arthyen, it was plain that your thoughts of being discovered at Cragnuth would be at the front of your mind, but I am not sure whether you had sensed my foreboding regarding the other matter that I have mentioned above. While your men-at-arms scurried about their business, you had accompanied me to the stables, where I began to saddle Elwine. There had been much activity here, as your men saw to their own mounts. One by one, the horses disappeared from their stalls, and it was not long before only the horses belonging to Cragnuth's garrison, along with Acha and Elwine, remained.

You had already given instructions to your men that they should leave the great gates of Cragnuth as soon as they were ready to do so, and that all should regroup in the forest where their original encampment had been located. I had been astounded, and impressed, by the speed at which your army decamped itself from our walls, and made off to the safety of the dark forest. All who were left were injured, and I promised you that I would ensure that they would get safe passage out of Cragnuth when they were fit enough to do so.

We tended our horses in a quick silence. If the scout had been correct in his estimation of their arrival, there would not have been much time left before my father and Margh would appear on the lowlands. As ever, I could see by your face that you

wished to speak of something. I can always tell when words wish to utter forth from your lips, my dear Arthyen, and I can always sense when those words are hard for you to say, hence their difficult passage across your lips.

I had placed my hand on your forearm as I prepared to mount Elwine for my journey out to meet my father. I did wish you good speed, and told you that I did hope to be able to travel to the valley, as soon as I could escape from my father's watchful eye.

It had been then that the words came forth.

"My Lady Ethna," you had begun. "I do have a thought in my head that does warn me that your father brings news to you that shall tear at my heart".

"I fear, My Lord," I had replied, "that it shall tear at my heart also, but I also fear that there will be nothing that can be done for me".

You had laid your hand across my cheek. "My Lady, there is always a solution to every problem, but it can sometimes remain hidden to those who seek it".

"I think then, that my solution is hidden in some dark place, My Lord, for I cannot see it - though I have searched many times", I answered. I had felt a lump rising in my throat, at the thought of what news could befall me later this day.

It had been time to leave, but I had not been sure as to how to depart from your company. I am embarrassed to record that I did wish to feel the softness of your lips upon mine before we did part, but as a woman of noble birth, it was not fitting for me to cause such a thing to occur. I found it impossible to consider further, and - instead - I did announce to you that it was time to leave. With my foot in Elwine's stirrup, I did lever myself into her saddle. I sat in fear of what was to soon to take place, but before we urged our horses to leave the comfort of their stable, you did take my hand in yours, and did raise it to your lips, placing a soft kiss upon it's quivering flesh.

We left the stables together, and slowly rode down to the main gate, where we walked our horses under its great arch, and out on to the lowlands that stretched before us. I turned Elwine west, as you steered Acha east.

And so we did part company.

I could see my father and cousin approaching towards the river, and turned in my saddle to watch you gallop Acha across the shallows, and into the darkness of the for-

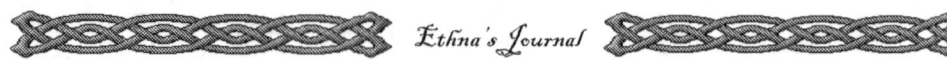
est beyond. It was clear that my father and Margh had also seen you, as they were close enough now for me to see them turn their attentions to your shape as it disappeared from view. I did prepare myself for the harshness of my father's tongue, and the cold leer across Margh's ugly face.

The ashes from the enemy pyre, were still smouldering, as were those from our own men's burial pit. Upon reaching my father, he stared at me icily before demanding of me, "What has been taking place here?"

I did gabble a reply, and told him all that had taken place yesterday. Upon mention of your name, his face turned purple, and he shouted with rage, as he questioned how I could let such a traitor as you enter the gates of his home. I was not surprised that it did not concern him that you had helped vanquish the enemy, and had saved Cragnuth from destruction. The distasteful Margh just sat in his saddle, and shook his head in sympathy with my father's raging, with a look of smug pretence upon his face. Upon seeing him again, I did realise that I loathed him even more than I had done a few days before, when he had left with my father.

My father urged his horse forward, pushing my own mare out of the way, as he urged his bony old nag into a gallop towards Cragnuth. Margh soon followed, but not before he had turned to me and thrown me a knowing smirk, at which I did merely turn my head away from his; my stare inadvertently settling upon the darkness of the forest.

Upon our return to the Hall, my father continued to vent his anger, when he came across the wounded that were sprawled around the brazier in the middle of the room. Orvin had shrunk into one of the dark corners of the Hall - I did think that he was perhaps the wisest of those present. He did know that the voice of ire would bring upon its wings a kick in the ribs, if he had remained within my father's shadow for too long. I, however, did not have that luxury. I did have no choice but to stand in my father's presence while he did shower me with insults and threats. The more he raged, however, the more determined I found myself becoming. I held myself firm before him, and my back stiffened as his words continued. I found myself clenching my fists as he spoke.

How dare he speak to me thus.

Steadily, I did remind him that some of those who lay wounded were men from Cragnuth, and that all of the men lying before him had given of themselves for the defence of his ancestral home. As I write this, I do recall how the bitter taste of loathing rose in my throat, and how my heart did beat as thunder within me, as I had

suggested - resolutely - to my father that perhaps he should give thanks to these men - some of whom may still leave this world - for their part in the defence of Cragnuth.

As soon as I had uttered the words, for all my bravery up until then, I found myself naturally recoiling in defence of his reply. I do admit, though, reader that I had not expected to feel the sting of his hand across my cheek in response, but that is what had followed. I had detected a low chuckle from Margh, as I had instinctively stepped back, and taken my own hand to that part of my face that had smarted from the attack.

Orvin emitted a low growl from the shadows, but I signalled to him with my other hand to remain where he was. It would not have been out of my father's character to draw his sword, and kill Orvin, if my faithful companion had come to my defence.

Is it so very wrong for a daughter to loathe her father so? I cannot see that any daughter could have *any* kind feelings towards a parent who shows nothing but such malice towards her. 'Twas always as such, as I have written before, but every day I have hoped that his feelings and actions towards me would change. I have always yearned for his love - for some slight notion of affection; a kind word, a loving look, but after all these years I am still searching and hoping. Perhaps, reader, they will never come upon me.

I had stood helplessly as I listened to my father bark his orders, that all those men in the Hall were to be removed to the stables. The men-at-arms who belonged to his garrison looked shocked at his instructions, but they did have no choice but to obey his command. So began the removal of those who had so gallantly and selflessly fought and shed their blood on that dark day of Yule yesterday.

I retreated to my bower and have been here ever since. I did stand at my window, gazing across the lowlands towards the forest to where I knew you would be. Not an hour or two after my father's return I did see several of the townspeople making their way back to Cragnuth across the lowlands. I could make out the towering figure of Tarek amongst them. As they passed under my window, I saw Tilda and two other girls from the kitchens, along with Airic and Beloc, who was our thatcher. Joining them was our carpenter, Aldfric, and Gryffyd amongst others. It was clear to me that you had sent these people back to Cragnuth for two reasons. One to ensure my father's household returned to how it should be, but also, if I am correct, to ensure that things could be made ready for the next attack. Tarek's fire and skills would be needed to sharpen and repair blades. The bowyer was needed to continue his work on the bows he had left behind. The fletcher was needed to maintain his work on

sorely required arrows. All who had returned had special tasks to their name, and all had been sent for a reason. I knew that they would all be busy in the coming days, and I did hope that our foe would not attack again until we had had time to prepare ourselves.

As darkness fell, I could make out several lights in the dense forest. They flickered in the distance, and I knew it was your men keeping a watchful eye for the enemy. It brought me great comfort to know you had not deserted us. It brought me even greater comfort to know that you were still there in my world.

The news I have been dreading since my father's return has yet to reach my ears. It is now late, and I feel sure that it will not come today. As I write these last words, my bruised cheek does still ache, and I shall hope for a better day on the morrow. My dear companion, Orvin, is here with me, and I shall take to my bed knowing that you are not too far away. I wish you a restful night, Arthyen.

Until tomorrow.

Thirty-second Entry

I was awoken early this morning. Orvin hardly stirred in the darkness of the cold morning. As I sat up in my bed, he did whimper in his sleep, but did not awaken. I know not what did cause me to open my eyes so early. Perhaps 'twas a dream that had interrupted my slumbers - I remember not, but I do know that my stomach did feel unsettled, and I still cannot tell you for what reason.

It was bitter cold, and I wrapped myself in my cloak as I arose. The floor was icy against my feet, and my toes had quickly searched for my shoes. I could not help my teeth chattering in the coldness of my chamber, as I went to my window and looked out. Peering into the distance, I could see the lights were still dancing within the shadows of the distant forest. For a brief moment, I did wonder whether my father or Margh had noticed them the night before, but realised that they had probably been too busy at their drinking and dining to notice such things.

As I had passed my bed on the way to my door, I had gently stroked Orvin's sleeping head. He raised his head sleepily, yawned, and made as if to get up from his slumbers. I kissed his head, bade him stay where he was, and smiled as he did lay his head back down on my coverlet again.

I opened my door slowly and quietly - I know not why I was drawn to do such a thing - I did not know what hour of the day it was, but had guessed that it was long past the hour of midnight. The candle that burned at my bedside still had a few hours left before it would go out completely, but I could tell by its size, that many hours had passed since I had retired to my bed. I had wrapped my cloak around me,

and shivered as I looked down the dark corridor. The candles on the walls were also burning their last flames; their wax hanging from their metal frames like the icicles that hung outside from any part of the buildings they could get a grip. I wondered why I had left the warmth of my cot, but something within me had urged me on.

I approached the steps that led down to the hall - all was quiet below. I could not hear any snoring, and breathed a sigh of relief, as I had realised that my father and cousin must have retired to their own chambers, and had not collapsed where they sat as they so often have done before.

I had slowly made my way down the steps, my hands holding up my cloak so that I did not trip. All of our hounds were in the valley, deep in the caves, and the Hall seemed to be deserted. The only life appeared to come from the brazier in the middle of the room - it had recently been tended, and was still burning fiercely. I did wonder who had replenished its thirsty flames - perchance it had been Airic before he had retired? Or perhaps one of the kitchen girls had been given the responsibility before she could take leave to catch what slumber she could, before the morning's duties did begin again.

I did make my way swiftly, yet cautiously, towards the heat, and stood with my hands warming over the flames. My mind did wander to thoughts of you, sweetest Arthyen, as I felt the warmth begin to bring life back to my cold hands. I did make the mistake of relaxing my guard, as the comforting heat and musings of you did take me away from this place.

It was then that I did hear the sound.

In the shadows to the left of me I did hear the noise of shuffling footsteps coming towards me. I did freeze. Perhaps it was a mouse or rat scuttling around, seeking out scraps of food from this evening's supper? But no, I did know that the sound I did hear came from something much larger than a mouse or rat. How I did wish, then, that I had not been so foolish as to wander around without the protection of at least my dagger. I would not have thought that I would feel so unsafe in my own home, but at that moment I felt vulnerable, and - I do loathe to admit - afraid of what or who was approaching me.

I did edge around to the right of the brazier, in the hope of being able to catch a glimpse of something. The candles on my left were still burning brightly, but as I watched, to my dismay, one of them suddenly went out, as if caught by a draught. It was an eerie sight to behold, and I felt my lifeblood run cold within my veins. Whatever - or whoever - it was, did not want to be seen. I turned my head sharply to the

steps, and decided that I should try to escape back to the safety of my bower. Picking up my cloak, I did begin to walk quickly, my ears keen for any sounds that might follow. To my distress, I did hear the shuffling begin to quicken. It was very clear, now, that it was not my imagination, and that there was definitely someone there intent on some evil against me.

I began to run towards the steps - the fear in my belly began to make me feel sick. Had the enemy invaded our walls while we were sleeping without our knowledge? Had the guards at the gate been slaughtered silently as they stood watch? Would this night be the last time I would draw breath in this world?

I did reach the third step, when I did feel a hand wrap itself around my left arm, and drag me backwards again. For a moment, I did hold my breath before attempting to exhale into a scream, as I did think that this might awaken Orvin and cause his barks to awaken my father and cousin, even though I did think that this would probably not make any difference, as they would almost certainly not hear him in their wine-sotten stupor.

A hand being placed over my mouth, however, had immediately halted my efforts.

Oh dear Arthyen, I did bite down so hard on that hand that I did draw blood, and could taste its bitterness upon my tongue. The hand withdrew sharply, and I heard a man grunt behind me. I did so want to turn to face my attacker, but will admit to being too scared to do so. I did kick out my leg behind me, to try and catch my assailant off guard long enough for me to try to run up the steps again.

My foot did not meet any resistance but did just kick the air behind it. I tried again and this time I did feel it make contact. Again, a grunt, but this time there was great anger behind the sound. I did pull away from the grip on my arm, and make my escape up the steps. I did not hear any footsteps following me, but did keep on running. I did not turn around, and when I reached the corridor, I just ran until I came upon the door to my bower. I flung it open and ran inside, shutting it firmly behind me. Leaning against it, I did struggle to catch my breath.

By this time, Orvin had awoken, and was standing beside me growling. He could sense danger outside my room, and I could only hope that whoever had attacked me would think twice about entering, upon hearing Orvin's warning.

However, it was not to be. For, as I did try to regain my composure, I felt the latch on my door lifting against my back, as I did lean with all my strength against it. Orvin became rigid, his ears were flat against his head, and his lips curled, baring his

teeth as he growled even louder. My eyes did instinctively locate the whereabouts of my sword, where it lay across the stool by my bed, but my dilemma was whether I could reach and draw it in time before my assailant burst his way through my door, and was upon me.

Who was he? And what did he want of me?

I shall attempt to put to parchment all that followed, in a way that shall leave you in no doubt as to the terror that I endured.

I had made up my mind to cease leaning against my door, so that I could collect my blade in readiness of what may befall me. At the very moment that I did move, the door burst open, and with such speed, Orvin did leap upon whoever it was whom had entered my bower. I could do nothing, but watch in horror, as I heard Orvin yelp, and collapse to the floor, before being kicked by a booted foot across the room into the corner. I did not know whether my companion was wounded, or dead, but he remained very quiet and still, where his body came to rest after it had hit the wall.

Who did stand before me in the shadows from the corridor?

Dear reader, it was my loathsome cousin, Margh. And it was then that I did fear what would befall me in the next minutes, for he edged towards me with a strange look upon his face. His eyes were fixed firmly upon me, but oozed a malice that I had not detected before. It was clear that he was not within the realms spun from too much wine either, for he did seem steady on his feet, and approached me with a sharpness that would not be possible, if wine had surged within him. This did concern me greatly - I knew that if he had been drunk, that I would have a better chance of being able to fight him off, but as he stood before me, it was plain to see that he was completely sober and that his senses were keen.

I backed away from him demanding, in as clear a tone as possible, that he should leave my bower at once.

He did ignore my request, and merely stated, "I warned you that I would slit his scrawny throat", nodding in the direction to where Orvin had been kicked.

I had glanced across to where poor Orvin lay. Great sadness did I feel, but I did remember the conversation to which Margh had referred, and replied with as much boldness that I could muster, "Then I shall have to cut out your heart, cousin, for that is the oath I did make. There are no dogs here to eat it, but I fear that it would be too shrivelled to make a worthy meal for them. Perhaps I should leave it for the

rats, for I know that they will eat anything. The poison within such a heart as yours would do Cragnuth a great service by disposing of such pests".

Margh had laughed quietly, and continued his approach; one bony hand clasped around his dagger where it was tucked into his belt, the other clenching itself into a fist. As he did walk towards me, I could do nothing but back further away, trapping myself against the wall. There was no escape, and I did fear for my life.

"I was alarmed to hear of the visit of the traitor at Cragnuth, My Lady", he spat. "I must admit that to hear that my future wife has entertained such a person in my absence irks me somewhat".

It was the first time I had heard mention of being Margh's wife, although, as you know, I have realised that this was quite probable for many days. This knowledge, however, could not have prepared me for the feeling of disgust that I did feel on hearing the words uttered from my cousin's own lips.

"My Lord Arthyen is *no* traitor, cousin. His presence here, as you are well aware, was to help protect Cragnuth. I do not like your tone of voice, and do not like your presence here in my bower. I would, again, demand that you leave," I did answer.

"I do not think you are in a position to demand anything, My Lady", he had persisted. "By tomorrow evening you will be my property, but I have decided that I shall not wait that long to take that which belongs to me".

The sickness did return to my stomach as I realised my fate. My situation was indeed, more serious than I had predicted - tomorrow I was to be given to my cousin in marriage. So soon? I did wonder when my father was going to have the decency to speak to me about it. A few minutes before the event, no doubt? More urgent, however, was the realisation that tonight my cousin had come to take my virtue by force.

My impending doom did encourage many ideas of escape to rush through my mind, but all were clouded by the immediate danger in which I did find myself. This evening, this man before me had one thought in his own head, and it was a thought that I did find both repulsive and frightening.

As I have written, by edging away from him, I had found myself with my back against my wall. There was nowhere for me to go, but remembering my blade, I did creep sideways across the wall towards my stool, but Margh, if nothing else, was certainly not dim-witted, and he realised immediately what I was trying to do. He swiftly

darted forward, removed my sword from where it lay, and tossed it to the other side of the room.

This creature was going to try to take from me that which I did not wish to give, and I did feel great anger at his despicable intentions. My head was still spinning with thoughts of how to escape his evil clutches. With one hand, he did grasp both of my arms around the wrists, and held them together. With his other hand, he did begin to slide my cloak from my shoulders, and did run his fingers across my shoulder to my neck where he lingered threateningly. I did think that he would throttle me, but he merely lingered for a moment, before his hand did brush down the front of my neck and began to trace my breastbone.

The touch of his fingers made my flesh crawl, and I did at once realise where his hand was going. I did begin to struggle more, but his grip was strong. I did try to kick his shins, but he did dodge out of the way. I cried out, but he did place his hand over my mouth, and thrust his face towards mine and hissed, "I should be quiet, My Lady, for I would hate to have to silence you myself".

He released his grip on my wrists, and did place that hand around my neck and squeezed.

"I would rather that than suffer your advances further," I managed to gasp.

Margh eased his grip around my throat, and grasped my left arm, "Ah, but that would be too easy, my dearest cousin", he whispered in my left ear, before he took the fleshy part between his teeth and did bite down on it. It made me wince, but I was determined not cry out and show my discomfort. I felt him lick my left cheek, and down the side of my neck. I tried to hit him with my right hand, but he grasped each of my wrists, and pushed me back against the wall, my arms outstretched. As he bent his head towards me in an attempt to kiss me, I did take the opportunity to raise my right knee sharply upwards into his groin, with much force. This did have the affect that I wished for, and he released my arms, and did bend over in great discomfort, clutching his balls, but not before I had snatched the dagger from his belt.

Reader, I could have killed him then. I could have plunged the dagger into his black heart, and could, indeed, have cut it out and fulfilled my oath. However, to kill in battle is one thing. To kill in cold blood is a different matter.

As Margh did slowly recover his composure, I did collect my sword from where he had thrown it, and stood behind him, dagger and sword drawn and did calmly demand, "I shall ask you again, cousin, to take your most unwelcome lust away from

my bower."

He had straightened himself, and turned to face me. His face was contorted in anger and he spat out the following words: "Remember my sweet lady, tomorrow eve you shall be mine by the law of this land, and I shall have what is mine in the end. You may have won a minor victory here this eve, but tomorrow you shall lose the battle".

Hiding his obvious discomfort, he did do his utmost to create an air of disdain, and strutted past me, leaving my chamber at last. I slammed the door behind him and leant against it, before sliding down on to the floor, where I sat with my head in my hands and did weep. The uneasiness in my stomach did reach my throat, and I did retch on to the floor, before crawling in the darkness, to the corner where Orvin lay.

I stretched out a hand to his prone body, and did search for a sign of life. There was a stillness about him that did give me such an overwhelming feeling of despair. Had my dearest friend of so many years really left me? Was he now sitting beside my dear Leif looking down upon me? I knew Leif would look after and love him, but I was not ready to let my faithful companion go yet, and - above all - I did not want him to leave like this. He should die of old age in his sleep, and not by the boot of such a man as Margh.

A heartbeat I did find, and I did sob loudly as I realised that he was still alive. Margh had not succeeded in taking Orvin away from me just yet. I did whisper his name, and heard a faint whimper in response. Dearest Orvin, I did hear your tail thumping upon the cold wooden floor. I have never understood how dogs manage to give this sign of greeting, even when they are in such distress themselves. I knew, though, that Margh must have hurt you in some way - I had seen the blood on the dagger's blade.

Upon realising that Orvin was still alive, this did bring a new hope within me, and I did fetch the candle from where it flickered next to my bed. Kneeling down beside my wounded friend, I did search for his injury. I could see the dark stain of blood on the floor, and did feel the sticky patch of fur around his chest. This was where Margh had dealt the cruel blow, before rendering my companion unaware as Orvin had hit his head on the wall, whence he had been kicked with such evil force.

From my first discovery of his wound, it would appear that it was not too deep, and I did rejoice that it would not be a difficult wound to heal. It became obvious that his silence had been caused by being stunned into a state of oblivion on contact with the wall, and not through a mortal thrust from the dagger.

As I did kneel beside him, stroking his head, and whispering words of comfort, he did slowly raise himself to his feet. His legs were shaky, but he did still manage to lick my face, at which I laughed with great happiness; the tears flowing down my cheeks, before giving him a gentle hug and a kiss on his head in return.

I did soak some cloth in my bowl of icy water, and did clean the wound, offering my apologies to him for the coldness of the liquid, before wrapping another piece of clean cloth around his wound in a fashion that was not very becoming for such a brave hound, but which would suffice in keeping the injury clean. I did wish that I could administer a healing poultice, but that would mean that I would have to wander the halls in the darkness again, in search of such ingredients from the kitchens, and I did not wish to run into my cousin once more.

I did tell Orvin that we were to leave Cragnuth as I did gather up as many belongings as I could manage to carry. I did dress, and, with one last look at my chamber - for I did not think I should ever lay eyes on it again - I did gingerly open my door, and check down the corridor to make sure that we were not being watched.

Quietly, and quickly, we made our way down the steps, and into the Hall. Pulling my cloak around my head, I did open the great oak doors, and we did depart down through the bailey towards the stables. There was no moon, and the heavy clouds hung above us, almost motionless in the night sky. The ice beneath my feet crackled as I walked, and I was glad to reach the cover of the stables.

Finding Elwine, I had quickly saddled and bridled her, before leading her out into the early morning air. I knew, by the colour of the sky in the east, that it would soon be dawn, and I did realise that I was running out of time to make my escape undetected. I led Elwine down through the village, and to the main gates.

I was concerned about getting past the guards, but I need not have worried. My actions over the past few days had earned me a reasonable amount of respect from the men of Cragnuth, and, after witnessing my father's treatment of the wounded men, it did seem that they did understand that my departure from the town must be for good reason. They did not question my arrival at the gate, and did open it without a word. I nodded my thanks to them, and they did bow in return, before quietly and swiftly closing the gate behind me.

I do hope that my father did not punish them harshly for letting me escape.

Mounting Elwine, and with poor Orvin at our side, we did journey slowly towards the forest, and the flickering lights therein.

You did make me most welcome, Arthyen, and I do thank you for not asking me questions as to my sudden arrival at your camp. I do thank you, also, for letting me write this now before I do try to rest, for I do feel that upon my awakening, there will be much to tell you, and much for me to do to prevent, what I feel will be your response.

Thirty-third Entry

*U*pon my arrival in the forest early this morning, I was confronted by your guards, but did not encounter any hindrance from them once I had identified myself to their satisfaction. I did make my way by torchlight to the hidden entrance, and down into the valley, passing the sleeping townspeople in their caves.

You had been understandably surprised to see me upon my arrival at your tent. It does seem that I do make a habit of awakening you prematurely, and once again, you had appeared at the entrance of your tent in a somewhat sleep-filled way. But – as always - you were courteous and, above all else, concerned at my arrival.

The first thing I had done was to ask you to send for Wilf. Dear Wilf has a way with animals, and I knew that Orvin would be in safe hands under the marshal's care. I had been hesitant to tell you of the exact events of the previous evening, and would only tell you only that Orvin had been injured after an encounter with my cousin. As I had sat in the warmth of your tent, with Orvin's head resting on my lap, awaiting the arrival of Wilf, I must have fallen asleep, for I did awaken suddenly at the sound of his concerned voice as he examined Orvin's wound.

As Wilf took my faithful friend away to his own tent, you had insisted that I sleep before attempting to tell you of the events that had befallen me that night. I did not have the strength to argue with you, and had gratefully lain upon your cot - its covers were still warm from where you had laid upon them, and your scent still clung to their fibres. I had curled myself up in that comforting warmth, and it was not long before I gave myself up to my slumbers.

Thirty-fourth Entry

I did awaken to find you asleep on in the chair by your table, your head resting on your arms, as they lay crossed across the map that was spread upon its cluttered surface. The candle was still flickering, and its wax was dribbling down the stem of the candlestick, hardening as it left the warmth of the flame, and became grasped in the coldness of the air.

I did feel guilty at your discomfort at having to sleep in such a way.

It had taken me a few minutes to realise where I was, when I did first open my eyes. The events of the previous evening had returned to my memory quickly enough, and I did sit up upon your cot, and shivered in the morning air. I had no wish to awaken you for, apart from not wanting to disturb your sleep, I had no desire to relive my experiences of last evening. I knew that you would wish to know what had happened to cause my sudden appearance at your tent, and I knew that I would have to tell you, but the thought did not appeal to me.

I had sat and gazed around your tent as you slept, but the overwhelming desire to empty my bladder, did cause me to wrap my cloak around me and step out into the gloominess of the early morning. There was a low mist that clung to the tents; its tiny droplets of water did dampen my hair as I made my way to a suitable place to answer the call of Mother Nature. Should I perhaps not write about such things in my journal? I do not see why I should hide such natural occurrences. This is, after all, a record of my life over the days about which I choose to write an entry. No, I shall continue to add such personal notes if I deem it necessary so to do. I hope I do

not offend those who may read this, but this natural need did have a bearing upon what did occur next.

I realised, after some comfort had returned to me, that the mist was thicker than I had first thought, and I found myself somewhat confused as to my exact location. I did try to retrace my steps back the way I had come, but I did find myself not outside your tent, but standing on a path that seemed to lead away from the encampment. I have no idea as to how I had found myself there, but for a reason I cannot explain I did follow it, and, even once it had become clear, I did proceed to walk further away from the safety of your tent, my sweet Arthyen.

The mist seemed to get thicker the further I did walk, and then I realised that I had come to the river. I knew not exactly whereabouts on the riverbank I was, but this was the same river where we had encountered the mystical Rhialdaron, and the vision of your father, and it made me somewhat apprehensive about being in this place on my own. I found myself wishing that I had taken more care when leaving your tent. I turned to return from whence I had come along the path, when I heard my name being called softly. It did cause a shiver to run down my spine, and the hairs upon the back of my neck to stiffen. I shook my head in disbelief, and did tell myself that the denseness of the mist was causing me to hear sounds that were not there. Sounds that would have been normal seemed to be louder, and even more mystical in the fog. I did try to convince myself that it was merely the sound of the fowl on the river that I could hear, as they quietly called to each other.

I continued to walk back down the path. My name was called once more, but this time I thought I did recognise the voice as that of Rhialdaron. I could not be sure, but felt almost certain that it was. I did stop dead in my tracks at this understanding, and slowly turned around. There was nothing there but grey swirls of damp mist. I felt something brush past me. This was too much like my experiences of the night before, and did make my blood run cold, as - indeed - it had last eve.

The voice did tell me not to be afraid; it said to follow the path towards the river, and that there would be someone there to meet me, and take me across.

I became more afraid. I began to doubt my senses. Could this person perhaps be 'The Boatman'?

I do fear 'The Boatman'.

I had heard stories of such a being in my childhood. The wandering folk who had oft visited Cragnuth on their way east, did speak of such a person; a figure shrouded in

 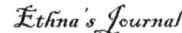
black, neither a face did you see, nor a bare hand did you touch. He would take you across the river – but if you did not cross his gloved palm with suitable payment, you did not even make half the journey across. He would toss you over the side of the boat into the cold, dark waters, and you would remain there forever; slowly sinking into the murky depths, with no way of escape. Before he did so, however, he would show himself to you - his hands were covered with pus-filled blisters, the nails black and flaking, but it was his face that was the most terrible. As you fell to the depths, you would remember the sight of flesh hanging from hollow cheeks, and the cold glare from the greyest eyes you had ever seen, as they stared at you from sunken eye sockets. His lips would part in a grin that showed rotten teeth, set in bloodied gums, and he would utter forth a deathly cackle as he let you go.

The more you struggled to reach the surface, the further you would sink - ever downwards. Fish would nibble hungrily at your flesh, as you tried in vain to swim to the banks. The arms of those already departed would wrap themselves around your body, and pull you into their bodies. You would become one of them. Once he had let you go, you would never reach the banks, and would remain in your watery grave until the end of time.

I did shudder at the thought of the dark, cold waters before me. You may offer the suggestion, reader, that a traveller should carry the correct payment before boarding such a boat. I should explain, however, that this not always possible; for the tale follows that the expected payment is never the same for one as it would be for another.

Readers of this journal - this vision did not make me feel any better.

But then, why should such a children's story be of any relevance to my current position? It was nonsense to think of such a thing. Here was I, a woman who had just taken part in a battle, and had killed for the first time, being afraid of a figure that lived in the pages of a tale to enthral children on stormy nights. This would not do, so taking a deep breath, I did as I had been bid, and turned, once again, in the direction of the river, and made my way slowly towards the bank.

There was no-one there, but then I had not expected there to be. All was quiet. Quite suddenly though, I did jump from within mine own skin, when two or three waterfowl took it upon themselves to launch their plump little bodies from the river, and take flight downstream. The sound of their exertions at trying to achieve flight did create such a din, that it did break my concentration. Oh, Arthyen, how I had longed to be back in your cot, wrapped in the warmth of your coverlet, and safe inside your tent. I did curse my body for waking me so early, and for causing me to wander so far from the safety of the encampment.

"Welcome daughter of Cragnuth", spoke a voice from nowhere. Such a low whisper it was too, that it could have easily been lost in the early morning air had I not been half-expecting it.

As had happened before, and as I have written about earlier, stepping-stones appeared before me. Again, the mysterious island did appear, and I did walk across to travel upon the same path as on the previous occasion. I could still see no-one, but could feel a presence around me. I came upon the archway, its dragonhead still glaring down upon all who dared enter. Your father's tomb lay in the middle of the room as before, Arthyen, quiet in its solitude.

The voice spoke again: "Beware daughter of Cragnuth, for what will come upon you is most malevolent. You must be prepared to meet this evil, and destroy it, before it can destroy you and those you hold most dear".

As I listened to the words, the room became darker, as a shape loomed from the opposite end. I did instinctively reach for my sword, but, as you know, it was not there. I could hear a dull flapping sound, like that of the wings of a giant bird. There before me came a creature I have never encountered before, but have heard of in epic tales. Of course, you and I had spoken of such a beast, and your father's tomb is watched over by many statues of such a creature, but I was not prepared to see such that came before me. Its leathery wings stretched across the room - how could it possibly fly in such a small space? More sorcery? Here I stood upon an island that did not exist in the real world, so it was no real surprise to realise that the columns around the room had disappeared into the mist, as this vision had appeared. Now, looking around, I could see a barren landscape; free of mist and dotted with rocky crags.

More importantly, there was nothing at all to restrict the movement of this beast that came down upon me. It was like a giant version of those little creatures that sat around your father's tomb, Arthyen, but this was far more fearsome, and it did emit a low sound, as it lumbered towards me. My first instinct had been to crouch down to avoid it, but something within me made me stand firm, and meet my adversary face to face.

Surely, if this was indeed just a vision, then it could do me no harm, and would return to its mystical origins as swiftly as it had appeared?

However, journal, it did not cease its progress, and as it approached I did see its skin more clearly - it was not unlike that of the snakes that slither through the grasses on the lowlands during the months of summer. Alas, I have never set eyes upon a snake

with skin so dark and evil. There was malice about this creature before me. As it was almost upon me, its huge jaws opened to reveal teeth of the most frightening kind, spittle stretching from its lower to upper jaw as it opened its mouth wider.

I have heard how these beasts emit flames from their mouths. So this was how it was all to end now? Was I to be burned in the flames of this flying creature with no-one knowing how I had met my end? There would be nothing left of me but charred bones, and these remains would sink into the cold waters of the river when this island once again cloaked itself against the eyes of those who pass by. My departure from this world, therefore, would be forever shrouded in mystery.

This was all too real to me. I could smell it; I could hear it; I could feel the breeze coming from its giant flapping wings, and most vividly I could see it. Perhaps, after all, this was not a vision, but a *real* dragon of myth and legend?

I did close my eyes as the dragon bore down upon me, and did wait for the searing flames to envelop my body. The air around me was stifling, and the creature smelt of decaying meat, which made me feel nauseous.

I waited and waited, but suddenly the air became cold again - bitterly cold. The dampness of the mist had returned. I opened my eyes, and the rocky crags around me had once again become the columns around the tomb. The beast had gone, and I was alone again. I did shudder. What had this vision meant? Is this the dragon that would come upon you, Arthyen, to challenge your bloodline for one last time? Why had it made itself known to me?

The silence was broken as the voice spoke again, "The Lady Ethna is now prepared. Be gone from here, and speak of this to no-one."

Meekly, I did turn and do as I was bid, but as I left through the archway I heard the voice of your father speak to me. "You are charged with much, sweet child of Crag-nuth, but I know that you will serve my son well. It is as it is written. Go with strength in your heart."

Before I could respond, I knew the island was disappearing once more, and did hurry back across the stones. As I did place my feet upon the banks of the river, the last of the stones had already gone from whence they had come.

I could hear my name being called, and did recognise your voice amongst the others, dear Arthyen. I had been missed, and a search party had been dispatched to look for me. I was glad to see you emerge from the fog in front of me, and did thankfully ac-

cept your embrace.

As we stood in that place, I did feel safe once more. What had just passed was a heavy burden on my mind, but I knew I could not share my experience with you. I have grown used to putting thoughts away until I am alone, and can then think about them more clearly and deeply. This was not such a time, and I will ponder my vision when solitude doth visit me again.

However, I did know of one onerous task still to be performed - that of relating the events of the past evening to you. I knew not how you would react to such news, and it did concern me greatly, but I realised that the truth would have to be told.

You sat quietly as I recounted my trip to the Hall at Cragnuth; the expression on your face grew darker as the story unfolded. By the time I had finished my account, you were pacing up and down inside the tent. I watched as you clenched your fists, and released them over and over again. Dear Arthyen, I did not think my tale would have caused you so much anguish, and I am sorry that it did so. Perhaps I should not have told you all that had taken place?

I had been sitting at the foot of your cot as I did tell my tale, and once painfully re-counted, you ceased your pacing, knelt before me, and asked most gently if my cousin had caused me any physical pain. I did shake my head. In truth, Arthyen, apart from the torment of believing Orvin to be dead, I did suffer but bruises to my arms, which are of no importance, and I did not think it necessary to confide in you about their existence.

You are in no way responsible for what did befall me, but you did insist on blaming yourself, by declaring that you should not have left me at Cragnuth when my father and cousin did return. I did implore you to cease in such self-accusation, but you did seem determined to lay the sole blame upon yourself. Nothing I did say could sway you from such a course.

I did wonder how my dearest Orvin was faring, and did voice this concern aloud. You did suggest that we should both pay old Wilf a visit to find out the answer to this, if I did feel that I was able to do so.

As we prepared to leave the warmth of your tent to search out Wilf's own, you did halt my progress by laying a hand on my shoulder. You did bend towards me, and did place your soft lips upon my forehead so softly, that it was as if one of the fairie folk had brushed their feather-light wings against my skin. Oh, Arthyen, my heart doth beat for you alone, and no-one else. I do feel whole when in your company, and

doth miss you *so* much when we are apart.

Wilf did greet us with his usual cheerfulness - a toothless grin, coupled with the gleam ever-present in his one good eye. He made us most welcome in his tent, and it did raise my spirits even more when I did see my hound standing in the corner, his tail wagging furiously at the sight of my entrance. He was being restrained by a piece of rope tied around his neck, and secured to the peg of the tent. I knew that poor Orvin would not be taking too kindly to such restriction, but Wilf explained to me that he had tied Orvin to prevent him escaping to seek me out, thus putting the poultice around his wound at risk of being loosened. Dear Wilf had cared for my faithful friend very well indeed, and Orvin seemed back to his old self - the wound was still bound, but Wilf had been able to see to this in a much more effective way than that which I had attempted in my rush to flee Cragnuth, and the clutches of my cousin.

I was pleased when Wilf told me that I could take Orvin back with me if I so wished, as he had administered all that he could. He told me that the poultice was working well, and that the gash had not been as deep as he and I had first thought.

You are indeed a noble and honourable lord, my dearest Arthyen, for tonight you did leave my presence, and did make a bed for yourself in the tent of one of those who has recently left this world for the greater one - the world that we shall all enter one day at a time unknown to us. It is a world that I have often thought upon, and one that I would like to think I should embrace with courage in my heart. I am certain that I shall meet my ancestors there, and can walk with them once again in green fields that are awash with flowers. I am sure that it will be a place where I can hold my head up nobly, knowing that I have done all that I can to honour my name.

And yet thoughts of my father do cloud my vision. If I were to meet him in such a place, would he still have such ill-feeling towards me? Should I still have such loath-ing for him also? It would seem to me that I should be tied to him forever, not only in this world, but also in the next. This is a troublesome thought, and one that I wish not to dwell upon. It shall be put away in the darkest corners of my mind, and I can but hope that I do not have to discover whether my prophecy will come true for many years hence.

Besides, now that I am alone, I can think upon my vision of this morning. Even though many hours have passed since the dragon did bear down upon me, it is as clear in my head now, as it was terrifying then. Such a giant beast it was that came before me, and if - as I so believe - I am to play a part in its destruction, I know not how I am to achieve this. If this beast is to be invoked by a wizard, then his magick

will be truly great, and surely cannot possibly be destroyed by such mortal beings as you or me.

As has become a habit of mine these last few days, when I am thinking, I find myself toying with your ring that still hangs about my neck. I do find that pacing back and forth, and feeling its metal against my skin, doth give me succour, and I find myself placing it on each finger in turn, as my mind turns over each thought.

I did walk to the tent's opening, and did lift its cloth to peer into the night towards where you had brought your place of rest next to mine. In the light of your candle, I could see your shape sitting hunched over your table, as you laboured into the night, no doubt with your plans for the expected battle to come. How I wish you were here with me now to give me comfort, and how I wish I could unburden my thoughts to you. I know, however, that I cannot, and that I shall have to be satisfied with knowing that you are not far from me. I hope that you can find rest yourself soon, my sweet Arthyen.

You cannot know that I have fear in my heart, for I know not how I am to live up to your father's prophecy. You shall never know that I have a dread in my heart that I shall fail the Lord Beroun, or you, his heir. What am I to do? If I fail in whatever destiny has planned for me, it could mean that you will lose your birthright, or worse, your life, and that would be too much for my heart to bear.

If I could wish for one thing, as I write this, it would be that I could trust in my fate, and could stop tormenting myself with these questions. I must learn that what will be, shall be, and that I must wait for destiny to deal her hand.

As I finish this entry for today, Orvin is sitting beside me with his head resting on my knee, his soulful brown eyes staring up at me, as I write these last words. It is good to have him back by my side.

Thirty-fifth Entry

Two days have passed since I did arrive at your encampment. My father and Margh have not yet managed to locate the valley - if they have even tried. The sentries at the forest's edge have not reported their appearance, and whilst I am thankful, I do admit to finding this rather strange. After Margh's advances on that dreadful evening two days ago, and my following escape, I would have expected a search to have taken place. I cannot understand why this has not occurred - it is a puzzlement to me. Your men patrolling the lowland's edge have reported that no-one has left the gates of Cragnuth, nor has anyone arrived. The place has been still and quiet. Something is amiss, but I cannot think what it is.

I knew that Margh would not have told my father what had taken place in my chamber between him and me; in truth, as far as my father is concerned, he - no doubt - is not even aware that I do even know of the plans that have been made for our union. Yet, I do now find myself wondering whether there *were* any such plans? Perhaps my cousin had merely used this as some kind of excuse - perchance to deliberately anger me, or even to simply justify his deplorable actions? This, as the time passes, has begun to seem more probable in my mind.

I did tell you of these thoughts, my dear Arthyen, and you did agree that it may well be the answer as to why no-one had come to search for me. In my father's eyes, it could well be that I am now just another traitor, and not worthy of his attention as a daughter any longer. As much as we talked, and tried to come to a worthy answer to this mystification, you and I could not dispel our suspicions that something else was

occurring.

It had been the arrival of the news that the gates of Cragnuth had opened, that had prompted us to ride with haste to the caverns to await further reports. We did hear that a bedraggled line of men was making its way slowly across the lowlands towards the forest. Eventually, as the first of these reached the guards, it became clear that this procession consisted entirely of those men who had been wounded, and whom my father had so unfeelingly sent to the stables to recover. Those who could walk were helping those who could not, for there were still a few who had to be carried over the shoulders of the strongest.

This sad and war-weary line of men slowly appeared at the top of the path that led into the valley. Again, this had mystified us. Why were these men were being sent away from Cragnuth *now*, on this day, for no apparent reason?

As you may have gathered already, reader, my mind tends to delve deeper into matters, and has the habit of looking beyond the surface. An answer to our puzzlement had thus come upon me, and I grabbed your arm, and whispered quickly into your ear. "I sense deceit, My Lord".

You bent your head nearer to mine and gestured me to continue.

"Think upon it, My Lord. Do you know exactly who these men are?" I asked you. "Can you recognise every single one of them under their hoods? Would it not be possible for *anyone* to hide themselves in such a way?"

I did notice the glint of realisation in those dark brown eyes of yours. You nodded.

"Halt!" you ordered. This had been such a sudden outburst from you, not only had it made Elwine jump, but I could not help but do so myself. "All you men come from Cragnuth today, halt! ...and lower your hoods!"

This command echoed up and down the line of men. It reached all those who were still in the cavern, and all those who had yet to enter through the hidden entrance.

Again, I heard you shout: "Show yourselves!"

I was so certain of my suspicions, and rode through to the forest beyond, where I did wait for you to join me.

It was not long before you were at my side, and did shake your head. Most of the

 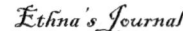
men had arrived in the valley; but there were still a few stragglers who were making their way slowly through the forest. I did urge Elwine into the cover of the trees on one side of the path, and did wait for their approach. You had done likewise with Acha and waited on the opposite side of the track. Upon their arrival in the clearing, you did make your presence known, and did order them to halt and lower their hoods. At this command two of them did *indeed* falter, and halt in their tracks. They stood motionless, their heads bowed looking at the path at their feet. They did not remove their hoods.

You did not acknowledge my presence, but I heard you call out to the two men, "It seems that a suggestion offered to me recently may indeed be correct". You had then urged Acha forward, and stood in front of the two figures as they remained where they had halted.

"My Lords Edric and Margh, welcome," you had addressed them. "To what pleasure do we owe your company this fine winter's day?"

There came no answer from the figures, and I watched as you drew your father's sword, and carefully placed its point under the hood of one of those standing before you. "Hmm. Rat had your tongue?" you had asked as you flicked the blade, and revealed the head of my cousin. "If not, then perhaps my blade may have it?" you continued, your voice full of undisguised loathing.

I saw Margh visibly flinch as your blade had flicked his hood back. To see him again brought such a feeling of fear and hatred within me, and I remained where I was; seated upon Elwine in the shadows of the forest. Yes, my suspicions had been correct; my father had used the wounded men as a cover, in an attempt to discover the secret entry to the valley. I can only assume that he had meant to find it and return to Cragnuth; perhaps even to send a messenger to the King for reinforcements to come and take you captive. I half-smiled to myself at the thought that he should really have known better - after all I *am* his daughter, and know very well how his mind doth work.

However, now a problem did present itself upon us. What were we to do with these two? Were we to blindfold them, take them to the encampment and hold them captive? I did fear that the sound of the waterfall would give away the entrance to the valley, and knew that this could not be an option. Through the branches of the trees, I looked across at you, Arthyen, and did hope that you had an idea of how to deal with them.

You had already removed the hood from my father's head, and remained sitting

astride Acha, your sword still drawn as you spoke to them. I could not hear what you were saying, and did wish to know what words were passing between you, but I could not bring myself to urge Elwine forward into the clearing. I did not want to see my father's glare of distaste upon me - I have grown tired of such expressions, and will be happy never to lay mine own eyes upon him again.

You had my complete trust that you would deal with them in a way you thought most fitting, Arthyen. It had been my father who was talking the most - he was walking backwards and forwards, and throwing his arms about as he blustered on to you. My cousin, however, stood perfectly silent. He was like a hawk hunting for its prey. As he stood with his arms crossed, I could see him turning his head, his eyes scanning deep into the forest - searching. He knew I was there somewhere, but he knew not of my exact location.

Perhaps as a true warrior I should have ridden out of the forest at great speed, and - with one strike of my blade - have removed his head from his shoulders? No, as a true warrior I would do no such thing; I knew there would not have been any honour in such an action, but merely a sense of self-satisfaction at the revenge it might have wreaked in those few short moments.

After a short while, the conversation had ceased between you and my father, and - replacing the hoods upon their heads - both he and my cousin had turned to leave the forest taking the route by which they had come. You had raised your hand, and silently - from out of the trees - six riders appeared from where they had been hiding, awaiting your bidding. They were to escort the pair of unwelcome intruders back to the lowlands, and to make certain that they did return to Cragnuth.

It was then that Margh turned, and his searching eyes seemed to locate me. I know not how he could see me, for I was well disguised, but I did feel that he knew exactly where I was. This surely seemed to be true, for - as he looked in my direction - I could see him open his cloak, and wrap his fist around the hilt of his sword. I do swear, even now - hours later - that he did slightly nod his head towards me, as if in acknowledgement of my presence, as his grip tightened around the weapon.

After they had disappeared down the track, I did emerge from my place of hiding, and did meet you in the clearing. I could see from your expression that you were not entirely content with the outcome of your conversation. However, you did smile when you saw me, and did tell me that they had gone for the present, and that they would not return, unless they wished to have their gizzards ripped out and fed to the crows. You did also tell me that you had suggested that my father, on their return to the comfort of the Hall at Cragnuth, should enquire of my cousin as to what had

really urged me to flee. I did wonder what Margh would offer for an answer, but was certain that he would already be thinking of some satisfactory untruths.

I did wonder what else had been said. For it was evident that you were neglecting to inform me of something that had passed between you and my father, and - laying my hand upon your arm - I did ask of you: "My Lord. What is it that has caused you the concern of which you do not speak? I know that there is *something* that you are keeping from me. Pray tell me what it is, so that I may comfort you".

You did shake your head, and did lay your hand upon mine, where it rested, and replied that it was nothing that I could remedy. Then, to my amazement, you did suddenly smile the broadest smile that I have seen upon your lips. There was a glint in your eye as you leant across to kiss my cheek.

"Come, My Lady Ethna", you then said. "There is much to be done in the camp tonight, and it shall all commence with a visit to the caves. There is someone there I need to search out."

Thirty-sixth Entry

he first thing you had done upon our return to the caverns, was to send word for extra men to stand guard in the forest, to further protect the secrecy of the valley - just in case our recent unwanted guests did not think your threat of disembowelment was an honest one.

As planned, we did, indeed, break our journey at the caves. Upon our arrival you did dismount Acha, and disappear into the first of the three caverns. You had insisted that I had remained seated upon Elwine, whilst you did go about your business. I had not questioned your actions, but had wished to visit my townspeople - especially little Hannel - and had insisted that I should be allowed at least to bid them welcome. Strangely, you did ask of me the whereabouts of Hannel, and upon my answer you could not refuse my request as it would seem that the person you did seek was not to be found in the same cave. My curiosity was raised, but I did have other things on my mind. I did, therefore, dismount Elwine, and search out sweet Hannel.

I did not have to enter the cave, for he had seen us from where he was sitting, playing his favourite game of stones with Meleri and Hafren, the daughters of Heulyn, whom I do not think I have mentioned before in this journal. She is the wife of Aldfric the carpenter, and comes from across the borders of our lands, further to the north. This land is not as far away as the birthplace of Tarek, but is still one that has not been visited by many of our townspeople. Like Tarek, Heulyn speaks in a different tongue - hers being very melodious on the ears. She has a temper to be avoided when in full flow, by all accounts, but I have yet to encounter such an outburst.

Her two daughters, Meleri and Hafren, are of eight and ten years, with hair as black

as the raven's wing, and eyes to match. They look just like their mother, and have certainly been graced with her love of talking. Ever since they learned their first words, their lips have never stopped. They chatter constantly, have smiles on their faces that never wane, and a sparkle in their dark eyes. They are two beautiful little girls, and I was glad to see they had taken poor Hannel under their protective wings.

Hannel had leapt up when he saw me, and did run and wrap himself around my legs as he always does. I had bent down and kissed the top of his head, and had wrapped my arms around his tiny shoulders. I was concerned to see him so thin - it had only been a few days since mine eyes had fallen upon him, but in that short passing of time, he seemed to have become more slight and pale in appearance.

Hannel took my hand, and led me to where Meleri and Hafren were sitting cross-legged, waiting for his return. He did sit down, and pulled my hand to make me sit beside him. This I had done, and for the next few minutes had joined in their game. The girls did nothing but ask me questions of the battle that had taken place. I had not thought it proper to speak too much on such a subject to such young children, and I knew that their mother would not thank me for it, so I did make a few comments, and did change the subject at the first opportunity.

To my relief, the girls' attention was soon distracted back to the game at hand. After a short while, you did appear at the mouth of the cave - your urgent, secret, business seemingly taken care of. I did beckon you to join us, and it was then that Meleri had poked her sister in her side, and did whisper something in her ear. At this, Hafren had turned to look; first at me, and then at you, and then did start to giggle uncontrollably. I have no idea why she did giggle so much, but did presume it was some childish comment regarding the friendship between you and me. I saw the look of puzzlement on your face, and did take your hand to urge you sit beside us for a moment. You squatted, and tousled Hannel's hair, as he wriggled his tiny body closer to mine. Poor Arthyen, you are not used to the company of young children. It must have been very hard for you to ignore the constant giggling and staring from Meleri and Hafren - they were indeed merciless in their attention. One day, I am certain, some unfortunate young men shall receive such deep attention upon themselves.

Upon our departure, Hannel had cried. It did upset me greatly to see those tears fall so freely down his pale cheeks. I would have hoped that by now, his feeling of loss for his mother would have eased a little more than it was clear that it had. I did not see his father or brothers during my visit, which made me sad and a little angry. It seemed clear then, that they were not caring for the youngest member of their family. If it was not for the fact that these are troubled and dangerous times, I would have been very tempted to take Hannel back with me to the encampment, and to have

looked after him myself, and treated him as my own little brother.

But I could not take him. I did know that, but what could I do with this poor crying child who had his arms wrapped around both my legs and would not let me move? It was Heulyn who had come to my rescue. I had not noticed at the time, but Hafren had gone to fetch her mother, when she had realised that Hannel was upset, and would prove troublesome in leaving. The girls were clearly used to his sadness and needy behaviour.

Heulyn managed to pry him away from my legs, and urged me to take my leave before he did escape her grasp. You and I did go, but with heavy hearts. It was clear that you did have sympathy for Hannel also - I could see it in your eyes.

Our encounter with Hannel seemed to dampen your spirits somewhat, dearest Arthyen, and we did ride back to your encampment in a contemplative silence. I do think that I know what you were feeling and thinking. I am certain that you were experiencing the same emotions as me. How could such a tiny boy create such a feeling of desperation, just by our being in his presence for such a short moment in time? What is it about Hannel that brings upon us such feelings of desolation?

We did return to your camp some two or three hours hence, dear Arthyen, but you have been involved in battle-plans since we did return, and you have left me to my own company. I do not complain about this solitude - it is pleasant to be by myself, as it gives me time to reflect on the events of the past few days. Despite the fearful uncertainties that I do face ahead, I do think that I have a path in front of me now that I wish to follow, and I do so with good spirits and a glad heart. I know that I have at last found the person to whom I wish to give my heart totally and without condition. I have discovered that there is someone in this world for whom I should gladly lay down my life should I have cause to do so. This realisation did come upon me suddenly, as I did stand at the entrance to the tent, and did watch you from a distance as you did give your commands to your young second-in-command, Caswyn. I did look at you in the fading light, the glow from the fires dancing on the metal of your blade's hilt at your hip. I knew then that my place was at your side, Arthyen. Long may I be allowed to remain there.

However, there is one thing that still doth puzzle me. As I write this, I still do know not why, or to whom you did make a visit upon our return from the forest.

Thirty-seventh Entry

I have not made an entry for these past few days, reader, but there is much news to tell, some of which is joyous to my heart, and some of it which rips at my very being to have to write.

Let me try to explain - I shall endeavour to put quill to paper as quickly as I may, without leaving out any of the details.

I had spent much of the day since my last entry visiting my people further up the valley. As usual, I had tarried a while with little Hannel, but had also made time to try to speak to all of the townspeople to enquire of their health and spirits. All seemed pleased to speak to me, but I did get the impression that they are impatient to move back to their homes, and I did get asked the same question repeatedly of when I thought this might be. I, of course, had no answer to give them, but could but make sounds of encouragement and hope. It is the coldest month of the year, and the caves are not the ideal choice of habitation for these people. This I know only too well, but I do *also* know that there is a high probability that Cragnuth will come under siege again before the month is out - the enemy will surely not let our small victory deter them from their course of destruction.

I know, also, that a much stronger army than we saw last time will most likely undertake the next attack, and that it is probable that Cragnuth will not survive as it did before. I am concerned for the safety of those who had gone back there on the return of my father and cousin, and I have begun to think of ideas for ways to get these back here to the safety of the valley. My entire thoughts, of course, I did not share

with those around me, for I do not want to worry them further, but it was important that I warn those capable of fighting, to be ever ready for a muster at a moment's notice in case their services should be called upon.

I did make it my business that I should discuss the problem of Tarek, Tilda, and the others who were back at Cragnuth, with you, Arthyen, upon my return later that afternoon.

My day did pass quickly, as indeed it always seems to do when you are in pleasant company, and enjoying yourself. It had been good to catch up with the town news from such gossips as Seren and Heulyn. I did write above, that I tarried with Hannel, but perhaps I should alter that to read that Hannel tarried a while with me, for he followed me everywhere all day, and did not leave my side, until Heulyn took him back with her to help prepare the supper, with Meleri and Hafren.

The sun had begun to set, Arthyen, as I began my journey back to your camp. Elwine picked her way down the path in the fading light, and we made our way slowly across the plain to the river. I knew my way now, and I was in no immediate hurry to get back to the camp before nightfall, for fear of getting lost. All three of us; Elwine, Orvin, and I, were confident of our road.

I was most surprised, however, to be passed by Lord Caswyn cantering in the opposite direction. I presumed he must be on some mission for you, and did bow my head as he approached. He did slow his mount down to a walk as he came close to me, and did bow his head in response, but I could not understand the broad grin on his face. This was something that I have never seen before on his arrogant young features. Yes, I have seen the smirk of someone who thinks he knows everything, and - on more than one occasion - the knowing smile of someone who thinks he is always right, but a broad grin ... never! I did assume that he was sharing a private thought with himself, and that he had merely forgotten to change the expression on his face upon encountering me. He is a strange young man - full of his own importance, but nonetheless, oddly likeable.

He had kicked his horse back into a canter, when we had exchanged our bows of greeting, and then did continue his journey back up the valley from whence I had come.

Apart from the usual sounds of the encampment, all had seemed peaceful upon my return. By usual, I am - of course - referring to the occasional bark of a dog or the noise of men talking and shouting. But then it changed. The sound of someone singing very loudly, in a voice that should really not be singing, does *not* come under

the list of *usual*. In my short stay here, I have grown used to the sound of some of the men singing at night, after supper, just before they retire to their cots. They sing songs of their homes, and of their loved ones. Or of battles won in other times and lands. For the most part, these men have voices that are melodious and pleasant to the ear, and their plaintive tones have oft brought a tear to my eye. It is easy to forget that these men and boys are away from their families, and that some have not seen their wives, children, or parents for many a long month.

The voice I heard upon my return, however, was not melodious. I did wonder whether its owner had been supping on a secret supply of ale, for it was the kind of singing that I used to hear upon passing *The Serpent's Nest* just before a body would be thrust into the street, before swaying from side to side, as it made its way down one of the lanes into one of the cottages.

As I had tethered Elwine, I did hear a shout from nearby that was clearly aimed at the singer. In no uncertain terms did this call instruct the other to cease his noise or be prepared to have something hot and unpleasant thrust where it should most certainly not be placed. This was soon followed by many other threats from around nearby fires, and I did smile to myself at the ease at which these men seemed to curse in my presence. They did not seem to think ill of uttering such foul threats, and I did take this as a compliment, for it did mean that they had accepted me as one of them. Either that, or they had simply forgotten that I was there. However, the singing ceased, and so did the cursing, but not before you, Arthyen, had reminded everyone that there was a lady present, and those responsible should be mindful of this in future.

Reader, my quill is wandering, and I do find myself getting lost in events. I shall take you to an hour or so later, if I may be so bold.

We had eaten supper, and you had asked me how my day had been. I did recount my visit with my people, and their questions of a possible return to their homes at Cragnuth. I did see you frown at the mention of this, and I did lay my hand upon yours, and did tell you that I knew that this would not be possible for many days yet... if at all. I did tell you that I had warned the men who could fight, to be prepared for battle at short notice, and you did nod in thanks of this.

You did ask me into the health of little Hannel, and I did describe how he had stayed by my side during my entire visit and that he had looked well enough. In truth, the boy was still not as healthy as he should be, but did seem better than when we last did see him.

I did mention also that I had come upon Caswyn on my return journey, and did wonder at your apparent embarrassment at this information. You did seem to look uncomfortable, or perhaps I could even say, somewhat guilty, and you did not offer an explanation of his whereabouts. Not that I would have expected one, as your business is yours alone, dear Arthyen, but it was all rather strange.

A few moments later it became stranger still, when there was a tapping on the tent entrance, and I heard the voice of the Lord Caswyn say, "Your orders have been carried out successfully, Captain". This was a very strange occurrence, his name having only just been mentioned between us.

At this statement you had risen sharply, bowed your head, kissed my hand, and had bade your goodnight, before striding out of the tent. I had followed briskly, but was only quick enough to see you and the young lord disappear into your tent, deep in discussion like two boys plotting some game of mischief.

I did glance around, but could see no-one else nearby, but was intrigued to notice that there was another figure waiting for you in your tent. Now it seemed obvious that Lord Caswyn had gone back to the caves, and had returned with the very person that you had so eagerly sought out on our last visit together.

I had been pondering who it could be, when quite suddenly and quite unexpectedly you did appear at the opening of your tent, and did look in my direction before slowly walking towards me. Such an easy gait you did have. Oh, but it was my turn to look embarrassed at being caught watching your tent, and I did run back inside, and was quite beside myself. I felt that if I ran back inside, and did busy myself that you would think I had not been standing watching your tent, but had merely been caught at that moment as I had been taking of the air outside. What foolery to think such a thing. Of *course* you would know that I had been standing there all the time. Oh no, what should I do?

I heard your tap on the material, "May I enter, My Lady?" you had enquired.

"But of course, My Lord. Please do," I responded as calmly as I could.

You opened the flap and, as you always had to, did bend to gain entrance through the low opening. Once inside, you did straighten and bow your head in greeting, before walking straight up to me, and taking my hands in yours. I was apprehensive for I knew not what was to come.

"My Lady Ethna," you began. "I have thought upon this for many an hour, and the

meeting with your father and cousin in the forest - and the obvious danger in which you find yourself - did encourage me to think upon it with more urgency than before, for I fear all may be lost."

I did look upon you, truly without knowing what you did mean.

"I am aware that I should speak to your father before speaking to you of such matters, but in the circumstances, I fear that it would not be prudent so to do," you had continued. "I can give you now, my heart and my protection, but I have nothing to offer you, My Lady, but the hope of what the future may bring. I have no lands or riches to give you - all that you see around you are all that I have to give."

I did then realise the meaning in your words, and I do swear that my heart did miss a beat within my breast.

"My Lord..." I began, but you did continue...

"I do pledge my oath that I shall honour you for the rest of my days upon this world, should you agree to take me as your husband."

I could not speak, for my voice had left me. I could find no words that would give a reply worthy of what I was feeling within me.

"What say you, My Lady?" you did ask, as you did kneel before me. "Shall we be united as one? Will you take this battle-weary heart as yours? Can I hope for your heart in return?"

I did kneel in front of you. "My Lord, I look for no lands or riches, for I need only your heart to sustain me. What I seek is before me, and I receive your oath, and pledge my own that, in return, I shall honour you until I should leave this world for the next."

I did caress your cheek. "I give you my heart gladly - it has been yours for many a day since."

"Then my wife you are happy to be?" you asked earnestly.

"I should be honoured to take one as brave as you as my husband, My Lord," I did answer.

You did place a hand on each of my cheeks, and did place a hearty kiss upon my lips

before you did jump to your feet, pulling me up with you. Your eyes did gleam with delight - they reminded me of Leif's look of joy after he had placed a frog within the covers of his sister's bed in gleeful anticipation of her disgusted despair at its discovery so many years before.

You did pace up and down, with one hand tucked into the top of your breeches, and the other rubbing the back of your head, as you explained that once all this war had been dealt with, you hoped that we could have a ceremony befitting such an occasion. But for now Father Lorcan would take our vows, to ensure that all was seemly in the eyes of the law.

"So it was he you did visit the other day?" I asked, nodding to myself as I knew this to be correct.

"Indeed it was," you had confirmed, "and that was whom Lord Caswyn was travelling to see tonight when you did pass on the road."

I nodded. The identity of the person waiting in your tent was now perfectly clear.

"Caswyn!" you called, and a familiar face peered round the flap of the tent opening.

You gave instructions for Father Lorcan to be escorted to the tent. I did shake from head to foot for it did suddenly dawn upon me what was about to take place. I had not imagined that the day of my marriage would be in a tent in the midst of a war, wearing clothes that were torn, old and dirty.

Father Lorcan arrived not many minutes later. I am not certain of his true thoughts of the occasion, for he has served my father for many years, and I am not sure of his true allegiance. Whether he did agree with what was to occur I know not, but in truth he did not show any signs of disagreement, and was quite well disposed to greet me pleasantly enough.

It would seem that Lord Caswyn was to be a witness to the occasion as he did take his place behind us as you did stand before me.

At that moment there came a tap at the tent entrance, and you did ask the caller to identify himself. It was a man called Ranulf who answered and he did immediately tell you that there was something outside that you should – perhaps - wish to investigate as a matter of urgency.

You did sigh. "Is it important, soldier?" you asked.

"I think so, my Lord Captain, sir," had been the hurried reply.

You gave me your apologies for the interruption, and - keeping a tight hold on my right hand - did lead me out of the tent, to follow Ranulf to the scene of the disturbance. Father Lorcan and Lord Caswyn did follow us. I could not help but wonder whether this tight grip was to ensure that I did not change my mind during this interlude, and decide to leave the camp under cover of the diversion. Dear Arthyen. Of course I would not do such a thing - I could not have. At that moment, I was still in a state of surprise and shock that what was taking place could be real. I would never have dreamed, upon awakening that morning, that by the same evening I would be your wife.

We followed Ranulf through the line of tents in the direction of the river. He did take us right to the river's edge before he did stop and point back up the valley.

A double line of flaming torches and lamps was making its way along the bank towards the encampment. As the line grew closer, we could hear the sound of chattering voices and happy singing. You did stand in front of us, alone in your obvious annoyance at this interruption. Your feet were apart, and your hand was on the hilt of your sword, as you did wait for the deputation to arrive.

The group did stop just short of you, and all fell silent.

"What goes on here?" you did shout.

All those who stood at the front of the group did turn and look at each other, as if expecting the person standing next to them to be the first to utter forth an explanation. I did hear a familiar voice making its way through from the belly of the group, as bodies were thrust to one side. Then a recognisable short, plump figure appeared at the front. It was Seren, the bread-maker, who stood before us, hands on hips and with a broad grin upon her rosy face.

"Now, 'ere, M'lord", she began, seemingly completely unaware of the anger that *I* could easily detect from the sound of your voice. "We did 'ear that there was something 'appening down 'ere in the camp, M'lord, that we folk would not want to miss".

I am sorry; Arthyen, but I did let forth an uncontrollable giggle. Of all people, my dear Lord Arthyen - Seren is well known in the town as being the nosiest, and worst gossip, of all that dwell in Cragnuth. Heulyn is close behind her in the running for greatest Cragnuth gossip, but Seren is the one woman who knows everything about everyone, and if there is even a whiff of plotting, she will be one who will sniff it out

first. It was clear that the noble young Lord Caswyn had not made completely sure of the situation when he had been to collect Father Lorcan. He must have let slip a loose word too many, before ensuring that he and the Father were completely alone.

You had turned to me at the sound of my giggle, and the anger upon your face did slowly change to a look of hopelessness at my uncontrollable mirth. I saw you glance across at Caswyn, who immediately lowered his gaze and began to shuffle his feet in the dirt, which did make me laugh even more. You had turned back to the people, and I saw your body relax as you did shrug your shoulders and did laugh out loud at the audacity of Seren, and the situation that did present itself.

"Then so be it", you did shout. "Let us make this an open secret! The more witnesses the better!"

I was amazed at the obvious confidence of my people that the event upon which they had all invited themselves, would – indeed - actually take place. Was there *really* no doubt at all that I would not refuse the offer? Were my feelings *really* that open for all to see? I blushed red as a berry.

Before long, word had spread around the camp, and soon all was music, singing, dancing and laughing. There was to be no feasting, for there was no extra food available, or ale for drinking, but the people did make the best of what they did have, and there was much merriment. These things will come, upon the end of our trials, when we do bless our union in front of your people, when you do take up your rightful place upon the throne of Graelin. For now, the people will make their own merriment - we have enough gifted musicians who have brought along their instruments on which to play; some from Cragnuth, and many others your own men. I do believe that I did even spy some jugglers amongst your soldiers; one of whom I am sure was tossing three daggers in the air with much cleverness and skill.

Meleri did present me with a circlet of ivy that she had made and Hannel did give me one that he had made by threading tiny red berries together. Both of these I did place upon my head and I did thank them for their sweetness. To take a husband in the middle of winter does mean there is a great lack of flowers to place in one's hair as is the usual custom.

Dear Orvin had some ivy tied around his neck too, and did look as handsome a hound as ever there was. Hannel bent in front of Orvin, and as his little fingers tied the stems together, Orvin did wag his tail happily and did lick little Hannel's face furiously, which made Hannel laugh, and splutter, as he tried to wipe away the enthusiastic tongue.

So, dear reader, my dear Arthyen's secret was out, and all was well. Father Lorcan had stood patiently waiting for the crowds to quieten down, before he could proceed with the ceremony. I do remember, now, that I did promise earlier in this journal, to write a few more words about Father Lorcan, and I do offer my apologies for not having done so. I shall try to rectify this now.

Father Lorcan is a likeable man, but can be rather stern in his outlook. I imagine that most men of the cloth are likewise, but he is the only one I have come across in my life, so have none with whom to compare him. He is a tall, thin man in his older years, with greying hair that does hang loose upon his shoulders. He has, what I believe is quite common amongst his kind, and is termed, so I am told, a tonsure. When I was a small girl, I can remember in our lessons, that the top of Father Lorcan's head did shine in the candlelight, which did afford us much delight, for we could not believe that such a thing could happen. His head was like a polished stone, like those that are found on the river-bed in the summer months when the waters are low, and you can wade across in safety. Being a girl, of course, I did not attend lessons as often as the boys, but I was allowed to attend a few from time to time, to learn my letters.

I know not from whence Father Lorcan did come, for he has always been at Cragnuth for as long as I can remember. I know that he was not born there, but I know not when he did arrive. I must remember to ask Seren, for she is sure to know of such things.

Father Lorcan doth speak slowly in a very deep, soft voice, and it is sometimes very hard to understand what he is saying at all. When I was younger, he also had the habit of falling asleep when taking lessons – something that he still does today, so I am told, but more frequently than in the days when I was trying to learn. To a child it was most amusing, but as one grows up, it can become rather irksome, if one is trying to hold a sensible conversation.

I am sorry, dear reader, for I am wandering from my path again. It is a bad habit of mine I know, and I am sorry for keeping you waiting.

The townspeople had set their torches and lanterns into a path that led from the edge of the camp to the river. I did walk upon this path to meet you, where you did wait for me under the great oak tree that bent its gnarled branches out across the river. The minstrels did play a tune to accompany me, as I made my way towards you.

When I did reach you, we stood facing each other, and I did place my outstretched

hands in yours. You did lay a coin in my palm, as a promise that what riches you may have you will share with me. We did make our pledges, and I did take you as my husband, Arthyen. We had no rings to exchange, but with Father Lorcan's blessing, we are now bound to each other, and only death can part us - albeit until we can meet again.

Such an evening of dancing and merriment did follow, before - at last - both of us weary of such rejoicing; you did lead me to our tent. What did follow I shall not record in detail for it is too personal to share, but I do hope that my inexperience in such matters did not alter your expectations of me. You did seem well-versed in the ways of the marriage bed, and - try as hard as I could - I could not help but wonder with whom you had shared such intimate closeness before. I do know, however, that whoever she or they were, it is of no real concern now, for you are here with me and that which you give to me, I shall treasure and nurture for the rest of my life. My beloved Arthyen, it is such a wondrous feeling to lie next to the one you do love with all of your heart.

We did spend much of the next three days in our own company, leaving the tent only once or twice a day to take the air, and walk Orvin to the edge of the camp. I cannot describe how good it is to be able to walk arm in arm with you, my husband, quite openly without fear of recrimination.

Thirty-eighth Entry

I shall write this as a new entry, for I fear the previous one did go on for too long.

It was just before mid-morning on the fourth day, that a rider had come charging through the camp towards our tent. We could hear him shouting that he carried an urgent message for his captain, long before he did arrive - somewhat breathlessly - in our midst. Sliding from his sweaty mount, which then stood head bowed, thoroughly exhausted from its gallop, he had told you that the enemy had been seen a few miles away, and was approaching Cragnuth in great numbers, and that it would be only a few short hours before they did arrive. He did tell you that there must be four times as many as had attacked before, and did venture to add, "There are too many for us, my Lord Arthyen."

In answer you had replied, "That is for me to decide, soldier. I would welcome you not to voice your opinions so openly for all to hear."

The messenger had begged your forgiveness for such an utterance, at which you had dismissed him, and immediately issued orders for your men to muster, and be ready to ride out. I, too, had made preparations to leave.

You held up your hand and said, "No, Ethna. You shall not ride with us this time. Will you give me your word that you shall not follow us?"

Dear Arthyen, I had shaken my head at your request. "My Lord," I had begun. "I can

give you my word that I shall not ride into battle with you, but I cannot give such an oath that I shall remain here at the encampment."

You had looked at me with a frown etched upon your face, but I had continued, "I fear that this will be the end of Cragnuth, husband. I need to be able to lay my eyes upon it for one last time, before it is gone forever. I give you my word that I shall remain in the forest, but please grant me leave to travel thus?"

"My Lady", you replied. "As my wife, I would rather you remain here in the valley. Do not forget that your father and cousin are still within reach of you, battle or no battle. I fear that they could take you whilst the enemy does attack, and whilst my men and I are preoccupied with war. Remember that they do not know that you are wed to me, and I am certain they will not take too kindly to finding out. It is a dangerous place for you to be."

"Perhaps you should leave Cragnuth to its fate, husband?" I offered. "My father does not seem to be prepared to offer you the hand of friendship, so why should you help him? It may be your lands that our town does stand upon, but my father has decided that you are a traitor, so why not merely let him suffer for his ignorance?"

"I do not think you would really wish me to do that, My Lady", you replied.

I knew that you were right. As much as I may loathe my father, I did still love my home. Although the great Lord Edric is a detestable, cruel, man he is still of my flesh and blood, and - try as I might - I found myself not being able to wish such a fate upon him.

As we spoke, you had been preparing yourself for battle. I had watched as you had dressed yourself for the fight ahead. You did have your back to me when I spoke next, and you did halt in your preparations. I did notice your shoulders droop, when I said, softly, "But what of those people still within the walls, Arthyen? How can they be saved?"

"My dearest Ethna," you replied, as you did turn to face me. "I know not what we can do for them, for they are out of our reach. I fear that they may be lost, for I cannot believe that your father will let them leave."

I knew that this was the truth. All I could do was hope that my father would also have had the foresight to have sent out a scout, and that upon hearing the news that the enemy was bearing down upon them in such great numbers, he would have the decency to let his people leave. I did know that it was like hoping for the impossible,

but where there is hope there is a possible future.

You did then add, "I fear that the words spoken by the scout are true, Ethna. If, in truth, the enemy do come upon Cragnuth in such numbers, then we shall not be able to defeat them, and it would be foolish to even try."

All that did happen next is but a blur in my mind, for so much did occur at once. We did take our leave of the camp, and I did ride by your side past the caverns where, as before, Orvin and Vala were left in the capable hands of one of the townspeople. On through the caves we did ride, and out through the waterfall. I do remember that it had begun to rain - it was as if a gate had been opened, and the clouds were trying to wash away all that was below. A great wind did roar through the trees, and I can remember thinking that it seemed as if it was the end of the world.

We did wait at the forest's edge in silence.

Looking across the plain towards my home. I could see that there was no movement. The banners were soaked, and clung to their masts as if in respect of what was to come. I longed for the great gates to open, and to see Tarek and the others making their escape, but they remained closed.

We did hear them before we did see them; a great thunder of feet marching as one. It did seem as if the whole earth did shake beneath us. We could hear the distant beat of the battle-drum, as it beat out the footsteps. A black mass came into view to the east, and my heart did sink. The messenger had spoken the truth; there were too many of them, and I knew then that you would not order your men to attack. I did indeed realise that it would have been a fool's errand to do so.

Cragnuth was dead.

The enemy was nearly upon the walls, when the gates - at last - did slowly open. The rain was so heavy that I could not see clearly, but I could dimly make out figures leaving through them. There was no mistaking Tarek - his tall figure towering over everyone else - and I did silently urge them all on to safety. All were on foot, except for two, who did ride out of the gates a few moments later.

I knew these two riders must be my father and Margh.

Why the rain did stop then, I know not, but that is what did happen. As suddenly as it had begun, it did stop. The wind did drop, and all was calm, except on the plain in front of us. It was if the heavens were on the side of the enemy, for it did allow

them to send their lighted arrows of destruction into the very heart of Cragnuth, and soon the little roofs were ablaze.

I cannot lay any blame upon you, Arthyen, for giving the signal for your men to re-treat further under the cover of the trees. All horses and men took several steps back into the darkness of the branches, and we could do nothing but watch the horror un-furl in front of us.

The main body of the enemy were almost upon a tiny piece of land that did jut into the river, where those who were trying to make their escape had managed to reach, and I did turn my head away as the foe did cut into my people.

The noise was deafening. I did not wish to look, but I did hope that somehow Tarek and the others might survive this attack. Turning my gaze back to that place, I could see that he, at least, was still alive. I could see him swinging a huge double-bladed axe around his head, as he sliced into his attackers. I did see that one of the horses was now without a rider, and was galloping across the frozen river in our direc-tion. I did not know what had happened to the other, and I did wonder what had become of my cousin and my father.

Most of the army had taken advantage of the open gates, and were storming into Cragnuth itself, leaving only a small number of their group at the place where my people were.

If only they could break loose and make a run across the river to safety.

The town was burning, and I did shut out any thoughts that did try and enter my head about those injured men who might still be alive inside the stables. It was only too clear that none would be so by the time the enemy did leave. I could only hope that their passing would be as swift as was possible. After surviving the previous bat-tle, it was too cruel to think that they would have suffered in pain these last days, only to have their struggle for life be cut off in such a way.

I did look to you, Arthyen, and did notice your own distress. It was clear to me that you did have no choice but to remain hidden, for if you were to go to the aid of those so near to us, our place of hiding would be discovered, and many more lives would be put at risk. But it was also very clear that this was an agonising decision for you. As a warrior, it was against your belief to sit and watch others meet their ends in such a way. My poor, dear warrior - it will take many days for you to come to terms with what took place before your eyes on that day.

"Closer," I did hear you whisper under your breath. "Come but a little closer, and my archers can reach you."

"The giant is doing well, my lord," I had heard Lord Caswyn say. "His axe does certainly deal a heavy blow upon the enemy."

You did nod your head in agreement, and in that moment I did think that all would not be lost after all. Perhaps Tarek would be able to save those left alive. You can imagine my horror, then, when I did see the great figure fall.

I did take a deep breath, and close my eyes. Silently I wept for my people, and the tears did roll down my cheeks. A breeze did pick up again, and it was not long before the acrid smell of burning did reach my nostrils. My home was alight and by the end of the day, all that would be left would be dying embers.

You did sit hunched in your saddle, one arm slung across its pommel. Such anguish you must have suffered, my dearest Arthyen. I did reach out my hand to touch yours, and you did flinch from your thoughts. You did look across at me and did say, "Forgive me, I did fail you".

"You did not fail me, husband, for there was nothing you could have done. I *do* know that, and I do not place any blame upon your shoulders," I replied.

Their destruction achieved, the black mass did soon leave Cragnuth to its fiery doom, and did turn onwards on their march to the west. Once all had left, you did signal your men to move forward. I did urge Elwine forward, but you did take the bridle, and restrict her movement. "You shall remain here, My Lady," you did say.

"I wish to see what has happened to my father, My Lord," I did offer in response.

"I would ask that you stay here, for I fear that what you may find will not be suitable for your eyes to see," you insisted. "You shall remain here with Leofric, and I shall bring you news when I have it."

You did then speak to Leofric quietly, and although I could not hear what you did say, it was plain that you were giving him orders not let to me out of his sight. You did then spur Acha onwards, and - with your men - did leave the trees, and ride out on to the plains before us. I did watch you ride to where my people had made their last, hopeless stand, and did see you dismount. After a short while, you did ride to the flaming town, leaving behind a company of a few men who did stand around the tree that stood at the bank's edge.

 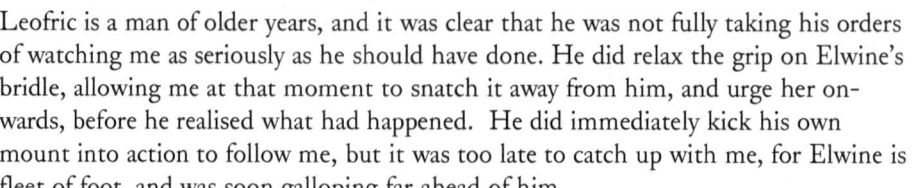

Leofric is a man of older years, and it was clear that he was not fully taking his orders of watching me as seriously as he should have done. He did relax the grip on Elwine's bridle, allowing me at that moment to snatch it away from him, and urge her on-wards, before he realised what had happened. He did immediately kick his own mount into action to follow me, but it was too late to catch up with me, for Elwine is fleet of foot, and was soon galloping far ahead of him.

I did reach the group of men, and jumped from her back. The men did not know what to do upon my arrival, and did stand closely together to prevent me from pass-ing. "Let me through," I did order.

But all stood still. I could hear the odd murmur pass up and down the line.

"Let me pass!" I did say louder, and with as much authority as I could summon in my voice.

"You did hear My Lady ask you to let her pass," a voice spoke from within the group.

"Tarek?" I did call out. "Is that really you, Tarek?"

"It is I, My Lady," did come the reply. "Will you men let the Lady Ethna pass!" he did shout, at which two men parted in front of me to allow me through.

Tarek did sit before me, his hand held against his head, as he did try to stop the flow of blood that did trickle down the side of his forehead. I could see that he did have many wounds on his great body. If he had not been such a giant of a man, he would - no doubt - have been dead from such an attack that he had obviously suffered. How-ever, here he was before me - alive - and I did smile, and hug him until he did groan from the pain that I did unwittingly inflict upon him, by pressing on a wound upon his shoulder as I did so.

My joy, however, was soon lost, when I did see what had become of those others who had tried to escape Cragnuth with him. It was clear that Aldfric, the carpenter, and Beloc, the thatcher, were both dead - their bodies had been dismembered and their limbs were strewn around them.

Gryffyd was sitting up against the great trunk, alive but wounded badly, by the look of the gash that ran down his head from just above his hairline to his chin. One of the kitchen girls was trying to stop the bleeding, but was not having much success at doing so. I did learn much later that this girl had been knocked senseless, and must have been mistaken for dead for she did survive without much injury. Unlike Tilda

and the other kitchen girl, for they had been killed by a single blow each to the head. They lay in each other's arms, half across the ice and half on the bank, their blood laying in a pool on the frozen water, slowly seeping into the ice.

My father and cousin were, at first, nowhere to be seen. Neither was our chandler, Airic. I could see the body of a horse lying on its side near the bank of the river, where it had obviously been trying to escape across the ice. I did wonder if I would find the body of its rider underneath it, and did slowly - and somewhat hesitantly - approach it, for I did not know what I would find. You can imagine my amazement at finding, not my father or Margh, but Airic. I did see that he was still alive, although his arm did lay in an odd way out to his side. It would seem that when he had fallen, he had been lucky enough to fall into a dip in the earth, so that when the horse had collapsed; instead of being crushed, it had merely covered him as he lay in this dip.

I did call out for some men to move the dead horse, and give Airic some aid, and four men did do as I bid. They did say nothing, but kept looking at each other, as if they were sharing a secret betweenst them. It made me feel uncomfortable, and I did feel as if something was yet to unfold at this place. I did stand, and face those who stood in the circle. It was as if no-one dared to say a word to me, but it was clear that there was something that they all wished to say.

It was the gaze of these men, that led me to look on the other side of the tree. What I did find there made me understand their reluctance to speak. For there I did, at last, find my father.

He was fixed to the tree by the lance that did pierce through his body, and deep into the trunk behind him. The soldier who was speared in a similar way beside him was already dead - his entrails hanging from the gash in his stomach. I could see that my father was obviously, for all intents and purposes, also a dead man, although it was plain that he still had a few hours yet to suffer in his pain. I approached quietly, and stood in front of him, the circle of men standing silently.

"Father?" I heard myself question, as if I had been expecting him to answer me with words that would banish all hatred from within my heart. Of course, there were no such utterances from his lips, and he just raised his head slightly, and did stare at me.

Perhaps he was expecting me to cut him down from his agonising position. Upon realising that I was about to do no such thing, he spoke in the softest way I had ever heard him do.

His breathing was laboured, but he did manage to say quietly: "My daughter, you would release me from here, and comfort me in my dying hours?"

"Father," I began. "You have never shown me any kindness, for as long as I can remember. You have clearly laid blame at my feet for the death of my mother, and that of my brother, your heir. I have received no love from you, and yet you now expect me to show you such a caring?"

I recoiled at my words. I wish I could have taken them back as soon as they had been sent forth, for now was not the time to show such bitterness. I could not understand how I could be so cruel at such a time, and it did make me feel ashamed.

I began to walk away, and I did hear him weep. But I did keep walking away, for I could not bear to hear it. I knew there was nothing I could do for him to make his passage from this world a peaceful one - not now, with his flesh so mutilated and raw. There was but one thing I could do to release him, and my conscience pricked at every nerve in my body. Could I do such a thing to my own flesh and blood?

I did remove an arrow from my quiver, and did place the nock on my bowstring. Turning, I did raise my weapon, and - inhaling deeply - did eye my mark. My bow arm did shake, and the fingers pulling on the string did falter. I exhaled, and relaxed the string. I could feel the eyes of the circle of men upon me, and I inhaled again, lifted my bow, found my mark once more, and this time let my arrow fly.

"I release you from your pain and suffering Father, for I would not let even a mad dog suffer its last hours in such a way," I said aloud, as the arrow sped through the air. "May you find peace wherever you are going, my Lord Edric. I know not where that shall be, but I hope you find contentment there. Fare thee well."

The weeping did cease, as I heard the thud, and I knew the arrow had found its mark. I turned once again, picked up my bow bag from where it had fallen beneath my feet, and did make my way towards the men. The circle silently parted to let me through, this time, without a word from me, and I did make my way a little further upstream, where I did fall to my knees, and empty the contents of my belly on to the frozen riverbank.

Agonising moments did pass as I did try to understand and believe what had so recently occurred. My whole body did shake, and I could do nothing to stop it. Perhaps I should soon awaken, and realise that all this was but a terrible dream?

"You did the right thing by your father, My Lady," and I did recognise Tarek's deep

voice.

"Did I, Tarek?" I asked, still staring down at the frozen earth. "I hope you are correct, as I do wonder whether those men think I did murder mine own father. I fear that they think I am cold-hearted."

I had looked across at Tarek to where he was squatting beside me, obviously in great discomfort from his own injuries. "I am not cold-hearted, Tarek," I had said. "I was trying to release him from the stares of those men, from the pain inflicted upon his body by those who really killed him before I did. Was that really so wrong of me, Tarek?"

"I have heard no such utterances, My Lady", Tarek replied. "As you say, it was the enemy that killed your father. Your arrow released him from his torture. It was a brave act of a daughter to do such a thing."

I did look back towards the scene I had just left, and did see that the men had removed both bodies from the tree.

"Brave, Tarek?" my voice trembled. "I am not sure that brave is the word."

I could no longer stay there, and did stand and gather my things. As much as I did respect Tarek and feel glad that he was still alive, at that moment I did not wish to talk to anybody, or see anyone. I needed to be alone. And I needed to stop my shaking.

I did also see you, Arthyen, galloping back towards the tree. How I would so like to have been embraced by you, and to sit cradled in your arms, but I did need to cope with my feelings alone. So I did take my leave quickly, and as courteously I could manage, and did make my way across the ice slowly, as - after the rain - it had begun to melt slightly, making the walk across more treacherous - and on to the forest where I knew I would be able to hide in its safety. As I had approached the forest's edge, I had turned to see that you had reached Tarek. You had dismounted, and I could see that Tarek had a hand on your shoulder, and was preventing you from following.

Dear Tarek - he really is a good man.

And what of my slimy toad of a cousin, Margh? I did learn later that he had climbed into the tree to escape the slaughter below, and was to be found there later, having befouled himself, and in a state of shock, but otherwise unharmed.

Thirty-ninth Entry

Upon reaching the safety of the trees, it did become quite clear that I was not as alone as I had hoped that I would have been. Word had reached the townspeople about the fall of Cragnuth, and the forest was dotted with their figures, as most stood silently and watched the flames in the distance. Some of them were weeping, but I do think that most were too shocked to show any emotion. As I made my way past them, I did see Heulyn. I did feel great sadness for her, when I did look upon her face, for she would not know yet that her children were now fatherless, and that she would have to face the world alone, for – as you will recall - her husband, the carpenter Aldfric, was one of those who had been killed.

I had spoken to no-one during my search for solitude, and when at last I did find myself quite alone, I did sit and reflect upon the horrors of the day. I could not weep, for I had no tears left. I did lie upon the needled floor of the forest, and did curl myself into a tight ball, and await such a time that I did feel that I could once again be among others.

The sun began to set, and the forest around me was becoming darker, when I did decide that I should perhaps make my way back to the safety of the encampment. The path that I had taken in my search for solitude was not one that had been familiar to me, and I did know that I should return along it before darkness enveloped me completely. Once at the forest's edge, I knew that I would be able to find my way back along the, by now, well-trodden path to the waterfall.

My cloak was still damp from the storm earlier, and it did not offer much protection

against the bitter coldness that was returning with the setting sun. However, I did give thanks to the small protection that it offered, as I stood staring out across the lowlands before me. I did see the river glistening under the orange rays of the dying sun, and it seemed strange that only a few hours earlier, this peaceful scene had been the stage for such bloodshed and destruction.

Looking further, the horizon did seem unfamiliar; for where the mighty keep of Cragnuth had stood, there was now nothing but the smoke trails that did rise into the sky, and the glowing embers upon the ground - all that did remain of my home.

A cold, wet nose nudged at my left hand, and I did recognise Orvin's whine. I looked to my left, and did see a group of riders slowly approaching along the edge of the tree line, a familiar grey leading the way. You did dismount, and I was most welcome of the extra layer of cloth that you did wrap around my shoulders, before you did ask me gently, "You are ready to leave this place?"

I weakly nodded, and you did mount Acha, before stretching out your arm to help me on to her back behind you. No other words were spoken between us, and the other riders did sit in silence and wait for us to leave, before following on behind at a respectful distance. Their faces showed no expression, and it seemed that they were avoiding eye-contact with me.

Once through the waterfall, we did make our way down the path with the torches collected from inside the great cavern. We did not stop at the caves, but did continue on our silent journey into the valley. You did signal your men to ride on ahead, and they spurred their horses into a canter homeward. It seemed that they all sighed as one, with a great relief at being able to leave us under such difficult circumstances.

You walked Acha slowly, for there did not seem to be much need to hurry on such a night as this. My hands were cold, for I had mislaid my riding gloves many hours earlier, so I did tuck my hands into the front of your cloak to gain some warmth for them. They did tingle, as they did slowly come back to life from the heat of your body. I rested my head on your back, and did hold tightly around your waist as we returned to the camp.

Those we did pass did acknowledge our return, as we rode through the array of tents. You tethered Acha next to Elwine, who was quietly dozing, and I did slide from Acha's back slowly, patting her rump, as my feet landed on the ground. You did begin the process of bedding her down for the night, and I did check on Elwine whilst you did so; gently stroking her soft mouth, and teasing the long whiskers that did hang from her bottom lip. I did bid her a good night, and did enter into our tent.

After not too long, you had joined me and did immediately walk to the brazier to warm your body. I recall that I did shiver at that moment, for you did bring with you such cold air - it followed you in from outside as if trying to invade our warm space.

Neither of us seemed able to take food that night, and we did take to our bed. As we had lain together, you did tell me that I should not punish myself for what had occurred. It was clear that I must have loved my father, for if I had not, I would not have taken the action that I did. No-one with love in his or her heart could have left someone to die in such a way. If, as I have so often told you, and – indeed - have written here on these pages, I *did* have such hatred for my father, then I would have been able to walk away from him in his dying hours, leaving him to the mercy of time, as it did take his life slowly, agonisingly and inexorably away from him.

Thinking deeply about what you had said, did seem to make it clearer to me. And it did seem to make sense. Perhaps, then, I *did* have a love for my father; the kind of love that cannot be washed away, but which lingers in your heart, through whatever life doth deem necessary to toss at it. It is the sort of love that you do not know you carry within you still - it is long since buried, and oft thought of as lost.

I did not speak for a few minutes, for I did not want you to know that I was weeping again; the tears were silently running down the side of my eyes, as I lay on my back in your arms. I was scared that you would feel their dampness upon your skin, but if you did, then you did not speak of it.

After a few moments, I did tell you of the thoughts that had come to me on that afternoon, after the battle had finished. I did think that it was because my father had missed my mother so much, that he was so ill-humoured. I think that he may have been wishing to join her, from the very moment that she had left this world, taking my brother with her. Being in the position I do find myself now, with you, dear husband, it does make me look upon life with a different view. Now that I have someone who is so dear to me, I can understand what it must be like to lose that someone so suddenly, and so cruelly. It did not make my father's behaviour and treatment of me excusable, but - in a way - it did make it understandable.

And so, journal, after another day of death, it would appear that I did learn one important thing. That despite the ill-feeling and mistreatment that he did show to me over the years, that my father was - after all - my father, and, in truth, then perhaps, through all this, I did love him.

You will recall from my previous entry, that I did learn of Margh's avoidance of injury or death - it was as you and I did lay together on this evening, as I record now, that

you did tell me of this lucky escape of my cousin. I did shudder at the sound of his name, and did ask of you about his present situation, and you did inform me that he was presently under guard here in the encampment, until it had been decided what was to be done with him.

I did ask whether he had been informed of our union, and you did reply that you did not think so, and that you had given precise instructions for no-one to talk to him, or impart such news to him. For that, at least, I was thankful. For I would rather that he doth not know. Why? You may ask. For surely, if he were to know, then he would no longer bother me with his irksome attentions? Although I would dearly like to believe this, I am certain it is not correct to think so, as I have the very strong suspicion that his reaction will not be one of calm acceptance. I can still recall the look in his eyes when he tried to take my honour, and I can remember him toying with the hilt of his dagger that day in the forest, when I was sure that he could see me deep within my hiding place.

No, my cousin, the so-called *noble* Lord Margh, is sorely not to be trusted.

Fortieth Entry

Today did start calmly, as I did not awaken from my slumbers until well after the sun had risen. I did lie upon our cot still half-asleep, and did watch you at your table, as you did stand over the map laid out in front of you. I was warm beneath the covers, and did cuddle myself up into a ball as I did lie upon my left side, and did watch you. You had not yet finished getting dressed, and did stand bare-foot, in your breeches, with your over-shirt hanging loosely around your body. I could not see your face as your long wavy hair was hanging down across your cheek, hiding your profile from my gaze. You did cease from your labours briefly, and did take a drink from your goblet, before looking across to where I did lay. Smiling, you did amble towards me, and did sit upon the bed, offering me a drink from your cup.

You did stroke the hair away from my forehead, and did ask, "You do feel better this morning, beloved?"

I did raise myself into a sitting position, and did take a sip from the goblet. "I do, thank you," I did reply. "My spirits have lifted a little since we did speak last eve, although they have not recovered fully. I have been able to take rest, and do feel better placed to face the tasks ahead on this day. How do *you* fare this morning?"

"I do feel better knowing that your spirits have lifted, Ethna," you had replied. "Such a day as you did encounter yesterday, should not be experienced by anyone, and I was greatly concerned about you last eve."

I did smile weakly at you, dear husband, for I knew that the day I would have to endure would not be easy for me. Firstly, I would have to visit my people, and speak with the elders. The future of our township would need to be discussed, now that the people had no homes to go to. One day, in the not too distant future, I would hope that they would be able to build another Cragnuth, but for now it would not be wise to even consider undertaking such a task.

Secondly, I would sit with Heulyn, and those others who had lost loved ones yesterday. I was not sure how I would be able to cope with their pain atop mine own, but as leader of my people, I know that I must carry *their* burdens also.

Then there would be a visit to the injured - dearest Tarek and the others. I did hope that Tarek would recover from his injuries, for he had fought valiantly to protect his companions.

Lastly, journal, I knew that I would have to visit the fresh grave outside the charred remains of our town's walls. My father's body would have been wrapped in cloth, and laid there next to my mother and brother, before the cold, wet earth was laid upon it. I did know, also, that this visit would possibly be the last time I would be able to be with my mother, my brother, Martha and Leif. I know not when I shall be able to visit them again, and this doth make my heart heavy with such a feeling of loss.

I did inform you of my plans, and you did tell me that - for the sake of safety - you would accompany me, but would wait at a respectful distance, while I did say farewell to my kith and kin.

Your company on such a day was most welcome. Indeed, I do not know how I would have managed without you there at my side.

We did arrive at the caves shortly before mid-day. It was such a beautiful day – the sun shone down upon the valley, and the blue sky was almost cloudless. Everything was still, for there was no breeze of which to speak. Yule seemed so long ago, and all around there were signs of the promise of new life. The birds were singing loudly, and we could hear the cock birds calling to the hens, and see them showing off their plumage in the hope of attracting a mate for the coming season. The ground was soft now that the snowfalls were leaving us again, and - with the sun getting stronger each day - the frosts, which visited still sometimes at night, were quickly melted away. Such was the day that saw us making our way slowly alongside the riverbank.

I did speak with the elders but briefly, as it had been decided that they would visit the camp on the morrow, to discuss the future of Cragnuth's homeless. I knew that it

would be a long meeting, and that tomorrow would be as arduous a day as today, but the matter *does* need discussing, and with much urgency, for the people cannot stay where they are indefinitely.

You did come with me when I did visit brave Tarek. I could see that he was in the capable hands of his wife, Myrna, who was fussing around him as a mother does a newborn. He was battered and bruised, and his wounds were plenty, but - dear man that he is - he welcomed us with a beam across his tired face, and we did sit with him for a while, and made much pleasant conversation.

Airic's arm had been strapped between some wood in a most uncomfortable looking position, and he did sit quietly in a corner while Bertha, the eldest daughter of Hildred, the midwife, of whom I have written before, when sweet Martha did leave us, sat next to him trying to encourage him to talk. I do think that Bertha may have a soft spot for our chandler, but I am not too certain as to whether he returns her affections. However, he is a very solitary man, and it would not be fair of me to make any such observations, for even if he did have any such feeling, I am sure that he would not make it known to others. I did not linger with them long, as I did not wish to intrude, but I did bid Airic well with his recovery, and did search out poor Heulyn.

I did find her looking ashen-faced. Her daughters were huddled beside her, and it was clear that none had slept much the night before. Seren was with them, giving as much comfort as she could. I do hope that Heulyn did not see her poor husband's body, for it was not a sight I would have wished upon her. I did sit with them for a while, holding Heulyn's hand. We did not speak, for there was nothing we could say to each other that could change anything, or make it all seem better. So there we did sit; our small physical contact seemingly enough to share our grief and understanding of each other's feelings.

You had touched me gently on my shoulder to urge me to carry out my final task of the day, for it would not be long before the sun began its own homeward journey, and did leave us in the realms of the pale light of its sister moon.

We did make our farewells and did enter the great cavern. Poor Elwine still does not like the waterfall, and I did have to coax her again this day, along the narrow ledge to the green forest beyond. As you did ride ahead of me, my gaze did settle upon the bow strung across your back, and I did shudder at the memory of yesterday. The vision of my father did appear before me, mine own arrow piercing his heart, and I did bring Elwine sharply to a halt. She did snort at my sudden rough handling, and did shake her head at the sharpness of the bit in her mouth.

You stopped, and had turned in your saddle at the sound of Elwine's disapproval.

"I cannot go on," I said. "I cannot do this."

You turned Acha around, and had walked her back towards where we stood.

In truth, I did feel guilt - guilt that it had not been I, Lord Edric's daughter and heir, who had wrapped her father's body in the burial cloth. It should have been me. I should have removed the mortal arrow, and should have cleaned his body ready for the grave. I should have acted like a daughter, and should have tenderly closed the lids over his dead stare. It should have been *I*, who did place my father's arms across his chest, and it should have been *I*, who did lay his sword upon him, before wrapping the cloth around his lifeless body. No, instead I did run, and leave his body for your men to tend.

My heart did race within me, and I did pour forth these thoughts on to you. You told me that it had been you who had removed the arrow, and that it was you who had ordered it to be bound in the cloth, side by side with my father's sword, for it was not to be taken as the weapon of death, but of loving release.

"I did not once lay a kiss upon my father, and nor did he upon me," I told you. "Why is it then that I do wish now that I could have passed my lips across his forehead, before he was laid beside my mother?"

"Because of the love we did speak about last night, Ethna," you replied caressing my cheek with your hand, "but I am sorry you shall not have your wish."

Taking a deep breath, and recovering my composure, I did announce: "Come, let us continue," and did gently nudge Elwine in the ribs with my feet, to urge her to walk on. We did then ride on, side by side to the edge of the forest, where we did linger a while to check that it was safe to cross the open lowlands. All seemed quiet, so we did continue on our way, arriving at the small burial ground not long after.

As you had pledged, you did leave me alone to bid my family and friends a last fare-well.

My goodbyes given, I did return to where you stood, holding our horses' reins, and did hold out my hand to you. You did offer yours to me, and I did take it gladly, locking my fingers into yours and we did walk back towards the river, leading Acha and Elwine behind us.

I did not look back.

My beloved Arthyen, I did so enjoy walking with you this afternoon. It was only for a short while, but every moment I can share with you alone is to be treasured, and treated with great care and fondness. I do lock away these memories in my mind, so that I can think upon them when I am troubled, or away from you. They are my comfort, and I know that I shall be calling upon them before we can be truly together without fear of being parted again.

It was getting late, so we did reluctantly decide that we should ride the rest of the way. As I lifted myself into Elwine's saddle, I did glance ahead of me. At first, I did not believe what I saw.

A rider burst forth from the darkness of the forest; the horse galloping steadily along the tree line for a while, until the rider seemed to notice us, and did turn his mount towards us. I did return both feet to the ground, and did concentrate on the figure.

You did turn to follow my stare, and did usher me behind your back, your hand clasped around the hilt of your sword.

At the time, I was not sure whether I did recognise the rider first, or if you did, but you were clearly agitated by his appearance. No more so than I, when I did realise that my cousin, it was, who rode towards us.

I did learn later that you had arranged for him to be released while you and I were away from camp. You had wished me spared the torment of having to see him again, and had thought this would be an ideal time for him to leave. You had arranged that he be taken by blindfold out of the valley, and turned loose on his oath that he would return to his father's manor, and not return to try to locate the camp. You did explain to me later how you had not expected him to come upon us, and to approach us as he did.

We did stand and await his arrival. He pulled up his horse harshly, and it whinnied with pain. He kicked it into a walk around us, smirking as he did so.

"My Lord Margh," you did say. "You did pledge an oath that you would leave this place, and return to your father. I do not believe that your father's manor lies in this direction."

"My Lord Arthyen. What luck has befallen me," my cousin hissed. "For I was, indeed, on my way home as arranged, but did notice with these keen eyes of mine that

you have something which belongs to me. I have merely come to collect it, and I shall be on my way as promised."

"There is nothing for you here," you did reply, your grip tightening on your sword. I could see the muscles in your back contract, as my cousin did speak his words.

"Ah, but there is," Margh had continued. "She hides behind your back like a skulking dog."

"Better a skulking dog than the dead rat you shall be," I did say, as I came out from your shadow, my sword drawn from its sheath.

Margh did laugh loudly, before he did speak with such an evil tone that it did bring a shiver to my backbone. "Your father gave you to me, wench. You did escape me once before, but not this time. Yet I do admire your spirit, to stand before me with such a pathetic little blade in your hand," he added, laughing again. "What are you to do with it, I wonder. Prod me?"

He did lean lower down in his saddle, and, with his last words directed at me, said slyly, "I am sorry that I am not tied to a tree, My Lady, but I think you may find me harder to kill, for I am able to move."

I did start to walk forward, but you did restrain me from doing so, before you did walk to where Margh had halted his horse. "You are too late, Lord Margh," you said calmly. "For the Lady Ethna has taken a husband, and I would ask you to be more civil in your addresses to her. As for her blade, you would be wise not to underestimate, it for it has only recently tasted blood and may well be thirsty for more. If you do not believe me then that is your choice; however, I do not think you should find this so pathetic." As you spoke, you drew your sword from its sheath.

"Your words have been distasteful and disrespectful. I demand an apology from you, My Lord," you continued.

I did hold my breath, for I knew not what my cousin would do. I did see his face turn red with rage, and his eyes narrow. I could see him thinking deeply about what he would do next, but he is no fool, and did know that he was not well-suited to engage in any fight with you.

"And to whom has she given of herself, My Lord?" Margh asked, poison oozing from his words.

You did not answer, but merely stood your ground, your hand still firmly clasping your sword, ready to use it at a moment's notice should it be necessary.

"But of course..." my cousin did say at last, as he straightened in his saddle. "It is clear to me now. At least I now know who it is who shall feel the sting of my blade. We shall meet again my Lord Arthyen, and then we shall see who shall take the prize."

My cousin did then pull his poor horse around, and with a hefty kick in the ribs did force it into a gallop back towards the river. Not until he had crossed it did you return your sword to its sheath or turn your back to him.

"Pay no heed to his words, Ethna," you had said, as you did take my own sword from my hand, and return it to its place by my side. "They were cruel and given only to cause discomfort. You must not let them linger in your head, for if they do, then he did succeed in his intentions."

"I do know that I should not, Arthyen," I did reply, "but it is very hard. Indeed, there is much truth in what he did speak."

"They were words spoken by a coward who did hide in a tree, whilst those below were being butchered, Ethna. Pay him no heed, I implore you."

My cousin had ridden from view, but I could not be calm. His threat to you weighed heavily upon my mind, for I knew that he would keep his promise. He is more malicious than my father was, and is a dangerous enemy to make. He is a slimy and odious creature, and he doth have a vengeful mind. Oh, when shall all this finish? Will we ever be able to live our lives, peacefully, without threat?

I have thought since our meeting with my cousin, of how he did have the audacity to speak the words he did. He did seem to have forgotten, that it was I who did halt his advances only days before – or perhaps I should write, to suit himself, he had *chosen* to forget.

A messenger was awaiting your return when we did arrive back at the camp. He had been under strictest orders not to allow his missive into any other hand other than yours. The relief on being able to discharge his orders, was clearly visible in his expression when he did hand you the parchment. As you read the words, you did wander into our tent, and it was clear that whatever was written upon those pages was of greatest importance, for you did pace up and down inside, as you did read.

The poor messenger was still standing to attention, as if awaiting further orders, and I did give him leave to find refreshment, but told him not to go too far in case he was required for a return message. His shoulders relaxed, and he gave me thanks, and did disappear into the maze of tents.

I did stand just inside the entrance of our tent, and did wait patiently for you to finish reading. I could not understand what was taking you so long, for I could see from where I was standing, that there was not much written on the parchment. I could only think that perhaps you could not understand it, and had to read it over and again to try to make some sense of it. Eventually, after much pacing, you did sit at your small table, and bang down the letter upon its surface. Then, with both hands on the table, you did thrust yourself up to a standing position again, before seating yourself once more.

I did approach you, and did lay a hand upon your shoulder. Your mind must have been many miles away, for this action of mine did startle you.

"What is it, husband?" I did ask. "What is written upon this parchment that does make you so agitated?"

You did not answer, but turned and looked up at me, before handing up the message for me to read its contents for myself. I did gasp, and did sit down slowly next to you, with my hand upon your shoulder for support. I read the words again; just as you had done so many times before.

King Ulmar was dead.

The King had died of natural causes in his sleep, and - according to the Lord Keowyn, who had penned this urgent message - those who had taken advantage of Ulmar's addled brain had been arrested in the name of the new King. The decree of banishment over you, Arthyen, was now lifted, Lord Keowyn had added.

I had looked across at you, and had asked, "and who is this new King?" But as soon as the words had left my lips, and I saw the expression on your face, I remembered and realised my mistake. I did lean across and kiss your forehead before kneeling down before you, "My King," I said.

"You do not have to kneel before me, Ethna, for you are my Queen," you did reply, taking hold of me around my waist, and pulling me up. "I will have none of it. For you are my equal, and have proved yourself to be so many times".

"You will tell the men?" I asked.

At first you did shake your head, and did tell me that in your mind this news did not change anything. However, you knew that your men should be told that they were no longer under an order of exile, and agreed that they deserved the right to know that the man they were following was no longer an outlaw, but their King. I do think you were mildly embarrassed at your sudden elevation in rank, and you did ponder upon your next actions slowly.

After many moments had passed, you did jump up and call for young Caswyn, who did eventually appear at the tent, after being summoned five or six times. After you had explained, and told him what needed to be done, the poor young man did look shocked, and did fall to his knees in a heap. This did make you laugh, and you did help him to his feet, before patting him on the shoulders, and sending him on his way. After a short while, the sound of cheers did reach our ears.

"It seems the news has gone down well with your men, my King," I said, smiling.

It became clear that the men's spirits had been greatly lifted by the news, and there was much joviality for what was left of the afternoon, and early evening. I do not think that poor Caswyn has had so many tasks to complete in one day as he had upon this evening. He seemed to be forever in and out of our tent. You did, eventually, have to instruct him not keep bowing every time he entered, and left, for it was not necessary. Besides, it was becoming rather risky, for each time he did bow he did manage to knock something over with his sword, as he would forget to hold it down to prevent it from swinging upwards every time he did pay his respects.

It is strange, now as I write this, that as we sat together, neither of us did refer once more to the fact that you were now the King. Nothing about you had changed, and you did sit as you had sat before and you did speak as you had spoken before. You were the same Arthyen to me as he whom I had seen at the gate of Cragnuth many moons before. I cared not, neither, for the sudden elevation that had befallen me, as your wife. In fact, as I pen this now, it is actually a rather alarming prospect, and I am quite happy to stay in the shadows for as long as is possible. However, I will take my place at your side when the time *does* come upon us, and will be extremely proud – if nervous - to do so.

This entry is being scribbled with haste, as you, Arthyen, do, yourself write letters. I am unaware to whom you are writing, but you have spent many a candle notch doing so. You are still troubled – I can see it in your eyes as you do stare out across our tent - for it is clear that the words that you seek are elusive to you.

Today I have become Queen, but on the morrow, the fate of my people will be determined. I shall end my entry here for today, reader, for I have much to think upon before the elders' arrival on the morrow. It has been a most strange day, and I do feel that in a moment I may awaken and find that it is all merely a dream.

Forty-first Entry

*I*t was many hours after I had taken to our bed, when I did -at last - hear you blow out your candle. I had been half sleeping, but in these last few days I have grown used to you lying beside me, and find that it is difficult for sleep to find me until you are there. I am surprised as to how quickly this feeling has captured me.

I could sense, though, that things were not right with you, and I did turn to face you. You were lying on your back, staring into the darkness above us. I did ask what was troubling you, and you did answer: "I am at a loss as to what to do with your people, Ethna. I need to move my men on, but we cannot leave the people of Cragnuth here, for they cannot live under their current conditions forever."

"Where are we marching to?" I did ask you.

"My men will follow the enemy's road, Ethna, but you will be staying with your people. I will not have you marching with us."

I did open my mouth to answer, but you did carry on, "If your people come with us, they will hold us back, and it would be far too dangerous a road to expect them to take. The enemy could attack without warning at any time, and your people would be vulnerable. It is best that you remain here until the danger is passed. If I am correct, then the enemy *does* march upon our stronghold at Calamar. Once they have overcome the castle, then they have almost complete power."

"You will leave me?" I asked you quietly. I was lying on my back, also staring into

221

the gloom of the tent. You had not changed your position. It was as if, whilst you did tell me that you would be going without me, you did not want to look at me. It did feel as if someone had stabbed me in my heart.

Oh, I knew it had been ill-judged of me to think that we would not be parted now that we were wed, but somehow I had hoped that you would let me ride by your side for always. I felt anger towards you then, for I knew that I could not persuade you otherwise.

"I am sorry, but I have no choice but to leave you, Ethna. It is too dangerous for you to ride with me. And yet, I do not wish you to remain here, for I am distrustful of your cousin's oath that he will not attempt to return. I shall have to trust that you will be safe."

I could not respond. I knew that you were right not to trust Margh. I knew also, that it would not be too difficult for him to locate the secret entrance, as it would have been impossible to hide the noise from the waterfall from him. He would only have to follow the same road that he and my father took days before, to come eventually across the little dell. Then, I do fear, that all will be lost, for he is most tenacious in his desire to have me as his possession.

"I have despatched a rider tonight with a letter for Lord Keowyn, warning him of the enemy's likely approach. Another will leave at dawn. Hopefully, at least *one* of them will get through."

"To what end?" I forced myself to ask, in the hope that you would not sense my anger at having to remain behind. "What can Lord Keowyn do?"

"Long before I did leave with my scouting party and come to Cragnuth, Lord Keowyn and I did make plans in readiness for an assault of the kind that is looming upon us now. We did know that it would only be a matter of time before such an attack would arrive," you did explain. "Remember, beloved, that the mighty wizard doth search me out. I am certainly a man with a following, for I have a wizard, a dragon, and now your cousin after my head!" you continued with a wry chuckle.

I did look across to you at this attempt at lightening the conversation. It had not achieved its desired effect, for it did make me more nervous about your leaving me. Dear reader, I could not help myself but to try to persuade my husband to let me travel with him.

"Why cannot I accompany you on your journey, Arthyen?" I asked softly. "I do not

wish to be left here. You have said yourself that you do not trust my cousin. What if he *does* come to find me?"

You did turn on your side, and did rest your head on one arm. Your other hand you did rest upon my belly.

"You are a great ally in battle, Ethna; of that I am proudly aware, but you must remain here in the valley. I can only hope that your cousin does not return, but you must understand that a battle is no place for a woman at the best of times, let alone for one who has shared my bed these last days, and may well now carry my child inside her. You are too precious to me, Ethna, to lose on the field of battle, and with a real possibility that you carry my heir, you become even more so. Do you not understand?" you said earnestly, as you did gently rub your hand across my belly.

This has been something that I have thought of often these last few days. Each time we have lain in each other's arms after you have given me your seed, I have wondered whether a child may have been made. The thought doth excite me each time, but it doth also fill me with fear. My mother did die in childbirth, and only recently I have lost my dear Martha the same way. The idea of having your child is the most wonderful thing – it would be the dearest thing I can give you – but it is also very worrisome.

"Remember also," you did continue, "that you are now also under threat from the same wizard who doth hunt me. Be certain that he will not make the same mistake that he made with my mother, and shall search you out if he knows that you are, indeed, my wife. He will not be so eager again to dismiss the possibility of there being an heir. Therefore, if you are not seen with me, you will not come to his attention. If he does know of your existence, then not being with me will heighten your chances of survival."

I could see the sense in what you did say, but it did not make my mood any lighter. Yes, I *could* be with child, but there is always the possibility that I am not. Yes, Margh had given an oath not to return, but there is always the possibility, nay, a very real probability, that he will ignore this oath and return to find me.

"And what of my people?" I asked.

"Until the stronghold at Calamar is secure, it is not safe for them to travel anywhere. I had hoped that they would be able to journey to the stronghold, but recent events have changed those plans."

You did bend down and kiss me, "I am sorry, Ethna, to bring such disappointing tidings to you, but I cannot think of any other way that is safe for you and your people at this time."

"When shall you leave?" was all I could say.

"I have ordered my men to be ready to ride out at first light."

"So soon?" I had meekly asked. You did remind me that the enemy had two days in hand, and that the situation was in need of urgency. I did remind you of the elders' visit on the morrow, at which you did sigh, and say that there was nothing we could tell them, and that you would stop by the caves, and inform them as you passed through.

I did tell you that I would do so myself, as I would be travelling with you as far as the river.

You did open your mouth to utter, what I am sure as I write this, would have been a refusal, when I did lay my finger across your lips, and repeat "I shall be travelling with you as far as the river, my husband. There is nothing wrong in that. I shall then return here, and await news of your victory, and of our reunion."

You did remove my finger, and kiss the palm of my hand. "I shall be honoured to have your company until we reach the river. Our parting will be one of much sorrow, but we shall both know that, although we are apart, we carry each other in our hearts."

Forty-second Entry

I did not have a restful sleep last night, journal, nor did you, my sweet Arthyen, for you did toss and turn until you could lie down no more. I did feel you go from my side, and I did turn and lay in the warmth that you had left on the cloth. You lit a candle, and did dress yourself ready for the journey ahead.

I did arise from our bed shortly afterwards, and did dress myself. We were silent in our preparations, for there was nothing we could say that would take away our sorrow and fear. I did leave you, and walked into the cold air to prepare Elwine. It was still dark outside, but I found Acha already saddled ready for you, and the man who stood beside her seemed surprised to see me throw the saddlecloth across Elwine's back. "My Lady," he did say. "I am sorry, but I was not aware you were riding with us, or I would have tended your horse for you."

I did tell him that the decision was a recent one, and that it was not for him to concern himself about. I did continue with saddling Elwine before returning to the warmth of our tent. As dawn's light crept through the crack in the tent flaps, it did find us at last both ready, standing with a shared silent thought of the day that did loom in front of us, and the parting that would bring an ache to our hearts, with the very real chance of never seeing each other again.

I did approach you and did take your hands in mine. I could hear the sounds of the men and horses outside as they stood awaiting your appearance from our tent. I could hear the sound of their low voices as they talked amongst each other, their armour creaking as they settled in their saddles, and the sound of the horses snorting

and nickering, chewing on the bits between their jaws as they waited patiently.

You and I did share a last embrace before you did lead me into the early light outside. The sun was low in the sky, and its light did shine upon the armour of those who stood near to us. I did squint against the brightness outside, as I mounted Elwine, and awaited your presence on Acha's back beside me. You did swing into her saddle, and urge her to a walk. With Orvin walking alongside Elwine, we did follow you. The men waited for us to take the lead, and with a signal from you they did follow, two abreast, out of the encampment, and along the course of the river. We did move at a slow pace, for not all the men had mounts. Those on horseback came first, and those on foot did bring up the rear. I did turn in my saddle just the once, and could see the line stretch out far behind us. I did see little Vala trotting alongside the unmistakable figure of Wilf, and I knew then that by the end of the day I would have returned with not one, but two dogs.

We did reach the river all too soon, and once there you did order your men across, whilst you and I did sit and wait. The last two men did reach the opposite bank, and you did turn in your saddle. I did lay my hand upon your arm, and did smile weakly at you. "Be safe, my husband. I do love thee, and do yearn to see you return soon. Look to the skies at night, Arthyen and know that I look upon the same stars as you. I shall miss you, but by looking at them we shall be united."

"I do love thee in return, Ethna. I shall hope for a safe homecoming and will miss you beside me. At night, I shall indeed look to the stars, and by day I shall listen for your voice on the wind. In battle, I shall speak your name, and it will keep me strong. In my dreams, you will come to me, as I will visit you in yours. Be safe dearest Ethna." You did nudge Acha into the river, and did leave me standing with Orvin and Vala as we did watch you join your men.

I did stand and watch you until I could see you no more. I did turn Elwine around, and only then did I allow myself to cry.

I did visit the elders on my return to the valley, and told of your decision. They did seem to accept your reasons, and all was well. I did stay with my people for a while, and went to search out Hannel. I had hoped playing games with him would help me forget my sadness, but try as I might, I could not help feeling such emptiness within me. Hannel and I did share an hour or so in each other's company, before I did take my leave, and make my way back to the encampment, where a few men had been left behind, due to their injuries not allowing them to accompany you.

I do now sit in our tent, Arthyen, and it is so empty without you. There is not

much of yours left here; only an old tunic that has long seen its best, and one or two books. There is still some wine left in your goblet from last night, and a crust of bread upon your table. Looking around, it is hard to believe that you were ever here. I cannot write much more today, reader, as I am tired and full of such an overwhelming sense of loneliness and despair. I do swear that even Orvin and Vala have a look of sadness in their eyes.

I shall lay down my pen, and go outside to seek out the stars, in the hope that you are looking at them too, wherever you are. I shall then lie down in our bed, and wrap myself in the coverlet in the hope that I shall be wrapped in the ghost of your presence.

I do hope that your scent will still be upon it.

Forty-third Entry

*I*t has been four days since you did leave me, and no word has been heard of your whereabouts. I did return to the caves after two nights in the encampment, for I did find it too difficult without you there. The men who have been left behind have been good and kind to me, and they did look after me well whilst I stayed, but I did not think it was fair to have to burden them with my presence. So, I did leave, and did bring Vala and Orvin here with me to the caves, and have been here ever since, among my people.

It has been good to be back with them, and to be able to talk to my old friends again. I have been able to see Hannel's little smile again, and that has brought me cheer. I have had too much time to spare to sit and dwell upon our parting, and being with these people has helped to occupy my mind. Alas, they cannot be with me for all the time, and it is in the darkest hours of the night, when all around are sleeping, that I do lay awake and think of you.

I am relieved that we have not yet seen or heard anything more from my odious cousin. Long may this continue, for I do not know what I shall do if he *does* suddenly appear amongst us.

I still have a great concern about Hannel, for he remains very pale and thin, but his spirits do seem to have lifted greatly since last I did see him. He is talking more, and does seem so much more ready and willing to smile. His eyes look brighter, and he appears to be a lot more like a little boy at his age should be. You must forgive me for writing again that Hannel is such a sweet little boy, but I do love him dearly. If I

am to be blessed with a son one day, then I shall hope for one as sweet as dear Hannel.

Tarek is definitely on the way to full recovery, for I have heard his bellows from one of the other caves as I have been going about my business. He has truly been telling many yarns, for there has been much mirth and cries of disbelief, at that time of day when the sun is just setting and the night beasts are beginning to awaken.

I do smile as I write this, as it does, indeed, seem that Airic and Bertha have something special between them for I have noticed the look in their eyes when in each other's company. It is a sweet thing to see a fondness of hearts blossom, and I am hopeful of their continuing bond. Perhaps we shall have another union to celebrate in the not too distance future, dear reader?

How I do wish I could hear but one word from you, beloved husband. I know not whether you are safe, or whether you are under attack. Every night since you left have I stood in the coldness looking to the night sky. Tonight, the clouds do cover the stars but I have sent you fond wishes on the night air, and I do hope that my words have reached you in your slumbers.

Forty-fourth Entry

I did have the idea upon awakening this morning, that I would journey to the camp to collect the coverlet from our bed. I did think that perhaps your scent upon it might help me to sleep better than I have been able to these last nights. The notion had come to me before, but I had dismissed it as being one of those silly ideas that youngsters have when thinking about affairs of the heart. However, I have recently been of the mind that perhaps it is not such a silly notion after all.

I have just returned, and it now lies upon my cot in the corner of the cave. It was strange, indeed, to ride amongst the deserted tents. There were just two pillars of smoke rising into the sky today, whereas a few days earlier there had been a hundred or more. There was no shouting, calling or singing. No dogs were barking and no horses were whinnying. I did not like it – it did seem like a camp full of memories, as if all those who did live there had left this world for the next. I did tremble at its silence. I could sense your presence in our tent, which did give me some comfort, but it was so empty inside. A spider had been busy, and had woven her silken threads from a half melted candle that stood upon your table across to the rim of the goblet where you had left it sat on the other side of the desk. Small clumps of dirt had begun to cling to the gossamer threads where they had managed to blow in through the tent flaps.

Oh, do come back, Arthyen. Return with your men, and breathe some life back into this place. It is so cold and barren here.

I had invited those who remained to join us at the caves, but they did seem content

enough to stay where they were. This I did accept with good grace, and I bear them no ill-feeling concerning their wish to keep their own company.

Forgive me, dear reader, but I must lay down my pen for there is a commotion outside that I wish to look into. It may be a message from you, Arthyen. I must go.

Forty-fifth Entry

It had not been a message from you. I had walked briskly through the cave until I heard an unmistakable voice, and did quickly walk into the shadows, signalling Orvin to stay beside me out of sight. I did creep along the wall of the cave towards the opening, and did listen.

I could make out the voice demanding to know of my whereabouts, and I did hear Tarek replying that I had left with the army many days before. Dear Tarek, I do trust that giant of a man with my life. The voices became low, and I could not make out the exact words, for a dog did start to bark also. It was clear that our visitor seemed not to believe Tarek, but eventually I did hear the sound of hooves walking on the loose stones outside, as they made their way further down into the valley.

Dearest reader, you may have already realised who this person was that came upon us this day. It was, alas, my cousin Margh, and it did fill my heart with fear when I did hear his voice.

Only after I was sure that all had gone, did I run into the other cave where Tarek was, and did ask him for more details.

"What did my cousin say, Tarek?" I did ask of him. I was afraid of what Tarek would tell me, although I already knew the answer.

"He did come for you, My Lady," came the reply, "but I do think that you knew he would?"

 233

"Yes," I replied sadly. "I have been expecting him. But I had hoped that my expectations would not become reality. Where did he go?"

"He has gone to the camp, My Lady, to see for himself that you are not to be found there any more," Tarek told me. "I do hope that once he has satisfied himself on that score, then he will leave again, and that will be the end of it."

"I do hope so, Tarek, I do hope so. I do fear my cousin greatly, and I do not think I shall be able to stop him if he were to try and take me away from here."

"I do not think your people would let that happen, My Lady," Tarek had insisted. "There is one thing I am not sure of, though. He did know of Lord Arthyen's departure, My Lady, but why has he waited for so long before coming here?"

"He did have to find us first, Tarek," I replied.

"So you think he was lost, My Lady?" Tarek laughed. "That would be typical for your cousin, My Lady, would it not?"

I had ignored dear Tarek's mirth, for I was sorely worried about my cousin being so close at hand, but then Tarek has no idea of what did befall me in my chamber at the hands of my cousin, and he did not know of the threat made at the ashes of Cragnuth.

"How many men doth he have with him?" I asked tentatively, for I had a feeling that he would have come well prepared.

Poor Tarek. He did see then that I was earnest in my requests of him. "He did have twenty men with him, My Lady, but who can know if he has any others outside in the forest. You do really see this man as a threat?"

"Very much so, dear Tarek," I did reply. "If he *does* find me, then all will be lost."

"We shall be ready for him, upon his return this way, should he think he will search these caves, My Lady. Fear not, for he shall not pass. Go now and find the darkest corner you can, but first make sure that Elwine is well disguised."

I was ashamed to hide. I did tell Tarek this, but he did shake his head in disagreement of my admission. He did tell me that there was no shame, and that no-one here amongst us could accuse me of running from danger.

"You have shown courage in defending your people, My Lady. Let us now repay that courage with your protection," he had told me. "My Lord Arthyen has put your safety into our hands whilst he is away, and, upon my honour, with our life we shall defend it."

And so, reader, I did hide. I did take Elwine to the dimmest place in the cave, and did cover her with a blanket, before Orvin and I did take to the back of another cavern where we did wait for Margh's return up the valley. Tarek had sent word for the men to take themselves to the caves' mouths, but they did not stand guard, but did simply mingle in with the women and children. No-one would have known they were posted deliberately, for they seemed to melt into the everyday life of the villagers, but I did know that one word from Tarek would have brought them together as one.

We did wait for what seemed an eternity.

At last, Margh and his men did return. I did hear the muffled sounds of talking and then I did hear Tarek growl that they would not pass. I did inhale sharply. It would seem that my cousin had, indeed, demanded a search of the caves. I did hold on to Orvin tightly, and did hold my breath. In my head, I could almost feel the grip of Margh's bony hand upon my shoulder, as I imagine him dragging me out of my hiding place.

I did hear wailing and weeping from inside my cave. I could not understand what it meant, but the sounds turned my blood cold. Had someone been killed by Margh's men? It was horrible having to sit so still, and not be able to see what was happening, but I knew that I had to remain where I was.

Then an eerie silence descended upon us, followed by a deep laugh, which I knew came from Tarek. Suddenly the whole cave came alive with shouting and laughing. It was as if I had entered a strange dream, and I could not understand what was taking place around me. Then Tarek had appeared in front of me, looking very pleased with himself. He did take my hand, and help me up, and did bow before me.

"They are gone from here, My Lady," he announced so proudly I could swear that his chest puffed out on his giant frame, like that of the cockerel that paraded around his hens every morning. "How they did run, My Lady. I did think we would be undone when your cousin demanded entrance to the caves, but you have the womenfolk to thank for their change of heart."

"How so Tarek?" I asked, confused.

"Ha," he had laughed. "The flux!"

I looked at him quizzically, and he told me that some of the women had decided to take matters unto themselves, and had wailed and wept and announced that old Morgwan had been taken by the flux. He did tell me how he had found it very hard to keep a straight face, as the women had shouted and screamed that it was now eight who had left this world in agony from the pestilence, and that all the people must be doomed.

Tarek did laugh so much, that his mirth was interrupted now and then by a gasp of pain as his movements did upset his wounds, but he was enjoying the moment so much that he did not seem to worry unduly.

"The last time I saw your cousin move so quick, My Lady, was when he scrambled up the tree to save his hide. I can tell you that his men did not have to be told twice to stay in their saddles! I do not think they shall be returning *too* quickly!"

I did feel such relief wash over me, and I did thank everyone for their kindness and quick thinking. I did laugh with my people, and I know I should be happy, but I cannot, now, feel secure. Now my cousin knows of our location, I shall not settle in my bed at night, and I shall not feel safe in this valley ever again, but I cannot let my people see my uneasiness. It will be against your wishes, Arthyen, but perhaps it is time for me to take my people away from here? I know not where to lead them, but I sense it is not wise to remain here.

How I wish you were here with me, Arthyen. I long to be able to lie next to you again, for only then will my slumber be restful, and without fear.

Forty-sixth Entry

The days have been passing slowly since you did leave. The visit from my cousin has unsettled me, and I find myself looking over my shoulder whenever I leave the darkness of the caves. I do imagine his eyes staring at me, and can still feel his bony hands around my neck. I do not like this feeling, but try as hard as I might I cannot rid myself of it.

I feel trapped. I do not wish to stay here, but did give my oath to you that I would. I do wonder now, would you wish me to stay if you did know of the visit from my cousin, and the threat we find ourselves facing?

Yet, perhaps the threat of the flux will keep him away, for he would not wish to put himself at any risk. Yes, perhaps I should trust that the women's clever thinking would deter him from returning, even he if is suspicious of Tarek's explanation. I do spend my hours arguing with myself over what course of action to take, and I do find myself breathing a sigh of relief on deciding that we are safe where we are; but then I do become wary again with mistrust of my cousin.

It was whilst I was walking aimlessly down the path this afternoon, my head full of such thoughts, that the message did arrive. I did not hear the horse at first, but Orvin's warning bark drew me from my thoughts. It did take a few moments for my head to clear, and for me to realise quite what was occurring, but as soon as I had realised, I had run as quickly up the path as I could. I did nearly trip a couple of times on the loose stones, but did eventually reach the messenger as I did hear my name mentioned. I was somewhat out of breath from the run up the hill, but I did manage

to announce myself clear enough, and the messenger handed me the message.

I did ask Tarek - who seems to have taken on the role of guard these days since you did leave, Arthyen - to take the exhausted rider, and give him food and water and a place to rest. Willard, Hannel's older brother, sheepishly appeared to look after the horse, that seemed to me to be on the verge of collapse. Tarek's self-appointed role is a very welcome one, for I do trust him with my life, and he is such a giant of a man, that many a foe would think twice before trying to engage him in combat.

I rather think that Willard's role has been thrust upon him without his really wishing to have it. Poor Gryffyd is still recovering from the wounds he received when Cragnuth fell, and Hamel - Willard's father - volunteered his eldest son for the role of keeper of the horses until Gryffyd is recovered.

Reader, perhaps you are anxious to learn of the message rather than the roles of various members of my village. I, too, was greatly anxious to read the message, but I did not open it immediately, but did walk back down the path away from prying eyes and tongues. Orvin had sat next to me - expectantly - as I did stare at the parchment in my lap. I was scared to open it, for I did not know whether it could be bad news about you, Arthyen. Orvin did whine and nudge me excitedly, his tongue lolling out of his smiling jaws. My hands did shake as I took the letter from my lap, and I did take a deep breath as I broke the seal and did begin to read. My eyes did first search out the name at the bottom of the message, for if it was not from you I did not think I could bear to read it. There, in the boldest writing, was your name and I did feel my whole body relax, for I knew then that you were still in this world with me.

I shall not tell you, reader, of that was written as some of it is for mine own eyes only, but I can inform you that Arthyen had reached Calamar safely, and had not met with any resistance.

The messenger had been sent ahead of you, husband, and an escort who would be arriving back at the valley to accompany my people, together with those of your men who had remained at the camp, back with you to Calamar. You would arrive in two days time, and - although it will be a treacherous journey - it is one that we shall all have to make to seek the safety within the walls of Calamar. How urgent this journey is, dear Arthyen. You are not to know how urgent, for you are not aware of Margh's visit here. You are not to know the fear that doth follow me every minute of the day – this fear that my cousin will reappear amongst us at any time.

Upon reading the news of your expected arrival, I did immediately inform Tarek of the planned journey, so that he could pass around the necessary instructions to the

people to prepare them for their road. We were to be kept busy in preparation, but there was one thing that I did need to do. I know not whether I shall see this place again, so I had thought I would make one last visit to the camp. I knew this would also allow me to inform those men still there of the plans, and I could also lay my eyes once more upon the oak tree under which we did make our vows.

As I told Tarek of my plans to visit the camp, sweet little Hannel had pleaded with me to take him with me. I could see no reason why I should not give him a ride on Elwine's back, and I did think that the air would do his body good, and to take him away from the hustle and bustle of the caves at such a time, would seem to be a helpful thing to do.

Leaving the people of Cragnuth in the capable hands of Tarek, and with Hannel sitting in front of me, I did take Elwine down the familiar path to the banks of the river, with Orvin and Vala trotting by our side. I shall forever have this day in my memory, for it is one that will be impossible to forget.

We did arrive at the camp, and I did inform those who were there of the message from you. I did enter our tent, and did gather up the few belongings you had left, wrapping them in your old tunic. I did then secure it to Elwine's saddle and did make my way towards the oak tree, holding Hannel's tiny hand in mine. We did stand under its old, heavy branches that would soon be coming to life with tiny buds of green, and I did allow myself some personal thoughts. It was Hannel tugging against my skirt, and the barking from both Orvin and Vala that did awaken me from my daydreaming.

"Men are coming", screamed Hannel in a frightened voice. "They are coming here very fast". He had pointed back up the river. Following his outstretched finger, I did see thirty or more riders galloping down upon us. It was clear, even from where Hannel and I did stand, that they were not coming upon us in friendly terms, and it soon became evident to me that they had some malevolent business with the camp.

They did come down upon the encampment, waving their swords in the air, letting forth screams and shouts of terror. The men who were there did not have a chance to defend themselves, and most were cut-down where they stood. The attackers did then go about burning the tents, with the flames from the two or three fires that were alight around the camp. Soon there was fire everywhere, thick grey smoke billowing into the sky.

So, my cousin had made his move, for I did recognise the voice of Margh shouting to his men, and I did gather Hannel into my body. He did attract my attention to an-

other group of people coming down the valley, and I could see the unmistakable figure of Tarek ahead of other riders, made up of some of the garrison of Cragnuth who had been left behind to help defend us, should it become necessary.

My people did soon arrive at the camp, and the fighting did commence. The smoke wafted across the field, enveloping all around it in its thick acrid smell. I could hear sounds all around me – shouting, horses screaming, the sound of metal upon metal, and the cry of wounded men. I did stand with sword and dagger in my hands ready for an attack, but I knew not from whence it would come. A shape did come looming out towards me, legs flailing in the air. The horse came screaming out of the smoke, the whites of its eyes rolling in its head. Fear was etched across its face, and blood poured from the huge gash in its neck. Its rider was already dead, but it was still galloping, and came thundering down upon me. I jumped out of its way, pulling Hannel with me, and watched as it crashed into the ground at full speed.

As I had steadied myself, I did hear the familiar voice of my cousin, but could not see him. My eyes searched in the acrid smoke, which did sting my eyes, and did make them water. Orvin and Vala were barking, and both did stand facing the same direction. Turning to follow their gaze, I did see a black horse slowly walk out of the smoke. It did snort and toss its head angrily, white spittle foaming from its open jaws, as its rider pulled hard on its bridle.

Margh!

He did sit upright in his saddle, his sword unsheathed and laid across his arm.

"Get down and fight, you coward", I spat at him, adjusting my grip on the weapons in my grasp.

Margh did throw back his head, and did let loose a loud laugh.

He did ride his horse around me in a circle – round and round he did go. I did have no choice, but to follow him around to keep him in my sights, and it did make my belly feel unsettled, but I dare not take my eyes off him.

I clung to Hannel, and kept him in close to me. He was such a brave young warrior – he did not cry or utter forth one word of fear. He did just stand very close to me, and did move with me as if we were one body.

The breeze wafted slowly across us, and the smoke did slowly begin to clear. I did bend down to Hannel, and did whisper closely in his ear, "When I tell you, Hannel,

you must run. Run as fast as you can, and stay with the smoke. It will help to hide you. You must try to take yourself somewhere safe away from here. Can you do that for me, Hannel?"

He had nodded enthusiastically, as if he was about to play a game of hide and seek. I did ruffle his hair "Clever boy", I did say. I knew he would not be able to run very fast, but, although one leg was shorter than the other, he still did have an unexpected speed.

"Go now", I shouted with a slight push on his back, and he did, without question, run into the departing smoke. It took him with it as it crawled across the levels.

Margh had been surprised by this sudden escape, but he did not even attempt to halt Hannel's progress.

"The boy is of no consequence, My Lady", he smirked. "My men can hunt him out and have sport if they wish, but I have my own sport here before me." And he continued to circle his mount around me.

His circling had made us unknowingly slowly move our positions, and I realised that we were nearly at the riverbank. Margh had his back to the river, and – therefore - was unaware of what was taking place behind him. A swirling mist swept down the waters. I knew what this meant, and was not surprised when I did see the island appear.

I did see a figure standing in the archway and recognised it as your father, Arthyen. He was standing next to Rhialdaron. They were not quite as they had appeared before, for this time they were wraithlike – I could see right through them. Through their bodies, I could see the tomb and the pillars.

Margh must have seen the frown upon my face, for he did stop his baiting, and did turn around in his saddle, before jumping his horse back and shouting "What sorcery is this, witch? Your father always said you had the power of darkness over you. He said you killed your mother and brother when you were born".

I did hear his words, but they did not linger in my ears. My eyes were fixed upon something very strange coming from the room where the tomb lay. A dark mass rose from the roof. I did think it was a flock of bats, but I have never heard those beasts make that sound before. It was a low, screaming sound. It made me shiver with fright.

I did hear Margh's horse neighing in fright, and did turn my gaze upon my cousin once more. Something had grabbed his horse's legs, and was trying to pull it into the river.

At first, I could not quite make out what it was, but then I did realise that hands were coming from the dark waters - just as in the stories I had heard told of the boatman. So the tales *were* true after all, there *were* such beings deep in the waters. A shiver ran down my spine.

Those hands were of the dead that do try to keep you from escaping from the cold dark waters. Their flesh was deathly white, and almost transparent - I could almost see the bones under the thin skin. Long fingers had gripped around the horse's back fetlocks, and seemed to be trying to pull the poor demented creature back into the waters. It did scream in terror, and snorted, and with its front legs did try and escape the grip upon it, but they did keep sinking into the soft, wet mud. It could not find purchase upon the earth at all, and it did seem that the wraiths would triumph in their task.

All this while, Margh had been digging his feet into his horse's belly to try to get it to move forward. He realised that his task was hopeless, so he did turn, and smite the grasping hands with his sword. He did cut them away from their wrists and at last their grip was released, enabling his mount to escape their clutches. I stood shocked, as I watched the ripped flesh mend itself before my eyes, before it again slithered back into the river. I could hear wails and moans from the deep waters, and I did look across at the archway where the two figures did still stand motionless.

The black mass was approaching us, and the screeching sound was deafening. I did squint at the creatures to try to see what they were. I could not believe my eyes when I did realise that they were tiny dragons, just like those statues that do sit around your father's tomb, Arthyen. These, however, were not as terrifying as the one I had met in my vision here all those days ago. No, in some strange way that I cannot describe, these small beasts seemed oddly welcome. It did seem that they were part of me, and I do believe that Rhialdaron and Beroun had sent them to our assistance.

I did stand motionless, with Orvin and Vala by my side, as the creatures did fly around me. Margh crouched in his saddle waving his sword in the air at them, as they swooped down upon him. It was impotent against them. They were about as big as the length of my arm, and did bite at him. And how he did shout and scream in fright. His horse did bolt, throwing him from his saddle, unseating him heavily upon the ground on his haunches. He was winded for a few moments, and the beasts flew around his body, their jaws biting upon his arms and legs, piercing his leather ar-

mour. He had dropped his sword as he had been thrown, and he sat where he had been unseated, and frantically waved at his antagonists, trying to reach his sword as he did so.

To no avail. They were relentless in their attack upon his body.

Some of the dragons had left the group around my cousin, and had made their way towards the camp. I could see them attacking all those who had come with Margh. How they did know the difference between my brave people of Cragnuth, and those of my cousin's I know not, but they did leave Tarek and the others alone and gave them no harm.

My attention did return to my cousin, who by now had been forced on to his back. There were eight beasts all over him now, and his flesh was gashed and bleeding, but he still thrashed around trying to push them away from him. His sword lay on the ground beside him, his hands too badly ripped to have any strength left in them to hold it.

His men all down, most of the other dragons did return to the island - all but ten that is. These did join those around Margh. The noise from the river did strengthen, and the dragons did begin to drag Margh towards its cold waters. He did struggle, but could not escape the grip of the jaws that did drag him along the ground. As his feet did reach the bank, I saw the hands emerge again, and they did wrap themselves around his feet and legs. He did turn his head to me, and did scream for help, but I could do nothing but stand and watch. The hands kept pulling him in, and the dragons did fly off back to the island.

The wailing from the river was so loud it made by blood turn cold within me - it was a sound that I shall never wish to hear again; this sound of the dead calling out for their victim. As my cousin slowly slipped into the waters, he did twist his body, and did try to claw at the ground with his hands, to stop his progress into the waters. He could get no grip in the mud, and his fingers did leave deep lines in the soft earth. As more of his body sunk into the water, more arms did wrap themselves around him. Soon, only his head remained above the surface, and he did cry out once more, before a hand did clasp itself around his mouth, and did pull him under. Ripples circled, ever widening, until they came to meet the bank and disappeared.

It was over.

Everything became strangely silent then, after the deafening noise of before. The dragons had all returned to their resting place, and the wailing had ceased from the

river. It was as if nothing had occurred here at all. As I heard Tarek and the others approaching, the island began to disappear into the rolling mist that had returned to the river. As it became shrouded, I could still see that Rhialdaron and Beroun remained at the archway.

I did raise my sword to my lips, and did drop into a curtsey before them. When I did rise again, all had gone from the river, but not before I did feel a strange warm air enter my body, and did feel it flutter in my belly.

I know not whether Tarek or any of the others did see the island, but if they did, they did not speak of it. They were all shocked at what they had witnessed, and been part of, but none of them seemed able to speak of it. Perhaps each one of them did not want to admit to the others that they had seen the beasts – perhaps they did feel that what they had seen was some sorcery that should not be spoken of, for fear of being struck down with death or evil spells. I know not, but I *do* know that your father did play a part in saving my life today, and that of my people, and for that, I shall be eternally thankful, sweet Arthyen.

I did look for Hannel. I sent Orvin to search for him too. Reader, I did roam the field shouting his name, but he did not respond. I had felt desperate, as I had run from bush, to tree, to boulder to see if he had hidden himself so well, and that he had perhaps fallen asleep. I could find no trace of him, and I had started to get an uncomfortable feeling in my belly. I became full of dread, and I did begin to feel that we would never find him, or that if he we did, that Margh's men would have found him first.

I heard Orvin bark, but it was Tarek who did shout my name. I did look across to where he knelt, and it was clear by his posture that he had found something and that it was not favourable. I could hear Orvin whining, and I did run across to where they were. Not my sweet Hannel, I did scream inwardly to myself, please let it not be he.

Following Tarek's glazed stare, I did see the tiny body lying face down in the dirt, near the borders of the camp, underneath the branches of a low bush. To begin with, I was not certain how you had left this world, Hannel, for you did not have any visible marks upon you. It was not until I did lift you, that I realised that your neck was broken. If you did trip, or if you were attacked, I know not, and shall never learn the truth, but you were gone from this world.

Hannel, my dear, sweet, little boy. What is this life that it can be taken so easily without redress? As I held you in my arms, I had wept freely. Your lifeless eyes stared up at me, and I closed them with my thumbs, and as I rocked you back and

forth, you looked so peaceful in your eternal sleep. Orvin laid down beside us, and lay his head on his paws. Poor Orvin had lost a friend too, and I could see the sadness in his brown eyes.

Close your eyes little one
And let sleep come upon you
Let it take you to lands far, far away
Where you can play safe little one
With your friends in the green fields
And go back to the river that you played in today

Close your eyes little one
And let sleep come upon you
Let it take you to lands far, far away
Where you can play safe little one
And can make chains of daisies
And climb in the trees that you climbed in today

Close your eyes little one
And let sleep come upon you
Let it take you to lands far, far away
We will watch over you little one
As you play in your dreams now
And look forward to seeing you at the break of the day

As I sang you this lullaby, Hannel, I knew that you could not be sent on your final journey by yourself. I knew that your mother and her infant would be waiting for you on the other side, but how would you find them? You had been such a brave little boy today, but you are so young, and would be so frightened to take that crossing by yourself. Although many other people would pass you on their last journey to their ancestors, and the road would be crowded, I was afraid that you would become lost. I could not face the thought of your tiny body being pushed this way and that, as the others made their own way through the heavy mists, so I gently wrapped your limp body in my cloak, lifted you in my arms, and began my search. Death seemed to be all around, and men were dotted across the field of battle. The dying men - some of whom had followed Margh – groaned, and some of the unfortunate horses twitched in the last throes of death.

My mind was made up, and I knew what I must do - so I had wandered slowly, taking care not to tread upon a lifeless body in respect of their ultimate sacrifice, or slip upon the entrails of some unfortunate.

Tarek and the other townspeople were gathering the bodies of your men, Arthyen, and of those from our town who had been killed. Before leaving the encampment for one last time, we would ensure that they were sent to the other world, as only true warriors deserve. With great sadness, and a heavy heart as I write this, I know that there will be many more mounds of bodies that will light up the dark skies in the days to come.

At that time, sweet Hannel, I had to treat you as the warrior you had shown yourself to be on this fateful afternoon. You had shown no fear, and I am proud of your bravery. I shall tell your father that you had been such a brave son in your last hours. In this, you truly did deserve a warrior's burial, and I had to endeavour to give you such.

To this outcome, I did continue on my search, and at last did find who I was looking for. He was lying at the bottom of the small pile of bodies, and although I knew him as one of your men, Arthyen, I did not know him by name. I know that I should have done so, for I did recognise him from my stay after your leaving, and I do know that he did tell me his name. I am sorry that I have no memory of this, and I do feel ashamed that his name has left me.

He did look a kindly man, who was in his more mature years, and I felt that he would take your tiny hand in his, and guide you across the swords, Hannel, into the afterlife, and into your mother's arms. I knelt down and placed your shrouded body on the soldier's chest, and wrapped the latter's stiffening arm around you, gently clasping his hand around yours. I have seen death many times before, and I knew by the time the flames were alight, that his arm and hand would be so tightly set around you that nothing would separate you from each other. I did unwrap the cloak from your tiny head, caressed your soft cheek, and placed one last lingering kiss upon your forehead, before covering you again.

A messenger was dispatched to summon your father - Hamel, and brothers, Willard and Rafe, and I did stay with you, Hannel, until they did arrive at the burnt remains of the encampment. I did stay for a while, as the flames of the fire took your spirit on its way to your ancestors, and then I did leave your family to mourn in solitude, and did return to my people in the caves. There was sorrow among us all for we all did love you Hannel, and will never forget your sparkling eyes and sweet smiling face.

Farewell, my sweet little boy. We shall meet again one day, of that I am certain.

 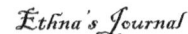

Forty-seventh Entry

Hamel did leave the caves to ride to Calamar to join the army today. It did come as no surprise when I learned of his departure. He has lost his wife, unborn child, and now his youngest son – all in a matter of weeks. He is a broken man, and I fear for his safety, as I can see that his mind is addled. He does not fear death, and I am worried that he will deliberately seek it. Willard and Rafe are being brave about it, and my heart doth ache for them. I know that they are worried for their father also, and do not expect to see him again.

The events of yesterday have cast a shadow over our hearts, and we have gone about our business in a quiet way. Your arrival, husband, is expected tomorrow, and I know my heart shall sing when I do see you again. However, I do know that you will be saddened by the passing of Hannel as much as we are. Perhaps Hamel shall come upon you on his journey, and shall tell you of the news himself. If not, then it will be up to me to share the sorrow with you, and I do not know how I shall be able to bear this burden.

Reader, even though the lives of those who did cause his death have ended, it will not soften the blow of Hannel's passing. For now, I must pack away my nib, for there is still much to do in preparation of our leaving on the morrow. Again, I do find myself recording that I know not when I shall be able to write again, but know that when I can, I shall certainly do so, for I have grown accustomed to letting you know of what occurs in my world. I do hope that one day this journal shall bring these days alive once again in someone else's eyes.

Forty-eighth Entry

s had been instructed in your message, Arthyen, I did take the people to the edge of the forest in readiness for your arrival. It did take a long time to pass everyone through the caves and out through the waterfall, especially those who did not wish to make that journey again after their ill memories of it before. We did have to bring our few livestock through also, and - although most did not prove to be too difficult - the swineherd, Jann, did have much trouble with his charges. The old sow, Agg, did present her master with great hardship, for she did not wish to enter the cave. He did prod and poke her with his stick to great extent, but it took the old swineherd's trick of tying a line to Agg's back legs and pulling her backwards, before she did repent and move forwards. He did then have to keep her moving at a great speed all through the caverns so that she did have no time to stop and think about leaving through the secret entrance behind the waterfall. I did think that we might have to leave our swine behind in the forest, for they did then start to root around in the forest floor, as only swine can do. We would not have time to stop and wait for them if they did do this all the way on our journey. They are slow walkers and *do* get preoccupied on their own business very easily.

I had roused the people just before dawn, but it was almost mid-day by the time all of them were assembled at the forest's edge. I did think what a motley group we did appear to be, as we did stand and talk amongst ourselves, awaiting your arrival. I did keep looking out for you across the lowlands. My stomach was turning over on itself and it did make me feel unwell. How I did miss little Hannel, for on an occasion

such as this, it would be he whom I would have sought out to spend time with in these waiting hours. He was such good company, but I shall not dwell upon his passing, for it will bring sadness to my heart, and I wish to remember him in the better times.

We did wait for what seemed an eternity, before one of our lookouts did announce the arrival of riders on the horizon. I recall hoping that it would be you, and not the enemy come upon us again. Why I did think that it could be the enemy, I know not, but I cannot assume that they will not reappear in our lives as suddenly as they did leave. They are on a mission to destroy, and will not stop before they have succeeded in their orders. I need not have concerned myself, though, for it was not long before I did recognise Acha, and the banners that did flutter in the wind above your heads. There were not many of you; about fifty I would estimate, but at the time I did think that hopefully it would be enough to escort us all to the safety of the walls of Calamar – if that mighty place still existed by the time we did arrive there.

Tarek had escorted me, and we had ridden into the open ahead of the others to greet you. We did stand just at the edge of the lowlands, and watch your approach.

With a broad grin upon your face, you did ride up to me, and did take my hand in yours before leaning across to place a firm kiss upon my lips. "Tis so good to see you again, beloved wife", you did tell me quietly. "The hours have passed so slowly without you beside me".

"So slowly I thought the days would stand still, beloved husband", I replied before raising your hand to my lips and kissing it.

"Your people are ready to take to the road?" you had asked, your eyes searching the darkness of the trees behind me.

"We are indeed, My Lord", I answered, as I had raised my hand as a signal for the exiled peoples of Cragnuth to come forth into the open.

"Then let us make haste, for we have a good few hours of daylight left to make good use of", you had said.

So, we did leave that place and did make our way to the safety of Calamar. When we had made camp, I did ask of you whether you had come across Hamel on your journey here, and you did say that you had not. You had enquired of me as to why I should ask such a question.

 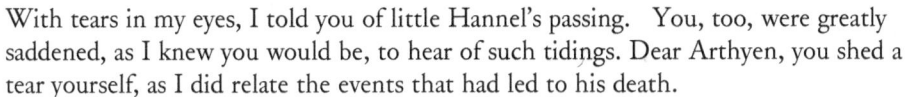
With tears in my eyes, I told you of little Hannel's passing. You, too, were greatly saddened, as I knew you would be, to hear of such tidings. Dear Arthyen, you shed a tear yourself, as I did relate the events that had led to his death.

I knew that you would not have believed my tale if you had not, yourself, seen the mystical appearance and disappearance of the island on the river. You were sorely angered to hear of my cousin's return to the valley, but seemed satisfied that he had met his end in a way that seemed to be justified, considering his wrongdoings. You did commend my people for their bravery and scheming, especially after I had told you about the women's idea of the 'flux'. This you had thought to be most ingenious, and it did raise a chuckle as you had supped your ale.

It was so good to sit with you again, dear Arthyen. So many days have passed since we have been in each other's company, and I did think that we would never do so again. However, here you were, sitting next to me as we did talk and hold hands in the light given forth from the brazier. You looked weary from your toils of the past few days. The days in the saddle had taken their toll upon you, I could see, and I did try and persuade you to take to your bed and rest, but you did not wish to do so just yet, for you did tell me that you wished to be in my company for a while longer. I did protest that you would still be in my company if you were in your bed, but you did insist that it was to be able to look upon me, and talk with me, that you desired.

I do recall that I did sleep so well that night - the most restful sleep that I have had since you had left. I smiled when you did tell me the next morning that it was the same for you also.

Now I come to remember it, I did feel ill that morning also and now, three days later, I must admit that I do still feel unsettled and do hope that I am not sickening for something. It is a feeling that I cannot describe, but I do feel very tired and sickly. If I have not improved in the next day or two, then I shall visit the apothecary, and see what he can suggest to raise my spirits. I am sure that he will have some tonic or potion that will make me feel better. I shall not dwell upon mine own discomfort, for there are many more important issues to be faced in the coming days.

Going back to our journey to Calamar, we did not meet many travellers upon the road apart from three or four wanderers who did not seem to have anywhere in particular to go; they just seemed to keep walking in whatever direction seemed to take their fancy. One of them in particular though, did make his mark upon my mind. He was a tall, lean man, of middling years I would say, and did seem higher in rank than his clothing did suggest. He did wear his long yellow hair in a braid down his back where it fell to just below his shoulder blades. His clothes were ragged, and his

body dirty from many days spent on the road. As we did pass him, he did raise his head to look at you and me, Arthyen. He did have piercing blue eyes, not unlike those of my evil cousin Margh. They did discomfort me, but I know not why. It was as if he could see into my very soul, as my own eyes locked on to his for that fleeting moment.

As we had passed him, he did stop walking, and stood; his stare upon us. I turned in Elwine's saddle and could not take my eyes off him. I could not, and even now, as I write this days later - still cannot - discern whether there was a malevolence about him or not. However, I watched him until he was but a dot in the distance, and it was you who had spoken my name to distract me from my gaze. I did look across at you, and did smile weakly in return of yours. I did ask you whether you had seen him, but you did not appear to have taken much notice of the man, and shook your head. "Just another traveller - like us," you said. "He is probably walking towards Calamar also. Perhaps you shall see him again there".

Oh Arthyen, I do hope, for some reason, that I will not. He discomforts me so.

Our long march passed without event, and I am pleased, and relieved, to report that we did all make it here without loss of life. I have never been this far away from my home before, and it has been a journey of discovery for me, for I did not know what the land did look like this far north. There were vast stretches of barren moorland, not unlike my beloved Blackditch Moor, but this land was also full of tiny valleys that did carve their way across the land. We did descend into, and climb out of, many of these places, with tiny streams that did cut their way through the valley floor. They burbled and babbled as their waters raced down tiny outcroppings of shiny rock, as they made their way, I know not where.

We could see Calamar as it rose in the distance on the summit of a large hill. As we neared it, the land around became flatter, and the castle clearly had a very good sight of all that occurred around it. I did speak of this later to your cousin, the Lady Igraine, and she did agree with me, but did add that it did have its drawbacks also, for in the season of mists, these did cling to the castle, making it impossible to see anything of what did happen below the crown of cloud.

I could not have been prepared for the sight of Calamar. I do not think anyone could have described it well enough to me, for it is quite the largest town I have ever seen. Its castle battlements are larger than Cragnuth's ever were, by three or four times.

As we entered through the great gates, we made our way up the hill through the township that clung to the sides of it. There were so many people bustling to and

from their daily business. The traders shouted their wares, and the place was alive with noise and numerous smells. I was not sure where all our people would go, amongst the already crowded confines of the outer walls. Calamar was obviously full of homeless peoples like ourselves, and I was greatly concerned for my people's safety and comfort.

However, in times such as these that we find ourselves in, we have no choice but to seek the sanctuary of this place. Arthyen and I made our way further into the bowels of Calamar, and on up the winding path that took us to the great Keep above. Dismounting, we climbed the steps that led to the heavy doors, and were immediately allowed entry by the guards that stood sentry outside. They bowed their heads low as we entered. I was not prepared for what opened up before me as we went in.

Reader, I could but stand in awe at what sight befell my eyes. I stood and looked around; I fear that my mouth was wide open in surprise. My dear husband had to take my arm to awaken me from my bemused state, and prompted me with a slight incline of his head to follow him. The Hall is bigger than the whole Keep at Cragnuth; its walls covered in great tapestries. It is so big that it needs four braziers, set down its middle, to give adequate heat inside its cavernous expanse. As you had led me down the Hall, I had gazed around me, still with my mouth open in wonder at the size of the place, and the ornate decorations that did hang on its walls.

As we had passed them, the sentries posted around the edges of the room stood to attention; other members of the court did bow before you. At last, I did recognise the Lord Keowyn standing at the rear of the Hall, a young woman at his side. I took this lady to be your cousin, the Lady Igraine. When we did at last reach them, Lord Keowyn did bow, and your cousin did curtsey, in welcome. You did ask them to stand, and did embrace Lord Keowyn warmly before placing a kiss on your cousin's cheek. You did then introduce me before wrapping an arm around Lord Keowyn's shoulder, and taking him off into the far corner of the room, leaving me with the Lady Igraine.

Forty-ninth Entry

Life inside the great stone walls of Calamar is busy with the arrival, almost every day, of a steady trickle of those people who have lost their homes to the terror that has swarmed across the land. Every small space seems to have been taken by some family or other, in their quest for safety from the enemy that has laid waste to their homes. I do feel somewhat guilty that my own people have now taken more space within the walls, and yet - as I wrote in my previous entry - what else are we to do?

As I did write yesterday, upon our arrival here, you did escort me to the Great Hall to meet the Lady Igraine and Lord Keowyn. Lady Igraine has been most gracious in her acceptance of you as her new King, and also of me. She is the only surviving child of your uncle, the late King Ulmar. It would seem that there were three other children - the eldest son had been killed many years before, and of her two sisters; one had died in childbirth, the other having developed a fire in her blood which did take her two winters ago.

After our supper, we did walk along the ramparts that do surround the Great Hall. A hundred tiny fires flickered all around the mound upon which it did stand. There was a constant deep rumble of voices, as the town's many inhabitants went about their business below us, with the odd shout, loud singing, or barking of a dog. Looking into the distance to the east, I could see an orange glow in the night sky.

The enemy encampment.

Upon our arrival, Lord Keowyn did report that the enemy had arrived three days ago, but have not moved since. It is clear they are waiting for something, or perhaps someone, before they do make their attack.

In the pale moonlight, I could make out a hill a little further to the east, the rocky crags at its top silhouetted against the eerie light. It looked familiar to me, and did make me shiver as I did remember it had come to me in my vision the last time I had been on the island. I then realised who the enemy were awaiting, and did know that what was to come would either be the end of all I knew, or the beginning of peace in this land. I know also that the outcome of the coming battle is somehow in *my* hands, and the burden of such knowledge weighs heavily on my mind, and my heart. Even more so, for I am bound by my oath that I cannot mention that which I saw to anyone, not even you, my sweet Arthyen.

As I looked across at you tonight, whilst the moon did cast its light down upon your weary face, I wished I could tell you everything that had occurred on that misty morning many days ago, and have you tell me that everything would be alright, but I knew that I could not. Above all, I cannot let you sense my terror of what may yet come to pass. I did place my hand upon your cheek, and did brush a lock of hair from your eyes, before placing a soft kiss upon your lips. Your beard tickled my chin, and I giggled and pulled away from you. You had pulled me towards you, and I tucked my head under your chin. We had stood like that for many a while, looking out over the ramparts at the glow in the distance.

The new day did come upon us all too quickly, and I did not wish to leave the comfort of our bed and the warmth of your arms. I did know that any day, or hour, soon could herald the end of all that we have, more so now than at any other time in the past.

Fiftieth Entry

*I*t had been the Lady Igraine who did start this day on its eventful path. She had come upon me as I did return to our chamber, after taking our morning meal. I had been feeling somewhat unwell, as was usual these days, and did wish to lay upon our bed for a short while until the uneasy feeling in my belly did fade. We did pass in the corridor, and she did remark upon the odd look upon my face. When I did tell her how I did feel, and that I would have to visit the doctor, she did usher me into our chamber, Arthyen, with such a look of delight upon her own face, that I did wonder what she was about to tell me. I had been unprepared for the words that did utter forth from her lips, but upon reflection, I am not sure why I had not thought of them first.

She did ask me, quite openly, but in a soft voice lest we could be overheard, when the child was due. It had taken a few moments to penetrate into my head what she did mean, and then I realised that the feelings I had been experiencing these last weeks were exactly as those described by dear Martha when she did talk to me about the infant she was hoping would be the girl she and Hamel had longed for. Alas, of course, neither of them did survive (as I have related before in this journal). I can remember poor Martha did endure much with this last child, and she did make sure that everyone around did know of her sufferings, for she did not have any such occurrences with any of her other offspring. I am still recovering from the loss of her friendship, and it does hurt to remember her passing, but as I write this I can grin at the recollection of her grumbling every day about how unwell she did feel.

Lady Igraine did not seem to grasp, at first, that this news was a shock, and did chatter on about how exciting it was that the King already had an heir. And did he know?

And what had been his reaction to the news? She did ask so many questions all at once, that all her words seemed to melt into each other, and I could not possible answer any of them.

I did sit on the edge of our cot, Arthyen, and did remain quite silent, for I knew not what to say. My head felt it would burst with all the questions with which sweet Lady Igraine was quizzing me. It was indeed an exciting time, but to carry a child whilst our futures were so unclear? Surely, this was not the ideal time to bring an infant into such an uncertain world? I felt confused. Yet elated that I did carry within me such a wondrous thing.

Lady Igraine at last seemed to realise that the news was a surprise to me, and she gently sat next to me on our bed, and did take my hand in hers. She said not a word, but did wait for me to speak first. I turned to face her, and holding tightly on to her hands, I did tell her not to mention the child to anyone. She had seemed shocked that I did wish to keep it a secret, but I did explain to her that it would put unbearable pressure upon your shoulders, if you did find out, and that it would be more probable, than not, that you would send me away from Calamar, and its imminent danger. I did not tell her the complete truth about why this could not happen, for I could not - reader, you know I am under oath myself on this matter, but I knew that you, husband, would surely send me away, and then I should not be able to fulfil my destiny as foretold by your father.

I did make her swear an oath that what had occurred between us that day would not be shared with any other. I know, by the expression upon her face, that she did not fully understand why, but she did do as I had bid.

I did stand and go to the window, and bathed in the warm sunlight, with one hand shielding my eyes, the other caressing my belly I did turn to the Lady Igraine, and smile. "I can but hope that one day very soon I shall be able to tell the King that I do carry his child, Lady Igraine. There is something that I need to do first, and then I shall tell him. Until then, you and I shall have to keep this to ourselves. I know you cannot understand, but it is all I can tell you for now. I am sorry."

Lady Igraine had nodded, curtsied, and left the room; I fear in a rather confused manner, her demeanour was subdued. I had hoped that she and I would make a good friendship, but I fear that my behaviour may have caused a barrier between us. I can only hope that one day I shall be able to tell her of the reasons behind my actions.

I did not have much time alone to spend with our unborn child, Arthyen, for soon after the Lady Igraine had left, you did enter our room with urgency in your gait.

You did announce to me that scouts had brought news that the enemy was moving towards Calamar, and that it would be upon us by mid-afternoon at the latest. Preparations, at this fortress, were well under way for the expected battle ahead. My dearest Arthyen, I felt so much guilt within me for not telling you of the child that grew within my body, as I watched you, with great urgency, dress yourself in your armour.

I aided you in securing some of the buckles, and did quietly query your participation in any battle that may occur. Even though I knew what your reaction would be, I did suggest to you that as King, surely it was not your place to take part in warfare directly. The answer you did give was as I had expected. It was of the utmost importance that you did ensure that your men saw that you were not afraid to stand in battle with them, and that just because you were now King, it did not mean that you would hide away in the safety of the walls of your castle. I would not have expected it any other way, my dearest husband; my King.

Journal, mine own demons did continue to plague me. As I did stand and assist you, my beloved husband, prepare for battle, I did struggle with my own thoughts. I did have no means of knowing exactly how I was to take part in the coming events, but whatever it did involve, how could I do what was expected of me, now that I did carry my King's heir? I did toil with these feelings while you did dress, and eventually did console myself with the notions that, if the vision of your father did – indeed - know my fortune, then he must also know that I would be with child. I did feel comforted that this must be the truth, and that it was what I should believe. So be it, I *would* believe.

When you were fully armoured, we did go back to Great Hall and did await further news of our foe's approach.

It was clear, when our assailants did arrive upon the lowlands that did stretch from Calamar's main gate, that not all of their numbers had come. There were but one to two hundred of them that did come upon us.

It was obvious to you, dear husband, that these attackers had been sent to merely taunt the castle, but you did ride out with your army, now greater in numbers since joining with the garrison here at Calamar, and did engage the enemy. However, as did the enemy, you did not ride with all of your garrison. No, you did play the enemy at their own game, and did not reveal how strong your company was.

Standing on the great ramparts, the sun was blinding. Lady Igraine had joined me briefly to watch Lord Keowyn, you and your followers, ride out into the fight that

would, nevertheless, fury outside the walls, but she could not watch the carnage that would surely follow, and had retreated through the throngs of people to the Hall to await the arrival of the injured. Raising my hand to shield the sun's harsh rays from my eyes, I looked down upon the battle that raged beneath the battlements.

It was not long before I followed in Lady Igraine's footsteps.

Even though the numbers were not as they could be, this first battle was no less fierce, and the Lady Igraine and I had gone to the Hall where we and other women-folk were to tend the wounds of those brave men who had managed to make their painful way to us. Those who could not walk perished in the midst of the fighting, as we had not the men enough to spare to aid those injured a safe passage. Many brave warriors died in our arms, and many shall face a life with scars not only on the surface but also deep in their minds. They have spoken of such a horrifying enemy that it does chill the heart.

Then suddenly there was quiet and a stillness in the air. It was over, and - my sweet Arthyen - you were safe.

News of the victory had reached those waiting within the city walls. Emerging from every crook and cranny where they had been hiding, women and children were filling the battlements behind the bailey, waiting for the return of their husbands, fathers, sons and brothers. The victors had begun their return through the great gate, and I could see that you were at their head.

The throng did pass us on its way to meet the riders with a great cheer upon their lips. Igraine and I had become separated, and I did have to move back into the Hall. You did not see me as you passed by, and I could not get to you through the crowd, but could but watch as you dismounted, and removed your helm. I pushed my way through the jubilant throng. At last, I was through, and stood a few feet away from you. Was it the sense of my presence that caused you to turn towards me?

Oh, how exhausted you did look, Arthyen. The battle-lust that had so recently surged through your body was now leaving behind such a weary figure. I walked slowly towards you, my eyes holding your gaze, and 'twas as if the people around me did not exist; their excited chattering did fade into silence. Still looking into your tired eyes, I did take up your right hand in my left, and did remove the blood soaked gauntlet. Raising your hand to my lips, I did kiss your palm, before laying my own hand in yours, turning it until our fingers could entwine. I did tenderly kiss each of your fingertips. My eyes still sending those unspoken words known only to us, with the back of my right hand, I did caress your cheek, my forefinger then tracing gently

across your lips.

The first battle is over, and you are still in this world with me. I will not think of the next battle until it comes upon us, but I do fear that it shall do so within the next day or so. Tonight, we did see the familiar orange glow on the horizon that did rise from the encampment of our foe, and by the range of the light; it is plain that there are many enemy swords still to vanquish.

Fifty-first Entry

It was on the second night after that first battle, that the dream did visit me in my sleep. I saw a circle of standing stones atop a hill, and in the midst of this circle a lone figure did stand, surrounded by grey clouds from which fine rain did fall. In the distance I could hear the beat of drums, each strike loud in my ears, although I could see no drum-bearers from where I crouched behind a small outcrop of rocks. From afar, I could hear the unmistakable sounds of battle raging below. In my dream world, I did turn and see far below me the tiny figures as they did fight their bloody struggle for survival. I did see the enemy retreat into the distance, and upon hearing a voice from within the circle of stones, did turn my head around again in time to see a hazy figure emerge from the greyness.

I did awaken from my dream to find my right hand clenched, as if gripping my sword. I found myself damp with sweat, and my mouth was dry with fear, and it did take me a few moments to realise that I had left my dream, and was back in the sureness of lying next to you, Arthyen. I did sit up, and did see Orvin asleep at the foot of our bed, his nose and mouth twitching as it did when he was himself dreaming. Looking across at you, I could see you were also far away in sleep, and did envy both of you for your peaceful rest.

I did get out of bed, and wrapped myself in my cloak, walking quietly to the window, where I did stand, and stare out across the lowlands towards the glow in the sky.

Something deep within me knew that on the morrow I would have to follow the path towards that destiny of which Beroun had spoken. I wished so much that I could return to sleep, but I knew that I would spend the next hours in darkness, and alone with my thoughts. I could hear you quietly breathing, and did wish to lay next to you and wrap myself around your body, but I did not wish to wake you for you would need as much rest as possible before the toils of the day that I knew was to come. I did decide, instead, to take the air, and did leave our room quietly to make my way to the ramparts, where I did wander slowly around, my cloak wrapped tightly around me to keep in as much warmth as possible. The only people I did meet were the sentries on watch. They did seem surprised to see me, but did bow courteously, and did enquire as to my welfare. Once I had convinced them that I merely could not sleep, and that all was well, they did leave me to my thoughts.

So, dawn did find me there on the battlements, and as the sun rose, it did bring with it a faint breeze which did gently sweep across the walls, bringing the banners back to life in its wake. Cockerels began their early morning calls, and soon the town below the fortifications became alive with the smells and sounds of a new day.

I did return to our chamber to find you just stirring. Poor Orvin was sitting by the door awaiting my return. I do not know how long he had been sitting there, but did praise him for not rousing you with any concerned barks. I did not tell you about my dream, and that I had been awake all night, for there was no need for you to be concerned with such things. I lay next to you as you did open your eyes, and did greet your awakening with a smile. Dearest husband, how I do love thee with all of my heart.

I did spend the morning most uneasily, for I was in constant anticipation of the news of the enemy's approach. I did find myself unable to settle, and every time someone did enter the Hall, I did expect him to bring such news to you. Eventually, though, as I had known, such intelligence *did* come, and I found myself oddly thankful for this, for it did release me from my fretting. The task was now at hand, and I could concentrate on the path that I knew I had to take.

How was I to leave the safety of the castle walls? If you, Arthyen, became aware of my motives, I would be undone. There was no possible way that I could slip away until you had left. I would have to wait until the battle had commenced, but it would be difficult to leave in the throes of battle. I would have to ensure that the Lady Igraine knew nothing of my plotting, and would need to go from her company without raising suspicion. I settled upon the ploy of absenting myself from her company by feigning sickness - in my condition it would not be unduly surprising. It was not an ideal plan, and I did not wish to be full of such trickery, but it was the only

way I would be able to leave unseen, and unhindered.

So journal, this is exactly what I did.

Your men mustered, you - along with the army of Calamar - did leave the sanctuary of its walls. I watched as you, and Lord Keowyn, disappeared through the gates and out into the flat lands, followed by your men. As you had all walked your mounts through the town, the crowds had parted to line the way. An unnatural silence fell upon the fortress; the only sound to be heard was the odd sound of armour clinking or a horse whinnying or snorting. It brought a shiver to my bones; it was as if the whole place had fallen into mourning its dead. I knew what everyone was thinking in this silence – who would fall on this day, never to return to his family?

Slowly, the line of men left the gates. My thoughts were with them all, but, of course, especially with you, Arthyen. Silently, I wished you well on this day.

At last, the waiting was over. But suddenly, I felt oddly light-headed, and had to briefly lean against the side of one of the stalls for a moment, while I gathered my strength. Before I could continue, I had to summon up the bravery that appeared to have suddenly left with your passing into the field of battle. This would not do. I could not falter now.

It was time for me to saddle Elwine and follow my fate. Rallying my resolve, I did equip myself with as much armour as I could find, but that which remained did not fit very well. However, it would offer me some protection, and I did welcome it. And so, reader, with my bow, sword, and dagger, I left the great walls of Calamar.

Once outside the great gate, I led Elwine as close to the walls as possible, away from the midst of the battle, and guided her in the direction of the hill. My helm did not allow me to see much of what was taking place on either side of me, but I could hear the sounds well enough. Elwine forced her way through the mass of bodies, and I did smite that enemy that did stand in our path until I did reach the foot of the hill. Reining Elwine around, I did look back upon Calamar, and the fight that did rage on before it. I searched for your banners fluttering on the staffs of their bearers, for I knew that if I found them, I would find you.

I did see you in the thick of the fighting. What occurred next, however, I could not believe. I did cry out your name loudly, as I did see the great Acha fall. She did rear briefly, before her legs did buckle beneath her grey frame, and I did see your body crash to the ground as you tumbled from her falling body - everything seemed to be in slow-motion. My task was now forgotten - I could not leave you. I urged Elwine

into a gallop towards you, and did jump from her back, running as fast as I could in the armour that was heavier than to that which I was accustomed, towards where you had fallen, my voice screaming your name over and over. I fell to my knees beside you, sliding along the bloodied soil.

Removing my helm, I looked down upon your face. Your eyes were open, but did seem to stare lifelessly into the sky above you. I wiped away the crimson liquid that had begun to dribble slowly from the corner of your mouth. I shook your shoulders to try to rouse you, but you did not respond, Arthyen. I did look to the same skies and did cry out, the tears running down my cheeks, falling from my chin on to your face, as I did cradle your lifeless head in my lap. I could not believe that I had lost you so suddenly. So cruelly. All it had taken was one brief moment of time. One moment I had seen you sitting tall in your saddle; the sunlight gleaming on the metal of your blade. And then, in the time it takes to blink, you were lying here on the ground.

The battle carried on around us, but the sounds of war faded, as I rocked you back and forth, my dear husband. Would your eyes now never look upon the son who did lie here in the warmth of my belly, next to where your head was resting?

Shadows formed over us, and I realised that figures had intruded into our tiny place of solitude amongst that huge battle. I did quickly take your father's sword in one hand, and drew mine own. I did stand, shouting as I did so in a voice so loud that even I was afraid.

"You filthy sons of whores," I heard myself scream, as I swung my blade above my head. "Do not dare come near us!" I felt the sword hit flesh and I did withdraw it and swing again with my other hand, turning around as I did so. I know not what powered my strength, but I did crouch and lunge at anything that came near me. Perhaps it was you who did help me, Arthyen, from wherever you were now? Or, perchance your father did lend his strength to the blade? Whatever - or whoever - it was, it did serve me well. I do not know how many enemies I did slay that after-noon, but all I did know was anger - such a great anger was within, that my husband had been taken away from his unborn child and me. I knew not how we would face life without you, or if we would live beyond the end of the day, but I *did* know that I would take as many of the enemy with us as I could. I did hold no mercy upon them, and if they approached me they did die by your father's mighty sword, or mine own.

The news had spread that the King had fallen, and, in the event that you might still live, as would normally occur, a guard soon surrounded your body, to protect you

from an enemy's mortal blow. If, by some small chance, you *were* still alive, they would defend you to the death; of that I was certain, and their circle would be impenetrable against enemy weapons. I did feel exhausted and forlorn, and did wish to do nothing but stay with you, but I knew there was *something* I still needed to do, and that I would have to leave you in their charge.

So, my dear Arthyen, I did kneel before you and did kiss your forehead. I did inhale such a deep breath and did wipe my wet eyes and running nose with the sleeve of my dress before standing once again. If my face was, indeed, as dirty as my hands and clothes, then my face would look no worse. It mattered not. I did look at the backs of those who did guard you, husband, and did see such brave, honourable men; men who would die themselves to save their King. Now, it was to be my turn once more. I did place the helm once more upon my head, and - with your father's sword still in my right hand - I did turn to face the circle.

"Let me pass", I ordered.

Unspoken, the men did part, and through that gap in the circle that did open before me, I did remount Elwine, and did restart my journey to the hill and the fate that did await me.

A great, grey cloud had descended, and did hang low over the top of the tor. I dismounted Elwine, and kissed her muzzle, before turning to begin my journey up the hill on foot. In the near distance, I could hear Tarek call out to me to stop. But I ignored him, for I knew that I must climb. I shut out his persistent shouting, and with my head held as high as I could muster under the weight of my helm, I began my scramble up the side of the slope. Your father's sword was heavy, and I did have to carry it over my shoulder. I did tuck up my skirts to enable me to tackle the loose stones and shingle at the base of the hill.

It did take much effort to walk up the slope; the weight of your father's sword added to the heaviness that my armour did cause, and the fact that the ground beneath my feet was slippery, and I did constantly lose my footing, did make it more so. I was about halfway up, when I stopped to remove my shoes, for I did think I would have a firmer grip on the earth if my feet were bare. Turning back the way I had climbed, I could see that Tarek and Caswyn were following me. I do hold them both in such high regard, but I did wish they would turn back. The task ahead was one that I needed to bear on my own, but I knew I could do nothing to stop them from following.

Looking beyond them, just as I had seen in my dream, I could see that the enemy

seemed to be retreating. My eyes sought the circle of men that remained unmoved, as they stood protecting you where you had fallen. I knew they would take you from the field of battle, once safe passage to the gates was certain.

It was not long before the weight of my hauberk became too much for me, and I did remove it willingly, followed by my helm and gauntlets. I did leave them where they fell, and did continue on my way up the tor. My skirts did fall down around my ankles constantly, so I did stop, and rend off as much material as was necessary to allow my legs to move freely up the slippery slope.

Reader, I do not know what - or who - did control whatever did take place upon that hilltop that I did find myself climbing, but upon nearly reaching the top I did feel the earth beneath my feet start to move. I believed the ground would split, and take me into the very heart of the earth below. It did shake around me so much, that I did have to steady myself from falling and did sit down upon the grass.

I did see them then. Creatures of the dark soil did slither from every place around me. Worms of all sizes did weave their way across the earth, their muddy bodies slithering along the broken ground. I could feel their coldness on the skin of my hands where I had placed them beside me to steady myself. Worms do not cause me any distress, but to see so many of them in one place, and on such a day as this... it did unnerve me.

It would seem that it was known that I was there. What is more, it was clear to me then, that my presence was not welcomed.

I would not be beaten back by such spells, and stood amongst the writhing mass. Resuming my journey up the hill, I did enter into a cloud of grey mist that did swirl down over the peak. Looking back, I could no longer see Tarek or Caswyn for they had disappeared into the gloom. The dampness of this cloud did seep into my clothing, and did make me shiver with cold. It was quiet. An unnatural silence did surround me, with the sounds of the battle below reaching my ears no more.

I climbed a hundred or so paces, and did leave the dampness of the cloud, where I found myself into fresh air once more. I was near the upland, and caution overcame me. I knew not what was awaiting me atop this tor, but I knew it was dangerous, and was possessed of a great magick. I listened hard for any sounds, but none did come to my ears.

So, I did walk on a bit further.

What did occur next I feel you may not believe, but I shall record it nevertheless. For I shall hope that you do realise that events on that day were strange and, therefore, open to the most unusual occurrences.

At first, I did think it was a heavy rainfall, but the force with which this did hit upon my head and shoulders was beyond that capable of water alone. I do wish that Tarek and Caswyn had been with me at that moment, for they would then have witnessed this most frightening trickery for themselves.

Hundreds of toads did rain down upon me, journal. You may gasp in horror at my writing, or you may laugh out loud at my apparent madness, but as I write this I do swear upon my honour that I do record the truth. They did fall from the sky above with such evil force, that I did have to crouch, and defend myself against their malicious assault upon my body.

I did begin to cry, I do admit to you. On this day, I had lost the man I did love more than anyone in this world, I had had the beasts of the underworld slithering over me where I did sit, and now toads were assailing me from the skies above! This was, indeed, powerful sorcery, and I did wonder what I would encounter next.

As the toads did land upon the earth, they did jump off into the grass, their sounds of obvious distress loud on the still air. At that moment I did think I would return down the hill, back to Calamar to grieve your passing, and mourn the loss of our life together. To forget about my vision, and the destiny that lay before me. Either course of action might mean the end of my life also. There was no assuredness that what I was to undertake upon this day would make any difference. However, this feeling did pass – I could not falter. I did owe it to you, dearest husband, to do as I had been bid by your father. This was the least I could do, and it did pale in comparison to the sacrifice for which you had recently given yourself.

Inhaling deeply, I did continue, eventually creeping on all fours, as I did reach the flat summit. Peering slowly over the ridge, I did make out the ancient standing stones ahead of me.

I knew these rocky crags from my vision. I did clamber around the huge stones that were scattered around the rim of the plateau as quietly as I could, and crouched as low to the ground as possible.

From within the circle of standing stones, I could hear a low chanting - a single, male, voice.

In the stones' midst stood a figure, his back turned towards me. He possessed a tall, lean, body, which stood naked as the day he did first come into this world. The long yellow plait that did hang down to his shoulder blades did seem oddly familiar, and was not unlike that which belonged to the traveller whom we had passed a few days before. I did not think this could be possible. I could see that his skin was covered in symbols, but symbols that I did not understand. He stood with his arms out-stretched to his sides, as if summoning something.

I hid behind a rock.

I could hear the beating of great wings from the other side of the hilltop, but could see nothing. Then I knew what it was immediately, for at that instant my vision be-came reality. As the stench of burning flesh and rotting meat did meet my nostrils, I could see the tips of bat-like wings as they did flap upwards. Each time they did ap-pear I could see a bit more of them, until at last the great beast managed to lift its hideous body over the top of the hill. It did fly low over the crags, the tips of its gi-ant wings only just clearing the ground. I could see its yellow eyes glowing, as it took in all around it, looking for its prey. Upon seeing it, I knew there was nothing I could do to it that would stop this beast from continuing its journey over the hilltop and down into the lowlands below.

I knew then my destiny; I had been given the task of destroying the sorcerer who had slain your father, Arthyen, and here he did stand, in front of me. With terror in my heart, I did know also, that he *knew* I was there.

It was then that I did instinctively reach out for the comfort of Orvin, and stroked the soft hair upon his head, when the recollection returned to me that I had left him safely within the walls of Calamar. In the briefest passage of time, after which this memory did return to me, I looked upon a dog that did sit next to me, with its tongue lolling out of its mouth. This great black beast turned its head slightly up-wards to look at me, before returning its gaze to the figure amidst the standing stones. It seemed perfectly at ease in my company and - oddly - apart from the first shock of seeing such an animal I, too, was at ease.

I have no idea from whence it had come, journal, but I have heard of strange black dogs that do roam our lands, although I had not seen one myself or personally known of anyone who had encountered such a thing. It had oft been the subject of Tarek's many tales on stormy winter nights, that did chill the blood, and cause sleep to evade the listener. Looking upon this animal now, however, it strangely did not cause any chills or discomfort.

This beast was much larger than Orvin, and heavier in body, and - as I crouched behind the rock - it was almost as big as I was. Its fur was long, thick, and as black as a starless night, and it sat silently and still beside me. I welcomed its company, and did rest my hand upon its shoulders, burying my fingers deep inside its warm fur. Its presence beside me seemed to take away the disquiet caused by my situation.

Far below in the lowlands, I could hear the screech of the dragon as it spewed out its flames of destruction on all who were unfortunate not to have been able to seek shelter. I felt that my heart did stop beating when I did think of you, Arthyen, for I had no idea whether your protectors had managed to take your body away from the great beast's fury. However, journal, I had to clear my head of all thoughts other than of what did stand before me. My hand did clench the fur of my new companion, but still he did not flinch from my touch.

Footsteps.

I could hear footsteps, softly making their laboured way over the rim of the hill, from where I had myself, emerged earlier. Gripping the hilt of Beroun's sword, I did turn my head slowly, and eased my body round so that my back was against the rock. A cold sweat overcame me, and I sensed that my other hand had become free. I know not where it could have disappeared to, but the black dog had gone from my side. I became confused as to where I was; my mouth had gone dry, my heart did beat fast, my belly did toss, and I found myself breathing with short sharp breaths. I pressed my body into the rock behind me, as if willing it to swallow me up from this place.

The footsteps were still approaching and then I did hear my name called in a low whisper. I immediately recognised Tarek's unmistakable voice. I had quite forgotten that he and Caswyn were following me up the hill. With relief that the footsteps belonged to friend rather than foe, I did respond as softly as I could, and was greeted with the sight of both men crawling towards me. Their company was *most* welcome, but I knew not how they could help. We sat huddled behind the rock as the fine rain soaked through to our very skin. I could hardly speak for my teeth were chattering with the cold. Their faces and hands were scratched and bloodied, and both men looked shocked. I did wonder whether they had met with such strange happenings as I had done on my climb, for their wounds seemed freshly made, and most unusual for wounds of battle. They did not seem inclined to talk, and seemed uneasy with their own thoughts. Unlike me, they had had the choice, and - looking at them then - I was sure they had wished that they had not followed my path.

"You need not follow me further, dear friends", I whispered. "The task that doth lay before me is for me alone, and I doth know not how all this will end. I have no de-

sire to cause you to come to harm. I doth urge you both to return down the hill and to the safety of Calamar".

I had paused, as once again the sound of the dragon reached my ears. I added slowly "Although, I am not sure that there is still safety within those walls".

It had been young Caswyn who had answered me, almost as soon as the last words had left my lips. I have grown to like this young man very much. Many weeks ago, reader, when he first came into my acquaintance, I remember that I did find him arrogant, but over time I think that this conceit has softened. I am quite certain that involvement in the battles of recent days, has caused him to realise that life in this world is – indeed - a fragile thing, and is to be fought for at all cost. I do believe that it has caused him great astonishment to realise that life does not revolve around costly clothing and a pretty horse. Dear old Wilf said once that it would come as a shock for him to see battle, and I think he was right, for the young man who sat shivering before me was definitely not the same as he who had questioned my arrival at the camp all those nights ago.

"I am here to serve you, My Lady, on my King's instructions", he did say. "However, I would not leave even if I could, for I know you to be a worthy charge, and I would offer my sword for your protection of my own free will".

I did smile weakly and, taking his cold hand in mine, did thank him, before turning to my dear friend Tarek. "And what of you, Tarek?" I asked. "Why do you follow me to this place? Have you had not enough of pain?"

"I did take an oath to watch over you in the King's absence, My Lady, and that oath still stands", came the reply. "But like the young lord here, I would have it no other way, and am honoured to stand beside you."

I did thank the great man also, but could not smile when he asked, "So, My Lady, what is the plan?"

For I had no plan. We could all hear the strange chanting that came from the figure amidst the standing stones, where he still stood with his back to us, and his arms outstretched.

There this person was, standing unguarded and alone; surely, it would be so easy. All I had to do was to send one well-aimed arrow, and all would be finished, but after all that I had endured to reach this place, and all that my companions had suffered also, this would seem too simple a resolve.

But I had to try.

Quietly I prepared my arrow. I knew it would not be as straightforward as usual, because my bowstring had been dampened in the rain. Slowly, and as silently as I could, I stood and took aim. Tarek and Caswyn remained behind the rock, with weapons drawn in readiness, as Tarek explained, "An assault may be required to finish him off".

I pulled the string back to my cheek, took steady aim, and released the arrow. It flew through the fine rain straight towards its target, but just as it reached its mark the figure jumped to one side and caught the arrow in his left hand. Strangely, he did not turn his head, but merely remained where he stood. I felt nauseous, and threw myself back down behind the rock. My companions looked quizzically at me, as I sat stunned at what had taken place.

"It is hopeless," I stammered, and I told them what had occurred. Both men turned pale, and I placed a hand on each of their shoulders. "I urge you both to leave this place, dear friends", I said. "The King is dead, and I do not hold you to your oaths now that he is gone. Go swiftly, for I fear the sorcerer knows of our exact location now".

They did not look at each other, but together they didst shake their heads in refusal. So be it. It would seem that we had an unspoken accord.

We decided upon a suitable attack, and it was agreed that we would separate and attack on three sides. Tarek and Caswyn crawled slowly away on their bellies, to other rocks that were dotted around the hilltop. I followed Tarek briefly until he had placed himself, and then I continued on my way further around. I found myself shielded in some bushes behind a large boulder. On looking carefully through the branches, I could see quite clearly the face of the man who stood so powerfully in the ring of stones. It was, indeed, the man we had passed on our way to Calamar, and now I knew why I had felt so uneasy about him then, and why I had had no desire ever to meet or see him again, when suggested that this might happen by my beloved Arthyen.

Suddenly, quite unexpectedly, the figure did drop into a crouching position, and did turn his head this way and that, not unlike an animal does when it has sensed danger and is trying to remain unnoticed. He was alert. I could see that in his expression, and his gaze darted about the hilltop. There was nothing for it, but for me to stand and challenge his power.

Reader, I have no recollection of how I felt at that moment. I can remember taking a very deep breath into my chest, and standing to my full height, with Beroun's sword in one hand, and mine own in the other. I must have looked a wild sight, for my dress was in tatters, my wet hair clung to my shoulders and back, and I knew that my face was streaked with dirt and blood. I took one step forward, and the sorcerer, remaining in his crouched position, turned his head to look straight at me. Another step forward, and he unwrapped himself to stand at his full height. I noticed Tarek appear to my left, and Caswyn to my right. The figure in the standing stones continued to stare at my approach, and seemingly ignored my companions.

We slowly walked towards the ring of stones, getting closer and closer until we reached the outer rim. I do not think we paid any attention to the fact that this man stood before us, totally naked, and covered with the strangest symbols we had ever seen, for we all knew that he was possessed of a great power and malevolence; he who stood before us was not necessarily a true image of what really existed. There was something at work here very much more powerful than a mere man.

I put my right foot across the rim.

The figure responded at once. He reached out his left hand, and then his right, and I heard my companions scream in terror. Looking first at Tarek, and then at Caswyn, I saw them raised to the skies, their feet running in the air, and their arms flailing around. Both had dropped their weapons, and I could see that where they lay on the ground, they were glowing red with some magickal heat. My companions were tossed around in the air above, at the whim of their captor.

There was nothing I could do, for as he did play with my loyal companions, he did not take the fix of his eyes away from me. When he had finished with them, he did toss them to the sides and they did fall from my view. I knew not whether they were alive or had fallen to their deaths down the hillside. But I *knew*, then, that I was alone.

I heard the familiar sound of the wings flapping to my right. I turned my head slightly, to see the great beast appear over the top of the hill, and the sky became darker as its shape lumbered closer. It flew over me, and the force of its wing beats did nearly blow me over where I stood, but I dug my heels into the earth, and stood firm. It circled overhead three or four times, before landing behind the ring of stones on a large outcropping of rock. It looked down upon the wizard, and stood - with its great wings curled into its body - patiently awaiting its master's unspoken orders.

I took a step forward, and the sorcerer's hand shot out in front of him, motioning as

if to turn an imaginary key. I felt a sensation as if something was turning my insides into a knot within me. It did cause me great pain, and I did fall to my knees in such distress. This I tried to avoid, for it did render me vulnerable, but the ache was beyond anything I had ever encountered, and with each turn of his hand it did bring another twist, tighter than before. My antagonist began to sing, very softly to begin with, but then his voice did get louder and louder. I have no idea what song did come forth from his lips, for it was in a foreign tongue, as were his incantations, but it did not seem to possess kindly words or a gentle meaning. I noticed the dragon rocking its head slowly from side to side with the words, occasionally a puff of smoke arising from its large nostrils. It was as if the song was sending the beast to sleep, for its eyes seemed to become heavier and heavier as the song continued.

The torturous touch of sorcery that had been thrown down upon me had ceased. I raised my head to see the wizard standing very still in his circle, his head hanging down with his chin touching his naked chest. He was still uttering the words that seemed to be lulling the great beast. Slowly standing, I took another slight step forward. No response came. Another step, and another, until I was standing within a sword's length from him.

I knew this was quite probably a trap, but what else could I do, reader? There was such a foul stench from his body, that it did cause me a great desire to be sick, but I did swallow back the bile, and did try my utmost to compose myself.

"You dare to come into my presence?" He spat out the words, raising his head as he did so, to look at me with the piercing blue eyes I remembered from when I did first see him on our road to Calamar. He cocked his head to one side and then the other. His hair was matted, and seemed to be moving of its own accord, which attracted my stare towards it. It doth cause the skin on my own head to irritate upon writing this, as I think back to that day.

I did not avert my eyes from his icy stare, thus acknowledging this threat, but stood firm, and returned mine own stare back to him. I did not answer his question.

"You are, indeed, very foolish to tread in this place", he continued, after he had realised that there would be no answer from my lips, and no withdrawal of my body from where I did stand in front of him. "I see that even your black dog has deserted you".

"Oh yes, I did see him here", the wizard said when he saw the look of surprise on my face at the mention of the black dog, for I knew not how he had known of its presence, as it had been well hidden behind the rock with me. "Do not forget that I see and hear all that I need and wish to, My Lady Ethna. But no do excuse me", and he

made a low bow in front of me, deliberately exaggerating the movements as he finished his sentence, "forgive my rudeness. I should, of course, address you as your Majesty, I believe?"

He knew my name also, but I was beginning to realise that this foul man was, indeed, not going to be such an easy foe to vanquish as I had at first hoped. However, had I *really* expected anything else, I do wonder?

I opened my mouth to speak, but it had become dry, and my voice had left me. I cleared my throat before attempting to try again, but before I could, the wizard started to giggle like a small child. Not the innocent laugh of a child at play, but that of a child after a wicked deed has been done.

I shall add quickly here, reader, that I do not mean any child of whom I have had the acquaintance, but one of those who have been possessed by evil spirits as told to us when we were, ourselves, young. Just as those children who have, until recently, sat around the campfires at night, with their arms around each other, or perhaps clinging to their mothers' skirts, as dear Tarek told his stories.

The wizard was still bowing low before me, when his giggling began. Quietly at first, then gradually getting louder, as he unfurled himself again into a standing position. Quite suddenly, and most unexpectedly, he jumped at me, and stood not a finger's distance away. He stood so close that I could not move - his toes were touching mine, and he sneered down at me as he said, "But of course, you are not going to be Your Majesty any more, are you, sweet thing?" and he placed his bony forefinger under my chin, and scratched the skin roughly, "for Arthyen is dead, is he not? And if he is dead, then you are still just a mere lady, are you not?"

I then felt his other hand clasp the flesh of my belly in his fist. "I see though, that there is still one more heir of Beroun to deal with."

I shrank away from him, and could feel the anger building up inside me. Each of my hands gripped the hilts of the swords that lay in their grasp.

"You will have to deal with his mother first," I growled, as I raised both my arms together. "Tell me, wizard, does your blood run red, or does it run as black as your heart? Perchance, I shall see, when I have wrenched it from your body, and have laid it on the dirt before me".

I felt something warm and wet on my toes, and with disgust realised that he was relieving himself on my feet. He continued to stare at me for a reaction, but – again -

he received none from me.

I crossed my arms, and placed the swords on his shoulders – one swift move, and his head would leave them. However, it was he that moved swiftly, and brought up his arms, and brushed mine away as if they were mere feathers. The weapons spun from the force of his touch, and went spinning to the farthest edges of the stone circle.

The wizard clicked his fingers, and I saw the dragon open his eyes. It snorted angrily, and fidgeted upon its rock. It did then stretch out each wing in turn, and flexed its muscles, before neatly folding them again against its body. It was ready to do its master's bidding, and I did fear what that would be.

Another click of his fingers, and the circle in which we were standing became suddenly enveloped in flames. My weapons lay outside the flames, and I found myself trapped inside this circle with him. I prepared myself for the end that had seemingly arrived.

Unexpectedly, he turned his back to me, and returned to the centre of the ring. I took the opportunity to shake my feet, and wipe them upon the grass. I heard him chuckle.

I watched as he raised his hands, and upon this command, I saw the dragon unfurl its wings, and - with one giant beat - launch itself into the air.

Turning once more, he threw out his left hand towards me. It was then that I did begin to fill dizzy, and my legs began to shake beneath me. I took a deep breath, and forced myself to think of something else. If I could make myself concentrate, I was sure I could beat this sorcery.

I took myself back to the first time you arrived at Cragnuth, Arthyen – I made myself picture every detail of that day. I took myself back even further, to the first memory I have of my childhood there. I pictured the glory of Cragnuth, as it nestled on the top of the rocky crags, with its banners flying in the warm wind that blew across the lowlands in the summer. I heard the call of the geese, as they made their journey over our battlements, to settle on the river below us.

Rhialdaron stood before me. I could see her quite clearly, and felt her place her hand upon my head. She bent forward slowly, and placed a kiss upon my forehead. "All is not as it appears to be", she whispered in my thoughts. "We are with you. We shall give you the strength you need. Trust in us".

I concentrated harder, and Martha's face passed through my thoughts, grinning broadly. She looked so happy, with her new infant swaddled in her arms. The vision of Martha faded slowly, and the face of dearest Leif appeared next, his golden hair gleaming in the sun. He laughed, and blew me a kiss, and I felt it land upon my cheek. As it did so, he disappeared from view. I shut my eyes, and heard the muffled sound of my father's voice. As it became clearer, I opened my eyes again and saw him standing before me with his hand wrapped around that of the woman who stood beside him. I have never before seen this woman, but I knew it to be my mother. I could see myself in her face – she had the same eyes as me, and her hair was long and dark like mine, as it flowed down to below her waist. In her arms, she cradled a baby – my twin brother. She gave the baby to my father, and walked over to me. "Sweet daughter", I heard her speak softly as she smiled and embraced me, before placing her lips on my cheek in the only kiss I have ever been given from her.

I did not want her to leave me, and did try to keep her embrace around me, but she slipped through my grasp, and returned to where my father and brother stood. I blinked and they were gone. I then felt a tug at my sleeve and, looking down, saw my sweet little boy, Hannel. It was good to see that he looked happy and well, as he smiled up at me. He took my hand, and gave me a tiny white flower, before he himself faded into the ethers.

I shall leave this entry for now, reader, for what I have just recounted has brought a tear to my eye and an ache to my heart. In addition, it is long past the hour of midnight, and my body is tired from sitting at my writing desk. Forgive me for not having the strength to continue more tonight, but I must lay myself upon my bed.

Fifty-second Entry

*I*ournal, to continue:

The sound of the mad cackling from the sorcerer returned me to the hilltop, but I felt stronger. My legs did not shake, and I no longer felt dizzy. He seemed confused that his sorcery had appeared not to have had any affect upon me. In my hand, I felt the delicate touch of the petals of the flower that Hannel had given me whilst I had briefly left reality. I did not, and still do not, understand how that flower came to be in my hand, but there it was, and its scent was, indeed, potent.

I felt an unknown power rush through my body, and I stood tall in front of my opponent. I spoke, but the voice that did come from my mouth was not that of mine. "You dare to try and take the life of the heir of the throne with your dark sorcery, little man?"

I was as shocked to hear this voice as the wizard who stood before me. Suddenly he seemed to look so small and puny in his nakedness. His scrawny little body seemed easy to break. There seemed to be recognition in his face at this voice. I noticed, also, that as this recognition came upon him, the dragon that did fly over our heads seemed to lose its strength, and faltered in its flight.

I do confess, journal, that I was as confused as the wizard appeared to be, at the sound of the voice that had uttered from my lips. I did not understand how Rhialdaron

could possibly speak through me.

My antagonist nervously scratched his arms and chest as if being irritated by small bugs. He seemed not to know what to do. He hopped from one leg to the other, and scratched at his head. Again, he tried to throw a spell my way, but it had no reaction upon me.

"You?" he spat. "I thought you were gone from these lands. Gone from this world. I vanquished you many years ago".

"It is clear that you did not", the voice from my lips replied. "It would seem that your magick is not as powerful as you have always thought, brother".

He wailed, shook his head violently, and then shouted in anger, which did make me shudder. The whole area seemed to shake with his temper. His attention to the dragon had gone completely, and it fell to the ground with a loud thud. To explain, I can only liken it to flying a kite on a windy day - when the wind suddenly drops, and the delicate structure seems to lose its strength, and comes to the ground as if it were a stone dropped from on high. There seemed to be no life in the beast, but I knew it was still with us, for I could hear its noisy breathing, and a gurgling from its throat.

"Look at you standing before me, Kegan", my voice continued. "Your body covered in symbols that mean nothing. Do you think those that come upon you will look at you, and think you are a great wizard covered in symbols of great sorcery? You are an evil little man, brother. It is time for your wicked light upon this earth to be snuffed out".

"And you think that by your words I shall be crushed?" Kegan had replied with poison in his voice. "You think you can overpower me in the body of this weak woman? She has no weapons, no magick".

"She has the sword of Beroun, little brother".

"You forget, sister, that it lays out of reach", he replied mockingly.

"I think not," was the reply.

Realising his mistake, he tried to reawaken the dragon. Through me, Rhialdaron laughed. "It was always your failing, brother, that you could only work one spell at a time. A true sorcerer can do many things at once. You have put all of your attention

on to me, and your vessel of destruction has become useless."

Through the flames came your father's sword, Arthyen. It flew to my hand, and I grasped it tightly. It did not seem to feel as heavy any more, and gleamed in the light from the fires.

Those flames did not seem so tall now either, and they seemed to be losing their strength as the minutes did pass. The sorcerer was agitated at his sister's sudden vocal appearance on the tor. Kegan really *did* seem scared of her and her power. Desperately he chanted words, gabbling them as fast as he could in a desperate attempt to awaken the dragon from where it had fallen. Slowly it raised its head, but it did not appear to have any energy left within its body. I could almost feel sorry for it as I watched it struggle to its feet, but I knew that it was not real; just a vision created by this man who stood before me.

Rhialdaron whispered inside my head, "I must leave you now, Ethna, for I cannot kill my own kith and kin. To do so would make me as bad as he in the eyes of the law of my people. It would bring dishonour upon our ancestors. It is enough that I have brought him to his downfall".

I shuddered, and pleaded with her not to leave me.

"I have given you the chance to do what has to be done. My brother is agitated, and cannot focus his mind on more than one thing at this time," she spoke silently. "Act now, and all will be resolved".

I felt her leave me, and I fell to my knees once more. I heard the wizard laugh. He seemed to think it was all over, and that he would be able to take me now that his sister had left.

I inhaled deeply, and stood up.

Anger and deep loathing filled me.

"For my people, I will crush you". I spat the words at him. "I shall conquer you in the name of those of my people that you have caused to leave this world. For them, and my unborn son, and my husband, you will breathe your last breath upon this earth this very day".

I slowly began to walk towards him, the sword ready in my hand.

"Prepare to die, foul little man. I shall not speak your name for it would burn my tongue to utter such a blasphemy".

I heard my own name called to my right, and turned my head slightly to see Tarek appear. He looked shaken and bruised, but seemed to be uninjured. There was no time to greet him properly, with the delight that I did feel, now I knew that he was still alive, so I raised my right hand to halt his approach. "Leave me, kind Tarek, this is my task, and I must do it alone".

My opponent was giving all his attention to the beast where it lay. He had summoned the energy to get it to stand, and it was reviving quickly now. There was no time to be lost, and I quickened my pace. I raised the sword above my head, and brought it down upon him. Just as the blade was about to pierce his flesh, he jumped to the side and the metal crashed to the ground. He laughed again, and I felt his foot kick my side. It unsteadied me, and I almost fell, but I managed to keep upright. I swung the blade up towards him, and caught him on his shoulder. He cried in anger, and spat at me, as he babbled continuously at the dragon. I could not afford to take my eyes away from my opponent, so did not know what the beast was doing. I had no need to, for I did then hear the unmistakeable sound of a wing beat, and I realised that he had succeeded in raising it to the skies again.

"My Lady", I heard Tarek shout. "Watch your back from the beast".

A chill ran down my backbone, and I felt the hairs on the back of my neck stand up. I could not - dare not - turn around to face the beast, but did continue to attack its master. Again, I raised the sword, and brought it down upon him, this time catching his arm. It did knock him backwards slightly, but he continued to babble the words to control the dragon.

I did feel no shame in attacking an unarmed man, for this man was perfectly equipped to defeat me without steel. I *had* to silence him.

He jumped around me, and tried to grab my hair to pull me down. Again, the blade swung, and he had to jump out of the way. "I will cut out your tongue", I hissed.

He stood, and waggled his tongue at me, but then looked startled, as he stared behind me. I felt a rush of wind at my side, and saw a dark shape lurch forward and launch itself at my enemy. The black dog had reappeared, and had its jaws firmly clenched around the left arm of Kegan. He cried out, and tried to shake himself loose of the teeth.

Again his power over the great beast in the sky seemed to wane, and I could hear its wings frantically trying to hold it amongst the dark clouds above us.

I rushed forward, and lurched the sword upon Kegan. I heard him gasp, as the metal pierced through his chest, but he could not fall, for he remained skewered upon the blade. The black dog released its grip upon the arm, and retreated a few steps, where it sat itself down upon the ground, its tongue hanging over the side of its bloodied jaws.

Kegan looked at me with the shock of disbelief in his icy blue eyes. They seemed to dull as I watched the life fade out of them. I twisted the blade around inside him, before putting my foot against his hips, and pushing him off it. He fell to the ground on his knees, but he would not give up his life that easily, and did begin to chant the words once more.

I bent down in front of him, and - ignoring the disgusting fleas that brought his hair to life - grabbed a fistful of it, and raised his head. I was amazed as to how light his body was, and managed to raise him up to a standing position, where he stood, his legs buckling beneath him. I placed the blade of my sword on his shoulder, before letting go of his hair, and as he began to fall again, with both hands on the hilt, I swung it into his neck. His whole weight was hung upon my blade, and I urged it further into his flesh and bone. It was a slow death, and he must have been fully aware of the sting of my sword, but I did not care. To rid our world of this evil monster was all that was important, and at that point I had no feelings of remorse as his headless body crumpled to the ground. His vile, little head fell to the ground, and rolled to a halt some feet away, but I was horrified to see that his mouth continued to utter the same words. I drew my dagger, and, reader, with repulsion, I did open the jaws of the severed head, and did slice out the tongue as I had so recently promised to do. As I did so, there was a deafening noise behind me, but I was too tired to react.

There came upon the hilltop an eerie silence.

I did turn to look for the dragon, but it had gone. Tarek did tell me later that as soon as I had relieved Kegan's head of its tongue, the beast had disappeared into a thousand tiny pieces of dust, that had been taken away on a gust of wind, that had blown across the tor at that very moment. It became clear to me then, that the sound I had heard, was - in fact - the demise of the beast.

The black dog left soon after the death of Kegan. He did stand, bark twice, turned and disappeared into the closing darkness.

I stayed upon the tor all night, journal. Tarek did look for Caswyn, and had found him dazed and confused, but alive, on the other side of the hill. They did stay apart from me, and did leave me to my thoughts. It was over. The enemy had been over-thrown. But what was to become of me now? My husband was dead and my beloved Cragnuth was gone. Where was I to go? And how was I to bring up our son alone?

There was much I did need to think upon, but on that night, all I wished to do was sleep, for I was exhausted in mind, spirit, and body.

Fifty-third Entry

J awoke to the sound of the dawn chorus, and an early morning chill.
Shivering, I wrapped my arms tightly around my body, and tentatively
opened my eyes to look around the tor. After a few minutes had passed, I
realised that I had fallen asleep with Kegan's severed tongue in my right
hand. Disgusted, I threw it away from me, where it rolled slightly in the dust before
coming to rest some way in front of me. I wiped my hand against my dress, to rid it
of the dried blood that had stuck to my palm. I continued to wipe my hand, as if to
try to purge it of the very skin that had been in contact with the disgusting piece of
flesh. I felt dirty and tainted, and wished to place my whole body into the freshest
spring water I could find, where I would stay whilst the waters took away the stain
and odour of evil that was upon me.

I had fallen asleep against one of the standing stones, and my back did ache from
where it had lain against the bare rock. Stretching myself as much as I could, I
stroked my belly gently, and arched my back to loosen the muscles that had tightened
during my fitful sleep and, slowly standing, I realised that my legs were aching from
the walk up the hill the day before. Dear reader, I cannot describe how alone and
desolate I felt at that moment.

Ahead of me, I watched as a pair of crows bickered over which of them would take
the prize of the tongue that they had between their beaks. It had not taken long for
them to find it, and they argued over it bitterly, for it was a much-prized piece of

flesh. Another two or three were busy pecking at Kegan's head. I looked away, not out of disgust, but out of despair. I knew that I would have to take my leave of this place, and make my way back down the hill, back to Calamar. I did not know what I would find there, but I knew that you would not be there to greet me, Arthyen.

I am not one to dwell upon my discomforts, reader, and I know that I have already told you this, but my body did ache so much that I was not certain how I would walk down the hill without fear of falling on the slippery rocks. I slowly bent to pick up Beroun's sword from where it had lain by my side; Kegan's blood long since dried upon its blade, causing its normal gleaming surface to be dulled. From the other side of the ring of stones, Tarek and Caswyn approached, and - seemingly from their appearance - the two of them had both endured as unrestful a sleep as I. We embraced each other as the old friends we had become, for no-one could experience such a day as we had yesterday, without becoming either dead, or firm friends from that day on.

What a sight we must have been, as all three of us returned from the hill that morning. All of us were tired, sore, and each one of us seemed to have developed a limp of our own. As Tarek and Caswyn went ahead of me, I watched the bundle at Tarek's side bouncing off his leg, as he walked unsteadily down the slope. Kegan's head would be displayed on a spike at the gates of Calamar, as a warning to all those who might dare to challenge the city's rule.

Whilst I had been on top of the hill, I had known not what had been occurring below me on the lowlands, and in the castle. I had heard the dragon's roar, but could only imagine what I might find, if I made it back down the hill alive. Here I was now, and I could see the devastation that had been caused by the great beast's attacks. The land around the castle walls was charred where Kegan's device of destruction had rained its deadly flames down upon it the day before.

Any bodies that had been left were burned beyond recognition, and we picked our way through the remains of both our own kind, and that of our enemy. I could only hope that you, sweet Arthyen, had been safely removed from this field, before it became a place of flame. We had been half-way across the battlefield, when it was a blessed relief to welcome the arrival of an escort from Calamar come upon us, with three spare horses to take us the rest of the way.

Once inside the gates, the first task was to enquire as to the whereabouts of your body, dear husband, for I wished to spend some time alone with you, before facing your council. I urged my mount on through the gathering crowds in the market place, and eventually arrived in the main courtyard near the Great Hall. Tarek and Caswyn had long since disappeared amongst the growing throng of people, and the

news soon spread from one to another of the events that had taken place the day before. Dear Tarek will certainly have much to tell in his stories after this.

Lord Keowyn greeted me as I dismounted, and I can recount that he had looked visibly shocked when he did see me, and did show much concern for my well-being, but I assured him that I was well in body but wished to pay my respects to the King. He did try, somewhat clumsily in his embarrassment, to thank me for what he called, my heroic deed, but I was not listening to such things as this. It did not matter. My tears would not be abated for much longer a period, and it was of the utmost importance that I did need to be on my own with you, husband.

Fifty-fourth Entry

ord Keowyn had smiled with sympathy, bowed his head at my wish and had escorted me across the courtyard through the hall doors. I did not pay much close attention to the direction in which he was taking me, for I was not, and as I write this, am still not, familiar with the arrangement of the castle or its town. It was not until the last corridor, that I began to recognise where I was. Lord Keowyn had bowed low, touched my arm, and retreated into the shadows of the passageway before I could utter my surprise at being brought to my own bedchambers. I could hear the sound of Orvin whimpering and scratching against the door, and I could not understand why he should be locked up inside my chamber, for he should have been allowed downstairs to the Great Hall to be with the other hounds.

I wished to open the door and let him free, but I also wished to see you, Arthyen, before I could carry on with any other daily business that would need to be tended to. I knew I would have to consult your council at some time soon, to talk about my position now that you had gone, but before I did so, I needed to be with you alone for a time to gather my thoughts. However, upon hearing my poor Orvin whimpering, I opened the door, and let him free to jump up in greeting. He jumped around like a puppy, and his tail wagged so much I thought it would come apart from his body.

Peering in through the open door, I could see that our chambers were dim; the drapes had been pulled over the windows, allowing only a thin shaft of light to pass

through, and it took me a while for my eyes to become adjusted to the darkness of the room. I could hear the faint sound of breathing, and as objects in the room became clearer, I could make out a shape lying on the bed. A rustle from the corner of the room alerted me, and I turned to see an old woman shuffle her way towards me. She curtsied and announced herself, through missing teeth, as Matilda.

"'is Majesty is sleepin' Ma'am", she lisped. "'e bin wake most of night frettin' 'bout you. I 'ad to give 'im a right potion to get 'im orf".

It had taken me a while to understand what she had just said - not her words, but their meaning, and it was after much shaking of my head that I realised what Matilda had actually told me. I could not believe that you were still alive, for I had seen you lying on the ground only the day before, and it had seemed so plain to me that all life had left your body.

I felt light-headed then, reader. My legs seemed as if they would carry my weight no longer, and I had to lean against the bed for support, for I did feel I would fall to the floor. Making a clucking sound, Matilda stepped forward to assist me, and putting her arms around my waist, led me towards a seat. She was fussing over me - I could hear her concerned voice, but I did not hear her words - my mind was too confused. The only words that echoed in my head were that you were alive, Arthyen. You had not left us alone in this world. Round and round these words went, until I believed that my head would burst.

The room stopped spinning, and I became calm again, although my heart still beat faster than it should. I stared across at the bed at your body, as it lay under the coverlet. You lay on your back, the covers pulled to your waist. Your head was bound around the forehead, and I could see a dark stain where the blood had seeped through. You looked so peaceful in your slumber.

"He is really alive?" I asked her. I felt my eyes misting. "This is not a dream? I could not bear it, if this was such."

Her face softened, and she took my hands in hers. As she replied, she gently shook them up and down, "'Tis not a dream Ma'am. I promise 'ee that 'is Majesty is only sleepin'."

I could not help but laugh and sob at the same time, journal. I grasped Matilda by the shoulders, and placed a hearty kiss upon her left cheek. In that moment, the heavy weight of sorrow and despondency lifted, and I was beside myself with joy that you had survived after all, and had not left your son and me alone in this world.

But then the cloud descended upon me again. "What of his wounds?" I asked quietly.

She seemed to be hesitant at answering my question, and a sense of foreboding washed over me once more.

"It is not just the wound to his head that ails him, is it?" I continued, holding my breath, as I feared the worst.

"No, Ma'am", she replied slowly, under her breath as if to try to hide the truth. "A small cut ☐ when 'e fell by all accounts, Ma'am". I could see she was struggling for words. "But☐.", she had faltered.

I took hold of Matilda's arm, pulled her to the farthest corner of the room, and demanded from her the full extent of your injury. Her resistance at telling me was scaring me, but I asked her for the truth in as calm a way as I could muster. Had I misunderstood her? Had she meant that you were alive, but would still die from your wounds? That would be too cruel. I could not bear that. To have you back after all this, only to lose you again? No, it could not be - it would be far too unkind. We live in a world full of pain and sorrow, of loss and despair, but surely, after everything, you and I did deserve *some* life together?

We sat on the window-seat, and Matilda told me the full extent of what did ail you, my husband. Slowly she told me that when your men brought you back to the castle, you were as if asleep. When you returned to wakefulness, and had tried to move, you found that you could not, as you had lost all sensation in your body, from your neck to your toes. Something dreadful had happened after your fall from Acha on the field of battle. Nothing could be done for you, but to bring you to your bed. Matilda had been charged with watching over you. She told me that it had not been easy, for you became irritated and angry at having to lie in such a hopeless manner.

"I lay no blame on 'is Majesty," she told me. "But 'e did curse sommut rotten, Ma'am. 'is words even made *me* blush".

I half-smiled at her, and - trying not to show my agitation - patted her on her hand. "Go on, *please*," I implored her.

It would seem that some feelings of life had returned to your feet and lower legs, and you had tried to rise from your bed. This had made you more agitated, for whilst they did have feelings, the rest of your body would still not move.
Matilda went on to tell me that, as the day wore on, my absence had caused you

much distress. No-one could explain where I was and you could not understand why Orvin was here, but that I was not. You had dispatched men to search the castle, riders to search the battlefield, and had eventually concluded that the enemy had taken me.

I am so very sorry that I had caused you such distress, sweet husband, but you must understand now, I hope, that I did think that you had taken your last breath of life in battle. When I had sat with your head in my lap, before I climbed the hill, you did not appear to show any signs of life at all. I am *so very sorry*.

It was after you had become so convinced of my fate, and had spoken so clearly of the evils that could have befallen me, that Matilda had then decided it best to administer a sleeping potion, but that had not been the easiest of tasks. "Several attempts I made, Ma'am, but 'is Majesty kept 'itting the cup out of me 'and", she explained.

At first glance, Matilda does not look like the kind of woman you would wish to have in charge of the care of your husband, let alone the King. She is a thin, scrawny woman of middling years, who has clearly not worn the age of time very well. She has lost most of her teeth, and appears to survive with two in her top gum, and one in her bottom gum, although the latter would seem to be holding on for dear life, for it does wobble so as she talks. She has a short upturned nose, and dark, almost black eyes, which are framed by very bushy eyebrows. In fact, journal, and I hope she will not read this, for she may become offended, she is a very hairy woman indeed! There are hairs sprouting under her chin, and I believe she will also develop more hairs on her top lip by the time the next two or three years have passed.

In all this, though, she is a lovely, kind, and caring woman, and she has taken care of you, Arthyen, in my absence. She has made you comfortable, has sat with you since they brought you here, and has seen to your every need. It is quite clear, from her explanation of what had occurred, that you had not been easy to care for. I am most grateful to her, and words will never be enough to thank her.

However, it was all I could give her, and I patted her hands and *did* thank her, from the bottom of my heart.

She shrugged her shoulders, and looked embarrassed. "'Tis nothing, Ma'am. 'Twas my position to care for 'im. I tell 'ee, though, I wish me own 'usband showed as much carin' an' concern for me, as my King does for 'is Queen".

Matilda did try to encourage me to have a rest myself, for she said I looked worn out, but I did tell her that I would rest once I had spoken to you, and she nodded her un-

derstanding, and left the room, slowly closing the door behind her, so as not to make any sudden noises to disturb you.

I approached the bed quietly so as not to awaken you, and - gently leaning on the soft fabric - stretched over to look at you as you lay in the shadows of the canopy. I wanted so much to awaken you, but knew that sleep was the best cure for you now. I placed a kiss upon your cheek, so softly that it would not disturb you.

Poor Orvin had been ignored since I had entered the room, so I left the bed, and took him to the window, where I did sit with him for a while, and did whisper to him all about the black dog I had met upon the tor.

The sun had moved around further to the west, and the light through the window had lost its brilliance, when I heard you stirring. I jumped up, nervous as to how I would find you. I slowly and silently approached the bed.

"Is that you, Matilda?"

I did not respond.

"Matilda?" you asked again.

"She is not here, husband", I replied tentatively.

I heard you gasp and choke back your emotion at hearing my voice. "Damn this body!" you cried out as you tried to move to see me. "I thought you were gone".

"As I thought so of *you*, Arthyen".

"Come closer, sweet Ethna, for I cannot move my head to see you. Let me look upon your face, for I have missed it, and thought I would not lay eyes upon it again in this world".

I approached.

"A fine state you do look, My Lady", you did try and smile, but your eyes gave away the sadness within you. "I thought I had lost you, beloved, for no-one could find you".

I did climb on to the bed and bent over to kiss you, before lying beside you, and tucking my arm across your chest.

"I am here, Arthyen, and I shall stay beside you now for many years to come".

"I thought you had been taken, Ethna".

"Husband, I had to follow the path your father told me of". I did then tell you of my meeting with Beroun, and how I had been bound by an oath of silence. I told you what had occurred upon the tor, and of the bravery and loyalty of Tarek and Caswyn.

You listened in silence.

As the story did unfold you wept, and when all was finished, you did say, "I am sorry you had to face the nightmare alone on the tor, Ethna. A lady should not have to face such terrors, and I am sorely humbled by your bravery. And all the while, here I lay as feeble as a newborn".

"I was supposed to do this on my own, Arthyen", I replied, stroking his cheek. "There would have been nothing that you could have done, for it was my path alone. It was meant to be."

You tried to move your head to look at me, but could not, and asked for a drink. The goblet by the bed was empty, so I climbed from the bed and took it to the pitcher, which stood on the table near the window. I heard you quietly say that you had wished that you had died in battle, rather than have to face the years without feeling or control over your body. I did not say anything, for I knew you had not wished me to hear.

Reader, no, I did not tell him then about our child - it was not the right time to do so.

Fifty-fifth Entry

Over these past few days, I am greatly relieved and happy to write, journal, that my dear husband's strength has returned slowly to his legs and arms, and he did leave our bed three days hence, eight days after my return, for the first time since that fateful day.

Beloved Arthyen, your movement was shaky, and your pace had been slow, but you did manage to walk across to the window in our room, and sit upon the settle underneath it. You are not one to sit idly, sweet Arthyen, and it was a difficult task to keep you from pushing your recovery too rapidly, but it has been such a pleasurable few days whilst we have been able to spend so much time together, alone with our own dreams and wishes. We have been able to sit together, and while away the hours of these warming days in our own solitude; something we have not been able to achieve very often since our first meeting. You have had some business of the council to attend to, and I have sat and given you my opinion when you have asked me of it. You do place much worth on my involvement, and I am grateful for the trust you do have in me.

I am shyly embarrassed to record that there has been much feasting and drinking in my honour since the death of Kegan. On the night after my return I had been ushered away from you, down into the Great Hall where I had been confronted with a sea of happy faces, already rosy with the effects of ale. The council did offer a toast to me for my deed, and all in the Hall raised their mazers to me. I felt my cheeks

redden, and did offer a toast also to Tarek and Caswyn for their help upon the tor. Again the Hall, as one, raised their drinks. The drinking and feasting soon continued, and I took my leave as soon as was reasonable for me to do so without appearing rude. I wished not to cause offence, and - as far as I am aware - for no-one has told me differently, none was taken. But I had wished to return to you, Arthyen, as soon as I could.

Such celebration has been continuing for these past few days, every night by all accounts, across the town in taverns, in houses, and even in the streets. It has all been good humoured, with only the odd occasion of a fight breaking out due to some careless tongue speaking out of turn. It is as it always is when ale is passed around. Tongues get looser, and tales start to drip from them with such ease, that can cause such offence so quickly and simply. A bad deed undertaken against another person, which both parties may have thought long forgotten, suddenly rear their ugly heads once more with the aid of the relaxing brew.

It has been a bright, warm, late spring day today, and you did manage to walk to the courtyard, and sit with me in the warming sunshine. The blossom on the tree under which we did sit, was in full bloom, and as the gentle breezes caught the branches, we were covered with occasional showers of delicate pink petals. It was on this day that I did tell you that I do carry our child. Of course, my news was received with great delight, and you did kiss me so heartily that I nearly fell backwards off the seat! Then we did laugh so loudly that our mirth did cause some disquiet from those who were passing. They were probably wondering whether their choice of King was, after all, a good one, no doubt. Someone is such a high position should act with more decorum, I am sure!

You have teased me constantly since my return, saying that once your body has fully recovered, and after your official coronation, you will hold such a feast and toast my heroic deed personally as Arthyen, King. You will also announce the news of your heir, to make it a double celebration of peace and life. I have implored you not to do so, but you insist, with a glint of mischief in your eye also, that, as King, you have a moral and honourable duty so to speak. I know your words have an element of truth, however. I am well aware that the people need to rejoice in victory, for it does encourage good morale amongst them.

Fifty-sixth Entry

On the morrow, you are to be crowned King in the sight of all your people. The crown of the Queen shall be placed upon mine own head one week later. More of this I shall, no doubt, tell you in another entry, but before that doth happen, you and I, sweet Arthyen, shall take our vows in the presence of the court, and all those who dwell within the walls of Calamar. Of this, I can be sure; my own people shall mingle with yours, and the day will be one of great rejoicing and feasting.

Today, to escape the frantic preparations of your coronation, you and I did sit together on the bench under our tree for most of the morning; my arm wrapped in yours, with my head upon your shoulder. We sat in silent contemplation and watched the tiny blossom cascade around us. Orvin did his best to try to catch some of the petals as they fell, but I do not feel that he had much success, but he seemed to have enjoyed himself snapping his jaws in a vague attempt to thwart their tempting downward fluttering. What a blissful way to spend a sunny spring morning, and I hope that we shall have many more like this one in our days together. It does seem hard to believe that so much has occurred since that autumn day I first saw you at Cragnuth; battles have been won, but many lives have been lost, and I can but hope that, at least for the foreseeable future, we can have peace in our lands.

Whilst Arthyen did attend to some business this afternoon, journal, I did take the opportunity to run down into the marketplace to buy some biscuits. I had the sudden taste for the crumbly rich texture and went on the hunt to find some. I spent

some time looking at all the wares for sale, and eventually found some fruited biscuits being sold by a young girl, who was chatting idly to a young man as he leant over the table to get as close as he possibly could to her. He was so obviously besotted with her, that he had not noticed I had walked up behind him. The girl cleared her throat as a warning, and he jumped up and back, his face as red as an apple. I smiled, and offered the girl my payment, and she smiled back and pocketed it in the pouch that hung at her waist, before turning her gaze once more to the young man. Clearly, neither of them realised who I was, and it did not concern me at all.

Growing up in Cragnuth as the daughter of a Lord, I have long been used to guards standing to attention, and townspeople bowing or curtsying wherever I go. But there I knew everyone, and it seemed somehow easier. Here, it is different, for there are many people I do not know and I find it awkward on occasions when I come across someone who gets flustered at meeting me, and attempts to bow or curtsy when they are suddenly faced with the woman who will soon be their Queen. I know it is unfair of me to come across the people in such an unguarded way, and perhaps the old council members are correct in their wishes for me to be escorted wherever I go, but for these last few days before my coronation, I wish to remain as Lady Ethna. Therefore, when I come across someone who knows me not, I find it most welcome to be able to appear ordinary in his or her eyes, and blend in with my surroundings.

So, upon making my purchase, and leaving the two young lovers to their wooing, I rushed back through the market, and on up the steps to the courtyard with the biscuits firmly in my grip. I was sure that they would not be as good as Seren's, but, as I have told you much earlier in this journal, Seren makes some of the most delicious biscuits I have ever tasted, and I am certain that there is no-one else alive who could better her method of mixing and baking them. However, this is beside the point. I merely add this event, journal, to record how wonderful it was to wander freely through the town this afternoon. It brought back so many memories of my time at Cragnuth, and it was good to feel so liberated from the many burdens that have rested so heavily on my heart over the last months. I feel truly happy for the first time in many a long day, and cannot help myself from shouting out greetings, and waving at familiar faces and, also, to those who bow before me.

As I have written before, I am not sure that those members of the council, who prefer to uphold the old ways, approve of my wandering around unchecked and unguarded. But I will not be told to whom I may or may not speak. I will not be prevented from playing hide and seek with a group of children if I so wish, or for sitting with the women as they spin their cloth outside their tiny shacks, and talk in quiet tones on such interesting tittle-tattle such as the behaviour of the wife of someone who has strayed from her path of fidelity. Some of those who are living within the

protective walls of Calamar are my people, and I will not cease to speak to them just because I am now to be Queen. Besides, the day of my coronation has not yet come upon me, so those stuffy old men of the council can throw me glances of disapproval as much as they wish. They can sit and fidget with their fingers outstretched across their swollen bellies, and frown to their hearts' content, for it means not a thing to me. When the time comes for me to act with the demeanour that befits the station of Queen, then I shall, but for now I am still Lady Ethna, and I shall make the most of these days while I can.

I discern that you disapprove of some of my wilful actions, dearest husband, but I know also that you understand my wish to hold on to as much of my freedom as I possibly can, until it is gone, as I know it, forever. Deep down, I believe that you do feel the same, husband, and I am sorry that for you it is harder. For you to be as you were before will be impossible, for you are soon to be King, and will have to leave much of your old ways behind, for you will be more confined with the business of council than be able to roam around the lands as once you did. It is clear to me also, that you are full of apprehension about your coronation tomorrow. Like me, attention is not something that you favour, and I know that you will be much relieved when darkness falls, and the day is done. As, dear reader and dear husband, will I.

Kegan's head is still in residence upon its spike at the gates of the city. The persistent pecking of the crows has eaten most of its flesh away, but still it sits there being pelted by stones, rotten fruit, or anything that the townspeople can lay their hands on as they pass through the gates. Hungry beaks have long since stolen Kegan's icy blue eyes, and the empty dark sockets stare out across the lowlands. Beloved husband, you did see him for the first time this evening, when we passed through the gates to take a gentle ride across the lowlands together.

You have not been out of the castle since peace was restored, and - with four guards accompanying us at a respectful distance - we took our horses out across the lowlands to the foot of the tor. I know you are deeply upset at the loss of Acha, for the grey mare had been your constant companion for many years, and through many battles. Although a magnificent beast - as black as the darkest night, the horse that you were mounted upon today is no match for the gentle Acha, but you bore your melancholia well.

"I shall never be able to show my thanks for what you did face upon the tor, Ethna," you said, as we halted our horses at the base of the hill. "Although it would seem that it was written that you should face Kegan as you did, it was still with the utmost bravery that you did so. If it was not for you, then all of these lands would be ruled under the dark wizard's magick, and I do, with fear, imagine what would have become

of this place," you continued as you stared back towards the castle.

"One of the things I think about most," you had carried on, as you stared across the lowlands. "On that night you were missing, and I knew not what had occurred with you, I remember thinking that before I left the castle walls that last time, I had not spoken with you."

"I do not understand," I asked you.

"On the eve of battle, words that should be spoken should come forth from a warrior's lips, for he may not be given another chance to utter them", you explained. "It is something that all warriors know so to do to their loved ones, before leaving for battle. I did not do so, Ethna, and I have oft thought about it since. If you had not returned to me it would have made our parting even more unbearable, for I forgot to say them. I did not tell you how much you have become a part of me. I know not how I could have suffered to live, knowing I had lost you without speaking such words".

I stretched out my hand towards you, and wrapped my fingers around yours, giving your hand a gentle squeeze. My dearest, gentle Arthyen, you turned to look back at me with sadness in your eyes. "It is in the past," I told you softly, smiling gently. "There is no need to think upon what evil may have been, for it will *never* be. Be assured, I know what the unspoken words would have been, for they were in my heart already, and are still there."

You had reached across then, and had run your hand down my hair, but our quiet moment was soon interrupted, and gentle reader, in such a way as to cause my blood to run cold as it coursed through my body.

Startling us both from our peaceful moment, an eagle came screeching over the top of the hill. As it soared down from the skies above, it cast a giant shadow around us where we sat upon our mounts. It brought a chill to my bones, as the events of the past few days were still fresh in my mind, and, for my part, the sound of this bird was too reminiscent of Kegan's beast, and the terror it wrought down upon us. As I ducked involuntarily, I watched you inhale deeply, and flinch in your saddle. In the briefest passage of time, we had both realised where our minds had taken us, and upon realising that it was but a bird, we both visibly breathed a sigh of relief. Somewhat shaken at our vulnerability, we urged our horses onwards at a steady walk, and slowly made our way back to the castle, where we would rest before the solemnity of the ceremony that is to be held tomorrow.

Fifty-seventh Entry

oday you were crowned King. I watched with pride as you knelt before the throne, and had the golden circlet placed upon your head. When you arose, and turned to face your citizens, there was a great cheer from within the Hall, which rippled down the rows of people, until it reached the great doors at the back. Then I heard another cheer erupt outside, as the crowds there received the message that you were now their King. I could hear the sound of cheering outside for many moments, after the first had echoed around the Hall.

I could see your eyes searching the faces of the spectators, and when your gaze settled upon me, you smiled, and beckoned me forward. I curtsied, returned your smile, and crossed the Hall to you. Taking my hand in yours, you had kissed the back of it, before wrapping my arm in the crook of yours, and placing your hand over mine.

Dearest Arthyen, I could feel your body trembling, as we walked down the middle of the Hall together to the great doors, which were pushed slowly open by the guards as we approached them, and out into the sunlight where we stood together for a few minutes, while the crowds cheered again. I could see that you were tired, and I implored you to return to our chambers to take rest before supper. There would be many people to dine, and you would have to possess the sharpest mind in their presence. Now you are King many favours and questions will come forth, and you will have to sharpen your wits to be ready for them. Now will be the time to make your character known, for you will be sorely tested for any weaknesses by those who may

have aspirations to oppose your rule.

You did not need much persuading, dear husband, to retire for a few hours. Your pace quickened, as we retraced our steps down the Hall to the archway that gives access to the corridor to our private chambers. I had to suppress a giggle, and check your speed, for your desire to be absent, I felt, was becoming a bit too obvious.

"It is not that I wish to abstain from the kingly duties, Ethna," you explained earnestly once we had entered our rooms, away from the prying ears and eyes of anyone else. "Perhaps my eagerness to escape the Hall *was* misplaced, but I do feel ill at ease with the council still. I have memories of their treatment to my uncle whilst he was alive and although I know his main antagonists have been disposed of, I am still unsure of the others. I wish to speak to Lord Keowyn alone, Ethna, before we dine tonight."

"As you wish, husband," I replied, understanding fully, and not feeling at all upset at your desire for me not to be present. "You wish me to find him?"

"Indeed not, fair maiden, but I would request that you dispatch one of the guards to do so".

This I did, but did add that I wished to speak with the Lady Igraine also. I have neglected her lately, since my return, and I am hoping that she and I can resume our friendship, now that events have taken their course, and the truth has been revealed. Besides, whilst Lord Keowyn and you, Arthyen, were talking politics, it was my hope that the Lady Igraine and I could discuss our own thoughts on our futures.

Whilst you and Lord Keowyn debated the character of those of the King's council, that is exactly what we did - not only the blessing of our own vows, Arthyen, but also the Lady Igraine's planned union with Lord Keowyn.

It will be in three days time that you and I shall renew our vows. I have been poked and prodded by so many needlewomen in the past few days, that I do feel like the very pincushion from whence the pins did come. I should perhaps not reveal here the exact details of my gown, for if this journal were to be found by someone it would spoil any surprise I may have, but I cannot keep it a secret for I am about to burst with excitement. Reader, it is made of the softest and lightest pale blue velvet, trimmed around the sleeves and neck with the softest fur. A thin covering of lace hangs from my shoulders, and down the entire length of the dress, which falls away behind me. Upon this lace has been sewn a hundred or more tiny pearls. My head shall be covered with a veil of the same lace, topped with a simple bronze circlet

woven with some of the wildflowers that can be found sheltering against the walls of the castle. My feet will be covered with deerskin shoes, that have been dyed the nearest blue to match my gown.

I am to walk from the great doors of the Hall, down through the sea of people who shall be witnesses of our union. You, dearest Arthyen, will wait at the far end for me, where we shall meet, just as the sun begins to set, and I shall place my hand upon yours, as we stand before Father Lorcan once more. We shall exchange our words of promise in the sight of all those members of the court, and there will be no doubt, then, of our union amongst those of the council who perhaps were distrustful of it ever taking place before.

Fifty-eighth Entry

What a wondrous few days it has been, dear reader. The official blessing of our union took place three days ago, and tomorrow I shall have the crown of Queen placed upon my own head.

Our vows were exchanged in sight of those who may have doubted that such a ceremony had taken place before. This time they would be taken in front of all of our people, and I walked down the Hall as the musicians played a joyful tune. My way was covered with freshly laid rushes, herbs, and petals, that scented the Hall with such a heady smell, it reminded me of summers at Cragnuth when we used to gather in such things for our own Hall. I remember that I blushed to see so many people filling the great expanse, and it seemed to take an eternity to reach you. I could see you standing at the far end, your crown upon your head, and your dress of that of King. Your father's sword hung in its sheath at your side – its metal gleaming in the light from the candles that were placed around the Great Hall. My King, you looked so handsome, and I felt a flutter in my belly as our son kicked inside me. At last I found myself standing beside you, and you took my hand in yours, as we faced Father Lorcan.

This time, you did place a ring of gold upon my finger, and did pledge your troth, as I did for you in return. Father Lorcan laid his hands upon our heads in turn, and renewed his proclamation that we were now husband and wife. When the ceremony was over, we walked together, hand clasped in hand, and moved slowly down the

Great Hall to the open heavy oaken doors. A jester capered in front of us, scattering freshly gathered leaves and petals on our path, as he led us to the crowds outside. Into the darkness we emerged to a great roar of approval from those well-wishers outside, who had not been able to squeeze themselves in to witness the blessing inside. A thousand candles lit the bailey, musicians played, and acrobats performed their art with great skill.

We returned to the Hall for a feast of great proportions, as the festivities continued outside. I do admit to having a twinge of sadness on several occasions, as I remembered those who could not be with us to share our joy – Martha and Hannel, in particular, would have *so* enjoyed themselves. Martha would have been grinning from ear to ear, boasting at how 'she knew as much - that we would be wed', and little Hannel would have probably been sitting on my knee throughout the feast, or playing under the long table with Orvin. I also missed my mother – a daughter should have a mother present at her marriage, and – strangely – I missed my father. He, at least, would surely have been puffing out his chest at the thought of his daughter marrying so well. In fact, that would probably have been all he was thinking about.

There were celebrations that did continue until well after the sun had set, and it was not until the early hours of the next day, that Arthyen and I did manage to sleep, for the feasting and dancing could be heard all around the courtyard.

I shall curl up with my husband - my King - tonight, journal for the last time as Lady Ethna. I am nervous of tomorrow, and of the responsibilities that will come with it. I will do the best I can to be as good a Queen as is possible. I shall support my King, and defend him to the best of my abilities.

As we are resting, Kegan's head still sits upon his spike by the main gates. Tonight the moon will be throwing her pale light upon the picked bones of his skull, as he continues his eyeless stare across the lands he tried, and failed, to take for his own.

Fifty-ninth Entry

Forgive me, dear reader, for not writing for such a long time. Arthyen and I have been so busy with matters of the court, and have spent much time enjoying our time together. The seasons have changed, and with the autumn now upon us, it will soon be time for me to become a mother. Our child has been testing his muscles, and his kicks have given us both great amusement in the last few weeks. We have spent many a time watching his tiny feet and hands as they have pressed against my swollen belly. I will not say that it has not been uncomfortable, for he has caused me much discomfort as his time draws near, but I do not mind his constant fidgeting, for I know that it means he will be strong.

As I pen this entry I do think it may be my last for some time, if not forever. I shall try to occasionally pick up my quill, and tell you about events as they take place if I think they may be of interest to you. I fear, though, that my time may be taken up with other duties, and - of course - motherhood. I will try to let you know how my life with Arthyen doth progress, but I really do not know whether I shall be able to do so as much as I would wish.

It is late, reader. The candle has nearly burned out, and it has been a long day. I find myself not wishing to say goodnight to you, for I know I shall miss these scribblings. 'Tis a sad thought after all this time, for I have grown used to your company. I have never seen you, and will never see you, reader. I do not even know whether anyone

will actually ever come across this journal, but to think there may be someone out there who may read this, has kept alive my desire to recount, this albeit brief episode of my life. It has been a long road since I first put ink to parchment, and my life has changed considerably since it began – I have changed also. Through all the sadness and loss, my life doth now appear to be taking a new path, and I am excited at my future. I have grown stronger and wiser.

I am tired, I am repeating myself, and I know that now is finally the time for me to bid you farewell.

Peace and life's blessings to you all,

Ethna

Reader, I cannot leave without writing one last thing ... you have afforded me great comfort through these troublesome times, and have borne witness to my fears, hopes, and desires. I give my heartfelt thanks to you.

Tis I, Arthyen, son of Beroun and King of Graelin who doth now take up the quill.

I write with great sorrow in my heart, for my beloved Ethna did pass into the other world to search for her ancestors nearly one year ago. I did not find it in my heart to look upon her belongings until this morn, when I did lay eyes for the first time upon this journal. I did not know that our early days had been recounted in such depth, and it has brought back many memories to my weary head, and tired heart. I do remember that day our eyes did meet for the first time, with such clearness of memory even now. It has brought tears to these tired eyes of mine, to recollect those times. Her lovely face is forever in the forefront of my mind.

For my Queen's efforts in recording those days, and for those of you who may follow them, I do feel it right and proper that I do try to give her journal an ending. To begin, I shall endeavour to recall what did happen to some of those named therein. But you must forgive me if I neglect to mention someone, for I am old and my memory is not as keen as it once was.

Although many of those mentioned in my beloved's journal have left this world, they did go in peace and most did leave their own heirs to carry on their good name.

Ethna's beloved Orvin did leave us in his sleep at a ripe old age. I do not think my

Queen did ever truly recover from his loss, for he had been her constant companion for many years. She did lay him to rest in the shade of her favourite tree in the courtyard garden here at Calamar. It is where she used to sit reading in the long days of summer, while he did take his place at her side. I do oft sit there myself now, for it doth bring me closer to them both. In truth, it is where I sat whilst I read this journal, and it was there that we had sat when she told me she carried our first child.

Little Vala did return with Wilf to Cragnuth many years ago, when Ethna's people returned to rebuild their town. Wilf returned to his duties as marshal, with the aid of Gryffyd who, as expected, took over the role upon Wilf's death. Vala outlived him, but she joined him not long after. Sadly, over the years she could not hear very well and became completely blind in one eye, and lost most of her sight in the other. Her decline came rapidly, but she still managed to wag her tail in greeting when we visited Cragnuth.

Old Seren took up her baking skills again, and every time we visited Cragnuth, upon our arrival, Ethna insisted on paying her a visit. I have to admit that I do agree with my wife's undying protestations that Seren's biscuits were the best in the land.

With Ethna's agreement, and complete approval, the Lord Keowyn and Lady Igraine were given Cragnuth as their home as a wedding gift from us, and they have lived among her people in great contentment. By all accounts, they are most respected, and much to Ethna's joy, Cragnuth has thrived under their watchful guidance. They were blessed with five children, of who four have survived. To their most obvious distress, and ours, their eldest, their only daughter, died when she was but three years of age.

Tarek lit the fire of his smithy once more and up until the day he died, his tales continued to enthral all who gathered around the campfires to listen to him. Of course, by the time his life on this world had ended, he had many more stories to add to his long list, and - although I am sure his experiences on the tor were greatly embroidered - I am aware that it is still one of his best-loved sagas, and one that I know is still told, by his eldest son, to this day.

Airic, the chandler at Cragnuth, returned there with Bertha, and resumed his work of making the candles to supply the light to the castle once it was rebuilt. He continued to keep his own company, and crept around the Great Hall in the shadows, much as he had done when my beloved Ethna lived there. Upon our visits, Lord Keowyn and Lady Igraine often commented to us of his strangeness, but they were never left without light, and contentedly accepted his self-inflicted seclusion. He and Bertha did not have children, but still live there happily in their winter years.

I must, sadly, add here, also, that Hamel - father of Willard, Rafe and Hannel - was never seen again. Willard remains here at Calamar, whilst his brother, Rafe, returned to Cragnuth upon its rebuilding. Both are married, with children of their own, and have both become strong men, despite the grief that marred their younger years. They are sons to be proud of and I am sure Hamel would be content with how they entered into manhood so nobly.

My dearest Ethna and I did visit Cragnuth on many occasions, and always managed to slip away and visit the valley. As King and Queen we were never allowed to travel far alone at Calamar, but once back at Cragnuth we could slip away without worry of being followed. As most of those at Cragnuth knew of the valley's existence, we could enter the forest, and through the waterfall to the entrance of the valley, without having the fear of letting slip its exact location to prying eyes.

Whoever may be reading this may ask whether we did see the mysterious island again and I can answer this simply. Yes, reader, we did.

Exactly one year after her night on the tor, Ethna insisted that we pay a visit to the valley in the hope of laying eyes on the island once more. She seemed to instinctively know that it would reappear before us, and after that first time, it became a regular visit once a year on exactly the same date. Even when her belly was heavily swollen with our third child, Githa, did she insist on travelling to Cragnuth to see the island.

Every year, upon our visit, although we knew deep within our hearts that it would not fail us, we still half-doubted that it would appear. However, as always both Rhial-

daron and my father, Beroun, were standing at the gates to welcome us. We never crossed the stones, but stood on the banks of the river and silently paid our respects in thanks for their assistance on the tor, and in saving the lands from the evil grip of Kegan. I think Rhialdaron spoke to Ethna, but no words were ever spoken aloud. Ah, and always my Ethna looked so serene on our return journey through the valley after the visits.

She brought forth our third child, our second daughter, into the world at Cragnuth and I do swear that Githa has been blessed with something special as a result. She is able to see things that others cannot, and has - on more than one occasion - predicted events well before they have occurred. To some, she would be thought of as a sorceress - and this does cause me some concern - but to all of us at Calamar, and at Cragnuth, we know it to be a precious gift. Ethna thought, up until the day she left us, that Githa would have a destiny to follow, just as she herself had all those years before.

Of those of my men, whom you may know of more than others, I shall mention Caswyn. When he joined my army, Caswyn was but a young man, green of the experiences of the world. I know, at first, many thought him arrogant, my Queen included, but it became clear that this was just an unfortunate and misguided judgement of him. He was merely young and easily embarrassed, and in defence of this, he portrayed himself wrongly. However, he became a man in those few months, and is now one of my most trusted men-at-arms; a captain in my army, and much admired by those under his command. He recovered well from the incident on the hilltop, and it was not long after that his heart found that of a young maid at Calamar. Poor Caswyn took much teasing about his wooing, but he took her as his wife, and brought up, very well, three children of his own.

And, what of my Queen?

My dearest, courageous, Ethna did live until her fifty-eighth birthday, and she did leave this world without suffering pain for too long an age. I am bereft at her loss, but thankful that the start of her journey caused her to endure as little discomfort as possible. Her passing into the other world came one warm autumn evening as she sat in her much-loved spot, under her favourite tree in the courtyard. I had been sitting next to

her, with her hand curled in mine.

My Queen never complained when she felt unwell, but throughout our last few weeks together, I had seen discomfort etched upon her face. At night, sleep had become more elusive to her, and I knew she tried so hard not to disturb me in my slumber. She had not realised that I, too, lay awake with her.

On that evening, we had slowly walked to our normal seat to spend some time together, before I left to attend some late business. Her steps had been slower than usual, and she leant upon me more heavily than was I was accustomed to. Although it was still warm in the sun, there was a cooling breeze that wafted around us, and I sat close to her, with my own cloak wrapped around her too. She had laid her head on my shoulder, and talked of her beloved Orvin and of her hopes for our children. I knew, deep within my heart, that our time together was drawing to a close, and I took her hand in mine, and held it gently as she softly spoke. Each word seemed to tire her, and her speech became slower; the need to take a deep breath after each word becoming more urgent.

We talked of past times, and - as we often did - we spoke of those days when we first met. She shivered, and I had pulled her closer towards me. She pointed out the half-crescent moon in the sky, and said: "Look, Arthyen, the moon is impatient to show herself to-night. The sun has not yet set in the far west, but she is already revealing her pale face to us".

There had been two barks, way off in the distance. The sound penetrated through the everyday hum of Calamar. My Queen had lifted her head slightly, and had asked me if I had heard them. "'Tis the black hound, Arthyen", she whispered. "After all this time, he has returned". She looked up at me, her face more deathly in its paleness than ever before. We spoke nothing more of it, for we both knew what it foretold. With dread in my heart, I stroked her cold cheek, kissed her forehead, and urged her to lay her head once more upon my shoulder.

I had stared ahead of me, and had silently pleaded for more time with her. I did not want to be left alone – I knew not how I would live without her at my side. She had become my

confidante, my companion, and my advisor, as well as my wife. She had a keen eye, and her instincts were strong - I had long trusted her judgement, and had oft consulted her for her opinions. She was never afraid to tell me when I was wrong, but she was quick to commend me when I was right. I have known no other woman like her, and was ever proud to trust her with my life.

She never recorded this in her journal, reader, but Ethna had been born a daughter of the moon - she had come into this world one winter's night, when the moon was at her fullest. Hence, I looked up at the sky, and wondered whether the moon had appeared at the same time as her golden brother, on the evening of her daughter's departure, so that she, too, could see my Ethna's face once more, before she was gone forever upon these lands.

Softly I had heard Ethna speak, and I felt her weak grip on my hand give a slight squeeze. "Do not linger long before you join me, husband, for I shall miss you until we are together again."

Reader, I know not when I realised that there had been a longer pause than usual after this last utterance, but I slowly became aware that her body had become limp against mine. When we had first stepped out that late afternoon, the sky was blue with the promise of more warm weather on its way, before winter descended its barren hand upon the land. In those last moments, as we had sat, it began to change. Unexpectedly, dark clouds had swept across the sun, taking away what warmth there had been. It was at that moment, as they did so, that I knew she had gone - she had left with that warmth - and her passing had left me in the cold gloom. I sat with her lifeless body for many minutes, before one of my advisors came looking for me. Even though I knew that my beloved wife had left on her last, long journey, I had continued to talk to her, stroking her head as I did so. My advisor, realising that she had gone, had shuffled off in great haste to the Hall, to return shortly afterwards with our sons. There was nothing I could do, but follow helplessly and forlornly, as they gently carried their mother's limp body back to our chambers.

We did have many good years together, journal, but I do miss her today, as much as I did when she did leave me. I know she waits for me, for I do hear her breathing next to me

as I lay my head upon my pillow at night. I am ready to join her. I am to celebrate my own sixty-fourth birthday this year, but I do not know how I shall face it without Ethna by my side. Each day becomes harder, and every day I remember those last words that left her lips. I feel guilt at leaving her waiting for so long, and I feel desperation that this body of mine does not give up, but continues to live.

When my time does at last come upon me, I know that there will be many different things that I shall miss, but none can possibly compare with how I miss my beloved Ethna. I could never replace her, nor would I wish to. My pledge to her in front of our people was not only until death, but far beyond. My heart yearns to see her again – I long to hear her voice, and feel her hand in mine.

I am ready to hand the crown and kingdoms to our eldest son, Hannel – I know he is ready to receive them, and will be a great King. He is, of course, the son who Ethna did carry on that day she climbed the tor to face her destiny. I do think that their experience together upon that high top, whilst he was still in her womb, did give him the bravery he doth possess - a courage his mother held until her last day upon this world.

I am sure, also, that his name comes as no surprise to all that do read this, for you will know of the love we both did hold for that little boy who touched our hearts all those years ago. We had no hesitation, whatsoever, in bestowing upon our first born, such a valiant name.

You will not know, of course, that Ethna bore me five children. Two sons and three daughters - Hannel, Edythe, Githa, Edan, and Leoma are the names we gave them. All of our children, except our second and last daughters have wed well, and are happy in their lives and have produced sons and daughters of their own. I am not suggesting that our dearest second daughter, Githa, is unhappy in her life, but just that her chosen path is different from the others. She left Calamar in her seventeenth year - it did not come as a great surprise to us, but was worrisome nevertheless. One morning, she packed what few belongings she wished to take with her, and walked through the great gates. Ethna was greatly distressed at her daughter's sudden leave-taking. It was a worry that gnawed at her every day for years to come, but she could but hope that her second daugh-

ter's path would treat her well.

Githa would not tell us to where she was travelling, but we had seen purpose in her dark eyes. As I have already written, her mother and I both had always known that her life would not follow a normal path, and I hope, still, that wherever her destiny did lead her, that she is content. Since she left, we have seen her but twice - the last we saw of her was on the occasion of her sister, Edythe's, union. It was on the morning of Edythe's leave-taking for the ceremony at her husband's manor, that quite unexpectedly, Githa arrived at Talamar. She had taken all her family by surprise a few years earlier also, when she had done likewise, on her elder brother's wedding. It is only too clear that her powers are very strong.

Githa is most like her mother in temperament. She doth possess her mother's inner strength and courage, and is - in this way - most like her out of all our children. Of all our sons and daughters, it is Githa who looks the most like me, however. She was born with a head of dark wavy hair, and I can remember, even to this day, how Ethna announced upon our daughter's arrival how much she resembled me. I find myself laughing fondly, now as I write this, when I recall how Ethna told me quite firmly that our newest daughter's ears looked just like mine, and how her wailing for milk reminded her of my singing!

Pausing here, I must add that I do find it most odd that she did not return to her home upon her mother's passing. After the past two occasions, we had all expected her to do so. It has, ever since, caused me great anguish to think that, perchance, some ill has befallen her.

Edythe, our eldest daughter, has her mother's laugh. Even to this day, sometimes, when I hear her, I feel as if Ethna is with me again, and I have often halted in whatever task is upon me at the time, to turn to search for her. When she smiles, Edythe's mouth curls at the ends, just as her mother's did, and her eyes sparkle with the same mischief. To look at her sometimes it is like looking at my Ethna, for Edythe's expressions liken to hers so much. I do not often see Edythe these days, alas, as she is busy with her own life five day's ride from here.

 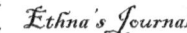
Little Leoma is sweet and quiet, and she possesses the tenderest of hearts of all five of our children. I think it was she who suffered most upon her mother's leaving. Many people have told me that it is because she was the last of our children. Leoma was very close to her mother, and I think that because Ethna knew she would be the last child she would bear, a special bond grew between them. Leoma came to us late in our lives, and is the youngest by eleven years. She is but fifteen years old now, and it was as if Ethna knew that she would leave while Leoma was still at such a young age. Ethna never really forgot the lonely childhood that she herself had encountered, without the love of a mother, and I think she bestowed upon Leoma more tender attention, because this thought was so fresh in her mind.

As for our two sons - Hannel has his mother's dark eyes, as well as her valour. Over the past year or two, I have included Hannel in all matters of the crown. There is nothing that he does not know regarding the realm over which he is to rule. He has been party to all decisions, and I have over these years, encouraged him to come forth before council and make his own edicts. I know him to be fair in his judgement, and trust him implicitly with our lands. My dearest Ethna would be proud of her tall, lean, eldest son, as he prepares to take our Kingdom of Graelin into the future.

Edan is our fourth child. He is a warrior of high regard upon the men, but is, unfortunately, a little impulsive. At twenty-six, he is still quite young, however, and I am certain that with age he will become less headstrong. I think that it is Edan who takes after me the most. His actions often remind me of how I used to behave, and upon more than one occasion when his opinion has been asked for, I have known exactly what his answer will be, for he thinks exactly as I do.

What more of me do Hannel and the others possess you may ask? I would like to feel that they all possess my sense of honour, fairness, and duty. I do know the kingdom will be safe under the care and direction of Hannel, and I can only hope that his heir will be as good a ruler as I know his father will be. I know he has the full support of his siblings, and that none bear any malice towards him. They will be by his side for future years to come.

And so, dear reader, my own time in this world is, surely, nearly at its close. My life has been filled with sorrow, but also with much joy and happiness. If you have shed a tear whilst reading any of this journal, then you are not alone, for my Queen and I shed many also. If our story has touched your lives, then it doth mean that all we suffered for the good of our kingdom has not been in vain, for hopefully it will mean that such evil shall not pass the realms of men again.

I now lay this journal to rest, and replace it back in its dusty corner for whoever may find it first, and leave it for them to do with what they wilt.

May all who read this be blessed with peace.

Arthyen
King of Graelin

THE CENTRE FOR FORTEAN ZOOLOGY

So, what is the Centre for Fortean Zoology?

We are a non profit-making organisation founded in 1992 with the aim of being a clearing house for information, and coordinating research into mystery animals around the world. We also study out of place animals, rare and aberrant animal behaviour, and Zooform Phenomena; – little-understood "things" that appear to be animals, but which are in fact nothing of the sort, and not even alive (at least in the way we understand the term).

Why should I join the Centre for Fortean Zoology?

Not only are we the biggest organisation of our type in the world but - or so we like to think - we are the best. We are certainly the only truly global Cryptozoological research organisation, and we carry out our investigations using a strictly scientific set of guidelines. We are expanding all the time and looking to recruit new members to help us in our research into mysterious animals and strange creatures across the globe. Why should you join us? Because, if you are genuinely interested in trying to solve the last great mysteries of Mother Nature, there is nobody better than us with whom to do it.

What do I get if I join the Centre for Fortean Zoology?

For £12 a year, you get a four-issue subscription to our journal *Animals & Men*. Each issue contains 60 pages packed with news, articles, letters, research papers, field reports, and even a gossip column! The magazine is A5 in format with a full colour cover. You also have access to one of the world's largest collections of resource material dealing with cryptozoology and allied disciplines, and people from the CFZ membership regularly take part in fieldwork and expeditions around the world.

How is the Centre for Fortean Zoology organized?

The CFZ is managed by a three-man board of trustees, with a non-profit making trust registered with HM Government Stamp Office. The board of trustees is supported by a Permanent Directorate of full and part-time staff, and advised by a Consultancy Board of specialists - many of whom who are world-renowned experts in their particular field. We have regional representatives across the UK, the USA, and many other parts of the world, and are affiliated with other organisations whose aims and protocols mirror our own.

I am new to the subject, and although I am interested I have little practical knowledge. I don't want to feel out of my depth. What should I do?

Don't worry. We were *all* beginners once. You'll find that the people at the CFZ are friendly and approachable. We have a thriving forum on the website which is the hub of an ever-growing electronic community. You will soon find your feet. Many members of the CFZ Permanent Directorate started off as ordinary members, and now work full time chasing monsters around the world.

I have an idea for a project which isn't on your website. What do I do?

Write to us, e-mail us, or telephone us. The list of future projects on the website is not exhaustive. If you have a good idea for an investigation, please tell us. We may well be able to help.

How do I go on an expedition?

We are always looking for volunteers to join us. If you see a project that interests you, do not hesitate to get in touch with us. Under certain circumstances we can help provide funding for your trip. If you look on the future projects section of the website, you can see some of the projects that we have pencilled in for the next few years.

In 2003 and 2004 we sent three-man expeditions to Sumatra looking for Orang-Pendek - a semi-legendary bipedal ape. The same three went to Mongolia in 2005. All three members started off merely subscribers to the CFZ magazine.

Next time it could be you!

Project Kerinci, Sumatra - 2003
In search of the bipedal ape Orang Pendek

How is the Centre for Fortean Zoology funded?

We have no magic sources of income. All our funds come from donations, membership fees, works that we do for TV, radio or magazines, and sales of our publications and merchandise. We are always looking for corporate sponsorship, and other sources of revenue. If you have any ideas for fund-raising please let us know. However, unlike other cryptozoological organisations in the past, we do not live in an intellectual ivory tower. We are not afraid to get our hands dirty, and furthermore we are not one of those organisations where the membership have to raise money so that a privileged few can go on expensive foreign trips. Our research teams both in the UK and abroad, consist of a mixture of experienced and inexperienced personnel. We are truly a community, and work on the premise that the benefits of CFZ membership are open to all.

What do you do with the data you gather from your investigations and expeditions?

Reports of our investigations are published on our website as soon as they are available. Preliminary reports are posted within days of the project finishing.

Each year we publish a 200 page yearbook containing research papers and expedition reports too long to be printed in the journal. We freely circulate our information to anybody who asks for it.

Is the CFZ community purely an electronic one?

No. Each year since 2000 we have held our annual convention - the *Weird Weekend* - in Exeter. It is three days of lectures, workshops, and excursions. But most importantly it is a chance for members of the CFZ to meet each other, and to talk with the members of the permanent directorate in a relaxed and informal setting and preferably with a pint of beer in one hand. Starting this year-18-20 August 2006 - the *Weird Weekend* will be bigger and better and held in the idyllic rural location of Woolsery in North Devon.

We are hoping to start up some regional groups in both the UK and the US which will have regular meetings, work together on research projects, and maybe have a mini convention of their own.

Since relocating to North Devon in 2005 we have become ever more closely involved with other community organisations, and we hope that this trend will continue. We also work closely with Police Forces across the UK as consultants for animal mutilation cases, and during 2006 we intend to forge closer links with the coastguard and other community services. We want to work closely with those who regularly travel into the Bristol Channel, so that if the recent trend of exotic animal visitors to our coastal waters continues, we can be out there as soon as possible.

We are building a Visitor's Centre in rural North Devon. This will not be open to the general public, but will provide a museum, a library and an educational resource for our members (currently over 400) across the globe. We are also planning a youth organisation which will involve children and young people in our activities.

Apart from having been the only Fortean Zoological organisation in the world to have consistently published material on all aspects of the subject for over a decade, we have achieved the following concrete results:

- Disproved the myth relating to the headless so-called sea-serpent carcass of Durgan beach in Cornwall 1975
- Disproved the story of the 1988 puma skull of Lustleigh Cleave
- Carried out the only in-depth research ever into mythos of the Cornish Owlma
- Made the first records of a tropical species of lamprey
- Made the first records of a luminous cave gnat larva in Thailand.
- Discovered a possible new species of British mammal - The Beech Marten.
- In 1994-6 carried out the first archival fortean zoological survey of Hong Kong.
- In the year 2000, CFZ theories where confirmed when an entirely new species of lizard was found resident in Britain.
- Identified the monster of Martin Mere in Lancashire as a giant wels catfish
- Expanded the known range of Armitage's skink in the Gambia by 80%
- Obtained photographic evidence of the remains of Europe's largest known pike
- Carried out the first ever in-depth study of the *ninki-nanka*
- Carried out the first attempt to breed Puerto Rican cave snails in captivity
- Were the first European explorers to visit the `lost valley` in Sumatra

THE SMALLER MYSTERY CARNIVORES OF THE WESTCOUNTRY
Jonathan Downes - ISBN 978-1-905723-05-8

£7.99

Although much has been written in recent years about the mystery big cats which have been reported stalking Westcountry moorlands, little has been written on the subject of the smaller British mystery carnivores. This unique book redresses the balance and examines the current status in the Westcountry of three species thought to be extinct: the Wildcat, the Pine Marten and the Polecat, finding that the truth is far more exciting than the currently held scientific dogma. This book also uncovers evidence suggesting that even more exotic species of small mammal may lurk hitherto unsuspected in the countryside of Devon, Cornwall, Somerset and Dorset.

THE BLACKDOWN MYSTERY
Jonathan Downes - ISBN 978-1-905723-00-3

£7.99

Intrepid members of the CFZ are up to the challenge, and manage to entangle themselves thoroughly in the bizarre trappings of this case. This is the soft under-belly of ufology, rife with unsavoury characters, plenty of drugs and booze." That sums it up quite well, we think. A new edition of the classic 1999 book by legendary fortean author Jonathan Downes. In this remarkable book, Jon weaves a complex tale of conspiracy, anti-conspiracy, quasi-conspiracy and downright lies surrounding an air-crash and alleged UFO incident in Somerset during 1996. However the story is much stranger than that. This excellent and amusing book lifts the lid off much of contemporary forteana and explains far more than it initially promises.

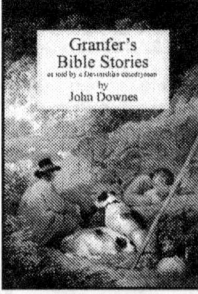

GRANFER'S BIBLE STORIES
John Downes - ISBN 0-9512872-8-1

£7.99

Bible stories in the Devonshire vernacular, each story being told by an old Devon Grandfather - 'Granfer'. These stories are now collected together in a remarkable book presenting selected parts of the Bible as one more-or-less continuous tale in short 'bite sized' stories intended for dipping into or even for bed-time reading. `Granfer` treats the biblical characters as if they were simple country folk living in the next village. Many of the stories are treated with a degree of bucolic humour and kindly irreverence, which not only gives the reader an opportunity to re-evaluate familiar tales in a new light, but do so in both an entertaining and a spiritually uplifting manner.

FRAGRANT HARBOURS DISTANT RIVERS
John Downes - ISBN 0-9512872-5-7

£12.50

Many excellent books have been written about Africa during the second half of the 19th Century, but this one is unique in that it presents the stories of a dozen different people, whose interlinked lives and achievements have as many nuances as any contemporary soap opera. It explains how the events in China and Hong Kong which surrounded the Opium Wars, intimately effected the events in Africa which take up the majority of this book. The author served in the Colonial Service in Nigeria and Hong Kong, during which he found himself following in the footsteps of one of the main characters in this book; Frederick Lugard – the architect of modern Nigeria.

**CFZ PRESS, MYRTLE COTTAGE,
WOOLFARDISWORTHY BIDEFORD,
NORTH DEVON, EX39 5QR
w w w . c f z . o r g . u k**

Other books available
from
CFZ PRESS

CFZ PRESS

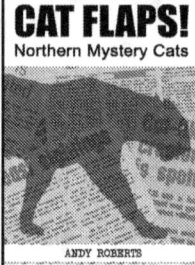

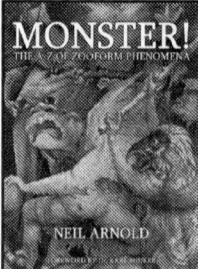

Other books available from
CFZ PRESS

CFZ PRESS

DARK DORSET CALENDAR CUSTOMS
Robert J Newland - ISBN 978-1-905723-18-8

£12.50

Much of the intrinsic charm of Dorset folklore is owed to the importance of folk customs. Today only a small amount of these curious and occasionally eccentric customs have survived, while those that still continue have, for many of us, lost their original significance. Why do we eat pancakes on Shrove Tuesday? Why do children dance around the maypole on May Day? Why do we carve pumpkin lanterns at Hallowe'en? All the answers are here! Robert has made an in-depth study of the Dorset country calendar identifying the major feast-days, holidays and celebrations when traditionally such folk customs are practiced.

CENTRE FOR FORTEAN ZOOLOGY 2004 YEARBOOK
Edited by Jonathan Downes and Richard Freeman
ISBN 978-1905723140

£12.50

The Centre For Fortean Zoology Yearbook is a collection of papers and essays too long and detailed for publication in the CFZ Journal *Animals & Men*. With contributions from both well-known researchers, and relative newcomers to the field, the Yearbook provides a forum where new theories can be expounded, and work on little-known cryptids discussed.

CENTRE FOR FORTEAN ZOOLOGY 2008 YEARBOOK
Edited by Jonathan Downes and Richard Freeman
ISBN 978 -1905723195

£12.50

The Centre For Fortean Zoology Yearbook is a collection of papers and essays too long and detailed for publication in the CFZ Journal *Animals & Men*. With contributions from both well-known researchers, and relative newcomers to the field, the Yearbook provides a forum where new theories can be expounded, and work on little-known cryptids discussed.

**CFZ PRESS, MYRTLE COTTAGE,
WOOLFARDISWORTHY BIDEFORD,
NORTH DEVON, EX39 5QR**
w w w . c f z . o r g . u k